Red Fern Press

Red Fern Press books may be purchased for educational, business, or sales promotional use. For more information, please e-mail the marketing department at redfernpressquery@gmail.com.

First Edition

Cover design, Jaime North // Photography, Joyce Snyder

ISBN 979-8-9887672-7-5 (Kindle)
ISBN 979-8-9887672-8-2 (Paperback)
ISBN 979-8-9887672-5-1 (Hardcover)

For my brother and the endless adventures we
dreamed up as we traversed the cool creeks,
dark woods, and grassy landscapes of our childhood.

Acknowledgements

Thank you to my editor, Andra Paitz, who is a constant and tireless advocate for the best story she can possibly evoke from the depths of my soul. Thank you for organizing chaos. To my daughter, an endless source of inspiration, and my mother and stepfather, who believe in me, always. To all the early readers of *Newcross*, in all its iterations, thank you for your time and support. And to my MFA professors and authors Christian Kiefer and Brian Conn, thank you for your sage advice and always believing it was possible. To my friends and family, you are the source of all my joy and the energy that keeps me going, thank you. To Jaime North, books are, indeed, judged by their covers, so thank you for making mine worthy of consideration. And to Joyce Snyder, good photographers take photos; great photographers capture the soul. Thank you for being the latter.

Content

Suggestions for Further Reading

The Third Period by Steph West (Red Fern Press, 2025)

Clean Break by Steph West (Red Fern Press, 2025)

Coming Soon

Book 2 of the *Newcross* trilogy, *Bounty*, by Steph West

Newcross

Fin

New York City

2020

1

Do You Want to Know Who You Are?

New York City, 2020

Detective Fin Baker scanned the reeking New York City alley filled with trash, glass bottles, cigarettes, and a homeless guy but no suspect. A sense of déjà vu crawled up her spine.

Have I been here before?

As the noisy night gave way to an even noisier morning of horns blasting and flights roaring overhead, she caught a glint of metal under the stuffed dumpster beside her. Her worn leather jacket crinkled as she leaned over to discover a bloody dagger lying underneath.

Looks antique.

She snapped on a pair of latex gloves and knelt. The leather strap tied to the knife's handle was trapped under the leg of the rusted bin.

How the hell is that caught?

Her hanging badge thumped against her chest when she leaned back to see if anyone was watching.

Just do it.

Before curious eyes could catch her, she lifted the impossibly heavy dumpster with one hand while flicking the leather band with the other. She softly put the big metal box down and surveyed the alley again.

No one saw. "Evidence over here," she called over her shoulder.

The NYPD evidence techs turned and nodded. Fin stood and stepped back as an eager young man with a camera and an evidence bag ran over. After a few flashes lit up the area, he reached under the bin, grabbed the dagger by the leather strap, and dropped it in the bag.

As he wrote on the label, he asked, "You see anything else while you were under there?"

"Nope, looked clean to me."

"All right." He tapped the bag. "Thanks, detective."

As he returned to the team, her attention drifted to the tall, strong man in yesterday's navy blue suit and gray tie. His clothes, the gun, and cuffs gave off an alluring vibe as he accepted the new evidence the tech handed him.

Fin wandered over to him.

"Sorry you had to wear yesterday's suit," she whispered, tucking her long, dark hair behind her ear.

Without taking his eyes off the dagger, he whispered back, "You know, if you let me leave my stuff at your place, then less people would suspect we're sleeping together."

Her shoulders tightened up at yet another mention of their relationship status. "That's quite a leap of logic." She put her thumbs in her back pockets.

A glare passed between them.

"So, it's a family drama." He ticked his head toward the crime scene with barely concealed irritation. "Brother and sister. She tried to kill him with the dagger you found under the dumpster. She told the cops down at the station that it's a family heirloom. Maybe 1920s-ish. Pretty fuckin' epic, actually." But he didn't sound impressed.

"Did he live?" She eyed the puddle of blood a few feet away. When he didn't answer her, she glowered at him. *Silent treatment, really?* She cleared her throat. "Hodge. Did he live?"

He huffed. "Barely. Gives a whole new meaning to sibling rivalry."

"Well, I don't have siblings, so I wouldn't know." Fin half smiled at him. *Nothing?* "Actually, I don't know if I have any family."

He glanced at her, softening a little. "I still can't believe the foster home didn't have anything except that bracelet."

Reaching over to her left wrist, Fin caressed the compass carved into the turquoise stone set inside a leather band. She would never tell Hodge, but it emitted a faint glow that only she could see. "Uh, well, sort of. There was a note with it in my basket."

She admired the raw beauty of the turquoise but frowned as it got ice cold. The hair on her arms stood at attention.

Feels like someone's watching me.

She looked around, squinting at the small crowd that had gathered near their crime scene. Inside the police area, a stoic man in his late twenties with chin-length, jet-black hair and what looked to be Italian roots mixed with something else stared back at her. He flicked his eyes away when she noticed him.

2

She crossed her arms and drummed her short, manicured nails against the weathered leather of her jacket.

"Who's that guy?" She nodded to the mystery man.

"Transfer. Name's Riggs, I think."

A taser rested on his hip where a gun should've been.

"Why no gun?"

"Huh?" Hodge nodded his thanks to the last of the departing evidence crew.

"Why doesn't he carry a gun?"

"No idea." His face darkened. "Why don't you fuckin' ask him."

"Nice." She dropped her arms to her sides as Hodge stormed off after the technicians. *This isn't working.*

She peered around the alley, then back to Riggs and the small crowd behind him. They seemed like the normal tourists who gathered at crime scenes. New Yorkers didn't give a shit about this kind of everyday occurrence. But tourists, well, this was invigorating for them. Out of the ordinary.

Who's that?

Across the street, a man dressed in a brown duster, combat boots, and a cowboy hat was walking furtively down the sidewalk. His coat billowed, revealing an automatic rifle slung across his body, as he turned a corner and disappeared.

"What the fuck?" She darted through the crowd and dodged a few cars as she crossed to the other side of the street, ignoring the honking horns and yelling cabbies. Cupping the Glock on her hip, she put her back against the corner and peeked into the alley.

She crept forward, checking dumpsters and trash piles until she reached the end of the lane.

No one's here.

This wasn't the first time she'd seen a person who almost immediately disappeared. A therapist would call her crazy, but the psychic she visited claimed it was ghosts.

Either way, it's not normal to see people who aren't there.

She relaxed the grip on her gun. "Fuck."

"Fin!"

She spun around as the cowboy swung a steel pipe at her head. Ducking, a rush of air brushed her hair. After launching her shoulder into his gut, she grabbed his waist and pushed until they fell. She jumped up and pulled her handgun.

"Drop it!"

He gave her a wretched smile, featuring a shiny gold tooth, then disappeared. When her perp evaporated, she caught sight of another man standing off to the side. His dark Clark Gable style hair swept high above his blue, almost clear, eyes.

"Don't move." She veered the gun at him, aiming at center mass.

"Hello Fin." He adjusted the tie knotted against his Adam's apple.

"Hands!" she yelled.

He put his hands up and gave her a submissive nod.

What's with his skin? It's practically translucent. "How do you know my name?"

"Because." He turned his hand to display a glowing turquoise ring. A cane appeared from nowhere under his hand, and he double tapped it on the ground. "I'm your father. And you, daughter, are in great danger."

~~~

"What?" Fin bolted upright in bed, slapping the man next to her in the head.

"What the fuck?" Hodge jerked awake and sat up.

Was that a dream?

Squinting at her cell phone on the nightstand, she reached over and brought it to life. The time, 4:03 a.m., glowed on the screen. Her breath evened out as she took comfort in her familiar, organized, white bedroom. The illumination from the blue neon Eat sign pointing down to the diner across the street gave her room an ethereal glow.

"How did I get here?" She twisted around to Hodge, who laid back down.

"What are you talking about? We've been here all night."

"We have?"

"You were just dreaming."

Didn't feel like a dream.

The bed dipped as he scooted closer and touched her back. "Fin?"

"He said he was my father."

"What?"

"There was a man. He said he was my father." She wiped the sweat from her face. "It felt so real." *It was real. Wasn't it?*

4
~~~

Hodge's cell dinged from the nightstand on his side of the bed a moment before hers did.

"Shit," he said.

They grabbed their phones and got up.

Hodge made a beeline for the bathroom. "I'll hop in the shower real quick and head out. If you show up a few minutes after me, we should be good."

"Okay. Except . . . aren't those the same clothes you had on yesterday?"

"Shit." He scooped up his rumpled navy blue suit and gray tie from the floor. "We need to talk about this. I don't even have a fuckin' drawer."

"Mmm hmm." His eyes were boring a hole into her, so she busied herself by getting a towel and handing it to him with a half-smile.

He snatched it and walked into the bathroom. Thankfully, the shower started without another painful conversation about where their relationship was going.

Fin twisted her neck side to side, making it crackle. Tracing the grooves of the compass with her index finger, she eyeballed the bathroom. *I've never had a dream that felt like that. Never.*

After stripping down to nothing, she dropped her bracelet on the nightstand next to her black military watch and headed toward the bathroom. On her way, she tripped and slammed her big toe into her dresser. The precisely organized butterfly figurines on its surface clinked as they danced and toppled over.

"Fuck!" Reaching down and grabbing her foot, she twisted her body and collapsed onto the bed. A crimson tear drop leaked from under the injured nail.

"Don't do it," she whispered. She shook her head slowly as that same drop of blood retreated and slid back under her nail. The skin knitted back together, and her pain disappeared within seconds.

That is so not normal.

Deciding yet again to ignore the unexplainable, she let go of her foot and sat up straight. She repeated the mantra she'd been chanting since she was five years old and first noticed the strange things that happened to her. *It never happened.*

Wait, what did I trip on?

Tip-toeing back to the end of the bed, she gasped. Her alleged father's cane was lying on the floor. *How did it get here?* She picked it up and ran her hand along the smooth silky black surface, admiring the antique look of it and the turquoise stone in the crystal handle. It was worn but regal. Classic.

Getting an idea, she checked over her shoulder. *He's still in there.* After taking a deep breath, she rapped it twice on the ground like he had and waited.

Nothing.

She cringed with embarrassment. *Well, what did you think would happen?*

Shaking her head, she walked over to her closet, threw the cane in, slammed the door, and turned toward the bathroom.

Maybe it's Hodge's.

Straightening her shoulders, she walked into her bathroom and stepped into the shower.

~~~

As soon as Fin stepped out of her black Jeep Wrangler and laid eyes on the New York City alley, she recognized it. "Holy shit." She strode past the evidence team to the dumpster, bent over, and peered underneath.

The dagger.

"What the hell?" She stood quickly, her brown leather jacket crinkling. *If it wasn't a dream, then what was it? A premonition?*

After putting on her latex gloves, she quickly lifted the weighty dumpster and freed the leather band. Softly putting it back down, she hollered, "Evidence over here." *A 1920s dagger.*

Fin passed a female tech as she made tracks to Hodge. *Wait, last time it was a guy. Why is it different?*

She glanced over her shoulder as the woman took the photo, bagged the dagger, and marked it for processing.

What's going on?

Hodge arched an eyebrow as she sped over to him. "What?"

"Was I in bed all night last night?"

His eyes flared as he glanced at a tech who fidgeted next to him. Hodge gave the younger man a nod to leave.

As the tech beat a hasty retreat, Hodge whispered, "We're trying not to have people know we're sleeping together. Which would be easier if you—"
~~~

"If I let you keep your stuff at my place, yeah, yeah, yeah," she mumbled. "Hodge, seriously, was I in bed all night? Or, I don't know, have we worked this same case before? Or a really similar one in this alley?"

"Why would we work the same case twice?" Confusion and concern warred with each other on his face. "Are you okay?"

"Uh . . ." She adjusted her shoulders and put her thumbs in her back pockets. "Yeah. Fine." *I'm not fine. How is this happening?*

Staring at a puddle of blood a few feet away, she asked, "Did he live this time?"

"This time?" He scanned her face. "Fin, what's going on?"

"Just tell me if he lived." Her eyes pleaded for answers.

"No, he didn't."

They stared at each other for a moment.

"You're freaking me out," he said.

I'm freaking out. Fin gave a slight shake of her head. "It's fine. I'm fine."

The female tech interrupted them by bringing the bagged dagger to Hodge and asking him a question.

Ignoring them, Fin turned to the crowd with the eerie sense that she was being watched. She homed in on the tall, stoic man she'd seen before. He turned away when they made eye contact.

She sprinted toward him, but the small crowd consumed her. By the time she got to where he'd been standing, he was gone. Twisting to face the other side of the street, she searched for the pipe-wielding cowboy. As if on cue, he crashed through the crowd with an automatic rifle on his side and disappeared down the alley.

"Holy fucking shit." She took off after him, gripping the handle of her Glock as she peeked around the corner.

Nothing.

She slowly followed him, checking dumpsters and trash piles as she went. But he wasn't there.

No, something happens.

She remembered to duck, and a *whoosh* of air whistled over her head. Fin turned and rushed her assailant, tackling him. After rolling off to the side and jumping up, she pulled her handgun.

"Drop it!"

When he disappeared again, she turned to the man claiming to be her father.

"Impressive, I didn't even have to warn you this time." He grinned at her. "You learn fast. That's good."

"What's happening? Tell me."

"I'll show you, Fin, if you really want to know."

"I, I—"

"Don't wait too long to answer or you're going to have a much bigger problem to deal with."

"Like what?"

He smirked as something rustled behind her.

An aggressive gust of air pushed her backward a step as a shadow briefly blocked out the early morning sky. Her gun followed her gaze up to rust-colored talons as big as her head and a crimson and cobalt wingspan that covered the alley.

What? The? Fuck?

A creature, which looked like a colorful pterodactyl with a tail and head of a bright blue scorpion, landed in front of her. Sitting on its back as though he were riding a horse was the gold-toothed man. He yelled at the beast, "Wound, not kill."

"How—" She could only croak out one word.

Surprisingly fast for its size, the tip of the scorpion tail impaled her at the shoulder.

A scream tore through Fin's throat as her gun fell and rattled across the cement.

The monster lifted her off the ground but released her just as quickly. A fierce warrior's cry rang out from behind her as she fell to the pavement. She twisted in agony toward the sound to see her father holding a teal stone sword at his side. He wore a triumphant expression as he admired the lopped-off scorpion stinger at his feet. The beast and its rider had both disappeared again.

Her father asked, "Fin. Do you want to know who you are?"

"Yes." She gagged, fighting down vomit from the pain of the scorpion's sting.

"When I drop you back, pack your bags. We've got work to do. Your mother, Nellie, needs you. And so do I."

He stepped closer and touched her arm.

~~~
~~~

Fin startled violently, slapping Hodge in the head. Her hand flew to her shoulder, and she clutched her blood-soaked New York Rangers tank top at the site of the intense pain.

"Fuck, what the fuck?" Hodge bolted upright.

She struggled to catch her breath, turning away from him to hide the blood from his curious eyes.

"Sorry," she whispered, as he flopped backward.

She sat up and dropped her legs over the side of the bed as pain lanced through her body. She froze until it began to ease, comforted by the cool hardwood floor underneath her bare feet. The pain faded as the wound healed completely.

Fin peered over her shoulder to the nightstand on Hodge's side of the bed just before his phone dinged.

"Shit." He groaned. The bed swayed when he grabbed his phone and jumped up.

As he hurried to the shower, she stared at the wall, or rather, what was leaning against it. Feeling magnetically drawn to it, she stood up and grabbed her father's cane.

It wasn't a dream. Tears stung her eyes as she stared at it.

Nellie is my mother's name.

"Where has she been?"

And why do they need me now?

2

Did You Expect Something Different?

Walking back into her bedroom, Fin made sure Hodge was still in the shower. She dressed quickly and fastened her watch and compass bracelet onto her wrist. After clipping her badge to her hip, she pulled her sweaty hair into a ponytail. He'd probably take another ten minutes. She needed to be gone by then.

I can't explain this. Not yet.

She glanced around. *Everything I need is packed and in the living room.* She squinted curiously at the top drawer of her nightstand. *Should I take it with me?* She crossed the room, opened the drawer, and pulled out an aged, yellow envelope. Caressing the soft paper, she barely remembered the foster home counselor who gave it to her when she turned eighteen.

She had . . . what? Brown hair? No, auburn and long. Always wore that turquoise pendant.

The envelope crackled as she opened it and touched the old, torn paper inside. The faded ink on the note was ready to disappear completely.

No fingerprints.

She didn't doubt the crime lab's results. But honestly, how was it possible that the note, the envelope, and the bracelet had absolutely no fingerprints or oils or anything traceable on them?

Noticing something for the first time, she eyed the handwriting on the page. "Hmm." She clutched the note and envelope in one hand, then grabbed her father's cane and hurried to the living room. After dropping the cane with her gear, she took out a sheet of paper and pen from her small desk and wrote the sentence that was on the letter: This child's name is Fin Baker.

She laid the two notes side-by-side. "Huh." *Similar handwriting.*

Touching them at the same time, Fin closed her eyes as warmth spread through her chest. *Maybe my mother's handwriting is like mine.* Maybe Nellie also had the same smile, the same love of pasta and wine after a tough day, or cold Chinese noodles for breakfast.

I'll take it with me. She carefully folded it and slid it into her back pocket.

"Are you ready?" a male voice asked.

She spun around, instinctively reaching for a gun that wasn't there, and faced the man claiming to be her father. "How are you doing that?"

His haunting blue eyes crinkled at the corners. "You'll see."

Shaking her head, Fin stepped over to the safe she'd had inserted into the wall when she moved in. While using her thumbprint to open it, she said, "I'm packed. Ready. Start talking."

"What would you like to know first?"

She pulled a bullet proof vest from the safe and dropped it next to her backpack and leather weekender bag.

"Why am I dreaming the same thing over and over?"

"What makes you think you're dreaming at all?"

She scoffed as she reached back inside the safe, grabbed her loaded standard issue Glock, and holstered it at her right hip. "There's no other logical explanation for this."

He cocked his head. "There is another explanation. I don't know that you would call it logical. Humans tend to believe that it's necessary for something to be logical for it to be true."

"Humans? Aren't you human?"

He gave her a cheeky smile, cleared his throat, and changed the subject. "I think you already know, in your gut, that you weren't dreaming." He peered around her tiny apartment with its space efficient furniture and black and white design. "Clean. Stylish."

She retrieved a sheathed knife from the safe, bent down, and pulled up her pant leg. "Did you expect something different?" After attaching it to her right calf, she popped up and raised one haughty eyebrow.

"I'm not sure what I expected." He had the good graces to look embarrassed. "I've watched you for years. But I don't think I know you at all."

She had to tamp down the darkness that burbled up inside her. *He's been keeping an eye on me but left me in a foster home?* She took in his stature with a mixture of anger, hurt, and confusion.

He was a little more than six-feet tall, wearing the same clothing he had been the last two times she'd seen him. But now she noticed more details: classic black dress pants, shiny black shoes, a dark purple vest, white shirt, and black velvet jacket with a gold tie like an ascot cinched tight to his throat. A matching gold handkerchief flopped from his breast pocket. The short top hat he held nestled between his elbow and waist was made of a worn deep-brown leather. She appreciated the steampunk vibe, but the Clark Gable hairstyle reminded her of a plastic Ken doll. It hadn't budged an inch from its perfectly coifed position. And his skin looked too young for him to be a parent.

"How old are you?" She snatched her distressed leather jacket from the desk chair where she'd thrown it last night and slipped it on. "You can't possibly be old enough to be my father."

He tilted his head side to side. "Not sure how old I am, honestly. I quit counting after a million or so."

She gave him a heavy dose of side-eye. "A million years?"

"Several million probably." He shrugged.

Snorting, she offloaded the bags and dropped her gear. She tossed him his cane, which he caught with ninja-like accuracy, and headed to the bathroom.

"What are you doing?"

"You're full of shit. I'm getting in the shower and going to work."

He stiffened. "If you do, you'll be dead by dinner time, I assure you."

She stopped in her tracks and flashed her eyes toward him. "What did you say?"

"You think that attack in the alley will be the last? I know you're struggling with what's happening to you, but if you give me one shot, I'll show you this is real, and we can get to work."

Hodge's shower shut off, and she glanced nervously at the bathroom.

"Your partner won't even know you've been gone. I promise." He reached out his hand.

The cop in her wanted to call 911, to yell for Hodge, to pull her gun and arrest this man right here and now for breaking and entering. But the little girl in her, the one with unexplainable gifts and no family, needed to know. She gathered her things again before reaching out and clasping his hand, hoping that the truth of who she was would finally come to light.

3

Quite Unsettling

All Fin did was blink when her father's hand closed on hers, and now, here she stood at the end of a long gravel driveway under the heat of a noon sun. A gentle breeze cooled her face and lifted the ends of her ponytail. *I didn't feel anything.* She peered around at the pastoral scene with an unexpected reverence and breathed in the earthy air.

I know this place. How?

As she scanned the acreage and the small house and the barn that inhabited it, she noticed a slight turquoise haze emanating from the ground. *What is that?*

She didn't realize how hard she was gripping her alleged father's hand until he let go. She glanced at him and found his pale, gentle eyes affectionately studying her face. "You look quite a bit like your mother."

She gasped as unexpected tears squeezed her throat and pricked her eyes. "I do?"

He nodded. "Better end of the gene pool. Lucky you."

She gave him a quivering smile as a slight buzzing started to reverberate in her head. A heaviness that felt like mercury steeling into the pores of her bones began to weigh her down.

"What's happening to me?" She dropped to her knees as the heaviness in her body succumbed to the crushing gravity. The pale haze thickened into a rich fog and turned an intense color of sea blue she'd never seen. Her equilibrium felt as though she was both in a plane and on the ground at the same time. And she wasn't sure if the buzzing was something she was feeling or hearing. Her compass bracelet was so bitter cold that it almost burned her skin.

"What's . . . happening?" She clapped her hands over her ears and hunched in a vain attempt to escape the ravaging sensations.

"Fin?" Her father's voice sounded like it was coming through a megaphone from one hundred feet away. "Fin?"

"Help me!" She blinked back tears as the buzzing made the hair on her skin vibrate.

Hands brushed her hair as a necklace banged against her chest. Immediately, the thick fog returned to a pale haze, and she felt a wave of relief from the afflictions that had been racking her body.

"It's gone." Her hands dropped from her ears as she peered up at her father from the ground.

He nodded at her chest.

She craned her head down and touched a unique gold pendant with turquoise swirls that was as smooth as a river rock and easy to hold between her thumb and index finger. Its weight felt more appropriate for something double its size. "What is it?"

"I made it for you." He extended a hand to help her up. "There's a tremendous amount of magic here. Until you're trained to handle it, this pendant will keep it at bay. Hide you from the likes of Halo."

After taking his hand, she stood up. "Halo?"

"The man in the alley. He's the first one to hunt you, but he won't be the last. That pendant will protect you for now."

"Trained? Protect me? I—"

"Come." He spun on his heel and strode away.

She ran to catch up, blinking against the noon sun reflecting off the bright gravel driveway. Savoring the fresh country air over the hot dog vendor and underground sewer smell of New York City, she admired the tall grass and wildflowers that covered most of the property as they waved lazily in the light wind. On her right, an old and rusty sign sat crooked on its pole and read, Newcross 5 miles. Another sign next to it read, House for Auction Day After Tomorrow.

"Where's Newcross?" she called out to him.

"Ohio," he shouted back without turning.

"Like, the state of?"

"Indeed."

She finally caught up to him. *God, he's fast.* "New York to Ohio in a second?"

"Not even a second."

She jumped as something brushed against her ankle. "Where'd you come from? Are you lost?" Bending down, she checked the neck of the sleek black cat that rubbed against her leg. *No tags.* He leaned into her hand as she petted him. "I hope you weren't abandoned."

Her heart felt heavy for the stray. But when she noticed how quickly her father was getting away, she gave its fuzzy ears a parting scratch and dashed off. "Duty calls."

In front of her, an old house sat on the right side of the driveway, which was on the western side of the vast, grassy property. Its cracked, peeling paint had faded to a pale, tan color that reminded her of aged skin. The washed out red-orange door hung by a rusty hinge. Just before the house was an old barn that was also crumbling under the weight of time.

The black cat had raced ahead to her father who was quickly closing in on the property.

A strange sense of urgency in her spine spurred her forward, too. "What is this place?"

He glanced back and smiled but kept walking.

She wiped the sweat off her forehead, noticing how his face stayed perfectly dry in defiance of the heat of a Midwestern spring day despite his stiff, black velvet jacket.

He made his way up the few stairs that were still intact to the front porch before turning to wait for her. "This," he said with a dramatic pause, "is your mother's house."

She sucked in air too quickly. "Is she . . . is she here?"

"No. This was her childhood home back in the 1970s. It was in pristine condition then," he lamented.

"Where is she now?"

His eyes lowered as he opened the door for her.

With a lump in her throat, she walked past him into the small family home. Once inside, she sneezed from the gathered dust and wiped her nose with her hand. The rooms were empty. Their windows were laden with faded rose-colored velvet curtains. A musty scent of dampness and moth balls filled the air. She turned to ask a question and came face-to-face with a proffered handkerchief.

"Is my mother alive?" She took it and wiped her nose.

"No."

"Why did you both leave me?" The words spilled out before her brain could stop them. Uncontrollable tears flowed down her face. She hid her face in the white, silky square. *How dare he show up unannounced and unexplained with mysteries and strange animals and stories of her dead mother. It was arrogant. No, it was cruel.*

An unfamiliar male voice said, "She's not here, Auci."

Reaching for her gun, Fin spun toward the living room.

A tall-ish man with blond hair and golden eyes gripped a dagger and faced her father. *Auci. My father's name is Auci.*

Wait. She glanced over her shoulder at her father who was also standing behind her. "What? Twins?"

"No," he said. "Time. What you're seeing happened more than two hours ago."

"B-but that would mean—"

"That we are moving in time, yes."

"What?" Struggling to slow her breathing, she reached out and leaned against the wall. It was the only thing keeping her from falling. *Time travel?* "How?"

"I don't know the exact mechanics. It's simply one of our abilities. Our bloodline. Best not to worry about the 'how' of it all. Just know that we can. Now, watch." He pointed at the scene in front of them.

Her mind was scrambling to put it all together. *Pay attention.*

Her father from two hours ago and the man slowly circled each other around a dusty dining room table before coming to a stop.

"Interesting," said her father in the past. "You're protecting her, Oliver."

"I love her," the other man said, tightening his grip on the knife's handle. "I know who you are. Auci, the mighty auctioneer. I'm not scared of you."

Fin flared questioning eyes at her father. "You're an auctioneer? Of what?"

"Magical tools and trinkets." He gave her a slight smirk. "It's far more interesting than it sounds, I assure you."

Fin narrowed her eyes at him as she leaned away from the wall and stood of her own volition. "I have no doubt."

Auci's eyes flickered with amusement, and she turned her attention back to the events already in motion.

Auci of the past scrutinized the dagger. "I know that's not the Grim, which is the only thing that can kill me, so I'm curious what your intentions are."

Shocked, Fin asked, "Wait. There's only one weapon that can kill you? But that would make you . . ."

He nonchalantly lifted one shoulder.

She shook her head. "Immortal."

"I am immortal."

Fin couldn't help the huff that escaped her chest.

He rocked back on his heels. "Haven't you ever wondered where your unusual ability to heal comes from?"

The mocking expression dropped from her face like an anvil. "Am I immortal?"

"No," he said quickly. "You're part human, so you can be mortally wounded. Although, you did heal quite well from that flying scorpion sting." He eyed her with pride.

She fidgeted under his stare. *Immortal.* She shifted her attention back to Oliver as he pled with past Auci to "set her free."

"Who are they talking about?" Fin asked.

"My sister. Gunnar." Auci shuffled his feet.

Fin sucked in a breath. "I have an aunt?"

"Indeed. You're quite like her actually." He nodded to a dark, cobwebbed corner of the dining room. "Here she comes now."

Stunned, Fin turned back as a woman with dark blonde hair and emerald-green eyes appeared from thin air.

"Threatening to kill Oliver won't stop me." Gunnar had a firm, baritone voice.

Fin was immediately enchanted by her aunt, taking a step forward on the creaky, hardwood floor. She stopped when Gunnar's head snapped up and peered in her direction. *Oh no.* Fin held her breath and didn't move.

Auci creeped up beside her. "She can't see you."

"But she heard me."

"She sensed you. Another gift we hold."

A defiant Gunnar, wearing a green leather jacket and matching pants, turned back to past Auci and settled her hands on her hips. Her rugged leather boots were made to handle any weather or landscape. A sheathed dagger clung to a band around her thigh in addition to the cross-body bag that was lumpy with gear.

She looks like a fighter.

"What's in her bag?" Fin nodded to the satchel.

"Mystical assistance," said future Auci.

Fin cocked her head at him.

"We can't kill. So, we have to be creative."

Fin's eyes bulged. "Can I . . ." She gave a magical wave of her hands.

"I'm not sure what that was." Auci mimicked her gesture. "But if you want to know if you can wield magic, the answer is we'll see."

"That's not really an answer." Fin turned back to the arguing trio and noticed the warmth in Oliver's eyes as he watched Gunnar. "He loves your sister."

When future Auci didn't respond, Fin arched an eyebrow at him. "You don't approve?"

"Humans and their love." He put air-quotes around the word love.

She snickered. At the very least, her father had a sense of humor, whether he was aware of it or not.

"It mucks things up."

"I think your sister might disagree," Fin said. "Is she human?"

"Her form is human, yes."

"And what are you?"

"I'm similar to what your people call the Greek gods."

She gave a pointed look at his black velvet jacket and purple vest. "You don't look like a Greek god."

He ignored her with a sigh and continued, "Amon—our other sibling— is, let's say, molecular. He can take the form of anything in the universe, manifesting as whatever he wants."

"How do you know he's a he?"

"I don't."

"How do you know when he's around?"

"I don't. Unless he makes himself known, which he doesn't usually do. He's a bit of a trickster."

"So, the whole family is funny then?" she murmured before returning to the conversation in front of them.

Future Auci didn't deign to reply, but past Auci asked, "Do you know where the Grim is?"

"I'm not telling you anything." Oliver's jaw clenched, and his body tensed for the fight.

He's willing to die for her.

Fin's gut convulsed with guilt. Hodge would die for her because he was in love with her. Fin would die for Hodge because he was her partner. *Same result. Very different reasons.* She winced at the thought.

Gunnar said, "You can go, Oli. I'll be fine. Really."

Eventually acquiescing, Oliver walked out.

"Is this what we've come to, Auci?" Gunnar's face softened into a plea as her leather boots shifted against the dusty, hardwood floors. Unlike her brother, she was starting to sweat just from standing in the heat.

Fin asked, "Can Gunnar die?"

"There's never been anything that could touch the three of us until now. That's why you're here." Auci hesitantly faced Fin as though he was about to deliver bad news. "Gunnar is unhappy with her role, so she's the one who commissioned the Grim."

Auci nodded toward the play in progress, and Fin followed his gaze.

Gunnar paced as her face twisted with anguish. "I don't want this life. You forget, time and again, my body is human. I have to live with humans. You don't. Amon doesn't." Gunnar yanked her hair behind her ears. "For all eternity? I can't do it anymore. I can't breathe. I can't move. I can't stand this heat or the cold or the rain or the wet clothes against my skin or the dirt on my face."

Crying out, Gunnar snatched the knife from her thigh band and shoved it through Auci's chest with precision and strength. He didn't budge as she pulled the dagger out with a relieved sigh.

Fin stepped back from the violence. "You didn't feel that?"

"I don't feel anything." His emphasis on the word "I" made the contrast clear.

"But Gunnar does. That's why she wants out. She feels everything like a human." She shook her head. "Wait, if you're a non-human entity, how can you be my father?"

They stared at each other as the long pause turned into awkward silence.

"That's a story for a different day." He studied her face for a moment and gave a light smile. "But, rest assured, I am your father."

He tried to shift their attention back to his sister, but Fin had other ideas.

"Is Nellie short for something?"

A new warmth flooded his eyes as he patiently entertained Fin's question. "Penelope. Her brother, Boone, couldn't say the letter P, so it came out as—"

"Nellie," she whispered.

His expression of tender reminiscence died when he looked at his sister.

Fin followed his gaze.

Past Auci was clearly exasperated. "You've tried to escape your life hundreds of times over the last century. And I'll admit, several of your attempts were quite inventive. Slipping me that sleeping elixir back in the seventeenth century was particularly creative, but it won't work. It never works, GiGi."

Fin said quickly, "GiGi?"

Auci glanced at his feet, then back to Gunnar. "She calls me Auci. I call her GiGi."

"That's very…" she paused as she followed his gaze to his sister. "Human."

He gave one quick nod but said nothing as they both watched Gunnar stare at past Auci with clear eyes. She straightened her shoulders and said, "It will work this time."

Fin asked, "Why don't you just let her out of this?"

"I can't. I don't have the power to remove any of us from this life."

She racked her brain for a different solution. "Can you change places with her? Give her a vacation? I mean, there's always a way when you love someone." She held future Auci's stare as his face turned quizzical.

He turned thoughtful eyes back to Gunnar.

Unwilling to let it go, Fin said, "So, the Grim is her solution then. Her way out is to kill you?"

"She believes my death will release her."

"Will it?" she asked, taking in his pained expression.

"No," he said tersely.

"What is it exactly? The Grim."

"It's a dagger made from Death's femur bone."

Fin massaged her temples in disbelief. "Are you telling me Death is a person?"

"Death is an entity, yes, constructed from bone. No face, though. Quite unsettling."

Fin dropped her hands to her hips as she eyed the dirt under Gunnar's nails and the weariness of her eyes. "So, she's willing to kill you to get out of this situation. Or die trying."

"Yes," he said quietly. "But we can't kill each other. So she'll have to find someone else to do it."

"How Machiavellian." She eyed the way Gunnar and past Auci were circling each other like vultures. "Why didn't she have Oliver use it on you just now?"

"She doesn't have it."

"Where is it?"

"Amon stole it from her. Quite clever. He hid it in a pocket of time here in Newcross. He put enchantments around it, so neither of us can get it."

"Well, if she can't get it, and you can't get it, then you have nothing to worry about."

Future Auci gave her a patient smile. "We can't get it, but our descendants can. Her crew of people are already working on it as we speak."

Her lips parted with surprise as she twisted toward him.

That mother fu…that's why I'm here.

Hot rage bubbled up again, and Fin could barely contain it. "And I'm your descendant. I'm here to get the Grim for you before Gunnar's descendant gets it for her. You need me to save your life."

He dipped his head once, almost apologetically. "Yes."

"You son of a bitch." She stormed out of the house.

"Fin, wait." He followed her onto the crunchy gravel.

She clenched her fists, trying to control her anger. "You've been alive for more than a million years. And for twenty-eight of them, I've been alone, growing up in a foster home, wondering about you, my mom, my family. You could have appeared, at any time, and nothing. Until you needed me to save your life."

"Fin, I'm—"

"No," she screamed, whipping around to face him. "You don't get to talk to me like you know me. Like you have a right to ask me for a favor like this."

"I know your favorite food is Chinese takeout. But only the morning after. Noodles."

Baffled, she stared at him. "What?"

"I know you've been wearing that bracelet ever since your wrist was big enough that it wouldn't slide off."

"So what?" She turned in a huff and started walking again as he followed.

"I know that you sent it and the letter to a crime lab looking for evidence of your family. But there was none, and there never will be."

She slid to a stop in the gravel and glared at him. "Did you tamper with it?"

"I know you got a pink teddy bear for your fourth birthday that didn't have a card. And then a gift every birthday thereafter. Always with no card."

Her heart softened.

"I know you were exceptional at sports but chose not to play them." An unidentifiable mix of emotions swirled across his face. "I know that idiot boy, Kevin, broke your heart when you were thirteen and mysteriously broke his arm not long afterward." He twitched an eyebrow as one corner of his lip turned up a little.

"No. You didn't."

He shrugged.

She fought down her conflicting feelings as she and her father surveyed each other for a moment.

"I know you sat in that window of your room at the foster home and stared for hours into the street just searching."

Her eyes filled with tears, and she swatted them away.

"And I know you don't know how sorry I am, or why it had to be that way for you. But I promise, I will make sure you get all the answers you need. Even for the questions you don't know to ask yet."

As the mixing of tears with her mascara burned her eyes, she pulled out his handkerchief to clean herself up. She stared at her mother's house and took a deep breath. "So, only someone who's a descendant of you or Gunnar can find this thing?"

"Technically, anyone who can get through the entrance and beat the enchantments can find it. But only a descendant can bring it back. We think."

She quirked a skeptical eyebrow. "You think?"

"Amon has, let's just say, an interesting sense of how to mediate between my sister and me. And a deep appreciation for scavenger hunts. Operative word being scavenger. He likes to play games. Riddles."

He glanced at her, so she asked, "What?"

He tilted his head at her and then straightened up. "Amon quite loved your mother, like his own sister."

Her lips shimmied at the corners as she watched his face light up. *Every time he talks about her.*

He said, "I don't know for sure, but I suspect, given his affection for her—and subsequently you—that you may be the only one who can actually retrieve it."

Fin considered her father for a moment until it struck her. "That's why Halo wants me. Or any descendant, I presume. To physically take it."

"Halo and others like him, yes."

She touched her necklace, contemplating his request, her head nodding even before she spoke. "I'm gonna help you, Auci. But I want something in return."

"Anything."

"I want to see my mother."

He gave her a sly smile. "I can do better than that. I can give you the time and space to know her."

Fin couldn't help the fresh tears that sprang to her eyes. She swallowed them away and looked at him squarely. "What happens if you die, Auci? The Grim. This can't just be about me. Or Gunnar. You said you're here to protect humans. If there's no you, then what?"

"My job is to manage every mystical object in the world, particularly the most dangerous ones, like the Grim. If I die, those objects are released back into the world with no one to gatekeep them." His intense stare sent a shiver through her bones. "And humans, well, they've proven to be quite self-destructive with that kind of power. Plain and simple, your world will descend into chaos."

"So, you've got nothing but good news then."

He flicked a sarcastic grin at her.

She took a deep breath. "All right. I'm in. Where do we start?"

"From now on, Fin, it's not just where but when. In this case, you have a cousin in Ireland who will be integral to helping you retrieve the Grim. You must convince him to get on a plane and come to Newcross."

"Cousin?" She peered at him as she thought for a second. "Through Nellie's brother? Boone?"

"Correct."

"Does he know about me? Or who his father is?"

"No. And sometimes, when it comes to matters involving time, it's better to—even required to—let people discover some things on their own."

She shot him a questioning glance, and he gave her a nod. *Is that why he stayed away? Why he's being so cryptic with me now?*

She shook her head to clear it. "Even if I get him on a plane to Ohio, I don't know how to get to Newcross. Or where the Grim is."

"No, but Dawson knows how to get to Newcross. He's been studying it for quite some time now. And I will show you the rest."

She nodded tentatively. "We have a deal then."

He put his hand in his pants pocket and winged out his elbow toward her. But at her hesitation, he pulled his elbow back.

"I am sorry, Fin." His eyes grew heavy with remorse. "That you were so alone. I truly am. But if it helps, you were never really alone. Never."

What is it with these tears? Fin swatted them away and sniffed, taking his handkerchief from her jean's pocket and patting her face dry yet again. Tucking it away, she lifted her eyes to him.

He gave her an encouraging smile and tilted his elbow to her again. "Ireland, ten hours ago. Shall we?"

A quick swallow pushed down her doubts as she nodded. *I can't believe this is my father. I can't believe my mother is dead.*

But the mystery of how and why Nellie had died was still very much alive. And Fin would do anything in this timeline or the next to find out what happened to her.

She tucked her hand into the crook of his elbow and they disappeared.

$$4$$

I Have a Book on That Somewhere

Dawson Klooney poked his glasses back up his nose and swiveled between the dusty book in his hand and the tower of books on his desk. Hardbacks in all shapes and sizes were scattered everywhere, consuming his small office. Thankfully, his frosted glass door provided an escape to the vast library beyond, which made the room feel less cramped.

One index finger, with its bitten-to-the-skin fingernail, skimmed the spines in the stack as he brought the text in his hand closer to his face. The dust tickling his nose gave him a two-second warning before he sneezed. But even knowing it was coming, his hand still spasmed out into the literary Jenga blocks, knocking them to the floor with a loud thud.

"Crap." Dawson wiped his nose with the sleeve of his flannel shirt and sighed as a strand of his dark hair fell into his eyes.

After hoisting himself up from the squeaky chair, his brown leather hiking boots in pristine condition creaked as he knelt to start picking up the mess. He studied each cover closely, trying to find the book he'd been reaching for. "Where are you?"

"Right here," said a woman with a light, Irish accent.

Startled, his eyes jumped toward the sound.

Sophie's amused face was a pale canvas painted with freckles and bright red lips under a mass of long, auburn hair.

"How'd you get in here?" *I thought the doors were locked?* He waved her into his office, always happy to see his confidant and friend. More than that, she felt like family to him.

"What are you searching for on the floor, there, Indiana Jones?" Sophie gave him a lopsided smile as she crossed her arms over her Army green hiking jacket.

"Green notebook. Pocket sized." He held up his fingers to make a frame of its small shape. *I know the doors were locked.* "You know, you always seem to show up right when I need you. How do you keep doing that?"

She shrugged one shoulder and gave him an impish smile. "I must be clairvoyant."

"I have a book on that somewhere." He went back to shuffling through the pile. "Clairvoyance and other extrasensory perceptions are widely disregarded by the scientific community as, uh, well, make believe. A pseudoscience, like most paranormal beliefs."

He shot her a slightly abashed look, but her placid expression said she wasn't offended.

"And what about you, Dawson? Do you think all that stuff is make believe?"

He crinkled his forehead, considering her question. "Well, uh, as a connoisseur of information, I try to keep my mind open to all possibilities and viewpoints."

"Keep that open mind."

The warmth of her smile felt like sunshine, and his soul opened to its rays.

She would have told me if we were family, right?

"So, this green book we're on the hunt for, what's it about? Bigfoot?" She snickered when he flinched.

"You know Bigfoot makes me cringe." His shoulders shook with an all too real shiver.

"I don't get it." Chuckling, she shook her head. "Where'd this fear come from?"

"Campfire stories with my dads." He held out his hand like he was gesturing to a persuasive PowerPoint presentation. "They're smart. Too smart. Plus, if Sasquatches are real, and it seems likely they are, they've remained hidden for years, so they're smart and sneaky. Terrifying."

"Your idiosyncrasies are adorable."

She uncrossed her arms and knelt next to him to help sort through the books. He noticed that her earlobes were attached at the bottom. His fingers mindlessly reached up and touched his own attached lobes.

Only eighteen percent of the population has attached earlobes. "The little green book is actually my journal."

"Ah, yes, your whole life is in that book."

Surprised, he studied her for a moment. "Quite right. How did you know that?"

"Here it is." She plucked the little leather-bound notebook from the pile with her tidy nails and handed it to him.

"That's the one." Warmth pooled at the base of his neck as she smiled at him. The family vibe he got from her spawned a desperation in his gut to find his birth parents. Maybe he had siblings and cousins, too. *My adoptive fathers were amazing, but Sophie feels so familiar to me.*

"What are you hoping to find in the journal?"

He started to answer but was distracted by her deep blue eyes. *Mine are gray. But it's been statistically proven that eye color isn't a great indicator of associated gene pools.*

"Dawson?"

He took the book from her hand. "Oh, sorry, it's got my notes about Newcross."

"Right, the town that's on no map anywhere. A mystery." She bounced her eyebrows at him.

Dawson's cell phone vibrated loudly in his pocket, interrupting her ribbing.

He checked the number and swallowed hard at its area code. "New York."

"Who do you know in the States?"

"Umm." *I don't know how to answer that.*

He knew this moment was coming, but it still felt like a freight train running off the tracks. How should a logical librarian feel about a note that's supposedly from the future but planted in the past? He was open to knowledge, but the application of that knowledge was a little harder for him to handle.

Dawson stood as he answered his phone. "H-hello?" He pushed his glasses up on his nose.

"Is this the librarian, Dawson Klooney?" a female voice asked.

"Uh, who's calling?" Holding the phone with his shoulder, he started to flip through the green notebook.

"My name is Fin Baker. I'm a detective from New York City. I'm standing outside your library. Would you mind letting me in?"

"Wait, I'm sorry. Did you say your name is Fin?" His finger stopped on an entry in the journal that read, "Does Fin = End?" *The Fin mentioned in the note from the future is a name not the French word for end.*

"Yeah, why?" she asked.

"Oh, no reason." Clearing his throat, he closed the pocket-sized book with one hand. "Yes, I'm Dawson." *I can't believe this is happening.* Dodging books, he popped over to his small window and peered out.

Fin said, "Okay, so can you let us in?"

Gazing outside, Dawson immediately recognized the strange-looking man on the sidewalk but not the woman standing next to him. Aesthetically, she was pleasing to look at, with rich, dark hair pulled into a ponytail. Clearly athletic. *She'd have to be if she's a cop.*

She glanced over at his window, pulled a badge off her hip, and held it in the air. *All business.*

He gasped. "Yes, of course, coming now."

~~~

Dawson fiddled nervously with a pile of library books near the front door as Auci and Fin stared at him. Wondering what Sophie would think of his visitors, he looked for her, but there was no sign of her. *I thought she was right behind me.*

Dawson nodded in acknowledgement at Auci. "Good to see you again."

Fin gave them a strange look. "You know each other?"

"Sort of," Auci replied.

An awkward moment passed before Dawson realized the man wasn't going to fill in the blanks. "Oh, uh," he stammered, pointing to the man. "He's the auctioneer who took me to a strange house for the maps. The Newcross maps."

"Maps to Newcross, huh?" Fin cast an arch look at her companion.

Not sure what to make of the exchange, Dawson said, "Yes, I've been researching my family history. I'm adopted." When Fin's face took on a note of understanding, he continued, "I believe my biological family is from there. I only know a couple things about Newcross, but I think it's the key to figuring out who I am. I'm curious, though, you seemed to recognize the town's name. Have you been there? Do you know it?"

He tried to keep his tone light because he didn't want to seem too anxious for more information, but he was bursting at the seams. Checking over his shoulder, he looked back toward his office. *Where's Sophie?*

Fin shook her head. "No, I'm not familiar with it. But I'm pretty sure it's where my mother is from." A slight flush crossed her face. *Bit of emotion there.* "I was abandoned at birth outside of a foster home in New York." She stole a glance at Auci. "I'm on the hunt for my family, too. And it seems beyond coincidence we would be searching for the same thing at the same time in the same town."

"I see." *Is Fin my family? Or, wait, am I being investigated?* "Is this a police matter?"
~~~

"Oh, no, sorry." Fin waved away the notion. "This is definitely personal."

"Okay." He relaxed a little as he shuffled his curious eyes between Auci and Fin. "This is all very peculiar."

"Yes, it is." She flicked her eyes to the auctioneer.

"I've been investigating for a while, but I hadn't made much progress until you showed up." He gestured to Auci, who tipped his head in a slight bow. "That was a few months ago. Although I really appreciated it, I'll admit that it felt a bit strange at the time." He held up his hands. "No offense."

"None taken," Auci said. "I get that a lot."

Pursing her lips, Fin shook her head a little bit at Auci. *She seems annoyed with him. Like how I get with my dads.*

Dawson's experience with Auci had made him question his own sanity. He'd gotten what he thought was a scam email about an auction, so he deleted it. The next day, Auci was in his office, encouraging him to attend. The odd man knew Dawson was searching for family and said there might be maps up for bid that could lead to the town his parents were from. But when they arrived at the event, everyone in attendance seemed like they were from a different time. And they looked washed-out like ghosts.

To reassure himself, he went back the next day. There was no auction, no auctioneer, no people, no sign. And the house was a dilapidated mess with rotten floorboards that should've been impossible to stand on the day before.

"Dawson?" Fin leaned forward.

"I'm sorry." He scooted his glasses up and peered into her questioning, but warm, eyes. *Intelligent. Caring.* "What was that?"

"Do you still have the maps?" Fin asked.

"Of course. Let me make you a copy. I'll be right back."

Dawson headed back to his office, where Sophie was noticeably absent. *When did she leave? I must be out of it today.*

He grabbed the maps from his desktop but hesitated. *I wonder.* He opened the top drawer and retrieved a worn, plain envelope. Pulling up the flap, he considered an object that resembled a number two pencil made of rock with a turquoise stone at the tip. It had been in the same envelope with the note. When he had tried and failed to write with it, he silently scolded himself because it obviously had no ink.

It must be something.

He slipped the note out of the envelope and read it even though he had it memorized. "Go to Newcross. Fin." He absentmindedly rubbed the paper between his thumb and forefinger.

This kind of lead was what he'd been hoping for all his life. But now that the moment was here, he suddenly felt stifled. *Am I sure I want to know?*

Squaring his shoulders, he walked to the copier and ran the maps through. When he returned to his strange visitors, only Fin remained.

"Here you go." He handed the copies to her. "Where's Auci?"

"He, uh, had to leave. Work, auction, stuff." She fidgeted with the copies. "Look, I know this is going to sound crazy, but I need to go to Newcross to investigate, and I think you should come with me."

He sucked in a deep breath, swallowed hard, and exhaled. "That seems about right." *But use your brain, Dawson.* "But first, I'd like to call the NYPD to verify you're for real."

"By all means." She handed him her badge. "I'm with the seventy-fifth precinct. Give them my badge number."

"Thank you. I'll be right back." He took a few steps on the worn, tan carpet toward his office but turned back. "Fin?"

"Yeah?" She looked up from her phone as her weight shifted from one foot to the other. He studied her face for a moment. There was something in the shape of it that reminded him of his own.

"Do you think it's possible we're related?" He tried not to sound too excited as he alternately pointed at himself and her.

"I mean . . ." She seemed on the verge of saying something but glanced away. "Anything's possible, right?"

He gave a light, self-conscious laugh as his body relaxed. "Indeed."

She waved her phone in the air. "I'll research flights while you call New York."

"All right then." *Direct, but kind. I like her.*

He walked into his office and jumped at Sophie's presence. "Where were you?"

"I was around." She shrugged. "So, are you going to Newcross with Fin?"

"Yes, I believe I am." He watched her out of the corner of his eye as he went around his desk. "Did I tell you her name was Fin?"

Her sly smile declined his question. "I'm glad you're going." She granted him an approval he didn't realize he was seeking until she offered it.

He slowly picked up his phone from his desk. "Is there—" He paused as he considered Sophie's kind eyes, their similar earlobes, and her protective nature. "Is there anything I should know before I go?"

She blinked quickly.

Does she look conflicted or confused?

"Just go to Newcross," she said. "And maybe, sometimes, let your heart lead." Dismissing the subject, she busied herself nosing through his books.

Lead with my heart? I'm not sure I can. "I'm gonna call the NYPD. Verify Fin is a cop there."

"Smart." She tapped her temple then her heart before picking up the aged edition of *Through the Looking Glass* and walking out of his office. As she went, she hollered over her shoulder, "Maybe you'll finally get those year-old hiking boots dirty."

He peered at the boots he bought, remembering why he'd bought them. *Adventure.* They barely had a scratch on them.

"Right." He sat down at his computer, looked up the precinct's number, and dialed it.

"NYPD, is this an emergency?"

He hung up the phone. *Heart.*

A brush of fur against his ankle made him jump. He glanced down to find a black cat with bright, topaz eyes.

"How the . . . ?" He scooted his chair backward as he peered at it from distance. *How on earth did a cat get in?* "Sophie?"

He waited for her to come back only to realize she was gone again. He gingerly got down on his hands and knees and stared eye to eye with the purring feline. *Quantum physics?*

"Are you Schrodinger's cat?" he whispered. When it blinked, he pulled back a bit. "Magic or physics? A secret door, perhaps?"

All of them?

"You're a bit of a mystery, aren't you?"

He peered around the cat to the open library where only Fin stood.

"A mystery, indeed."

5

You're in the Right Place

After one flight across the ocean, one across the Midwest, and now this grimy coach bus, Fin was glad to feel it sway to a stop. As it did, notes of Fin's favorite tune came through her headphones. She let the words fill her with a melancholy that seemed appropriate for the dirt-filled scene outside her window. *Bye, Bye Miss American Pie. Drove my Chevy to the levee, but the levee was dry.*

Everything beyond the smudged glass was dry as the dust kicked up a cloud all around them. She peered at Dawson, who was sound asleep and drooling onto the torn leather seat. Fin tapped her phone and brought the music to an abrupt stop before tossing her headphones into her backpack and reaching across the sticky aisle. She gave his arm a nudge.

"We're here."

He jerked awake with a snort.

After standing up, she slid her phone into her back pocket, grabbed her bags and jacket, and threaded her way down the aisle toward the front of the bus.

When the driver opened the door, dust rushed in.

Shit.

Choking on the grime, she coughed and waved away the hazy air. Eventually, the dust settled and revealed a long, bright, overgrown pathway that seemed to lead nowhere.

What the hell?

She asked the older woman behind the wheel, "This is the road to Newcross? It's barely a trail, let alone a road."

"Mmm hmm," the driver grunted.

Dawson filed in behind her, yawning, and barely awake. "Definitely not in Ireland anymore."

"More like a fucking Stephen King novel." Fin grimaced at the bus driver, who was smug as she grabbed the lever to shut the door. "Super helpful, thanks."

Stepping off the bus, she slid on her aviator sunglasses under the glare of the afternoon sun and immediately slapped at a bug on her arm. Gravel crunched under her feet as she stepped away from the shiny metal vehicle, pulled the black hair tie off her wrist, and cinched her dark hair into a ponytail again.

"So, what? We just walk?" Dawson descended the rickety bus like he was moving through sludge and stood next to her with his bags slung over his shoulders. Both were down to their T-shirts in the Midwestern heat.

With a heavy diesel groan, the gas-guzzler pulled away and kicked up another cloud of dust.

"I mean, do you think Uber works here?" she asked dryly as she surveyed the miles and miles of trees and foliage that surrounded them.

They shared a discerning look.

After opening one of his maps, he glanced between it and the scenery around them.

"Okay, then." He cleared his throat. "Seems like that's the correct way." He pointed down the road, then put the map in his back pocket.

"You're sure?"

"About eighty percent."

"Eighty? What the—" She jabbed him with a side-eye. "Eighty? That's all? I thought you've been studying this for months."

"Statistically, eighty is pretty good."

"Can you get it closer to, like, a hundred?"

He turned his face up to the sky and bellowed obnoxiously. "Give us a sign."

Fin looked up, too. "Who are you talking to?"

"God. Buddha. Zeus. Universe. Whoever you believe in." He threw his hands up. "It's about as helpful as you telling me I need to be a hundred."

She grinned at him. *Sarcasm. I like it.*

"Let's go." He waved her forward and started down the road.

Following him onto the glorified goat path, Fin said, "I would have thought a librarian, who deals mostly in facts, would eschew religion and the sky gods they peddle."

He shrugged and slapped at a bug on his hand. "I'm sure most do. Although I definitely lean more toward facts, there are some things science can't explain. And perhaps religion is one of those things. Better to ask for help than to not. Even if it seems ridiculous."

"Like an insurance policy?" She tilted her head.

"More like a recognition that as humans, we simply don't know everything. And it would be the height of hubris to assume otherwise."

They walked in companionable silence down the long road, dodging overgrown trees until something caught Fin's eye.

"Oh, you've got to be kidding me." She walked off the side of the road into the high grass and investigated a mess of unruly foliage.

"What is it?" Dawson hollered.

"Hang on," she yelled back as she reached through the tangled brush and grabbed the ensnared object. She gave it a quick yank and yipped in surprise when it came tearing through the sticks and trees, the momentum knocking her on her butt.

Whoa. Am I even stronger here? "Fuck me." After dropping the metal sheet on the ground, she jumped up and smacked the dust off her clothes as Dawson carefully made his way over.

They leaned over to get a better look at the rusted green road sign that read, Newcross 2 miles, with an arrow pointing the direction they were walking.

Fin pointedly ignored Dawson's self-satisfied grin as he said, "Well look at that. A sign." He started trudging back to the path with his arms raised to the heavens. "Thank you!"

At his mischievous chuckle, she exhaled noisily, shook her head, and followed him. "Coincidence."

They walked in silence as they adjusted to the heat and dry air of May in southern Ohio. Fin paused for a moment and observed the large oak and hickory trees, the low-lying bushes, the black cat. She did a double-take.

Is that the same cat from my mom's house?

"Daw—" she started to call out, but the animal was gone.

"What?" His eyes followed her line of sight.

"Nothing." She gave him a weak shake of her head and peered into the woods one last time before they resumed their trek. Her stomach tightened with the certainty that they were going the right way. Tuning into her body, she focused on her breathing as she followed Dawson's lead.

Everything feels so strange.

It reminded her of the déjà vu she had felt as the bus made its way down the winding roads into Newcross. When they drove past the sign displaying the town's population—only 1,123 people—she'd asked Dawson, "Did you feel that?"

His nose had been deep in the pages of his green notebook before he peered across the aisle at her. "What did you say?"

"Did you feel that?"

"Feel what?"

"Like . . ." Shaking her head, she searched for the words to describe the displaced sensation she'd felt as soon as they'd disappeared from civilization, swallowed up into the hole of Newcross. "Like time changed."

She scoured his face for any flicker of recognition but found nothing.

"I'm sorry, no. But I'm pretty tired from the flight. So, maybe it's jet lag?" He shrugged one shoulder at her.

After so many hours traveling together, she would've been able to read him even if she wasn't a cop. The man had no future in professional poker.

"Dawson, wait." She ran a little to catch up as he slowed and peered at her.

"You doin' okay?" he asked.

She bobbed her head. "I could ask you the same thing."

"I slept most of the trip." He flicked at a bug on his neck.

"Good."

After a few moments of listening to the soft sounds of the woods, Dawson said, "You feel connected to this place, don't you?"

She sucked in a surprised breath but wasn't sure what to say.

"You seem more agitated or something. Especially as we get closer to town."

How does he know that? She touched the pendant around her neck. Even with it, she could still feel the pulsing power of Newcross in her veins; see a light blue haze lying low to the ground. *Can he feel something too?*

"It doesn't affect me like that." He glanced down to the ground, scuffing his shoe in the dirt. "I was hoping to feel it more. But the facts are all I seem to have."

I guess we're both struggling. "Just because it doesn't affect you in the same way, doesn't mean you won't find what you're looking for here." She reached out and lightly touched his arm.

He gave her a hesitant nod. "It's a lot of pressure. To hope a single town can tell you everything about who you are."

"You know who you are." She scratched at her arm as a sweat bee flew away at her urging.

"I know who I am without my biological parents." He adjusted the shoulder strap of his bag. "It's something else entirely to know who you are with them."

They walked quietly for a moment.

She peeked at him once, twice. *Just say it.*

"I don't think they're alive. If that's what you're hoping for."

Dawson closed his eyes for a second, then opened them and glanced at her. "You won't mind if I keep hoping."

"Of course not." She gave him a supportive nod as they continued down the winding road.

After a moment, he paused. She stopped and saw him looking down at his boots. "What?"

The corners of his lips turned up in a wavering smile. "My boots," he said.

"What about them?"

"They're getting dirty," he said. As he started walking again, she followed, uncertain what he meant, but sure that whatever it was, it meant something to him.

~~~

As soon as they crossed into the town proper, Fin's connection to the place coursed through her body and power gathered in her necklace. She reached up and touched the pendant, which seemed to have a life of its own in this place, pulsing like an artery.

"Finally." Dawson stopped and caught his breath. "God, I need water."

"Ditto." She wiped her arm across her sweaty face and grimaced at the dirt it left behind on her skin.

"How do you feel?" He pushed his glasses up on his nose.

"I feel . . ." She paused. *I can describe it. I'm just not sure I want to.* She flicked her eyes at him. "Powerful, I guess. Physically connected? I know that sounds stupid."

"Not stupid. The places we're from hold deep physical connections for us, whether we remember them or not. It's science."

"Are you eighty or a hundred percent sure of that?"

A loud laugh burst out of him, releasing some tension. She laughed with him, and her heart grew a little bit.

"You've got a bit of humor in you."
~~~

"Some days." She frowned as she took in the dirty town. "Truly filthy." She shook her head. "And that's saying something coming from downtown New York."

"Linus meets Oscar." He gave her a cheeky grin.

Together, they considered the slow-moving mothers with children hanging from their arms, the dust that never seemed to settle, and the inescapable heat that felt like you were melting from the inside out.

Thinking she saw someone out of the corner of her eye, Fin whipped her head to the left, but it was nothing. *Again.* A sense of unease bloomed in her as she looked at Dawson, whose expression had grown more serious as well.

She gave a quick pat to his arm. "Hey, the answers we're looking for, they're here."

He contemplated her briefly before returning his gaze to the town. "How do you know that?"

Her stomach growled an interruption. *Food.* She pointed at the diner across the street. "Cop gut." She smacked her abdomen. "But first, food and drink."

"Yes." He drew the word out as if the sound alone was a relief. *Hopefully, food will help us feel a little more normal.*

A very large man stopped beside them. "Fin!"

Startled, she turned and stared into a pair of sparkling, dark eyes under a gallon-sized cowboy hat. Affection emanated from the man, and the weight of the town seemed to lighten in his presence.

"I am Fin, yes," she said before noticing his badge and standard issue uniform. "You must be the chief here?" *Why do I feel like I know him?*

"That's right. Always been a smart cop." He tapped his temple. "It's so good to see you again!"

"Again?"

Pulling her into a huge hug, he squeezed the air from Fin's lungs. Her hands flailed about, uncertain whether to embrace him or slap him. Before she could decide, he released her from his clutches with a wink and reached out his hand to Dawson.

"And you're Dawson. Make sure you write this down in your green notebook."

Looking puzzled, Dawson shook the chief's hand.

The traveling companions gawked at each other, equally confused.

"Well, I owe you two lunch." He shook his finger at them. "On me this time. Don't you try and pull a fast one again."

He clapped his hands together. "Hooo-ey! Let's go." He jerked his head toward the diner and started across the street.

The cop in Fin wanted more answers about how the hell he knew who they were. But her hungry gut forced her to say, "Yeah, okay."

He's just so damn likable. Checking in with Dawson, she made a what-do-you-think gesture.

"I'm thirsty," he said. "And starving."

She agreed. "Let's go."

They crossed the street as Dawson jotted a few notes into his journal.

Tenderness spread across Fin's chest. *I'm glad we're in this together.*

"Gentlemen first." She swung open the classic glass diner door as a bell dinged and a burst of bitter air conditioning struck her face.

Dawson opened his arms and walked into the AC like a king. "Oh, heavenly twentieth-century wonders."

Chuckling, she followed him into the near-empty 1950s diner with black and white tiled linoleum. Everything was worn and aged with ripped red leather booths and stools that were new several decades ago. The walls were covered in clocks. Black clocks, red clocks, blue clocks. Some had faces and some didn't, but they all looked absurd. They ticked loudly and off-beat with each other at an unbearable decibel.

Another sweeping feeling of déjà vu rippled through her from head to toe. *I've been here before.* An unsettling silence blanketed the diner as she looked back to the walls with a gasp.

"Where'd they go?" she whispered.

The walls were now covered in vintage movie posters and record albums. All the clocks were gone except for one black cat clock with wide eyes that bounced back and forth in time with its swinging tail. It hung next to a booth occupied by a mother and her two small children.

"Excuse me?" Fin said, but the woman ignored her. *She must not have heard me.* "Excuse me?" she said louder but still got no response.

"Uh, Fin?"

She spun at the sound of the Chief's voice.

"Who are you talking to?" He tilted his head at her as she turned back to the booth, which was empty now.

"Holy shit," she said quietly. *It's like the ghosts. But bigger. More intense.* She turned back to the big man, but she didn't know what to say.

"How about we go to our booth, okay?" The Chief smiled graciously at her as she nodded.

She took in the now-full diner, buzzing with people and conversation. She passed an older man wearing suspenders at the counter drinking coffee and reading the newspaper. When he looked at his watch, his whole body jerked. "I'm late!" he said, jumping up and fumbling for his wallet.

"Whoa!" Fin's toe caught a piece of torn flooring, sending her flying. She slammed, palm first, into an old jukebox that was loudly playing a Captain and Tennille song. "Dammit." She shook out her tweaked wrist, relieved that it healed on the spot.

"Careful." The chief hustled up to her, took one of her hands, and snaked his other hand under her shoulder. "Let me help."

"Thanks." She went to apologize for almost falling into the bustling man, but in his place she saw six teenage friends. They were sucking on milkshakes and laughing at their cell phones. One lazily looked up.

"You okay, lady?"

She nodded and shot a glare at the offending linoleum square that caused her to trip, but the linoleum was gone. The floor was now swirled black and white epoxy.

What is happening to me? A wave of panic washed over her as she mentally chanted her mantras. *It didn't happen. Save it for another day. Keep moving, Fin. Keep moving.*

"I'm usually not so clumsy," she said as she remembered the Chief and mustered a smile. "And I'm hungry. I suppose."

"Well, you're in the right place then." He led her to a corner booth where Dawson had already gulped his ice water and was now working through hers.

"Thirsty?" she asked as she got her bearings and slid into the red, leather booth next to Dawson.

He kept drinking, unapologetically, as the Chief slid into the other side. Fin took a second to peer around again at the restaurant as she gripped the table to ground herself. *Okay, teenagers are here, the floor is epoxy, jukebox is there, vintage posters and records, one black cat clock. No woman and her children, no man rushing from the counter. Feeling has passed.*

"Drink, honey?" said a moseying waitress who could have come out of the sitcom, *Alice.* She snapped her gum as she waited for Fin to answer, pencil and pad at the ready.

"Just another water, thanks." Fin took a deep breath and exhaled. *I'm good.*

By now, Dawson had moved on to drinking the chief's water. Rather than being upset, the officer cheered him on.

"Drink it down, hooo-eeey!" The big man twirled his cowboy hat in the air and slapped it down on the bench seat next to him.

"Actually, a whole new round of waters," Fin corrected.

"All right." She popped her gum and ambled away, hollering at some other customers, "I'll be there in a second!"

Fin shook her head with amazement at Dawson when he slammed down the chief's empty water glass on the table.

"Oh, God, that was good." Dawson wiped at his chin with the back of his hand.

The chief clapped his hands together. "That was awesome."

The waitress returned and dropped the next round of drinks, ignoring the water that she'd sloshed onto the table in the process. "Impressive drinking." She winked at Dawson.

Fin exhaled a light laugh as she grabbed her water and slurped it down as fast as she could. *Fuck. Brain freeze.* She grabbed her forehead as her eyes clenched shut. She cracked open one eye long enough to see their waitress pull a pencil from her pile of hair and yank the little pad out of her apron. "Whatcha eatin', folks? Chief, I know your order."

He winked at her. "Oh, you know me too well, Laverne."

My God, this would never happen in New York. Fin picked up the menu and scanned the standard diner fare just as the chief spoke up.

"I know their orders. Cheeseburgers, fries, and two sodas. Coke for him. Root beer for her. No onions on his, extra pickles on hers. And what's the pie today?"

"Cherry and banana cream."

"Ooo, let's go cherry. A classic."

Laverne gathered the menus and swaggered away as Fin shot a suspicious look at Dawson, who gave her an identical glance.

How does he know what we eat?

"So, you're probably wondering how I knew what to order for you." The chief propped his elbows on the table. "Or even how I know you. 'Cause you don't know me, am I right?"

"Sums it up quite nicely." Dawson leaned back into the booth and crossed his arms.

With narrowed eyes, Fin said, "At first, I thought maybe you knew our names from our parents because we were born here." *Or I'd hoped anyway.* "But you know what food we eat, that I'm a cop, that Dawson writes in his green notebook, so it's more like we've done this before. But that's—"

"Impossible?" the chief suggested.

Yeah, impossible.

He leaned in and whispered, "It'll be best, moving forward, if you both remove that word from your vocabularies."

Fin shifted uncomfortably in her seat as the chief's lips dipped into a serious bow that spoke to her gut. *This is crazy.*

Laverne interrupted by delivering the chief's coffee, spilling the dark liquid over its edges, and settling a little ceramic pourer next to it.

The chief sat back and added cream and sugar. And then more sugar, and then more sugar. "My mama always said I was too sweet to need sugar." His good-natured grin returned, and he stopped to gauge their reaction as he sipped his coffee.

But Fin had other things on her mind. *I can't believe I'm gonna say this.* "So, time travel. That's what we're talking about? That's how you know us?"

"Sure." He set down his coffee.

"Wait, what did you say?" Dawson gawked at Fin.

"Don't freak out," she said. "Write it down."

His gaze played tennis, lobbing back and forth between the chief and Fin. Apparently coming to a decision, he pulled out his small notebook, opened it, and held his pencil at the ready. His face was a billboard of uncertainty.

The chief scrubbed at his chin. "This isn't my area of expertise. It's Auci's. But soon enough, you'll have that notebook filled with all kinds of things, Dawson. I promise." He looked at each of them in turn. "I'm just here as a guide to Newcross. I'll drop you off to Auci in a bit."

"How do you know Auci?" she asked.

"Who is he, really?" Dawson added. "I get the strangest sense about him."

"Not entirely sure who—or what—he is," said the chief. "I have a few guesses. He's told me some things. I know he's not of this world, not exactly." He took a long gulp of coffee. "That sounds crazy, I know. But around these parts you get used to things not making sense and you just go with it."

"Not of this world?" Dawson scoffed. "Wait, are you . . . are you two serious about all of this?" Panic flushed Dawson's face.

"Just try to keep an open mind and listen." She gave him a reassuring nod before turning to the chief. "So, what do you think he is?" *Let's see what he knows.*

"If I had to guess—and I do—I'd say he's more like an entity." The giant man tilted his head side to side. "Not good or evil. He manages humanity's special objects." He sipped his coffee.

"Do you know what he wants?" Fin asked, trying to assess how much he knew about her, specifically.

"Now, see, *that* is a good question," said the chief.

So, he doesn't know everything Auci told me. Just enough to help.

Before the conversation could continue, Laverne came over and started setting down their orders.

Fin reveled in the mouth-watering smell as Laverne placed a steaming cheeseburger in front of her. "Thank you." Her delight shifted to surprise as she glanced at the chief's plate. *Chef's salad?*

The waitress slid a big cup of Ranch next to his plate, and the chief beamed at her. "You are precious, Laverne, thank you."

Fin grimaced as he scraped out all the dressing onto his salad with his spoon, then licked the spoon.

The big man looked up when his work was done. "My mama said I'm gonna come back as a bottle of ranch dressing."

Fin puckered her brow as she shot a sidelong gaze to Dawson, who just stared at his food. She nudged him with her elbow. "Eat, you'll feel better."

He adjusted his glasses and grudgingly began eating.

Fin took her own advice and bit into her greasy cheeseburger. The melty cheese mixed perfectly with the well-done beef, the ketchup and mustard, fresh onions and tomatoes, and extra pickles. She grabbed a few fries and shoved those in her mouth, too, delighting in the added texture of the tender fries surrounded by crispy potato skins. She relaxed a little as the comfort food took hold of her.

Better.

She swallowed her bite and took a long swig of her root beer before clearing her throat to get everyone's attention.

The chief spoke before she could remind him of her question. "No, I don't know what he wants with you. Do you?"

"Not entirely."

"I do know there's something in it for you." He inclined his head to each of them. "Both of you."

"Our family." Fin's lips twitched a little at the memory of meeting her father. "I know."

The officer's gaze softened as he stared into his coffee before peering back at them. "But I don't wanna get your hopes up. They're not here, right now, in this time."

"In this time?" Frowning, Dawson leaned forward in his seat. "What does that mean, exactly? Where are they?"

"I can't really go into it. I'm sorry." The chief took a drink of his coffee. "But here's what I do know: I'm gonna take you both on a little field trip per Auci's request, then I'm gonna drop you at the old house where Russell and Clara Belle lived with their kids Boone and Nellie. You know the one."

The chief nodded to Fin.

Tears stung her eyes. She had to glance away to catch her breath.

"Is Auci dangerous?" Dawson asked.

"Depends," said the chief.

"On what?"

"Well, I don't know all the answers, but I do know this: Auci controls special objects—"

"Like what?" Dawson interrupted.

"Objects that affect time or people or circumstances. Mystical, magical, important objects. Like, amulets, talismans, stuff like that. He brokers them. Thus, the auctioneer." He cocked his head. "And sometimes, he does not so nice things to people who try to mess with them."

"He runs a black market?" Fin asked.

"Basically." The chief shrugged. "But really, he protects people. Imagine items that dangerous in the wrong hands."

"What about protecting humans from each other?" Dawson asked.

Interesting question. "Why do you ask?"

"Well, when I saw him at the auction, he wasn't the only one there that stood out to me. There was also a girl . . ."

"A girl?" Fin prompted.

Dawson bobbed his head slowly, staring at nothing. "Teenager, actually. She was small but seemed bigger because she wore a trench coach that was way too large. I don't know, she just had this scary look about her. Hollow. And so angry for someone so young."

"How young?" the chief asked.

Dawson cocked his head, considering the question. "Maybe high school?" He absent-mindedly rubbed his finger across the smooth page of his notebook. "She looked at me, but it was like she saw through me, like I wasn't even there. And she was searching for something, tearing through things. There was a boy with her, too. Big. I think he called her Lila or something when he was trying to calm her down. I couldn't really tell. And then the auctioneer—uh, Auci—said it was time to leave."

"So, did she find what she was looking for?" Fin asked.

Dawson shook his head. "I don't think so."

Before she could ask another question, Laverne laid down their pie slices on the table, the forks clanking against the small plates. The waitress patted the chief's shoulder. "I'll put it on your tab."

"Thank ya, Laverne." He tipped an imaginary hat at her before she walked away.

They all stared at the pie for a second.

Ask it. Ask it. Ask it. "Do you know them? Our family. My mother."

He gave her a weak smile but tucked into his pie with gusto. "Eat up! We've got a bit of a haul. And you've got some training to do, Fin, if I'm not mistaken."

"Training?" Dawson narrowed his eyes at her. "I thought you were just investigating your family, like me?"

The chief raised an eyebrow at Fin but jumped in to save her from replying. "Pie makes everything better, Dawson, have some." He pushed Dawson's dessert plate toward him before devouring a forkful of cherries.

Fin gave Dawson an encouraging glance, but he pushed the pie away and looked out the greasy window.

She glanced back to the chief. *He knows my mother. And a hell of a lot more than he's letting on.*

6

I Don't Know What I Believe

Fin glanced furtively at Dawson as they followed the chief the few blocks to the police station. They passed a barber shop with the classic red and blue swirled barber pole and a Dairy Dog claiming the best slushies and swirl cones in the region before she finally broke the silence. "Dawson?"

He didn't say anything, just kicked a wayward rock down a storm drain.

She sniffled and wiped her nose on her arm. New York City smog was one thing, but this country air was something else entirely. Her nose was a faucet that wouldn't shut off.

Dawson scuffed to a stop beside her, so she stopped with him. He wiped his sweaty brow with his shirt. "How much is there I don't know?"

"I mean . . ." She shrugged.

"I know I said I'm open to all kinds of beliefs and knowledge, but this . . ." He slowly took in the Appalachian town around him, shifting uncomfortably. "I don't know."

When he started walking again, she followed. "I'm sorry I was evasive earlier, but we *are* family. You can feel that, right?" She fished for some eye contact before glancing back at the sidewalk and artfully dodging what looked like spit on the worn cement.

He finally looked at her with a shrug, shifting the weight of his bags in the uncomfortable heat. "I'm not really the feeling type."

"Me, either." She grinned as they passed a grocery store called Gilbert's on their right. It was an old, dirty building that needed a good wash, and the parking lot was filled with mostly dirty, rusted pick-up trucks. Not a Yellow cab or Suburban in sight.

Dawson finally relented and said, "Yeah, though, to answer your question, I do think we have similar features that could be construed as being related. Pure conjecture. But you *know* we're family. How?"

"The auctioneer," she said as they came to a stop at a dirt road intersection. The chief had already crossed and peered over his shoulder with a grin. Fin nodded to let him know they were coming. "Auci. He told me."

Dawson turned away and nodded as they both checked for cars, but there wasn't anything except trees and dirt for miles.

"He's my—" She shuffled her feet and let out a half laugh, half sigh. *Can't believe I'm saying this.* "He's my father, Dawson."

His head snapped to her. "He's your—"

"Uh-huh."

"Wait," he said as he shook his head like he was trying to shake the information together. "If we're family, then Auci is my family too?"

"Uncle, I think," said Fin. She led the way, crossing over the uneven, pressed dirt to the other side as he followed. "And there's something else."

Even though she could see he had more questions, he had enough grace to give her the floor as they stepped onto a curb and then into a parking lot of the only gas station in town. They crossed it to the other side, where Fin could see the sign for the police station.

"There are things about me, Dawson. Unexplainable things." She shifted her shoulders. *This sharing stuff. For the birds.* "Well, unexplainable until Auci came along."

He gave her one brisk nod. "Okay. Like what?"

She considered the best way to explain her abilities. "I have extraordinary strength. And healing. Like, instantly. Auci said there's some other stuff I haven't figured out yet."

"Maybe that's what the training is about, then?"

They glanced at each other and she gave him an uncertain look that turned sheepish.

"I can see some things glowing, too."

"Glowing?"

She swept her arm in front of them. "All of the ground. There's like a glowing haze."

Dawson stopped between the gas station and the police station and surveyed everything around him, including the bar across the street, before landing back on her. She held up her wrist to indicate the compass bracelet. "This is glowing right now, too. Like a turquoise night light."

He grabbed her forearm to examine the bracelet. "Fascinating."

The chief hollered, "Hey, let's go you two."

Dawson dropped her arm, pulled out his green book, and started making notes as he shuffled along, before stopping quickly. "Do you have any powers like Auci's? You can't like, read my mind, can you?"

She laughed. "No, I can't read your mind. And I don't know what of Auci's I have."

They resumed walking toward the chief, who was leaning patiently against his cruiser.

Dawson asked, "What about the powers? Like you. Like him. Why don't I have anything?"

"I actually don't know the answer to that. And it's why we have to keep going. Answers. I have to have them. Don't you?"

Dawson quietly eyed her for a moment before letting out a slow breath. "I do."

"Me, too."

She quietly exhaled. *He's gonna be okay.*

After they made it over to the cruiser, the chief stood straight, spit out his toothpick, and a wide grin enveloped his face.

"So, where are we going?" she asked.

He nodded at her and Dawson as he opened his driver's side door and slid in. "Someplace I think you'll really . . . connect to."

Fin could only guess what that meant as Dawson slid into the backseat. She took the passenger side at the front, sliding down into the hot leather seat. She grabbed the inside handle of the passenger door and yanked it shut. Her window shattered as the whole vehicle rocked back and forth.

"Whoa!" Dawson exclaimed as he grabbed the back of her seat.

She shifted wide-eyed to the chief.

He had a grip on the "oh shit" handle, surprise infusing every facet and wrinkle of his face.

What the hell? I couldn't control that.

They blinked at each other before the chief said, "Quite a bit of strength you've got there."

"Sorry." Cringing, she swept the shards of glass off her lap onto the floor. Not knowing what else to say, she stared out the windshield as the chief started up the car. She could hear Dawson scribbling behind her.

As they got moving, a warm breeze swept into the car, giving them some much needed air.

I'm stronger here. Much stronger.

Hiding her unusual strength had always been a struggle. She'd had to learn how to control how much oomph she used growing up. Over time, she'd gotten it under control. But here, in Newcross, everything was different.

"Fin?"

Startled out of her reverie, she peered at the chief. "Sorry, what?"

A stomach flipping sensation crashed into her. Steadying herself against the door handle, she frantically checked her surroundings. The chief appeared ten to twenty years younger now. He tossed her an infectious smile as she noticed the car was also different. The aesthetic was older, and the technology was outdated. Just as suddenly as the world had changed, the vision shifted back to the present and everything returned to normal.

When the car pulled to a stop, she jumped out, wanting to feel the solid ground under her feet. *What's happening to me?*

As a thunderous roar filled her ears, Fin noticed a new blue glow in her peripheral vision. Her body vibrated as she moved toward a stunning lake with a waterfall that joyfully bounced off jagged rocks before falling into a deep pool of shimmering turquoise water. The ethereal scene was enhanced by colorful mushrooms sprouting everywhere. They were like exotic flowers dotting the dark crevices of the trees, logs, and hidden spaces. The lush landscape took her breath away.

I've never seen anything like this. I've never felt anything like this.

"Fin? You okay?" Dawson walked toward her, followed by the heavy footsteps of the chief.

"It's glowing."

Dawson's voice drooped with disappointment. "I can't see any of it."

"What is this place?" she asked.

The chief answered, "This is Blue Falls."

"This place is like . . . it's, it's—" she stammered.

"Your fortress of solitude?" When Dawson saw her confused expression, he explained. "That was Superman's home base. Your face. You look like that. Like you're at peace or something."

This must be difficult for him. Fin touched his arm to comfort him, and he smiled.

"I've never seen so many different mushrooms," Dawson said. "Many of these aren't native to Ohio. And the colors are spectacular."

The chief scanned the area with pride. "It's quite unique, isn't it?"

Dazzled by the eccentric beauty of the place, Fin tried to capture every detail of the opulence around her with her mind. "Feels like a whole other world."

Chief settled his cowboy hat on his head. "In the 1800s, the whole town was stunning like this. With the bright flowers and crystal streams. The people who settled here made it the idyllic country setting."

Fin couldn't tell him that she was seeing everything he was describing. The past and the present were intermixing right in front of her. The visions were more complicated and comprehensive than the fleeting ghostly apparitions she'd seen up until now. Newcross was making the special things about her exponentially more powerful.

She peeked at Dawson, whose expression was saying, "I know something's happening to you."

Sympathy clutched at her chest. *I wish you could see this.*

The chief continued, "And then one day, apparently, it just changed. Like someone flipped a switch. Nothing seemed to work the same way anymore. The snow was heavier, the water was dirtier, and the woods were drier. There were theories that it was black magic kind of stuff."

"And what do you believe?" Dawson asked.

Fin listened to them talk as she watched a new vision appear. This one of the auctioneer, who was walking through the woods toward the glowing lake in front of her. *It's like when Auci showed me Gunnar at my mother's house.* Past Auci was trailed by Gunnar as a figure emerged from the water. The liquid took on a semi-human form with indescribable features.

That must be Amon. The other sibling.

"I don't know what I believe," the chief said. "But the locals believe in the Three Siblings."

"Auci, Gunnar, and Amon," Fin said. She turned to both of them, her stare landing on the chief.

"That's right," the chief said, as though he was impressed. He popped another toothpick in his mouth.

He knows things about me. Maybe even things I don't know yet.

"What's their story?" Dawson asked.

The Chief answered, "Legend has it that the Three Siblings were created out of the earth in this very spot of the world."

"Created? By what?" Dawson pulled out his notebook before smirking at Fin. "Sky Gods?"

"Sort of, yes." The chief tilted his head as Dawson jerked his stare to the chief.

"I-I was joking," he stammered.

"I wasn't," said the chief.

An awkward silence blanketed the moment as Dawson slowly turned to Fin, who gave him a weak smile.

"Why three of them?" Fin spoke up to move the moment along. She studied the vision still in motion. The auctioneer waived his turquoise-ringed hand over the glowing water, bringing from it a glowing piece of turquoise rock and a piece of stone.

"Well, having three of them distributes the labor. If one was the thief, one was the hider, and one was the broker, that makes it harder for things to go sideways."

She glanced at the chief. "But the auctioneer holds all the real power."

"Yes," he said. "He's the master of his siblings and all mystical objects." The chief went on to explain the siblings' roles to Dawson.

But Fin was only half-listening because she couldn't stop thinking about her aunt.

"Gunnar has had to live as a human—as a woman—since the beginning of time," the Chief explained.

Fin felt the pain of that experience down to her bones. *It must have been hell for her. I'd want out too if it was me.*

The chief said, "She's described as cunning and agile. Whip-smart."

"She is," Fin whispered, her chest puffing up a bit.

Returning to the vision in progress, Fin watched as Auci created the compass bracelet she was now wearing. Reflexively, she touched it with a soft upturn of her lips. Their task complete, Auci and Gunnar disappeared from the vision and Amon began to melt away. He dissipated into a blue glowing cloud before condensing into a recognizable black cat on the ground in front of her.

She gasped. Under her breath she whispered, "You're Amon."

The animal rubbed against her ankles as Dawson exclaimed, "That's the second black cat I've seen in as many days. How did it get here?"

Dawson began to move toward it as Fin glanced at the chief.

"Anyway, Dawson," the chief continued as the curious librarian halted and turned back to the story. "It's believed humans started misusing mystical objects for power, money, stuff like that. And the more they got, the more destructive they became. They started excavating and exploring the planet and the Siblings started to run out of hiding places."

"Why not just destroy the objects if they're so dangerous?" Dawson asked.

Fin chimed in. "If they destroy everything, what happens when someone needs one for good reasons?"

"True." The chief tipped his hat. "But, also, you can't just destroy magic. Not without consequences. It's like gasoline or mercury—there's a way to do things. The better way to control it is to just not make magical things, but that's not gonna happen. So, instead, they hide the objects to keep them safe."

"Newcross," Fin and Dawson said at the same time.

She glanced down at the cat, who seemed to be listening to every word. *Would he speak up if we got something wrong? Would he help me the way Auci has?*

"Yep," said the chief. "Locals believe that in the 1800s, the auctioneer created a pocket of time here in Newcross where Amon could hide the objects. It's their home, after all. But the more magical things that were hidden here, the more the town absorbed the trace magic emanating from those objects. Especially the malevolent ones. That's where the town's strangeness comes from. It's believed to be both in the world and not in the world."

"Hmm." Fin bent down and picked up Amon, but he squirmed and snagged her pendant, snapping it off and flinging it into the tall grass.

She froze. "Oh, no."

Fin let go of the cat as she dropped like a stone to her right knee. She cupped her ears inside her hands. The violent buzzing vibrated through her whole body as her increasingly frigid compass bracelet zapped her skin. "Auci!"

"Fin?" She heard Dawson's voice, but it sounded tinny and far away. "Fin?"

At the familiar rush of air overhead, Fin's stomach clenched in anticipation of a fight. "No, no, no," she shouted.

The scorpadactyl screeched across the sky.

The black cat disintegrated into a haze before transforming into a large, fire-breathing dragon. But the agile winged scorpion dodged the flames, raced behind the dragon, and stung its neck. Amon collapsed into a blue cloud as Halo and the winged scorpion barreled toward the chief.

Chief! Gotta help. Powering through the incessant buzzing, she dragged her leaden body across the grass and searched for her pendant. *No luck.* "Fuck!"

The mythical creature dove for the chief, who pulled his weapon and fired. Although the bullets pierced the beast, they seemed to only infuriate the animal.

"Shit." Fighting what felt like twice Earth's normal gravity, Fin grabbed for her gun.

"Dawson, duck," the chief yelled.

The men hit the ground, but the scorpion grabbed the chief with one of its massive talons.

Fin crawled to her knees, which felt like moving through wet cement. She raised her gun and aimed at the scorpion's rider as they lifted off the ground. She fired three times, hitting Halo once in his right shoulder. He jerked on the reins of the scorpion, causing it to release the chief from twenty feet in the air.

"Chief!" she screamed.

He fell like a stone. But before he hit the ground, the talons of a giant blue eagle snatched him from the air and dropped him gently next to Dawson. Their ally disintegrated into a mist that moved like liquid air, chasing their enemies.

Halo and his creature sped straight for Fin.

She did her best to stand, but she was so wobbly that she could no longer aim her gun accurately. Since using her weapon wasn't an option, she ducked down and lifted her compass-laden arm. A surge of power exploded from the turquoise stone, knocking her attackers away with a powerful force field that looked like a transparent blue barrier.

In addition to the power surge, the stone had released something else too.

"What the fuck?" she whispered. *A caterpillar?*

Its vivid green skin had symmetrical rows of turquoise dots outlined in black running along the spine. It had two sets of eyes. The functional eyes were embedded into a yellow circle with a white dot and black outline. The fake eyes, looking almost identical, sat just behind that on its back.

What is that thing supposed to do?

As the blue barrier held Halo back, the wiggly caterpillar dove down into the grass once, twice, three times. Each time it paused to gaze at her as though it was trying to communicate something. Dropping to her knees, she dragged her sandbag of a body toward the creature. She finally reached the caterpillar as it blinked its big, black eyes at her and dove again into the grass. Following it with her hand, she grasped the pendant as the buzzing disappeared, along with the caterpillar and barrier.

She tucked the pendant into her pocket and quickly stood as the scorpion landed and Halo jumped to the ground. As soon as his feet touched the grass, he ran full speed at Fin.

Bring it on. The power of Newcross coursed through her body as she ran to meet him. When he closed in, she dropped like she was sliding into home plate and took his feet out from underneath him. He crashed to the ground with a thud. It took a second for him to stand after bearing the brunt of her strength.

"I know why you're here," she said.

In a deep and gravelly voice, he said, "Then I don't have to explain it you." He rushed her again, pulling a knife from his waistband.

She held her position. When he got close, she grabbed the wrist with the knife and twisted. Every bone in his arm snapped. She threw him over her shoulder, slamming him into the ground, making it shake.

Capitalizing on the opening, the scorpion jumped at her. Fin dropped to her back and kicked its underbody, hurtling it into the sky. Halo groaned as the chief ran up to them with Dawson in tow.

"Go to the house, Fin," the chief said. "Map's in the car. I'll take care of Halo."

"How do you know his—"

"Fin, go," the chief said. "I've got this. Keys are in the cruiser."

Glancing at Dawson, she said, "Let's go."

They headed to the car, but Fin stopped and called back to the chief as he flipped Halo onto his stomach and put a knee in his back, cuffing him, "Will we see you again? Maybe . . . in a different time?"

"Anything's possible, Fin. You should know that by now," he said as he stood, removed his hat, and wiped his brow.

She asked, "You'll help us if we need it? The younger version of you. If that's a real thing."

"Well, my mama always said I was a helpful fellow. At any age."

She huffed a laugh and headed back to the cruiser.

"But Fin?"

She turned back to him. "Yeah?"

"If you meet me in another time and I'm being particularly stubborn, there might be something that could win me over. It's in a paper bag under the passenger seat. Take it with you. Just in case."

She and Dawson exchanged a confused look.

"Oh, and take the case files that are with the paper bag."

She said, "Thank you, Chief."

"Booker," he said.

"What?" she asked.

"That's my name," he said as he put his hat back on. "Quincy J. Booker."

Fin smiled as she and Dawson walked away. They could hear his booming voice as they reached the car.

"All right, Halo, let's do this again. What does this make? Fifteen times I've arrested you? You slippery devil."

As Fin opened the passenger door, she wondered, *How does he know Halo? And how has he arrested that gold-toothed bastard fifteen times?*

7

Onward

Fin gently closed the cruiser's door and took in the old, broken-down house in front of them. Adjusting her heavy gear, she contemplated what was about to happen next. Tears sprang to her eyes as she thought of her mother.

"You okay?" Dawson asked.

She wiped her eyes quickly. "Yeah."

"So, what's in the chief's bag?"

She held up the bag she'd retrieved from under the passenger seat and unrolled it, peering inside and smirking. "It's a cupcake."

"A cupcake?"

Shoving her nose into the bag, she inhaled deeply. "Peanut butter icing. Chocolate cake." She rolled the bag closed with a shake of her head.

"You got the files?"

She nodded. "In my backpack."

They quietly stared at the house for a moment.

"Dawson, in the interest of full disclosure, you should know that I've been here before."

"You have?" His eyebrows jumped into his forehead. "When?"

Well, that's a damn good question.

"Um . . ." She'd never had such a hard time with words. Trying to communicate something she didn't fully understand was challenging to say the least. "I mean, you realize this whole thing—everything we're doing—defies logic. At least as we understand it, right?"

She held his eye contact and watched him think through what she'd said.

He pushed his glasses up. "I suppose."

"And it's only going to get stranger from here, I'm guessing."

"Stranger than a flying scorpion?" They both chuckled, and he let out a tightly held breath. "I'm okay. I'll be okay."

I hope so.

"So, when were you at this place?"

"I'm not quite sure, to be honest." *And that's the truth.* "I think I was here in this time. The house looks the same, anyway. One second, I was in New York and then" —she snapped her fingers— "here. I'm pretty sure it was time travel. God, that's weird to say out loud."

Apprehension pinched his face. "Okay," he whispered.

"So, I think that Auci brought me here through time. I thought I was re-dreaming the same moment over and over. But I think I was actually reliving the same moments because he kept taking me back to the same spot. Ish. I mean, I'm not sure."

He gnawed at his lip. "I, um, I've read a little on time travel and the like."

"And?"

"I mean . . ." He tossed his hands up. "Theory. Impossible, you know?"

Trying to encourage him, she said gently, "But this, it's not theory."

"Right." He stood a little taller, going into professor mode. "Um, so, there's lots of ideas about the nature of time and time travel. Multiple timelines. Parallel timelines. Multiple versions of the self and outcomes, depending on which line you're in."

"That multiple line thing sounds like something," she said.

"How so?"

"Uh, the re-dreaming I thought I was doing. What if I was re-living it? Then it might make sense that I was in—or maybe creating—different timelines based on different choices? Small things changed each time I re-lived it."

"Interesting." His face lit up as he pulled out his note book and started writing. "Creating multiple timelines based on choice."

She tilted her head, considering that.

"There is something, though," he said, eyeing her thoughtfully.

"Something?"

"Well, you," he said, flipping his hand to her.

"What do you mean, me?"

"You're not entirely human, are you? Because of Auci."

She stilled as she glanced at him. *Shit. He's right. I'm not . . . I'm not . . .* A wave of dizziness rolled over her, so she concentrated on breathing slowly.

"Maybe that's one of your things." He jotted down notes in his book. "Can you control it?" When she didn't respond, he peered up at her. "You okay?"

She swallowed hard and nodded. It was one thing to suspect she was more than human; it was something else entirely to know it. "We could…" she whispered before clearing her throat. "We could speculate all day."

"Right." He closed his book and gave her an encouraging smile. "I didn't mean to freak you out."

They each sat with their own thoughts for a moment.

I need answers. "We're just gonna have to find out for ourselves."

"Or we could turn around and pretend it never happened?" Tension and trepidation lined his face.

I feel that, too. "We could." They looked at the looming house. "But the answers we want are here. I know that."

They locked eyes for a long moment.

"Onward then?" he asked.

She squared her shoulders. "Onward."

As they started toward the house, Fin kept her eyes peeled. For what, she wasn't sure. Everything was quiet, except their shoes on the gravel, as they passed the abandoned, run-down barn.

"Do you think Auci's here?" Dawson asked.

"I do."

After they walked up the porch steps, they each took a deep breath. Fin reached for the door, which groaned when she opened it. She stepped through the door frame into the cool, dark entryway. Dawson filed in behind her, blacking out the sunlight and casting shadows deep inside the home.

"It smells old," he said. "Like a library."

"Must feel like home, then, huh?"

"A much-needed memory at the moment." He touched things delicately as they moved inside, eventually picking up a croquet mallet. "Wonder who played with this?"

"Who even plays croquet?"

"Right?" He leaned it against the wall as they crept further into the worn-down house.

Fin could see different details this time around. She stepped gingerly around the holes in the floors, pointing them out to Dawson, who dodged them. Despite the cobwebs and dust lining every surface, she could tell someone had taken pride in it before it fell into disrepair. The walls had few nails or holes in them, and the trim was made of quality wood, as was the banister and staircase. As she ran her finger over the banister, emotion crashed into her as a vision appeared. She watched as a ghostly woman from another time ran down the staircase with a small sweater in her hand.

"Take a sweater. It'll get cold!" The woman, in her forties or late thirties, was tall with dark blond hair. She shook her head and dropped the sweater on the banister then ran back upstairs and vanished.

Fin darted her eyes to Dawson. "Did you see that woman? On the stairs?"

Dawson walked over and inspected the staircase. "It's been empty since we walked in."

Lose the word impossible. What's left? She peered at him as she flicked her hair out of her eyes. "I started seeing things when I was a child."

"Oh." He poked at his glasses. "What kinds of things?"

"I thought they were ghosts, if I'm being honest." She lightly touched the banister again as she examined the empty space where she saw the vision. "I tried to ignore it. As I got older, I learned to pretend. Act like they didn't exist."

She twisted back to Dawson.

"And now?" he asked.

She shook her head. "They're not ghosts. I know that much." Looking around her, she took a deep breath and blew it through pursed lips. "I think I'm seeing slices of time."

"But that's—"

"Impossible?"

They peered at each other as that sunk in.

A familiar voice said, "Welcome."

They both whipped around to face the front door. Fin drew her gun, but immediately lowered it.

"Auci." She was relieved to see him. "We could've used your help at the lake. I called for you. You didn't come."

"You seemed to have it under control." A flash of pride crossed his face. "And now you've met Amon."

She holstered her gun. "Spirited fellow."

"Indeed." He greeted Dawson by inclining his head. "Dawson."

"Hello again," Dawson said.

Coming farther into the house, Auci said, "I heard you talking about the ghosts. If you'll allow me, I'd like to show you what that is." He glanced back and forth between the cousins, raising his eyebrows. "Interested?"

Dawson glanced at her with a quick nod as she gave an affirmative chin raise to Auci. "I want to know."

"The auction is about to begin then." With a flourish, he turned toward the front room where a table with a gavel was now standing in front of the large front window.

"Where the hell did that table come from?" Dawson inched closer to Fin as she moved toward Auci.

They watched as Auci took his place behind the thick, worn wood and picked up the gavel, holding it aloft and waiting for their final consent.

Dawson exhaled a big breath. "Let's do it."

She asked, "Are you sure?"

"Oh my God," he snapped. "You just said you wanted to do this."

"We just, I mean, this could be, you know. It. So, we need to be sure."

"Are you sure?"

She peered at the auctioneer, who was calm and ready. *I trust him.* "I am."

"Then I trust you," Dawson said.

Fin again gave the auctioneer a quick gesture to go ahead.

"We'll start the bidding at one dollar," Auci said to seemingly no one. "One dollar bid now two, do I have a two, now three, three dollars?"

She'd been to several law enforcement auctions and was always enamored with the musicality of it, the way the man with the gavel would run the crowd and send an item home with someone who really wanted it. Auci was better than anyone she'd ever seen. He was smooth and filled with an unexpected charisma that gathered weight and steam as his auctioneering got louder with every point of his hand. "Now five, do I hear six dollars?"

He worked the empty room as though there were dozens of people standing around. As his haunting voice grew louder and his eyes larger, Fin started to see people appearing around her. "Now seven, do I hear eight?"

"Do you see them?" She had to shout as the auctioneer and the crowd became so loud it nearly overwhelmed her.

Dawson inspected the room. "Who?"

The auctioneer reached his crescendo with a powerful slam of his gavel. "And sold!"

At the crack of wood on wood, a hundred people appeared. Dawson looked as frozen in place as she felt. They looked around at the people who clapped in slow motion for the winning bidder. Everyone in the room, which was now overflowing with chairs and furniture and trinkets marked with bid numbers, seemed to be moving at half speed. They were dressed from a different time, maybe the 1970s.

Fin locked eyes with the auctioneer, who pointedly looked out the window. Fin followed his stare, her eyes landing on a girl. A teenager, maybe. The girl, whose face looked like she had been in a fight, was excited as an older boy with a bruised, black eye gently hugged her. They were followed by the woman from her vision, only this time, the woman was bruised. *Why are they all beaten up?*

Fin felt inexplicably compelled to run to the teenage girl and hug her. *I know her. How?* She tried to move toward her, but her feet felt like they were in sludge. She glanced back to the auctioneer, who gave her a nod that seemed to confirm what she was thinking about the girl.

When Auci slammed down his gavel again, Fin and Dawson were back in the present and the auctioneer was gone. The old house was in the same condition as though nothing had happened.

"That was incredible," Dawson said, beaming with delight. "Better than the last time even. Because now I know what it is. Time travel. My God, can you believe it? That's what happened to me the first time, with Auci and the maps, and now this time. It's, my God, it's incredible." He whipped the little book from his pocket and frantically wrote some notes.

She wanted to respond to him, but she couldn't. *Don't you dare cry.* But it was too late. Tears slid down her face as she thumbed her necklace.

Dawson's expression morphed from excitement to concern. "What's the matter?"

Her voice wavered with emotion. "I just saw my mother."

8

Try and Stab Me

As Fin grappled with the emotions that pierced her heart at the sight of her mother, Auci appeared out of nowhere and asked, "Your powers are stronger here. You've noticed, yes?"

Fin dried her eyes and nose with her shirt as she shoved her feelings down. *He can be so abrupt.* "Yes. I'm stronger. And the visions are more detailed and last longer."

He nodded. "Newcross is the source of all my power. And therefore, yours as well. When we're here, we're more powerful."

"Even though the rest of my family are ordinary humans?"

"I wouldn't call your mother ordinary." A wistful expression flitted across his features. "But if you mean not magical, then yes, they're just human." He glanced at his feet.

"Do you miss her?" Fin asked quietly.

"I—"

"Wait!" Dawson interrupted. "That's why I don't have the—" Dawson fluttered his fingers like he was playing the piano in the air.

"Correct." Auci quirked an eyebrow at Dawson's pantomime. "You saw your father, yes?"

Fin spun sharply to her cousin. "Did you see your father?"

"The teenage boy who hugged the girl." Although it was a statement, Dawson's voice pitched up like he was asking for confirmation.

Auci gave one sage bow of his head.

Dawson explained to Fin, "I looked like him as a teenager. Our eyes are different." He touched his earlobes. "Ears are different."

"You okay?" she asked.

He nodded but changed the subject. "That was your mother?"

"It was." She put her hands on her hips. "Why did you show us that?"

"I promised you the chance to know your mother, didn't I?"

As she glanced at the banister, things clicked into place. "So, we're going back in time."

"Indeed," he said. "I found where and when Amon hid the dagger. The 1970s. The key is to retrieve it as close to when he hid it as possible to minimize anyone else finding it. But before you go, I need to train you on how to move through time. And how to manage the power of Newcross on your body."

"Right, yeah." She shuffled her feet. "That was, uh, intense at Blue Falls. I could barely move."

A little twinkle sparked in Auci's eyes. "I was quite impressed you were able to move at all. Truly impressive. You're quite strong. Even more than I expected."

"What happened with my bracelet? With the barrier and the—"

"I'll show you." He interrupted and moved to leave, but she stopped him.

"Hang on. What about the visions, the ghosts? What are they? What am I seeing?"

"Ah, yes, those." He turned back to her. "I assume by now you realize they are not ghosts or figments of your imagination."

"I do."

"Our family line can see through time. No matter where you are, you can stand in that spot and view everything that happened there like a slideshow going back as far as you want. We can look through the layers of time and step into whichever layer we want. It's how Gunnar finds objects. How Amon hides them. How I manage them."

"So, time travel?" she asked.

"Sort of." He tilted his head side to side. "It's more like we exist in multiple layers at once and we choose which layer to interact with."

"That's real? Multiple timelines? Time is . . . stacked?" Dawson was flabbergasted.

"Layered, yes. And multiples, yes," said Auci patiently as he turned back to Fin while Dawson scrawled words across the pages of his book. "You're existing in multiple layers right now. You're aware of this layer because it's the one you choose to interact with. But once you're used to it and have more control, you'll see and manage all the layers you can exist in."

He tucked his hands behind his back. "When the visions occur, your powers are breaking through your perception of what's logical. You've tried to ignore it, but you can't ignore what's inside you. It will eventually come out whether you want it to or not."

"That's true. Several personality studies on that actually," Dawson said without looking up from his notebook.

Auci glanced at him then back to Fin. "Obviously, this is more than just your personality."

After thinking for a moment, Fin asked, "Can they see me? The people in these other timelines."

"No. To them, you're like a blur or a ghost or a feeling of déjà vu. Their human minds can't comprehend you."

"But I live in this timeline. The present one."

"Do you?"

At Auci's cagey expression, she pivoted. "What about the buzzing? And how cold the compass stone gets?"

"That bracelet is powerful. Whenever we enter a layer of time, it releases the bitter air of the universe at the entry point. The stone absorbs the cold so you don't have to. It also acts as an early warning system for you, so you know when something is afoot."

She thumbed the bracelet. "And the buzzing?" She pulled the pendant out of her pocket. "What is this necklace preventing me from feeling when I'm here?"

Auci walked over and waved his hand with the turquoise ring over her necklace, fixing the broken clasp. He took it from her palm and fastened it around her neck.

"A much stronger clasp." He patted her shoulders. "Your bloodline means you're sensitive to the magic of mystical objects. Newcross holds a pocket of time with many mystical objects. Too many. It's heavy with magic, and you can feel every ounce of it. Because you haven't learned to control it yet, it simply reverberated in your body creating the buzz. The pendant absorbs that. I also added a feature that makes you invisible to those who wish to do you harm."

"Thank you."

His eyes lit with delight as he rocked on his heels. "You're welcome. But we're running out of time, and I should teach you the basics before you go to your mother."

At the mention of her mother, squishy feelings burbled up inside her. She was never going to get used to this new wellspring of emotion. "I assumed as much."

"Uh, hello, I'm here." Dawson waved his hands around. "Do I need to learn anything? I've got weird stuff, too."

Fin raised a questioning eyebrow at him. "You've got weird stuff? What stuff?"

He reached in his bag and pulled out the stone-like pen with a turquoise tip. "What is this thing? Why do I have it?"

Fin noticed its glow. "You've had that the whole time?"

Dawson grinned sheepishly as Auci said to him, "Hold up your green notebook."

Dawson pulled it out of his bag and presented it.

Auci waved his hand again. "Now, write down any question you have in the green book using that special pen."

"I already know this pen doesn't write," Dawson griped. "I mean, honestly, why does she get all the good stuff?"

The auctioneer's lip twitched, and Fin fought back a grin. *He's not used to people questioning him.*

Auci pointed to the notebook. "Just write down your question."

"So, it's like a magic eight ball?" Dawson waggled the pen like it was a ridiculous proposition.

She had to agree it certainly sounded that way, but the glowing tip meant it was special.

"Magic eight balls are not magic," said the auctioneer. "Write down a question. Any question."

Skepticism infused his face, but Dawson dutifully wrote out a question.

She sucked in a little breath as the page began to glow for her, but for Dawson, it was a written answer that appeared.

"Whoa," Dawson said.

"What did you ask it?" Fin leaned forward.

"What is the square root of one million?"

"That was your burning question?"

"Well, I had to ask something I know the answer to," Dawson said.

"You know the answer to that?" she and Auci asked in unison.

"Yeah." He shoved his glasses up. "Parlor trick for my librarians' work group."

Taking a step closer, Fin asked, "Is the book right?"

"Yeah."

"Whoa," she said.

"Amazing." Dawson inspected the pen and paper more closely.

She gave Auci a lopsided smile. "That should keep him busy."

Instead of replying, the auctioneer touched her arm. Now they were standing in the middle of the woods at a tree line that glowed softly.

She swooned a little, but her feet steadied her. "I don't know if I'm ever going to get used to that."

He reached for her but saw she was okay and tucked his hands behind his back. She peered at their surroundings.

"You can see the glow I assume?" asked the auctioneer.

"Yes. It's like the lake. I saw the three of you there. But it was a different time."

"I know," said the auctioneer.

"I thought you couldn't read minds."

"I can't. But I can detect when I'm being watched through time. You will be able to as well once you hone your senses."

She inclined her head to the luminous tree line. "What's the glow made of?"

"The stuff."

A laugh burst out of Fin. "The stuff? That's the best name you could come up with for it?"

He shrugged. "We were made from it, my siblings and I. It looks like a fancy stone, but it can be used to create anything in the right hands. Our family can see the trace of its power."

"The glow," she whispered.

"That's correct. Now, I want you to find when Amon creates this place. So, you'll need to go back through the layers of time. To start, let your mind wander a little."

"Just, like, start thinking about it?"

"Yes, it's all here." He tapped his head.

Fin gave him a dubious sigh and faced the tree line. She tried to relax her mind for a moment but felt his eyes boring into her. "Don't stare at me. Makes me nervous."

She aggressively returned his raised eyebrow. After he directed his attention at something else, she focused on the tree line. *It's all in my mind.*

She took a deep breath and closed her eyes. *Just see back in time. Easy. You can do this.* When Fin opened her eyes, it took only a few seconds before images started to appear. The first ones were recent, teenagers smoking and drinking. But the tree line was glowing, so Amon must have changed things before this time. *How do I go back further?*

"Just tell your mind to go back," Auci said.

"I thought you couldn't read minds."

"I can't."

She turned to him, exasperated.

Auci held up his hands to ward off a verbal onslaught. "I can see what you're seeing. I can see time shifting."

"Oh," she said.

She faced the trees again, took another breath, reset her body, and closed her eyes. As she exhaled, she opened her eyes. *Go back.*

Thousands of years of history flooded her vision, people and animals everywhere. Some coming right at her, some running away, some screaming, some laughing. The world was spinning. "Oh no."

She squeezed her eyes shut to block out the images, but it was too late. Her knees hit the ground and her ponytail swung against her neck as she vomited in the grass. Twisting her backpack off, she spit, coughed a little, then spit some more. She pulled out a bottle of water, took a sip, swished it around in her mouth, and spit it back out. *Thank God I have gum in here.* After fishing out a piece from her bag, she popped it into her mouth and started chewing. Her hands shook a little as she packed everything away and slung the backpack on before standing and facing the auctioneer.

"Better?" he asked.

"Much."

"Try again. And this time, control how much you allow yourself to see. Use your mind like a computer. Give it commands."

She faced the tree line once more and steadied herself. *Think smaller. Go back to the 1970s.*

Again, the images started to come fast and furious, like being on a mental scrambler ride, but at a hundred times the pace. She felt the sickness start to come again. *Slow down.*

The visions slowed.

"Oh." She still couldn't see through all the images to any specific one. *I have to narrow it down. Go to 1971.*

The visions slowed enough that she could see more details, but they still had confusing layers on top of layers.

Form a grid.

The conjured images separated into a grid pattern.

"Interesting," the auctioneer whispered.

Every day in January. At noon. Thirty-one portals appeared in front of her. She searched them, but there was no glow. *Now February.* Twenty-eight squares appeared. She scanned those. Nothing. *March.* Nothing. *April.*

"Keep going," Auci said patiently.

She flipped through the years slowly and patiently. She skimmed through 1972, 1973, and 1974. *Okay, let's try 1975.* She sighed when the first four months yielded no results. *Go to May.* Nothing. *Wait. There.*

"May twenty-second and twenty-third." All the other dates fell away except for those days. *Move through every second of May twenty-second and twenty-third.* She watched both squares carefully looking for the moment she'd seen, the one where the glow disappeared. *Faster.* The images came a little faster, but still nothing. *Faster.* The images sped up like they were on fast-forward. *There. In reverse, the glow was there and then gone.*

"Stop. Go back." She watched the moment play out again and saw a slight movement through the grass and the trees. Like an invisible wave moving through them.

"Amon," she whispered.

"Yes."

The mysterious wave disappeared behind the tree line and within seconds the glow appeared. "He hid it late in the morning of May 23,1975."

"Correct." The auctioneer beamed at her and scooped his head, urging her forward. "Now, step into it."

"Step into what?"

"Step into the portal."

"How?"

"Just simply step in."

Fin walked over to the square and tentatively put her hand through it. *It doesn't feel different.* "Can it hurt me?"

"No."

Her shoulders relaxed, and she started to step into the frame.

"Oh, Fin?"

She froze mid-step and twisted toward him.

"If you die in another timeline, you die in them all."

She yanked her foot back and stomped it on the ground. "Remember when I asked if it could hurt me?"

"You asked if the transferring between timelines could hurt you. It cannot. But the threats within the timeframe most certainly can. And if there's a chance that the danger on the other side can come through, the portal will close. And you can't re-open it until the danger has passed."

"What about the invisibility part? You said I'll look like a ghost or apparition to them."

"While you're searching through the layers of time, yes. But once you step into a square, you're very real in that timeline. They'll be able to see you just like everyone can see you right now. I may exist in multiple timelines, but I'm only fully visible in this one because I choose to be in it."

"But, wait, how do the other timelines keep going if I'm not in them? Do I just disappear?"

"That's a question for another day that I promise to answer."

"Okay. So, how fast can I move between times?" She gasped as the auctioneer appeared right next to her.

"That fast," he said. "Once you get used to it."

"So, you just moved through a square? That fast?"

"Yes."

"So, once I go through this square, I can be seen in that timeline?"

"Yes."

"Gotcha." She checked to make sure her gun was holstered and her knife was still on her ankle band. "Hang on." She reached down and untied the knife sheath and reattached it on the outside of her jeans at the thigh, then threw a glance at Auci. "I mean, hanging out with you has its challenges."

"That's fair." He nudged his head toward the tree line.

She moved to the frame again, but Auci said, "Wait."

She glanced back to him.

"If you're injured so badly you can't heal, I've heard it's wise to follow the white fox. The one with the blue eyes."

"What does that mean?"

"In my world, it's believed the white fox is a guide that leads the Gods and their kin safely to the other side. And occasionally back again."

He's genuinely concerned for me. Her heart squeezed at the realization.

"Foxes are clever animals and the only ones shrewd enough to cross swiftly and undetected between life and death," he said. "But be wary; the fox is a wickedly Machiavellian animal. It will help you, but some day when you least expect it, it will come round to collect payment for services rendered."

"Sounds like a CI," she said with a snorting laugh.

He peered at her in confusion.

"Confidential informant. They give us info but expect . . . you know what, never mind, doesn't matter." She waved away the topic. "So, the fox serves the same function as St. Michael for cops."

"Protector of the innocent," he said with a respectful nod.

Growing somber, she added, "He's supposed to guide officers to God after they die. So, they say."

"It's good to know you're protected," Auci said. A quiet moment passed between them. "I should have been there for you more than I was. I wish I had been."

Her eyes misted over, so she shook her head to prevent the emotion from escalating. "Thank you." She took a deep breath. "Well, no time like the present." Watching for any danger, she stepped into the frame slowly and carefully. She glanced back at him with a grin. "Am I good to go through, or do you have some other sage piece of advice?"

His eyes brightened as he returned her grin. "No. Not at the moment."

She tipped her chin at him and brought her other leg into the square. Once she was through, she looked over her shoulder. Auci and his surroundings were now featured in a frame that hung in midair while she was fully immersed in the new time. "Wow. Trippy."

As she investigated her surroundings, her feet slowly crunched through the much shorter, greener grass toward the tree line. She reached out her hand and touched the trees, but the texture was all wrong.

"What the . . . ?" The bark felt like liquid wallpaper. Her touch left a striking turquoise trail that quickly sealed back into the illusion of a tree. "It's not real."

She studied the mirage for a second, then looked around, finding a stick lying on the ground. Mentally going through her supplies, she pulled off her backpack and opened it. After taking out some fishing string and her work phone, she tied the phone to the stick. Once it was secure, she tossed her gear back in the bag and threw on her backpack. She readied the phone for its mission, opening the camera and pressing record. Standing a few feet back, she slowly started the phone toward the illusion to push it through.

"Fin!" Auci shouted.

She glanced up just in time to see the frame with Auci disappear as something moved to her right. It was a female wearing an oversized trench coat.

The teenager stiffened in surprise upon seeing Fin.

They stared at one another. The shape of their eyes were so unnervingly similar that Fin felt as though she was staring into a funhouse mirror. She pulled the phone off the stick and jammed it in her pocket as they circled each other, maintaining the same distance.

"Who are you?" The girl had long, mousy-blond hair hanging loosely around her face and dripping onto her long, black coat. "Are you Gunnar?"

Fin blinked, leaning back slightly. "How do you know Gunnar?" She thumbed her ice-cold compass bracelet and glanced at the girl's wrist, noticing a glowing almost identical bracelet.

The teenager eyed Fin's bracelet, then glared at her. "You're not Gunnar." Her young face contorted with rage. "Who are you? Why are you here?" The girl took a defensive stance.

Fin lifted her hands up to reassure the girl. "Whoa. I'm not here for you."

"You're here for the Grim?" Her green eyes were icy.

Fin had only seen eyes like those on serial killers and murderers. All of them looked the same in the eyes—a dark void, as though human emotion was removed from their souls. Or maybe, they had no soul at all. That's how the girl looked. And Fin would be lying to herself if she said she wasn't unnerved.

"Is that what you're here for?" Fin asked.

The girl's facial expression transformed quickly, going from angry curiosity to malicious determination.

Fin brought her right hand down and rested it on her gun.

In a flash, the girl's hands tightened around Fin's throat.

God, she's fast. Fin had only seen a blur before she hit the ground with the girl on top of her. The teenager punched Fin's rib cage with the force of a middleweight boxer. *I can't hit her. I could kill her.*

"Stop! I don't want to hurt you," Fin yelled. *God she's strong.*

When the girl pulled her fist back for another punch, Fin jerked up and wrapped her arms around her attacker's waist. Pulling her over, they landed sideways on the ground as Fin tucked her head to protect it.

The girl started punching from above into Fin's back, ribs, and kidneys, which made Fin want to throw up. But she was still too scared to fight back, knowing what her enhanced strength could do.

I don't know if I can control it.

But when the girl grabbed Fin's knife from her thigh band and jabbed it toward her rib cage, Fin instinctively grabbed the girl's wrist and twisted.

As the girl screamed to the sound of breaking bones, she dropped the knife on the ground.

Shit.

Fin yanked the compass bracelet off the girl's wrist and stood up, twisting away from the teenager. But the girl had disappeared into thin air.

"What the hell?"

"Fin!" shouted the auctioneer as the square reopened and he came through the portal towards her.

She faced him, pointing to where the girl had been. "A girl was here."

He checked her over for bruises.

"I'm okay," she said. "I broke her wrist. My strength here is—"

"You'll learn to control it." He noticed what she was holding.

"I see you found its twin." He bobbed his head at the bracelet.

"Twin?"

He gently took it from her and held it next to the one on her wrist. "They are companions, and they have the ability to interact with each other among other things."

A loud breath escaped his lips. "My sister stole it from me. She's very good at her job. My assumption is that girl is her descendant hunting the Grim."

"I thought that, too. But she thought I was Gunnar."

The auctioneer pressed his lips together, making them into a thin line. "Oliver."

"Oh, right, the guy from yesterday. The one Gunnar's in love with."

"He's helping her so she can stay insulated from me." He glanced at the bracelet. "My siblings can use the compass stone to move humans or objects or animals to another place in time. But once the compass is removed, it breaks the magic."

"So, they go back to where they came from?"

"Correct."

"They must've sent her here to show her where the tree line is. I think that girl might be the one Dawson saw at your auction. You saw her, too, right?"

"I did. And I suspected as much."

"What other things does the compass do?"

"Well, it does quite a bit more than just show you north." He slipped the companion bracelet onto his wrist and waved his hand over it. A small click echoed between them.

What am I feeling?

He gave her an appraising look. "Can you feel that? Like a pulsing?"

"Yeah, what's it do?"

"It's like . . ." he said, trailing off. "A GPS tracker. Each compass stone can find the other, no matter where or when they are."

She marveled her bracelet. "Cool."

"In moments of need," he continued, "you can also call on it to help you. Which is what you unwittingly did earlier at Blue Falls." A slight smile tugged at the corners of his mouth as he waved his hand over his bracelet again. A turquoise-colored projection of a wolf shot forth. It shook its fur, ready to work.

"Wow," she whispered.

"It will guide you where you need to go to get the help you need."

"Why is it a wolf?"

"The animal is a representation of who you are inside."

Fin snorted. "Why do you get a wolf and I got a caterpillar?"

"That's a good question to ask yourself."

She put her hands on her hips. "So, what, I can tell it where to go?"

"No. It doesn't show you where you want to go; it shows you where you need to go."

She thought for a second. "Yeah, the caterpillar kept diving into the grass."

"Where your pendant was. Because that's all the help you needed." He glanced at the wolf who sat in patient waiting. "There's one other thing the compass can do."

"Really a multi-purpose tool, huh?"

He puffed up a little with pride. "Well, I knew you were going to need it. And I want you to be safe."

Not sure how to react to the warmth in her chest, she asked, "What's the other thing?"

"It can act as a shield."

"Like the blue barrier from earlier?"

"Yes, and a real shield, depending on the need." He opened his arms. "Try to stab me."

She gave him a questioning look.

"Are you serious?"

"I am."

"Okay." She inspected the ground for her knife. Finding where the girl had dropped it, she flipped it so she grasped the handle. "You asked for it."

She lifted the knife, aimed for his chest, and stabbed.

He swung the compass bracelet up in front of him. The wolf morphed into a glowing blue shield in front of his body. Her knife bounced off, dropping to the ground and wrenching Fin's wrist.

"Damn!" She twisted around, flicking her wrist with irritation. "Okay, shield. Got it." She swooped down, picked up the knife, and put it back in her thigh band. "Anything else you need to let me know?"

"Yes, many things, but you've got enough for now." He took off the bracelet and handed it to her.

She took it from him. "You're not going to keep it?"

"There's someone else who needs it. You'll know when it's right. Trust your instincts. But if you give it to a human, they must activate it with their blood."

"That's"—she reared her head back—"that's disgusting."

"Mystical objects in the hands of humans can often only be activated with blood."

Dawson. "We should get back."

"Don't worry about Dawson. It'll seem as though no time has passed at all."

"How is that possible?"

"Because we'll go back to the same point we left. So, technically, no time has passed in that timeline."

"Oh, right."

"We need to do one more thing." Before she could move, he touched her arm, and they were instantly standing in Blue Falls.

She looked at him pensively. "What are we—"

"The magic. You must learn to bear it." Auci's expression left no room for argument.

"Auci, I don't know—"

"You do know." He was stern, like a chastising father, and it caught her off guard. "You're resisting it."

"I'm not. I just don't know how to overcome it."

"That's because you're fighting it, daughter."

Ignoring the little thrill that went down her spine at being called daughter, she said, "I don't understand."

"Stop fighting the sensations. Let them in. Use them. They overwhelm you not because they are overwhelming but because you're pushing against them. Stop resisting it. Let yourself become who you are. Take the magic in and use it."

He raised his turquoise ring hand in the air but hesitated. "Are you ready?"

She shook her head.

"Fin." He narrowed his eyes at her. "Are you ready?"

She sucked in a deep breath and let it out slowly through pursed lips.

He waved his hand, and the clasp on her necklace clicked before he floated it away from her.

She dropped to her knees, the weight of the magic felt like a one-thousand-pound blanket draped on her back. The buzzing was so loud it overtook her.

Auci said her name, but it sounded like a yell from a mile away.

Just as quickly as it came on, it was gone.

Feeling the reassuring weight of the necklace against her chest, she grasped the pendant and looked up into Auci's eyes. *He looks scared.* "You're not hurting me." She swallowed and blinked the blurriness from her eyes before letting go of the necklace. "Do it again."

"Are you sure?"

"Do it again."

He raised his hand.

When the pendant clicked and pulled away, the weight collapsed on top of her, pushing her to the ground. The buzzing felt like a motor inside her gut. *Take it in and use it. Take it in and use it. Take it in and use it.*

She visualized funneling the power into her center where the motor lived. The buzzing began to relent, and she felt lighter. She kept imagining a gathering of light and power inside her. The brighter it got, the lighter she felt. *Keep going. Keep going.* The buzzing was gone now, and it was replaced with a pulsing. When she opened her eyes, she realized she was floating in air.

"What the hell?" She dropped like a stone ten feet onto the hard ground. "Oh, fuck." Panting, she peered wide-eyed at Auci. "Why was I in the air?"

"The magic lifted you."

"I can fly?"

"No, but someday you might be able to use the magic to lift you. Sort of like an extraordinary jump."

He waved his hand as the pendant fell back to her neck with a click. "To keep you invisible."

Neither of them spoke for what felt like an eternity.

Eventually, he asked, "How do you feel?"

"Like I have a lot to learn."

He gave her a gentle smile. "You're getting stronger. Soon enough, you'll be able to exist in Newcross without the pendant. Now, we need to get back. I'll meet you there." He blipped out of existence.

Fin decided to stay for a moment, walking to the falls and feeling the power of the place, how much it felt like home. She knelt at the edge and reached deep into the water, grabbing a handful of the turquoise mud and pulling it out. "The stuff," she whispered. It glowed with spectacular brilliance. She mushed it in her hand. *It's malleable.*

Her hands twisted the clay and formed it into a butterfly shape. It hardened into stone. "Hmmm." She tucked it into her backpack, stood up, and opened the time squares. Almost as soon as she did, she was already back at the house looking at Dawson and Auci. *Wow, I didn't even—I barely even thought about it and I was here. I'm already faster.*

"Are my parents alive?" Dawson asked as he wrote. He groaned as she joined them. "Seriously?"

"What was the answer?" she asked.

"Information unavailable." Dawson shot a glare at Auci.

Unaffected, Auci shrugged. "It's rather got a mind of its own, hasn't it?"

Dawson looked disappointed as he addressed his next comment to Fin. "You were gone less than a second. Did you figure out how to do what you needed to do?" He waggled his fingers to imitate magic.

"Sort of. I'll fill you in later."

"Okay. So, now what?" Dawson asked.

Fin answered, "Now, we go back to 1975 and get the Grim. You ready for real this time?"

"I've literally been ready for the last five minutes."

"How do I take him back with me?" she asked Auci.

"You can't. Not that I know of anyway. I'm the only one who can move people through time without the compass. Even Gunnar and Amon have to use the bracelets."

"Are there any rules? With time traveling?" asked Dawson.

"Generally speaking, we try to do it as little as possible so we're not creating excessive amounts of timelines. Outside of that, three major rules: Don't kill anyone, don't save anyone's life, and don't materially change anything based on your future knowledge."

"That's all, huh?" Dawson smirked.

"Good to know." Fin stood up straighter and gave the auctioneer one crisp nod. "We're ready."

An auctioneering table suddenly appeared.

But before Auci stepped behind the podium, he glanced at her. "You realize I can't come with you? With the Grim still out there, it's too dangerous."

"I understand, but what if I need you?"

"I'll be watching." He paused for a moment. "Get to know your mother. She's . . ." His gaze softened. "Surprising. Quite like you. Or maybe, you are quite like her."

She blinked back tears, swallowing the lump in her throat.

He walked to his table, waved two mood rings into existence, and began selling it to the highest bidder. As he reached a crescendo, he slammed the gavel down. "Sold!"

In an instant, Fin and Dawson were transported to a bright, sunny day, late in the afternoon. Auci was gone but the auction house was filled with hundreds of people. A girl's laughter caught their attention, and they turned toward it. The girl Fin had seen through the window on their last trip was holding Auci's mood ring.

The woman Fin had seen on the staircase in her mother's house said, "Happy birthday, Nellie girl."

Nellie's megawatt grin lit up the world.

Fin's body shook with repressed sobs. She faced the other direction, pulling the handkerchief out of her jean's pocket and crying into it.

Dawson's hand squeezed her shoulder. "It's okay," he whispered.

It took her a moment to collect herself, dry her eyes, and shake it off. She glanced at Dawson, who gave her a knowing look.

"You alright?" he asked.

She affirmed she was then faced her mother and grandmother, absorbing every single detail. The middle-aged woman had bruises partially hidden under a layer of makeup. Nellie had bruises, too, and she kept nursing her side and stomach.

The boy Dawson thought was his father had a fresh shiner on his eye. He gave Nellie a hug and said, "Take care of it, sis," before letting her go.

"Thank you, Boone." Nellie's face radiated love for her big brother.

"All right, we better head home," said the woman. "Russell will be angry if I don't have your birthday dinner ready when he gets there." She added quietly, "If he gets there."

As the three walked away, Fin and Dawson followed. The time-travelers glanced at each other. Both had tears in their eyes.

"When are we?" Dawson wiped his eyes.

Fin was pretty sure she already knew, but she wanted to double check. She grabbed a flyer that listed the items for the auction and skimmed it for the date. Wiping her eyes, she swallowed hard as she followed Nellie with her eyes.

"May twenty-first," she said. "1975."

Nellie

Newcross

1975

9

A Girl Did This to You?

Newcross, May 20, 1975

"Nellie, just peaches," Clara Belle called out from her bedroom. "And be quick about it."

Nellie rolled her eyes as she finished tying her favorite shoes. Her mama had gotten them from the donation bin at church, but Nellie didn't care. She couldn't love anything more with their bright green Adidas logo and gold-stamped "Gazelle" on the side of the cream-colored leather. She felt special in them. And fast.

She hopped off her small bed and peered around the corner, down the hallway, and into her mama's room. Clara Belle wore a kerchief around her head as she started to make the small bed inside the cramped, musty bedroom she shared with Russell. Nellie always thought the smell wafting out was alcohol and drugs mixed with dirty sheets. Not by her mother's choice, who was in there folding hospital corners right now.

"It's close to dark, and I want you back before the sun sets," Mama hollered.

Nellie snuck out of her room and down the stairs so she wouldn't get caught wearing short jean cut-offs. Waiting until she was almost out the door, she shouted, "Okay." She grabbed the money on the table, tucked it in her pocket, and raced out the bright vermillion door and past the barn.

A faint yell from her mother floated through the air. "Penelope Anne, take a sweater. It'll get cold!"

Nellie ignored her and ran down the gravel driveway, kicking up dust and rocks. *I don't need a stupid sweater. I need to get Jonesy Wolfe's attention.*

Her stomach clenched in bright bursts as she twirled in the last rays of sunshine. She ran to the rose bush at the end of the driveway and bent down to breathe in the flower's fresh scent.

Straightening up, she sang at the top of her lungs, "Love. Love will keep us together." Pretending to hold a microphone, she seductively leaned against the bright green sign shooting up through the roses. It read, Newcross 1 mile, with an arrow pointing the direction she was going. She started dancing down the road. "Think of me babe, whenever, some sweet-talkin' girl comes along, singin' her song."

She stopped in her tracks as a black cat seemed to appear from nowhere and sat before her on the road.

"Hmm." She pranced up to it as its starry eyes blinked slowly at her. "And just where did you come from?"

She knelt and petted its shiny coat, resulting in a rumbling purr. "I'd love to do this all day, but I've got a boy to see."

After a final head rub, she started to sashay away but turned back to the cat. "Would you like to walk with me?"

The cat started to follow at a distance.

"Lovely." She danced a little more and called over her shoulder. "I'm going to call you Sylvester."

The cat trotted faster to keep up with her.

"You like that, huh?"

Nellie slowed a little for it to catch up and was rewarded with a silky brush of its tail against her bare leg. "I'm turning fifteen tomorrow. You should come to my party. All the stray cats will be there."

The cat meowed at her, and she smiled.

"Jonesy is the boy I'm going to see." She stopped and struck a pose. "He's one of the cutest boys in school. But he's my brother's best friend. Bleh."

She made a face, and the cat meowed. "Too bad for my brother. Because Jonesy is funny, smart, and a baseball player. He loves animals too. You'd like him."

She beamed down at the cat, who rubbed against her leg. After stooping to pet him again, she stood and took in a deep breath of country air as the sun continued its descent behind the hills. The cool, May breeze kicked up her long, dark locks. Resuming her walk, she ran her hand over the tall spring flowers. Their blooms tickled her palm.

On the other side of the road, oak and hickory trees lined the gravel road like an infantry unit, protecting a small ravine and all the birds who were chirping at twilight. A white rabbit bounced through the trees, reminding her of *Alice's Adventures in Wonderland*. They had just read it in school. The absurdity of the story reminded her of Newcross. Just like Sylvester appearing from nowhere, strange things happened in this town.

She gave Sylvester a Cheshire smile. "Wanna see somethin' cool?"

Sylvester tilted his head at her.

"Keep up, then!"

Nellie launched into a sprint through the tall spring flowers into a deeper thatch of weeds that engulfed her five-foot, three-inch frame. The plants whipped her face and arms as she darted into an oblong clearing hidden from the road. A large paper bullseye target on a standing wood frame waited for an arrow. Nellie grabbed the simple recurve bow and an arrow fifteen feet from the target, rolled into a kneeling position, took aim, and fired.

"Bullseye." Sylvester walked in front of her and sat down with a swish of its tail. "Not bad, huh?"

Lowering her bow, Nellie admired the target. "My brother built this for me. Keeps saying I'm a natural."

She winked at the cat and ran an affectionate hand across the arched wood.

"He gave me this bow and arrow set, too. Wanna know a secret?" She leaned forward. "I think Boone stole it."

The hairs on the back of her neck rose to attention, she stood and spun around, her bow at the ready. "What the heck?" She hadn't heard or seen anything, but she had the sudden sense that she and Sylvester weren't alone.

Weird.

"Did you hear something?" She turned to the cat, but it was gone. "Sylvester?"

She peered around as the woods went quiet. A herd of goosebumps pimpled her arm. *Everything looks the same, but something feels different. And where's Sylvester?*

Her eyes roamed the shadows deep inside the woods, but nothing had changed. She dropped her bow and took one small step toward the road and then another, watching the formidable weeds around her with a tightly held breath.

"Here kitty, kitty, kitty." She picked up her pace, knocking away the weeds then flowers as she kept an eye out for Sylvester and anything else that may want to follow her. "Here kitty, kitty."

Once she hit the road toward town, she broke into a light jog, casting a few over-the-shoulder glances as she went. But nothing followed. Whatever had pulled at her attention was as elusive as the mysterious, black cat.

She shook her head. "Newcross just keeps getting curiouser."

<center>~~~</center>

Nellie peered behind her and into the woods one last time before she turned toward Gilbert's Grocery on Main Street. Its white, wood edges were dirty and aged, but it held one very important thing: Jonesy.

Making herself presentable, she smacked the dust off her clothes and wiped errant sweat away from her hairline, drying her hand on her light denim shorts. She caught a glimpse of her reflection in a car window at the farthest end of the parking lot.

"What the heck?" Pulling a weed out of her hair, she wiped the smile off her face and replaced it with the most disinterested expression she could muster.

Don't look desperate. Or sweaty.

She wasn't Farah Fawcett on last month's *Cosmo* cover, but she wasn't bad looking either. She attempted to boost her chest with her hands, but it was useless. She pulled her tank top forward and studied her training bra.

Marci McKenna gets boobs at eleven, and I get this.

She let out a huge sigh and put her top back in place, doing one final check in the window. Behind her reflection stood a tall man in a cowboy hat close enough she could see the glint off his gold tooth. She whipped around to face empty air. As she caught her breath, she smoothed her hair and searched the parking lot, but whatever she'd seen was gone. She lightly flipped her hair over her shoulder as she let out a shaky exhale. *Maybe I imagined it.* Squaring her shoulders, she walked the last stretch to the store's door and pushed it open. A loud ding rang out.

Shoot.

She dashed inside and hid behind a display table with a two-foot-high stack of the newest creamy pasta sauce the stores were hocking. Grabbing one of the jars, she peeked around the saucy skyscraper to see the reason she had offered to go to the store for her mama.

Oh my God.

Jonesy's stormy blue eyes investigated the entryway from afar. He looked side to side, running his large hands through his dark, neatly combed hair. Seeing nothing of interest, he went back to organizing the deli meat and cheese slices in the cold section just ahead of her.

Baseball players are so hot.

Hiding her face with the jar, she ran from the front of the store to the cereal section. She put the sauce down on the shelf next to the Lucky Charms and grabbed a box of Golden Grahams. Putting it up in front of her face, she ran to the end of aisle and leaned forward to glance around the corner.

"Hi, Nellie."

She jumped back in surprise, dropping the cereal on his feet.

He leaned one hand against the end cap and propped the other on his hip. The short sleeve of his Gilbert's Grocery shirt was bursting at the seams against his muscular arms. He beamed at her, sending a shock wave through her body.

As the scent of his Old Spice cologne wrapped around her, heat flooded her cheeks. She ducked under his outstretched arm and darted to the canned fruits and vegetables area. Going to the farthest end, she pretended to be terribly interested in green beans. She snuck a peek around the corner at Jonesy, who was smiling to himself as he put the cereal back and grabbed a broom.

The armpits of his cotton shirt were wet with sweat as he moved the broom back and forth across the floor. His forehead shone with the same perspiration, some of which had made its way from his hairline down his always-smiling cheekbones to his angled jaw.

I wanna be your girlfriend.

The front door dinged again.

Jonesy turned to greet the new customer, and Nellie followed his gaze.

A cheerleader.

Nellie whispered through clenched teeth, "Marci McKenna."

The cheerleader's boobs bounced inside her tight, green tank top as her long, auburn hair swung against her pale, creamy skin.

Get a better bra you space cadet.

Her heart ticked up a beat as she pivoted her attention back to Jonesy, whose wide grin at Marci made her blood boil.

No you don't.

She grabbed a Hostess snowball package from an end cap and threw it at Jonesy's head, feeling a wave of satisfaction as it smacked against his temple. But when Jonesy and Marci swiveled toward her launchpad, the satisfaction turned into embarrassment, and she ducked behind the cans.

"Stupid Marci." Seething, she took a breath before investigating the situation again.

Jonesy chuckled at Marci's infectious laugh. It flitted lightly through the store as her breasts shook with each gulp of flirtatious air. She touched

Jonesy's arm and gave him a one-hundred-watt smile, which he returned generously.

I cannot believe him.

Jonesy flicked his eyes in her direction.

She darted behind the display of cans, towering above her head. After waiting a second, she leaned out in time to catch him saying goodbye to the cheerleader, who turned to speak to a middle-aged woman wearing a pretty turquoise pendant.

He started to sweep again, working his way toward Nellie.

Bursting with triumph, she smiled with more teeth than was strictly necessary as she leaned her forehead against the stack of cool cans. One of them wobbled at the weight of her temple. When she tried to stabilize the can of peaches, she accidentally knocked one out of place. The whole pyramid turned into Dominoes of destruction that came tumbling down in a series of loud, aggressive bangs. One of the cans dropped near her shoes.

She yelped and yanked her foot off the floor just as Jonesy wrapped his arms around her, pulling her away from the rest of the falling metal that came down in one final, thunderous rage.

"Are you okay?" Jonesy asked. His hands were hot on her waist as he pulled her toward him, gazing into her wide eyes.

"I, uh . . ." She locked eyes with him, her free hand wrapped around his taut arm.

I love you.

"Sorry." She jerked away and bolted as fast as she could out of the grocery store.

About a quarter of a mile later, she had to stop and catch her breath. The warmth of Jonesy's hands on her body was still racing through her and tingling in ways she'd never felt before.

She finally noticed the weight in her hand and laughed when she saw a can of peaches. *I'll steal a hundred cans of peaches if I can have Jonesy's arms around me again.*

"Love!" She shimmied as she started singing on her way home. "Love will keep us together, think of me babe whenever."

But the warmth lasted only a moment as a cold chill brought Nellie to a stop, and she took in the western sky.

Almost sunset. A half mile to go. Walking faster, she clasped her arms across her body. *Should've brought my sweater.*

Another strong chill made her shiver.

What the jeepers?

Stopping fast, she checked the leaves on the large oak trees for wind, but they were still. Her eyes scanned the woods to her right and the field of tall grass and wildflowers to her left. She listened intently, but everything was quiet. Even the bugs had stopped chirping. Bending down, she searched low to the ground.

"Sylvester?"

"You should run, Nellie," a voice whispered.

Nerves on high alert, Nellie stood slowly as she examined the tree line for a person.

A figure about her height emerged from the shadows.

Is that a girl?

Nellie fell into the dead stare of a girl slightly older than she was. Her heavy, black trench coat betrayed how small she was. Dishwater blonde locks hid most of her face, but her light eyes shone through like she was possessed.

Run.

Nellie kicked up dirt as she sprinted for home. The sound of fast footsteps behind her electrified her insides. Running off the side of the road into the tall flowers gave her more traction. She glanced behind her as the stalks slapped her skin.

She has snake eyes. "Mama! Maaaamaaaaaa!"

She ran harder, but the girl was too fast. *Crazy fast.*

Strong arms wrapped around her chest, and down she went.

Nellie's knees slid across the rocky dirt. One large rock ripped the skin like it was tissue paper. The air *whooshed* out of her lungs as her body hit the ground, and the can of peaches dug into her hip. Landing face-first, she bit her lip and blood exploded from her mouth. She desperately tried to breathe, but the girl's weight crushed her. She turned and saw her attacker's face just before a fist blasted her right cheek. The world became nothing but blackness and streaks of light.

As her body was pulled across the ground, the world started to come back into focus.

"We're going on a little trip," the girl said in a chipper voice.

No. She tried to speak but couldn't. *Can't breathe.* Turning her head, she saw rocks passing by and grabbed a large one.

"I'm gonna enjoy killing you."

"No," Nellie whispered.

Her mind began to clear as air returned to her lungs.

"No." Nellie jerked her free foot off the ground and kicked the girl's inner thigh, toppling her backward on top of Nellie, who swung the rock at the girl's head. But Snake Eyes skillfully dodged the attempt and the rock hit her shoulder.

"Get off me!" Nellie shrieked.

The girl coiled around and began beating Nellie relentlessly. She pummeled Nellie's body as Nellie tried to ward off the blows. Every swing was laced with the uncontrollable rage Nellie had seen in only one other person: her father, Russell.

"I said no," Nellie hollered. She kicked, twisted, and yanked her body with such force, the girl couldn't hold on. Seeing an opening, Nellie put all the strength she had in her right arm and punched right between those cold, green eyes. Blood spattered everywhere as the girl rocked backward enough for Nellie to scoot away.

"No!" Snake Eyes tumbled to the ground, clutching her nose as dark crimson blood streamed through her fingers. "You bitch."

Nellie flipped over and tried to stand, but pain ripped through her body. She crawled across the ground, her nails breaking on the rocks. "Help!" she screamed.

She hadn't gone far before the girl grabbed her ankle and snatched her back like a serpent. Sticks and rocks ripped at her bare stomach as she was jerked back to reality.

As Snake Eyes straddled her, she screamed, "Get off me!"

"Shut up." The girl cocked her arm back to hit Nellie again when a male voice yelled out.

"Lily, stop!"

Her attacker turned and sneered into the woods.

When Nellie heard the sweet sound of her mama calling her name, she hollered with everything she had, "Mama!"

Lily glared down at Nellie. "I'll be back for you." She got up and ran off moments before Clara Belle appeared through the tall grass.

"Nellie!"

Nellie sobbed as her mother swooped in, wrapping her in a sweater and hugging her.

"Nellie, baby, what happened?" Her eyes were filled with a potent mix of fear, anger, and worry as she scanned her daughter's face. "My poor girl."

"I'm not . . . I don't know. I'm not sure."

"Okay, it's gonna be okay. Let's get you back to the house. We'll call the police. And the doctor."

"Okay." She stood with her mama's help and looked behind her. "Is she coming back?"

"A girl did this to you?" She reconsidered Nellie's injuries and scanned the woods. "I don't—I don't think she's coming back, honey."

"Her name was Lily." Her gaze went to where the girl had disappeared, but there was only darkness. Trees. Bushes. No Snake Eyes. "She was scary."

"Lily?"

"Yeah. And there was a guy with her. He told her to stop."

"Did you see him?"

"No, just her. She had greenish eyes, like a snake."

"Come on, baby." Clara Belle wrapped her arms around Nellie's shoulders and helped her out of the tall grass. "Let's go get you some help."

~~~

Nellie stared at the cops gathered in the living room as the doctor put the final touches on the stitches in her left eyebrow.

"Thanks, Frank," Mama said. "You know I appreciate it. Apple pie?"

"That sounds delicious." He gave her mama a knowing look.

This wasn't the first time Dr. Frank came to their house instead of making them go to the hospital. Clara Belle always said if she'd gone to the hospital every time Russell beat her, folks would get suspicious. And Frank was her good friend, so he made house calls. So, she always baked him a pie in gratitude.

"So," a big voice said.

Nellie swiveled on the hard seat of the dining room chair to stare into a pair of sparkling, dark eyes on a very large man who had meandered inside.

"Hi," she said.

"I'm Officer Booker." The giant man smiled at her from under his equally enormous cowboy hat.

She couldn't help trying to return his grin, but her swollen lip prevented her from giving him the full smile he deserved.

"Just one more time, Penelope. This girl, you said you heard a male voice shout Lily?"

"Yes, sir."

"But you didn't see him at all?"

"No, sir."
~~~

"All right, then." He smiled so big she giggled. "My mama always said my God-given grin could make anyone laugh."

"She was right."

Officer Booker tapped his knee and grinned. "It was nice to meet ya, Penelo—"

"Nellie," she interrupted.

"I'm sorry." He tipped his hat at her. "It's nice to meet ya, Nellie. Thanks for the information."

She nodded as he tipped his hat again and walked away.

After Officer Booker sauntered over to the other cops in the living room, she overheard him say, "Strange things in Newcross."

You're tellin' me.

Something soft brushed against her ankle, so she glanced down at the black cat from earlier. "Sylvester? Who let you in here?" She reached down to pet the stray.

He rubbed against her hand and tilted his head at her with an affectionate slow blink.

Looking up at the sound of her name, she noticed the group whispering together and glancing in her direction every so often. She sighed and dropped her other hand to pet Sylvester, but once again, he had disappeared.

"Strange things," she whispered.

She had more questions than she or anyone else could answer, but two played on a loop in her mind. *Who's Lily? And why does she wanna hurt me?*

10

Is That a Potato?

Newcross, May 21, 1975

Nellie pressed the tip of her freckled nose to the cool glass and watched her mama pay for Russell's medication inside.

Pffft, medication.

Real pharmacies didn't have pipes, incense, woven rugs, and hippies who gave the peace sign when you left. This charade was all part of the story Mama tried to tell herself and everyone else about who Russell was and why she stayed with him.

She twisted around and kicked a stone onto the busy Main Street as the mid-afternoon sun heated up the day. *I would never marry somebody like Russell.*

Nellie winced as her aspirin started to wear off. Hugging her *Jaws* T-shirt against her rib cage with her arms, she let out a slow breath through pursed, bruised lips. Her entire torso was aching from the beating the mystery girl, Lily, had handed her. She touched her black and blue face.

Mama will have makeup to cover this.

She touched the back pocket of her flared blue jeans to feel the reassuring outline of the small hunting knife Boone had given her. Sighing, she reached into her front pocket, pulled out an aspirin, and popped it in her mouth, swallowing it dry.

How much longer is this gonna take?

Nellie swung back to the glass and peered into the store. Even from here, she could see the black and blue around her mama's eye that had worsened since this morning. There was too much damage for the makeup to do its job properly. The broken, red blood vessels against the whites of her eyes were a glaring reminder of their violent morning.

Noticing her daughter's stare, Clara Belle sheepishly held up an I'll-just-be-a-minute finger and hid her face with her hair.

As if I don't know what happened.

Nellie rotated on her heel back to the street just as Marci McKenna was crossing it and trotting up to her.

At least she's wearing a better bra today.

Eyes wide, Marci said, "Oh my God, what happened to your face?"

Nellie lightly touched her face again. "Just a fight. On my way home last night."

"A fight?" Her nose crinkled with curiosity.

"Yeah." Nellie tipped her head down so that her hair would cover her face. *Why do you care?*

"You don't seem like the fightin' type." Marci swept her long auburn hair to the side as she investigated Nellie's bruises. "I'm sorry you got hurt."

Nellie's forehead crinkled in surprise at the sincerity in Marci's voice. She found herself staring into a pair of concerned, blue eyes as Marci reached out and gently touched her arm.

"No, it's-it's fine." Nellie managed a quick smile along with a shoulder shrug. "Thanks, though."

"I actually know how to box if you ever want lessons."

"You know how to box?"

Marci's eyes lit with pride. "My brother, Tommy, is really good at it. He taught me some tricks and moves. We have an aunt in Utah. She's been telling us about girls disappearing and ending up dead. Can you believe that? They're questioning some guy. Ted something. Bundt cake or something, I think." She snickered.

Nellie did too. "Bundt cake." *She's kinda funny.*

"I saw his picture. Too cute to be a killer, but my brother said you never know. He told me it's kill or be killed." Marci's expression filled with darkness. But as quickly as the storm clouds in her eyes came, they left. "Anyway, he's been teaching me how to kick someone in the balls and stuff. I could teach you."

Nellie blushed at the mention of balls and giggled a little. "Yeah, okay." Nellie gave the cheerleader a shy smile.

"I could come by later?" Marci seemed to be holding her breath.

"Well, it's my birthday tonight. Maybe tomorrow night?"

"Yeah, okay." Marci's face brightened.

Nellie tried to hide her grin, but couldn't. *Dammit, her energy is infectious.* "Alright, well, bye then."

"Bye." Marci strolled down the street with her flip-flops slapping the concrete and her long, auburn hair floating in the late spring breeze. A few seconds later, she pivoted to face Nellie but kept walking backward. Giving her a bright, friendly wave, she called out, "And happy birthday!"

"Thank you," Nellie hollered.

Marci swung around and kept going down the street. The older woman Nellie had seen her talking to at Gilbert's walked up to Marci and draped her arm around the girl's shoulder, pulling her into a quick side hug.

Is that her mom?

Nellie watched them for a moment. *Hmmm, maybe she's not half bad.*

Her eyes shifted back to the street, scanning it quietly as she observed the overabundance of women and children. Tall women, short women, pregnant women, women with children. Women carrying groceries or running errands. One or two with a bruise here or there. Most of them walked with their eyes cast down like robots on a conveyor belt. While the men were where?

"I hate this town," she said under her breath.

Nellie cradled her aching insides once more as she turned back to the window and watched her mother's lean, athletic figure through it.

When Clara Belle pulled out some cash from her second-hand wallet, the clerk looked sideways at the dirty bills. Her mama half laughed and used a tissue to wipe one of the twenties before she straightened it out.

There must be blood on it.

Russell had thrown it on her mama's bloody face this morning after breakfast. She'd forgotten to put the syrup out, which was a punishable offense according to Russell.

After tossing the cash at her, he'd yelled, "Go get my drugs, you dumb bitch."

Nellie had jumped in and yelled at him to stop, but her injuries kept her from doing much more. When he came at her, she cowered in the corner.

She shuffled her feet as her eyes misted over. *Like a scared little kid.*

Thankfully, Boone had come in from feeding the animals and shoved Russell away. But her brother had gotten a black eye for it. The only person who walked away unscathed from the breakfast table this morning was Russell.

Nellie closed her eyes and dropped her head forward until her hairline rested against the cool glass. Taking a deep breath, she swore someone whispered her name. Eyes flying open, she saw her feline friend at her feet. "Sylvester!"

She bent down to pet him, and her ribs reminded her that the aspirin hadn't kicked in yet. "You're a mysterious fellow, aren't you?"

Apparently reaching its affection quota for the day, the cat sauntered off, so she stood up to check on her mama. But she was distracted by the window's reflection where she saw a teenage boy standing on the curb across the street.

Another mirage? She spun around to face him.

This time, the reflection she'd seen was real. He was about her brother's age but much, much larger with a dark mass of slightly unkempt hair. He took in the crowd around him for a moment before his eyes landed on her.

The uneasy weight of his surly gaze made her breath catch for a split second.

The stuffed Salvation Army bag slung across his shoulder and his worn blue jeans, stained T-shirt, and dirty brown coat made it look like he'd been traveling for a while. He readjusted the bag and crossed the street toward her without checking for traffic.

Her brain was telling her to run, but her gut kept her feet firmly glued to the ground. *Do I know him?*

After stopping right in front of her, the dust he'd brought with him swirled and glittered in the sunlight until it settled peacefully on the ground.

"Hi." She squirmed but didn't break his stare. "I'm Nellie."

He tilted his head, and the sun gave his hazel eyes an amber glow. He had a strong jaw and big hands. When one of his giant paws reached out toward her face, she leaned away from it.

"What are you doing?" she asked.

Retracting his hand, he looked surprised at her reaction and dug into the bag slung around his shoulder. From its depths, he retrieved a dirty potato and offered it to her. His face was so serious and earnest she didn't dare turn the gift away. She slowly took it from him.

"Thanks?"

He tipped his head at her as the door dinged open behind her. A cool rush of air lifted Nellie's hair as Clara Belle moved swiftly between her daughter and the new kid in town.

He took a few steps back.

"Who are you?" Her mother's arm created a bony barrier between Nellie's battered body and the teenager's massive one.

He answered in a thick, rich voice, "Grayson."

Oh my God.

Her mama reared back a little. "What did you—"

But he cut her off with a sharp turn of his back and walked away from them. Casually moving down the street, he was eventually swallowed into the normal movement of the town.

"What did he say to you, Nellie?"

Stunned, Nellie just shook her head. She couldn't tell her mother that once he had spoken, she knew exactly who he was. His was the voice who had told Lily to stop beating her. He was the one who called out and saved her life.

Grayson.

Her mama grabbed her shoulders and whipped her around, frantically searching her over.

"Okay, you're okay," Clara Belle reassured herself. "But what is that?" Her hands pried at Nellie's. "Is that a potato?"

Nellie studied the dirty root vegetable in her hand. "He went to touch my face, but I pulled away, then he gave me the potato."

Clara Belle winced, giving an almost imperceptible nod. "They're supposed to help with bruising."

"What?"

"Old wives' tale. Take a potato, cut it in slices, and put the slices on bruises. Draws out the toxins or somethin'. It helps."

Nellie gave her a confused look.

"It does." She conjured a hint of a grin with an embarrassed tilt of her head.

She's so beautiful when she smiles.

Gently rubbing a circle between Nellie's shoulder blades, her mama said, "Let's go grab the cupcakes, okay?"

Nellie followed her to their pale blue, Chevy truck. Gripping the potato, she scrubbed her fingers across the dirt and grime on its skin.

"Hmm," Nellie murmured as she climbed gingerly into the truck. She rode home with the potato cradled in her lap like an egg she didn't want to break.

~~~

After Clara Belle pulled up the gravel driveway and parked the vehicle, Nellie gingerly stepped out of the truck while her mama grabbed the cupcakes and groceries from the back of the cab. Standing there gripping the potato, she watched her mother walk up the broken porch and into the house as the sun started to set just beyond the tree line.
~~~

Nellie considered the porch's new crookedness and leaned against the truck for a moment. Russell had crashed into it last night when he drove home drunk. It wasn't the first time. She marveled at how something that was perfectly normal yesterday could be so broken today.

Boone appeared on the front porch, his black eye even blacker now, and hollered, "Let's go. We need to get to the auction house before dinner."

He was tall and athletic with chocolate brown hair and eyes to match. The best brother around these parts. Maybe anywhere.

"I know exactly what to buy you for your birthday, little sister. Come on, get ready for the best birthday ever." He waved her into the house and went back inside.

Nellie followed Boone's lead with the potato safely in her hand.

Why did Grayson save me? How did he know Lily?

The porch creaked under her weight as she pushed through the door, pausing in the small entryway with the staircase to the right. The banister was her favorite part of the house. She walked to it and touched it lightly. The house was pristine because there were consequences if it wasn't.

Mama had set the tray of fresh cupcakes in the kitchen. The little treats were now adorned with candles, ready for her birthday later that night. Looking around, it seemed as though her mother had taken an eraser and simply rubbed a little here and dabbed a little there and, voilà, a completely different home than the one from this morning.

Best birthday ever, huh?

She carried the potato into the kitchen, rinsed it under the faucet, and set it on the counter. After pulling a shiny knife from the drawer, she carefully sliced through the dimpled skin exposing the white flesh on the inside. She picked up two potato slices, slimy with starch, leaned her head back, and laid them gently on her eyes.

For some reason, she had thought turning fifteen would mean she'd know everything. But if the last twenty-four hours had proven anything to her, it was that getting older meant she had more questions than answers.

And all of them seemed to lead back to Lily and Grayson.

11

I Know Why We're Here

Grayson moved through Newcross with a strong sense of purpose, his hand gripping the nylon strap of the bag slung across his chest.

Just get to the flowers.

Each heavy footstep took him closer to a place where he could exhale. On the way, he scanned the street for stones that had a turquoise glow. Seeing one, he pulled out a small drawstring bag from his pocket, leaned over, picked up the stone, dropped it into the bag, and tossed the smaller bag into the bigger bag across his chest.

I'll figure out what it does later.

He kept walking with his eyes trained on the ground, only looking up now and again to make sure he was moving in the right direction. He passed the barber shop, the department store, the post office, and Gilbert's Grocery. An annoyed huff of air escaped his lips.

Gilbert's needs a power wash. Nothing ever changes in Newcross.

It was the same thought he'd had every single time he crossed the border from Kentucky to Ohio for the last two years. And that thought was always followed by, *I thought the same thing last time.*

He kicked a rock down the sidewalk and shook his head.

"Come here, Hailey." A woman yanked her young daughter out of Grayson's path and held her close as they sped past him.

He shot them a dirty look over his shoulder.

Same ol' bullshit.

Facing forward, he noticed all the other women tucking their children behind their backs or crossing the street to avoid him all together. It was an irritatingly familiar experience. Their superficial judgment brought a sneer to his lips.

They're never going to see me as anything else, so might as well own it.

He spit as he passed them, leaving a slimy mark that repelled the women around him. He felt smug at the fear in their eyes. It was a jolt to his insides, giving him a burst of energy.

But he stopped in his tracks when he came face-to-face with Marci. He'd seen her around and knew her name because guys liked to call out to her from their cars.

He knew a lot about Newcross and its people, but they never tried to know him. Not that he gave them much of a chance, hiding and traversing the town at night whenever possible. Normally, when people noticed him, they scurried away, but Marci had never been mean to him. So, he was predisposed to like her even before he noticed Nellie talking to her.

They must be friends or at least acquaintances.

When her wide eyes landed on him, she came to a hard stop right in the middle of the sidewalk. The corners of her lips jerked up anxiously, but her eyes were scared.

"Excuse me," he said gruffly, stepping to the side to accommodate her. After a few more strides, he peeked over his shoulder.

She was looking at him with a strange expression.

Regret pursed his lips. *Didn't mean to scare her.*

He nodded at her and felt a touch of relief when she nodded back. *She ain't so bad.* He turned back to the sidewalk.

When he finally got off the main streets, his soul relaxed a little. Taking the first dirt road to the left, towards Nellie's house, added a spring to his step. He inhaled the clean air and appreciated the dappled trees with a grin. Passing the oak tree where he'd carved his initials, he remembered how many times over the last couple years he'd hidden behind it and watched people go by. Nellie had quickly become his favorite. Often he'd wanted to step out on the road and say hello.

I would'a scared her.

Feeling something at his ankles, he jumped and glanced down at a black cat eyeing him with a tilted head.

Kneeling down, he said, "Hey there, little buddy."

He gave it a rough scratch behind the ears, really digging in. The cat purred its approval.

"Good, right?" He gently trailed his hand down the cat's back then stood. "Now listen here, kitty. You see a girl wearing an oversized trench coat and a pissed off stare, you run the other way, ya hear? 'Cause it won't end in anything good for ya."

The cat meowed as Grayson lifted his face, basking in the late afternoon sun warming his skin. He peered into the western sky, filled with warm yellow hues and streaks of clouds.

"I see you, Mama."

She was in an afterlife he'd never taste. His mama was the first and last person who had tried as hard as she could to make him believe he was loved. Right up until her painful last breath. Even the cancer eating her alive couldn't stop her from trying to love her kids.

His hand brushed the tips of the yellow flowers, and they tickled the bottom of his palm. A heavy breath slipped slowly from his lungs. He closed his eyes, remembering how he'd seen Nellie do this very thing with her hand many times. Why she did it, he wasn't sure, but for him, it felt like the flowers were hugging him.

Opening his eyes, he glanced around for the cat, but it was gone. *Must have headed into the woods.*

Remembering the stone he'd found on Main Street, he dug the small drawstring bag out of the bigger bag. After opening it up, he peered inside at the luminous rocks. Sifting through the pile, he searched for the one he'd just picked up, which was flat with swirls of brown and turquoise. Eventually, he pulled out the right stone.

"All right, my little friend, what do you do?"

He did a variety of things with it: putting his blood on it, whispering to it, whacking it against his hand, tossing it in the air, dropping it, and smelling it. When he squeezed it, some fluid came out. He jumped back to avoid getting wet and chuckled.

"That's new."

He tilted his head back and held the stone over his open mouth. Squeezing again, he tasted the liquid.

"Water. That could come in handy." He tossed it into the air and caught it. "I'll call you a water stone."

Holding his hand over the flowers, he squeezed the stone and let them have a quick drink before plopping it back into its respective bags. He frowned as the yellow blooms took on a darker shade as the sun dipped lower.

Time to work.

An anxious sigh escaped his lips as he dried his hand on his jeans and pulled out a sketched map from his back pocket. He searched the thick trees for the one he'd marked with a small X just under the largest branch's armpit. Finding it, he trudged over and touched the carving before examining the ground below it. The bouquet he'd laid on top of it had been trampled.

"Shoot." He quickly tossed aside the dead and broken foliage. "Sorry, Lisa."

He winced as a memory of her face lit up his mind. When she was murdered, Lisa Smith had been seventeen years old with rich, dark hair and bright, blue eyes. She'd worn a plain, black T-shirt and flared, bell-bottom jeans.

"I liked your mood ring."

Before Grayson buried her, he took the mood ring off her finger and cleaned it. When Lily fell asleep that night, he took a bus across town and left the ring at her parents' doorstep with a note that simply read, "I'm sorry."

He shook his head to clear the memory, walked back across the road, pulled out a switchblade, and cut a bunch of the fragrant florals. One of the flowers he cut much longer than the bunch in his hand, before plucking the bud off and using the stem to tie the whole bundle together. After inspecting them and deciding they looked pretty, he walked back across the road.

Placing the fresh, clean bouquet on her grave, he said, "I'm so sorry."

The ten bodies buried across town and in Kentucky pulled on his heart like he was connected to them with strings.

Burying them accessed the deepest, darkest part of him. For now, though, it was better for everyone if he just kept doing it. But it couldn't last forever. Newcross was only so big, and he was running out of places to dig the graves his sister compulsively filled.

I don't wanna do it no more.

"Shut up Grayson." His body twitched away the thought as he looked toward the western sky. Time showed its passing in the slow setting of the sun.

"What should I do, Mama?"

Rose had spent a lot of time before she died convincing him to watch over his twin sister. Even then, his mama realized that Grayson was the least of her worries. Lily held more anger in her soul than anyone alive.

Except Russell.

When their dad tried to rape Lily, it destroyed something inside of her. She tried to kill him for it, but her attack ended with Russell slamming her head into a wall. Grayson had stepped in and nearly killed Russell, but the bastard escaped, and they never saw him again. Lily only got worse after that.

He shook his head again to clear it.

After patting the X carved into the tree's flesh, Grayson trudged into the woods and down the hill. It was cooler in the thick shade of the trees. The shadowy enclosure of the forest felt like home, a place he could hide or even disappear. When something reflected in the late afternoon light, his feet halted in place. Kneeling, he picked up the delicate earring from the dirt and rolled it around his fingers. He'd seen it before. It belonged to Nellie.

Wonder when she lost this?

Grayson had a fascination with Nellie that his sister didn't share. Nellie felt like what family could feel like, maybe even should feel like.

I swear to God if Russell ever touches Nellie, I'll kill him. A vision of her battered face flashed through his mind. *Did he do that to her?* Grayson's hands clenched into tight fists at the thought, the earring digging into his skin. *Once a bastard, always a bastard.*

He'd expected to hate Nellie, given their family situation, but he didn't. And when he'd seen the makeup that barely covered the bruising on Clara Belle's face today, he felt connected to them both. His fists relaxed as he took a deep breath.

"Don't tell me you're thinking about her again."

Grayson whipped around at his sister's voice, shoving Nellie's earring in his pocket.

He shouldn't have been startled by her sudden appearance since they were deep in the woods at their regular meeting spot. She emerged from the shadows with a swagger he'd never seen on a woman. Violence seeped from her pores, which gave her small figure a greater stature.

Giving her a stern glare, he said, "I asked you not to go after her, Lily. Not until we know what she knows."

"She doesn't know anything. We didn't even know anything until that Oliver asshole came along."

"You really think the Grim is real?"

"It has to be. I can feel it."

"You can?"

"I mean, I can feel that we're special." She creeped toward Grayson. "Can't you?"

Of course I can.

"No." He flicked his eyes to the ground and back at her.

Her eyes sparked as she walked toward him. "You wouldn't lie to me, would you?"

He held her stare as he shook his head. "Never."

"Good." Stopping in front of him, she pulled out her switchblade from her black boot and pressed the sharp tip against her index finger. It started to bleed as she twisted the knife. "I hate this life."

Not knowing what to say to keep her calm, he simply stared at his sister. He hated that she wore that beat-up, long jacket and combat boots. They had come from one of the first girls she'd killed. Lily asked him to bury the body after she stole "that bitch's" clothes.

That bitch was Dusty Jenkins. *Nineteen. Brown hair, hazel eyes. Wore a cross around her neck. I put it in her mama's mailbox. Buried her in the woods behind her home so she could be with her family.*

"Maybe we don't need to do this."

She moved like lightning over to Grayson, sliding her bloody blade under his chin. "We're here for Mom. Don't forget that."

Her eyes blazed with a fierce demand for loyalty, so he lifted his hands in a surrender. "I know why we're here."

He held his breath as the blade pressed against his throat.

She lifted her injured index finger and licked off the blood. Looking at her hand, her face took on the gleeful expression of a child watching their favorite magic trick. Her finger was completely healed. With a snicker, she sliced the knife down the side of his neck, cutting open the skin.

"Fuck." He twisted away from her, grabbing the wound as warm blood oozed around his fingers. Drawing his lips between his teeth, he bit down. *Don't say anything.*

He waited a moment before wiping the blood from his hand on his pants and lifting the bottom of his T-shirt to clean his neck. Touching his perfectly healed skin steadied the rage inside him. With a blank stare, he faced his sister's smiling lips and dancing eyes.

"Haven't you ever wondered why we heal so quickly?"

Every day. "I guess I just thought we were lucky."

Her laugh sounded like glass breaking. "You're so simple, Grayson."

I'm not simple. He watched her carefully as she shook her head and put her knife away.

"Anyway." She waved the subject away. "We'll get the Grim from the woods behind their house, and then we'll kill them. For Mom. For us. Off with their heads!" She rained down more glass shard laughter as her eyes narrowed into slits. "Think you can handle that?"

I'm losing her. "Okay." He nodded his head to prove he understood and was onboard. "I'll scout it out tonight. After it gets dark. Then we can go back in the early morning when everyone's asleep and take care of it."

Nellie.

"Fine. Let's head back to the cabin. You've got some burying to do. And don't forget the kindling for your little night light while it's still daytime." She raised a mocking eyebrow at him and began to walk away.

His lip twitched into a curl at the familiar taunt. "It ain't a night light. I told you, it's for warmth."

"Don't worry. I won't tell anyone you're scared of the dark." She tossed a sneer over her shoulder. "Everybody thinks you're the dangerous one." Shaking her head, she chuckled.

He couldn't stop the shudder the maniacal sound prompted.

She disappeared into the shadows, but her laugh clawed at the cool air. He peered around him. The sun was losing its valiant fight against the night as late afternoon was preparing to become early evening. He started to pick up kindling as the woods fell silent once more.

It's gonna be a long night.

The Hunt

Newcross

1975

12

We're on a Treasure Hunt

Newcross, May 21, 1975

Fin couldn't believe she was really in Newcross in a whole different time. *This is surreal.* Considering Dawson's freaked out expression, he was probably thinking the same thing.

She asked, "You okay?"

"Yeah," he said quietly. "Just give me a second."

Fin wiped her brow with the back of her hand. She wasn't sure if she was sweating from anxiety or the heat as she and Dawson followed Boone, Nellie, and their mom to their car. On the way, her nose began to run and she sneezed, the country air igniting allergies she never knew she had.

"Okay, Dawson, the flyer said this is May twenty-first. Looks like, what? Late afternoon? Maybe four? Five p.m.? Amon hid the dagger late on the morning of May twenty-third." She grabbed allergy pills from the side pocket of her backpack, popped one, wiped her nose on her sleeve, and returned the box to its place. "Auci said he would give us time to know our parents, so we get today and tomorrow with them. Let's try and soak it in, you know?"

"Right."

She realized her family had pulled ahead and was almost to the truck, so she ran to catch up to them.

"Hi, excuse me." Fin waved at them as they slowed and turned to her. Up close, she could see that both Nellie and her mom were badly bruised. *Her mom's good at covering it.* Boone's eye was bruised on the skin with a few broken blood vessels in the eye itself. "Um, hi there. Hi. I'm Fin. This is my cousin, Dawson."

Dawson jogged up with a friendly wave. "Hello." He kept his eyes on Boone, watching him closely.

I get it. She did the same with Nellie.

"Hi," Nellie said.

I can't believe that's my mom. Fin had a desperate urge to hug her, but she knew it would seem weird and out of place. *Maybe not. It is the seventies.*

"Hello," the woman said. "I'm Clara Belle."

Clara Belle shook Fin's hand. A faint look of recognition passed between them. Fin knew what it was, but Clara Belle was confused by it.

"Do I know you?" Clara Belle's gaze touched on the gun holstered at Fin's hip and the knife in her thigh band.

I should have put those away.

"You don't, no." Fin quickly let go of Clara Belle's hand and pulled her badge off her hip to show them. "I'm a cop."

"I'm a librarian." Dawson showed them his work badge.

Clara Belle inspected their credentials carefully. "You're from New York and Ireland." She narrowed her eyes. "Quite a distance from Newcross. Must be somethin' special here."

"There is." Fin's emotions were getting the best of her. *This is so annoying.*

Dawson extended his hand to his father. "I'm Dawson."

Boone reached out and grabbed his hand. "Nice to meet ya." Boone eyed him with the same curious evaluation that Clara Belle had.

"Look, uh . . ." Dawson touched the back of his hair with his hand, really playing up his uncertainty. "We don't mean to be a pain, but we were wondering if you had a place we might be able to stay tonight? We hitchhiked here from the bus stop outside of town. We're on a . . . treasure hunt, I suppose, is the right way to phrase it. There's an artifact we believe is here in Newcross. Actually, we think it might be behind your property. The house up the hill, right?"

Nice improv skills.

He was playing on the attitude of the times. It was much more acceptable in the 1970s to hitchhike or to do any kind of wandering and ask for the kindness of strangers, than it would be in 2020.

"A treasure hunt?" Boone asked. "Cool."

"Boone." Clara Belle shook her head slightly, clearly trying to reel him in. "I think you're mistaken. There's nothing behind our property. Just a lot of woods."

"Well, we think it's past your property line," Dawson said. "We'd appreciate any help, honestly. And we'll pay."

"Yes, of course, we'd pay." Fin caught Clara Belle's eyes again and then Nellie's, silently begging for help. *It's me, Mom. I'm your daughter. Don't you recognize me?* "Actually, I'm here because we think the piece may have been stolen and hidden in the woods. And whoever did it may come back. They could be dangerous. One person in particular, a girl, long dark blond hair, wears a trench coat."

"Lily?" Nellie gasped.

Fin's breath caught with surprise.

"Her name's Lily?" Dawson asked.

"Do you know her?" Clara Belle asked.

They all cast uneasy glances at each other.

"We've crossed paths with her during our investigation," said Fin. "We don't know that she stole it, but we know she'll go to any lengths to get it."

Clara Belle's stare grew hot. "She attacked my daughter yesterday."

That's the bruising on Nellie. Fin's eye twitched.

Clara Belle stroked Nellie's hair as Nellie cradled her ribs.

"We're a little concerned she may come back," said Clara Belle. "You think it's because this thing is hidden behind our house?"

"We do," Dawson said.

"Can you protect Nellie from her?" Clara Belle's eyes bored through Fin.

"Yes," Fin said. *It must have been Lily I fought. If Nellie tangled with her, no wonder they all look scared.* "But the only real protection is for us to get that artifact."

"How long will it take you?" Clara Belle asked.

"Just a few days," said Fin. "We were planning on searching for it the day after tomorrow."

Clara Belle thought for a moment. "All right. You can stay in the barn. It's not a home, but it's warm and safe and you can sleep there as long as you need."

Fin and Dawson gave each other an undetectable, mini-fist bump.

A flurry of indecipherable expressions passed between Clara Belle and her children before she finally said, "We'll tell Russell she's a cop. Doing an investigation." She faced Fin. "He won't mess with a cop."

Is he the cause of her bruising? "Thank you for helping us."

"Yes, thank you." Dawson shifted the weight of his backpack.

Clara Belle gestured to the bed of the truck. "Hop in. We'll give you a lift."

The family piled onto the bench seat in the front while Fin and Dawson climbed into the bed.

Fin beamed.

Dawson had the same goofy look on his face. "I feel the same way."

They were home.

~~~

When they arrived at the now familiar house, it was alive with the sounds of clucking chickens, a barking dog, and a yowling cat. The paint appeared new, and the flowers were on vivid display. Everything looked clean and put together, no longer worn from time's passing.

Clara Belle stepped out of the truck and smiled at Fin and Dawson as they climbed out of the back and her kids tumbled out of the front.

"Don't worry about the animals. They're friendly and not all ours," Clara Belle said. "We leave out food and water for the strays. But the chickens are ours."

"Gotcha," Fin said.

Clara Belle's gaze extended beyond the barn to the deep woods behind her property. "So, what is this artifact, anyway? Do you really think it's back there?" Her eyes were questioning but trusting as they met Fin's.

"Yeah, we pretty much know it's there. Somewhere. It's a dagger."

"A dagger?" Her grandmother's eyebrows shot up. "But why hide something so small out there? It's rough terrain. Spooky, too."

Nellie and Boone nodded in sync.

"Well, we have a few theories," said Fin. "But it's an ongoing investigation. So, I can't really share much. I'm sorry." *I want to tell you so badly.*

Nellie darted away and shouted, "Fin, come on! We'll show you where you can sleep!"

Fin gave Clara Belle an apologetic shrug before following Nellie and Boone to the barn. She felt an energy rush at her mother's carefree attitude and exuberance. Even after a beating, Nellie seemed to take life in stride. And she was clearly excited for company and the idea of searching for treasure. Fin could feel her chest swell.

"And Fin?" Clara Belle shouted. Fin faced her. "It's Nellie's birthday tonight."

"Oh, okay, we'll leave—"
~~~

"Why don't you both come celebrate with us?" Clara Belle interrupted. "Have a real dinner. I'm sure you haven't eaten anything homemade in a few days if you've been hitchhiking."

Fin couldn't help the grin that spread across her face. "Thank you. I'm starving."

And she was. She realized she and Dawson hadn't eaten since their lunch with the chief, and her appetite was enormous.

"Yeah, me too. Thank you." Dawson tipped his chin at Clara Belle.

"Sure." She pointed to the small barn Nellie was leading them to. "Russell's daddy bought him an Oldsmobile Cutlass last year before he died. Russell only drove it a few days before he ran it into a pond. It hasn't worked since. If you can start it, you can use it."

Fin and Dawson glanced at each other before Fin said, "Thanks. We'll take a look."

Clara Belle resumed walking toward the house. "Dinner's in an hour," she called over her shoulder.

"How old is Nellie?" hollered Fin.

"Turning fifteen," she yelled back.

Fin and Dawson watched her walking away for a moment.

Dawson said, "I feel like she knows."

"I don't think she knows, knows," said Fin. "But she's got a feeling."

Clara Belle peered over her shoulder at Fin and smiled before going up the porch and into the house.

"Shall we?" Dawson gestured toward the barn.

"We shall."

When they walked through the barn door, they found Nellie and Boone putting hay bales together to form beds.

Nellie dropped a bale into place. "We'll get you blankets and pillows. The hay isn't so bad, I promise. It's actually really warm."

"Thank you." Fin sneezed once, twice.

"Oh no, are you allergic?" Nellie asked.

Fin shook her head, wiping her nose. "I don't think so. Well, maybe. I'm used to concrete and the city. It's okay, though. I have medicine if I need it."

"Oh good." Nellie finished putting together the hay mattress.

Fin surveyed the wall of random tools that included everything from axes to scissors. Taking in the rest of the barn, she noticed the hay, high ceiling, and the car.

"Is that the old Cutlass?" Dawson pointed to the back of the barn.

"Yeah, that's it," said Boone. "Russell put it in a pond."

Russell? He doesn't call him Dad?

Nellie seemed uncomfortable at the mention of her father, so Fin asked, "You okay?"

The girl's shoulder gave a weak raise. "Yeah, fine."

Although Fin desperately wanted to dig a little deeper, she let the subject drop.

Dawson and Boone took the cover off the car.

"Whoa," said Fin.

"It's cool, isn't it?" Nellie came to life again.

"Totally." Fin eyed the baby blue Cutlass with the matching leather seats. "You like cars?"

"I love cars," Nellie said. "I can't wait to drive."

Fin chuckled. "I can show you a few things."

"No way, really?" Fin felt warm on the inside as Nellie grabbed her arm in excitement. "I would love that!"

"Well, let's see about getting it started first." Fin and Nellie crossed the medium-sized barn to where the boys were ogling the old girl. "What do we think?"

Dawson put his hands on his hips. "Submerged in water, probably some electrical damage."

Unable to hold back his excitement, Boone said, "I take an auto shop class. We've got some old parts. And the auto store in town should have anything else we need."

"Great." Dawson happily shrugged at Fin.

He's loving this. Wonder if he actually knows anything about fixing cars?

Nellie said, "Well, while you boys work on the car, Fin and I can grab pillows and blankets."

"Sounds good." Fin gave Dawson a little wave and followed Nellie out of the barn.

"We don't get a lot of strangers 'round here." Nellie faced Fin with a skip in her step. "It's exciting there's a treasure hunt right behind our house. Can you imagine?"

When Nellie shook her body with exaggerated excitement, Fin chuckled.

Nellie said, "Although, it does seem like a lot of work for a knife."

Fin let out a small laugh. "It really does, doesn't it?"

"Sylvester!" Nellie ran up to a black cat and picked it up. "He's a stray. And my new friend. I invited him to my party. Look, he came."

I recognize that cat. Fin walked up and petted the animal. "He's lovely."

After giving it a quick kiss on the head, Nellie put the cat down and continued walking toward the house.

Fin stood there, watching Amon saunter away before dissipating into a blue haze. She followed the luminous particles as they floated toward her and circled her slowly before dispersing. How weird to know that he was family but without a human form. In spite of that, she had real feelings about Amon. They were the same as the ones she had for Clara Belle or Nellie. *Does Amon have emotions?*

Nellie interrupted her observations. "Don't tell mama, but I've already thought about being a cop one day, too."

"Really?" Fin began following her again.

Nellie shoved her hands in her pockets. "I don't like gettin' pushed around."

Fin tried to keep her tone light even though she was pretty sure she knew the answer to her question. "Who pushes you around?"

Nellie shrugged as she gazed at the house. "I just think there's a lot of people in this town who need put behind bars, that's all. Maybe I can be the one to do it someday."

"I have no doubt you can," Fin said as they made their way on to the porch.

The house was much different from the last time she'd been there. The steps were framed with wildly growing ivy and white tea roses. Herbs grew in windowsill boxes bathed in sunlight. A welcome mat lie in front of the door, which had a flower wreath hanging from it. To the left was a rocking chair and to the right was a small bucket with clothespins in it. She glanced beyond the porch to her left and saw the clothesline itself.

I would've loved growing up in a place like this.

"Do you like being a cop?" Nellie opened the screen door and looked back at Fin.

Fin thought for a moment. "I do actually. I'm good at it, too."

"What do you like best?"

"Helping people. People who can't help themselves. People who are hurting. People who can't defend themselves against"—she indicated Nellie's bruises with her eyes—"monsters."

Nellie set her jaw and squared her shoulders. "That's what I want to do. Monster hunting."

Fin admired her mother's gumption. "I think you'd be a great monster hunter."

Nellie's face glowed with happiness just as Clara Belle opened the front door.

Fin's grandmother stood there with blankets and a couple pillows. "Need these?" She handed them to Fin. "Nellie come inside and let them get settled."

"Okay, Mama." Nellie ran into the house as Fin took the offering.

"You let me know if you get cold and need more," Clara Belle said, holding the screen door open.

"Thank you." Fin smiled at Clara Belle. "Your roses are lovely, by the way. Tea roses are my favorite. Why white?"

Clara Belle shrugged one shoulder. "Not sure. Maybe they seem pure, I guess. Simple. Untarnished."

They looked at the rose bushes as the wind lightly blew the blooms back and forth.

Clara Belle said, "When Boone was ten, he thought I should have red roses for my birthday so he painted them." Fin let out a snicker, and Clara Belle joined in. "Killed almost all of 'em. But they grew back. They're tough. Roses can take a lot."

"Yes, they can." Fin eyed Clara Belle for a moment as the silence grew.

"Nellie's been talkin' about being a cop for a little while now." Clara Belle leaned her lithe body against the door frame. "She thinks I don't know. But a mother always knows."

"Always?" asked Fin.

A look passed between them.

"Always," said Clara Belle.

Fin cleared her throat. "She seems determined."

Clara Belle smoothed her shirt and touched her face. "I know you know he beats me." She leveled a stare at Fin. "He don't beat the kids, if you're wonderin'. I'd never let him touch them. Well—" she paused with a sigh—"'cept this morning. Boone. First time he's ever taken a swing at his Daddy. Didn't end so well. He's becomin' a young man now, ya know?"

"I understand."

"Just, you being a cop and all."

"I won't say anything, Clara Belle."

"Thank you." She started back into the house.

Fin stopped her by saying, "But just so you know . . ." Clara Belle faced her. "I'd never let him touch you. Or them."

Her grandmother half-smiled. "I believe you wouldn't, Fin Baker." She let the screen door close and walked into the house.

Fin swiveled to the front of the porch and surveyed the land around her. The city had always been her home, and she cherished its busy streets and bustling people. Now that she was here, miles and decades away, this was the most powerful and the most known she'd ever felt. For the first time in her life, she understood a phrase that one of her counselors used to say: *Where you come from is where all your power is.*

"Indeed." She inhaled the fresh air and knew she was home.

13

Happy Birthday to You

Nellie's delight at yet another win of the game of Twister came out in a champion's guffaw. *Even better to beat Boone. Such a sore loser.*

"Never again!" Boone shouted. "I'm tired of you winning, Nellie, you contortionist!"

Boone boxed up the game and stashed it on the lowest shelf of the bookcase in the living room.

"Here I come." Clara Belle walked out of the kitchen with a tray of fifteen candle-lit, chocolate-frosted cupcakes.

Excited, Nellie ran to the kitchen table and sat down to receive her serenade.

"Happy birthday to you." As Nellie's mama approached, the flames from the birthday candles illuminated her bird-like features and big, brown eyes. "Happy birthday to you."

Nellie draped her dark brown braid down the side of her right shoulder like heavy rope. She caught a glimpse of Boone stealing a spare cupcake from the kitchen.

"Hey," she hollered, briefly interrupting her mama's singing.

He shoved the whole thing in his mouth as they both laughed.

Rolling her eyes, Nellie gripped the paper-wrapped daisies that Fin had given her. She glanced at Fin, who was watching her intently. *She looks at me so strangely. Almost affectionately.* She peered at Fin and mouthed, "Thank you," as she did a little happy shoulder dance.

Fin mouthed, "You're welcome," back.

I'm so glad Russell isn't here. Probably drunk somewhere.

Boone tried to sing the last line of the song but instead spit out shards of cupcake.

Nellie's heart soared at the way her brother could always make her crack-up. But her good mood evaporated as her eyes widened at a sound outside. Nellie dropped her flowers to the floor and gripped the white-washed wood of her kitchen chair.

"Happy birthday, Nellie girl." Clara Belle set the tray down in front of Nellie.

Nellie pressed her back against the wooden chair so hard that it dug into her flesh. Keeping her eyes on the flames, she didn't move, worrying that once she did, it would unleash bitterness into the world. She could feel the danger in every cell in her body as the flames glowing on the cupcakes whipped the night air with a sense of urgency.

Nellie caught Fin's eyes with her own and silently begged her, *Please help us.*

Fin's face went from questioning to serious. She walked to the front window and looked out.

Of course, Nellie knew the revving sound outside was coming from Russell's truck. She could hear it a mile away. When the sound meant your mother was about to get beaten for no good reason, you paid it the attention it deserved.

Fin touched the gun handle at her hip while peering out the window.

Headlights crossed over Fin's face and body as the world around Nellie faded away into a fuzzy, frozen reality. Even her mother's voice seemed as though it was covered with paper and moving through a tunnel. Her school counselor told her going numb and reducing her senses was how she protected herself. That was probably true. But Nellie didn't know about all that mumbo jumbo. She was just tired of feeling scared all the time.

Not tonight, please, not tonight. Nellie whimpered, "Mama."

"It'll be okay, Nellie. It'll be okay." Her mama raced to stand by Fin. But as quickly as she got there, they both sprinted away from the window.

"Move!" Fin shouted.

Clara Belle grabbed Nellie and yanked her into the kitchen, tucking Nellie under her body.

Shut your eyes.

The roar of Russell's truck preceded a huge bang. The sound of splintering wood and bending metal was like a bomb going off. Pieces of flying glass assaulted Nellie's face and arms with a painful fury. Other shards attacked the wall and fell to the hardwood floor like delicately clinking China.

Nellie knew it was her father and his blue, rusted truck that had barreled into the front porch for the second night in a row.

"Goddammit, Russell!" Her mama jumped up from the shrapnel and ran toward the danger. Again.

Stop running toward it, Mama. Run away. Run away!

Nellie slowly opened her eyes, taking in little bits of information slowly. *I'm alone in the kitchen.* She peeked around the corner. *Chaos.* This time, the truck had run up onto the porch and crashed into the front door. The collision unhinged the door and broke all the glass in the windows across the front of the house. Everyone inside was crammed in the small dining room area.

Fin, hand on gun. Dawson, behind Fin. Mama, screaming at Russell from inside. Boone, behind Mama with a baseball bat. Me, scared in the kitchen, peeking around the corner.

The truck came to life again, backing off the porch and slamming down to the ground until it rolled to the driveway and jerked to a stop. It did all this while dragging the screen door, which was stuck to the grill like a splattered bug.

The shattered glass sparkled under the porch lights. It crunched like potato chips under her mother's feet every time she moved to scream at Russell.

Russell's voice got louder as he approached the house.-"Shut the fuck up! I'll kill you if you say one more thing, bitch!"

"Nellie! What's your address?"

She glanced at Dawson, who was holding their bright yellow phone to his ear with the curly cord hanging down by his side. She wanted to tell him—she really did—but she couldn't speak. *Say something. Say something!* But nothing in her head reached her mouth. Her tremors only got worse as the noise in her head echoed louder and louder.

"She's in shock," Dawson said to the person on the other end as he disappeared around the wall.

What's shock?

"Where's the birthday girl?" Russell yelled from just inside the door.

She started to breathe fast, too fast. Her counselor said it was called hyperventi . . . venti . . . something. She peered around the corner at her drunken father leaning against the door frame dressed in dirty blue jeans and his oil-stained work shirt.

Her mother screamed, "Get out, Russell! Get the fuck out!"

He slammed the door frame with his hand and shouted, "She's my fuckin' daughter, and I'm here to celebrate her birthday, you dumb bitch."

Fin's hand was firmly on her gun as she started to speak. "The cops are on their way. You need to leave. Now." As she spoke, she moved toward Nellie.

Please come for me. Please come for me. Please come for me.

Fin moved faster as a belligerent Russell fought the flimsy door. It soon lost its battle as they both crashed down to the floor. He struggled to stand with a stupefied look as though even he was surprised he'd broken it down.

Fin grabbed Nellie under her arm. "Let's go." She pulled her out of the kitchen. Fin's hand never left the gun as she guided Nellie through the rubble.

"I'm here for the birthday girl," Russell hollered as he swayed drunkenly.

His blurry eyes found her as Fin started to pull her through the hole that used to be the front door. Nellie was close enough that she could smell the alcohol reeking from his body. He looked like an insane Madhatter.

Her dad's face turned ugly with rage. "You ungrateful little bitch."

"Russell, leave her alone, goddammit," Clara Belle screamed.

Nellie froze and the whole world seemed to slow down as Russell started toward her. Her mama moved to try and stop him, but Fin was already there. She kicked him between the legs, dropping him like a stone, and kneed him in the face. When his head and body jerked backward, she kicked him in the chest, sending him all the way to the back of the house.

Everyone gasped.

Fin glanced at each person in the room before settling on her. "Wait outside, Nellie. Go. It'll be okay. Wave the police in when they get here."

Nellie could hardly believe her eyes. *No one's ever stopped Russell. And she kicked him across the house. Like, literally, across the house. She's stronger than any guy I've ever seen. How's that possible?*

But Nellie did as she was told and stepped onto the porch, the glass crackling under her shoes. The crisp night air filled her lungs, tasting like freedom, as Nellie stepped off the porch into the driveway and walked away from the yelling and screaming. She went to the flowers and reached her hand out, letting them touch the bottom of her palm and comfort her.

I need to be brave like that. Stand up to Russell like that.

Her father was a thief. Stealing from her and her mother and her brother the things that mattered most. Splintering their lives into unidentifiable fragments of pain that they had learned to live with, each in their own way, over the years. He was like a human fault line, unpredictable and destructive. He could turn anything into a weapon, including the people he claimed to love. Her brother had become a man too soon, and she hated that Russell had made Boone someone who would stab his father to death if he had to.

He's a monster, who's trying to make a monster. Nellie didn't believe Boone would become Russell, but who knows what anyone would do under the poisonous influence of someone like her father?

She sat down to wait for the cops but caught her breath as an eerie quiet descended like a blanket of thick, winter snow. Nellie's stomach gathered into a knot, and she snapped her head up, gazing into a pair of hazel eyes.

"Grayson," she whispered.

His body seemed as big as a giant's. Nellie sucked in a sharp breath and held it, watching wide-eyed as Grayson fully emerged from the darkness. When her lungs forced her to breathe again, she did but only to suck in another breath and hold it.

He could be here for the artifact. He could be here to kill us. Maybe I was wrong about him before when I saw him at the bus stop. Her gut convulsed as her eyes pooled with silent tears.

"Please don't hurt me," Nellie whimpered.

He approached her like a spider to its prey, a knife in his left hand.

Her head thumped in rhythm with her heart, and her limbs were heavy with pain. Closing her tired eyes, she pulled herself together with a deep, quiet breath. "Just do it fast."

"I ain't gonna hurt you."

Nellie snapped her eyes open. The pain in his stare made her wince.

He put the knife away. "Did Russell do that?" he asked, pointing toward the house.

She looked at the destroyed porch. "How do you know Russell?"

Darkness flashed in his eyes as he raked them across her body. "He do that, too? The cuts?"

After a confused second, she touched her face and arms, where small cuts were bleeding. She nodded. "When the truck broke the glass."

His jaw clenched as he twisted toward the house.

"Today's my birthday." *Why did I say that? It's like I vomit words around him.* She wanted to be his friend but didn't know why.

He turned back to her, his face softening. "Oh." He studied her quietly for a few seconds before a lightbulb went off behind his eyes. He reached into his pocket and handed her something. "Happy birthday, then."

"Thank you." She gingerly reached over and took the thing from his hand. *My lost earring.* Smiling, she let out a breath and started to stand. He put his hand under her elbow and helped her up as she asked, "Where did you find this?"

His body stiffened as he glanced down the road at the sound of sirens. "Cops."

Grayson held her elbow as he walked her toward the house, and she leaned into it, happy for the support.

"Sit here." He gently guided her down onto a piece of the porch that wasn't smashed into smithereens. "I'll be back." Grayson jumped onto the porch, and walked through the front door.

Seconds later, Russell came flying out, tripped, and rolled off the broken porch onto the ground. Grayson followed as Russell said, "You filthy, evil bastard. Why're you here?"

"I heard there was a party," Grayson said.

Fin, Dawson, Boone, and Mama rushed out behind him.

"Nellie!" Clara Belle ran to her daughter and hugged her.

Fin drew her gun and kept it at her side as she waved everyone toward Nellie, then stood in front of them as Grayson moved off the porch toward Russell.

The sirens announced the police were just a few minutes away.

Russell sneered. "You don't belong here."

"I guess I don't belong at all." Grayson stalked over to him. "Right, Dad?"

Everyone snapped to attention as Nellie and Boone shot alarmed looks at Clara Belle.

"He's not my son," she said quickly, reassuring them both. "He's Russell's son. With someone else."

Nellie suddenly understood Grayson's familiarity and why she trusted him. But also why he scared her. He was a piece of Russell, and her father was the worst beast she'd ever met.

Standing up, Russell squared off with Grayson and said, "Go to hell."

"I'll meet you there."

They raced for each other. Grayson tackled Russell, and they exchanged punches all the way down to the ground. The younger man's size gave him an advantage as he brought Russell to his knees, bleeding and broken. Grayson grabbed Russell's hair with one hand and pulled the knife from his jeans with the other, raising it above his head.

"This is for my mama," Grayson said.

"No, Grayson, don't!" Nellie burst from her mother's arms.

But Fin got there first. She kicked Grayson, toppling him, and snatched his knife before pointing her gun at him. "Don't move." Without taking her eyes off Grayson, she said, "Nellie, get back."

Grayson's face registered surprise at Fin's movements and strength. He glanced to Nellie. "But he hurt you."

"Doesn't mean I want you to kill him," said Nellie. "It's not the way, please." As much as she wanted to be rid of Russell, she didn't want Grayson to be a murderer. And now that she knew he was her brother, she wanted to get to know him.

Nellie began to walk toward Grayson, but Clara Belle grabbed her. "Nellie, no."

She shook her off. "He won't hurt me, Mama."

Boone said, "Stop, it ain't safe."

Fin chimed in, "Nellie, stop."

Nellie addressed Fin. "No. He won't hurt me. Please put the gun down. Please."

Fin lowered her gun but didn't put it away as the flashing red sirens lit up the night.

Nellie eased up to Grayson. "You don't need to kill anyone. And, anyway, I get the feelin' that's not who you are." She locked eyes with him. *So much pain.*

"All right," he said. "I won't."

"Promise me."

"I promise."

Clara Belle came up behind Nellie and took her arm as she spoke to Grayson. "You're the boy we saw in town."

"I am," he said gruffly.

"Why are you here?"

"To warn you. About my sister," Grayson said.

"Lily," Nellie said. "The girl who attacked me."

Grayson lifted his chin in agreement. "My twin sister." No one moved. "She's hell bent on hurtin' you all. So, I need to find the thing she wants to use against you before she does."

"The dagger?" Fin asked.

Grayson flicked his eyes at Fin. "How did you—"

"I'll help you," Nellie interrupted, moving toward Grayson.

"Nellie!" Clara Belle tried to grab her again.

But Nellie dodged and moved to stand by Grayson as two police cruisers pulled up followed by an ambulance. Nellie watched the bright, flashing lights as Fin and Dawson waved them in. Clara Belle gave her a squeeze before Boone walked up and hugged her, too. Nellie turned to say something to Grayson, but he was nowhere to be found.

"Grayson?" She jerked away from her mother and brother, searched the darkness, and let out a disappointed grunt.

He was gone. For now.

14

You Don't Like My Collection?

Grayson stood at the edge of the woods and watched as the police took everyone's statement. When the cops put Russell in the back of a cruiser, a satisfied smirk spread across his face. *I hope you get what you deserve, you bastard.*

He shifted his focus to Nellie, who kept peering behind her into the woods. She wrapped her arms around herself and pulled on her sleeve in a nervous manner.

I can't believe she wanted me to stop.

After all these years, he had gotten used to his sister's homicidal rage. Murder was like a sport to Lily. She prided herself on how she'd gotten better at hunting people, duping them into coming with her, and her technique for torturing them a bit before she delivered death. It surprised him to hear his half-sister tell him to do the exact opposite, to hear her condemn death, to hear her say that his moral compass was truer than he knew it to be.

Fin shined a flashlight into the woods and started his way.

"Shit," he whispered. Fin was no joke. *Nellie is safe with her. But I'm not.*

He quietly and quickly moved through the woods, down into the darkness. Studying the trees, he was grateful for the quarter moon even though it meant he would be easier to find. Its faint glow allowed him to see the trunk with an arrow pointing the direction he wanted to go. He had carved the arrow when they'd first started frequenting this area so they didn't get lost.

Going deeper into the forest, Grayson realized how dark it was. Chills ran up his arms and into his hair. *Don't be scared. Don't be scared.*

He startled when something snapped to his left. Just as he was starting to relax, a crunching sound to his right made him jump. His heart ticked up a notch. *Mama said to breathe. Just breathe.* Grayson let out a slow exhale as his eyes adjusted to the near blackness of the deep woods. He took one quiet step and then another. One more. Now he was moving again.

He wasn't sure how old he was when his fear of darkness first took hold or when his mama started putting a night light in his room, but he knew it had to do with Russell. Everything bad in the twins' lives started and ended with Russell.

Lily might have been bad even without Russell. The thought brought him to a halt. "Don't think that," he whispered. *It's too terrible.* "I'm sorry, Mama."

He started walking again.

His mama would never think, let alone believe, that Lily was rotten on the inside. She would always say that Lily had a tough life, so it was Russell who created the thing that hunted people every few weeks. Mama claimed that his sister was a good person deep inside.

Maybe not. "Stop that."

He shook his head, but the thought that Lily's violence had always been there taunted him. Maybe, though, it would have stayed dormant if not for their father. Russell dug up the dead thing, gave it life, and set it free. Like a match to a powder keg, that son-of-a-bitch unleashed whatever evil existed in Lily's soul.

He inhaled a sharp breath to clear those thoughts away as he stopped. The outline of the cabin where he and Lily were staying was visible, but all he could focus on was the fresh grave he'd dug this morning. He had more to bury. Lily had taken to cutting them up, filling a broken freezer with her trophies.

You have to stop her.

He used to appreciate coming here because Lily was his only family. After their mother died and they lost their house, this was the only place they knew. So, despite everything, it had become home. But now, things were becoming blurrier in his mind, and the clear lines of loyalty to his sister were slowly disappearing. How could he continue to be loyal to someone he knew was losing her sense of right and wrong?

Or already lost it.

His breathing picked up. *It's okay to be scared.* That's what his Mama used to say anyway. Through sheer force of will, he made himself walk forward.

As he got closer to the cabin, he could hear arguing. After picking up his pace, he was opening the front door within seconds. The smell of the rotting body parts always seemed more pungent when other people were around. *We're used to it.*

Two unknown men, who looked like Lily's kind of hooligans, stood behind Oliver.

Taking in the scene, Grayson asked, "Lily? What's goin' on?"

"Oliver here is disappointed in me." She made an exaggerated sad face at Grayson, then threw her head back and laughed.

I hate it when she does that.

Oliver was clearly frightened.

I get it. Grayson knew how scary this side of Lily could be. She was getting worked up, ready to kill, and her vitriol was aimed at Oliver. Trying to be a calming influence, Grayson said, "Lily, let him go."

She jabbed an accusing finger at their guest. "The compass bracelet Oliver gave me got me into a touch of trouble, now didn't it?" Her glare made Oliver flinch. "Who was the woman I fought?"

"Like I said, I don't know. There shouldn't have been anyone there." He squirmed under Lily's heated stare.

"That bracelet took me right to the entry point and now I don't have it," she said. "But you're lucky that I have an excellent memory. Point me in the right direction, and I'll find it again."

"That's what Gunnar was hoping for," Oliver said. "But this . . ." He eyed the broken freezer on the other side of the room.

Lily gave him an innocent smile. "What? You don't like my collection?"

Grayson winced as she pulled out her knife and began twisting it against her index finger, making it bleed. His lip twitched with revulsion as she walked seductively toward Oliver, who backed up.

Lily, don't.

The two henchmen stepped forward to stop him as Lily closed the space between them.

Grayson moved before he thought, stepping in front of Oliver. "Lily, stop."

Her expression went from the erotic pleasure of killing someone to the frustrated rage of a teenager who was blocked from her favorite thing.

But he knew the real anger came from the fact that he was the one stopping her. *Betrayal.*

"How dare you," she whispered.

His sister's voice had once been a source of joy. It was sunshine on a warm day and the peaceful sounds of raindrops. But now it made his skin crawl. *I'm losing her. Think fast.*

"He's working for Gunnar, and he's not what you want anyway. Just let him go. We need to focus on getting to the Grim. That's the real source of power."

Her posture softened, relenting a little.

He knew what she really wanted was the ability to wreak more havoc than she already was. And the Grim was the thing that would help her do it. *Keep talking.*

"We need to get it before they do. Nellie and the others know. I overheard them planning while I was scouting tonight. They're headed out in two nights, so if we go that morning, we can beat them to it."

Liar.

Lily took a step back, processing what he'd said.

He tried to appear convincing, but the truth was, he didn't know if they knew or not. He only wanted to have at least a day to warn them. To get to Nellie, to all of them, and tell them everything he knew about the Grim so they could get it before Lily. *Another betrayal. And she ain't gonna forgive me for that one.*

"Okay." She eyed Grayson, then Oliver. "How does it feel to be touched by the hand of God?" She tossed up a disgusted hand and shouted "Go!" at Oliver, who dashed out of the house.

She speared Grayson with her icy green eyes. "You better be right."

"I am." He tilted his head toward the henchmen. "They got names?"

"Carl and Luke." She pointed at one, then the other.

Grayson nodded, and they nodded back. Carl had red hair and freckles whereas Luke had the more classic American good ol' boy blond hair and blue eyes.

They don't look too smart.

Grayson asked his sister, "They talk?"

Luke pulled out a knife and picked his teeth with it while Carl adjusted his balls and smelled his fingers.

Maybe better they don't talk.

Ignoring the question, Lily said, "You should have been back sooner." She put her knife away and licked the blood off her finger, which had already healed.

Anxiety rabbited around inside Grayson's gut. Things were changing faster than he could handle. Lily was scaring even him, and he didn't know what to do with that. His heart ticked up a notch.

Breathe, Grayson, breathe. "I was scoutin' them out like I said I would."

"I don't believe you," she said.

He shifted his weight to his back foot. *Don't panic.*

She pulled out her knife and touched its point to her chest right above her heart.

He winced and shook his head.

"When did you start thinking it was okay to lie to me, brother?"

"Don't do that, Lily."

"You're lying to me." She twisted the blade against her skin, groaning in pain but also pleasure.

"Dammit, stop it!"

"Liar!" she screamed so loud his eardrums stung.

He lurched forward, grabbing for the knife, but she dodged and shoved it through his hand. As he screamed in pain, she laughed like he'd just told a hysterical joke.

She's laughing?

She ripped the blade out of his hand.

Grayson cradled the injury, trying to staunch the blood and wait for it to heal. *Breathe, breathe, breathe.*

His sister wiped the blood off her chest with her fingers and licked them clean. With blood smeared around her mouth like a toddler who was learning to eat, she said, "I don't think you understand how serious I am."

Something inside him shriveled when Grayson realized he couldn't see the pain in her eyes anymore. It had been replaced with something much worse. Something much colder. Madness. *Please, little sister. Please still be in there.*

"No, I do understand." He shook his hand and wiped the blood on his shirt as the last of the skin knit back together. Luke and Carl leered at him but didn't comment as he flicked his eyes from them to Lily. "You and me, sis. Stick to the plan, and you'll get what you want. I promise."

She narrowed her eyes at him for a second. "Okay." She wiped the blood off her mouth with her forearm. "We'll go the morning after next. But if I find out you're lyin' to me, I'll go to their house and kill them all. Then I'll find the Grim and kill you."

Grayson stood still as Lily walked into the closet-sized kitchen and opened the fridge. She had never threatened to kill him before, but mostly because of their healing abilities. Now, though, she knew she could kill him with the Grim. And she made it clear that she would.

He clenched his hands into fists as he listened to her rustling around in the fridge. His nails dug into his skin, drawing blood. After shutting the door, she came back with two beers and snapped the caps off. He released his fingers from their tight ball and forced an upward twitch of his lips. She put one of the beers into his healed hand then hoisted hers in the air, waiting on him.

He clinked his bottle against hers manifesting a cool disinterest on the outside as his insides swirled with rage and fear.

"For Mama." She leveled her eyes at his, slitting them into thin veils of hatred.

He could no longer tell if that hatred was meant for him or for Nellie and her family. *There's no saving her.*

"For Mama." Not taking his eyes off her, he sipped the cold ale, taking a small comfort in how it eased his dry, aching throat.

"Don't you have some bodies to bury?" She spun away, slapped the top of the broken freezer, and disappeared out the front door.

Grayson snarled at Luke and Carl. "Get the fuck out."

They followed Lily but not before giving Grayson a condescending once-over.

Grayson swallowed hard at a sudden realization. His sister wasn't doing this for their mother, for the pain she felt, or for the childhood they lost. Lily was doing this for herself. Because she wanted to. Because she liked the blood and the murder. And as horrible as things had been, now he knew that with Lily at the helm, it was only going to get worse.

Much, much worse.

15

It Stays Between Us

Newcross, May 22, 1975

"I already told you, it's nothing." Nellie was getting exasperated as she moved through the high school's freshman hallway. "I fell, that's all."

"Come on, that looks like more than a fall." Sarah pointedly looked at Nellie's bruises.

Nellie loved Sarah's long, straight hair, but she did not love this conversation.

A recognizable male voice said, "She said it's nothing."

Nellie swooned. "Jonesy," she whispered.

He swaggered up to her, his leather varsity jacket crinkling as he moved, making her ears tingle with delight.

Sarah flipped her thick mane. "Geez, Jonesy, no need to get huffy about it." She walked off to class yelling over her shoulder, "Just trying to help."

Nellie shouted back, "Thanks." She rolled her eyes and blushed as she noticed Jonesy's blue eyes staring down at her.

"She's a busy body." He smiled as he gently placed his large hand against her worn, gray locker.

"Yeah." Nellie shuffled her feet and glanced down at her flared jeans moving with her hips. She lifted her shoulders back so her fitted T-shirt showed off what little assets she had. Her mama said that being fifteen meant she was becoming a woman. She wasn't entirely sure what that meant, but if it had anything to do with getting Jonesy to kiss her someday, she was all for it.

She raised her head just as Marci McKenna bounced her way toward Nellie, making every boy turn and stare. Thankfully, Jonesy's back was to her so he couldn't see Marci's assets on display.

Of course this is the moment Marci finds me. What would Judy Blume do in this situation?

"Your face is still pretty beat up." Jonesy captured her attention again as he lifted his hand from her locker and brushed her dark hair away from her bruised eye. His hand felt cool against the warmth of her blush.

She was trying to concentrate on Jonesy, but all she could see out of the corner of her eye was Marci coming right toward her. *Come on, for real, right now she shows up?*

"It's got everyone curious. Last day of school. They need something to gossip about all summer."

"Oh." Nellie tucked her chin, wishing away the clicking of Marci's heels as she closed in. "Yeah, I know."

"O-Oh, I'm sorry," Jonesy stuttered. He pulled his hand back and tucked it into his jeans pocket. "I didn't mean to sound like I was gossiping. I'm not. I swear."

"No, it's okay. I didn't think you were."

"I should'a walked you home."

"What?"

Marci grinned at Nellie, trying to capture her attention.

Marci, go away!

"I should'a walked you home the other night from the grocery store." A deep frown crossed Jonesy's face. "It wouldn't'a happened if I'd been there."

She frowned. *Don't do that, Jonesy.*

The last thing he needed was to feel guilty about yet another woman getting hurt on his watch. He'd never forgiven himself for his mama's murder even though he was so little when it happened that he couldn't have done anything about it.

But try telling him that. "You were workin'. You couldn't."

"I wanted to."

Nellie scuffed her shoe on the floor. "You did? I thought you were talking to that cheerleader." *And watching her chest. Crap, here she comes.* Nellie kept her eyes on Jonesy, ignoring Marci.

"I wasn't interested in talking to her." He scuffed his shoe in response.

That's cute.

Nellie felt warm all over as he put his hand back on her locker and said, "Do you think we could—"

"Hi, Nellie." Marci smiled brightly and looked like she was waiting for reciprocation.

Marci freaking McKenna.

"Hey, Marci." Nellie kept one eye on Jonesy and one eye on what he was peeking at. *Judy Blume would say, "Wear a more fitted bra, Marci!"*

"Can I still come over tonight?" An emotion that Nellie couldn't quite identify flashed across the popular girl's face.

Nellie wanted to say no. She wanted to turn her back and ignore the redhead, making her go away from the boy she liked. But Nellie saw something on Marci's face and felt immediately bad for being so defensive about Jonesy.

"Sure, Marci." When Marci started bouncing excitedly, Nellie pursed her lips in annoyance. *Please stop, I'm begging you.*

"I'll come over after dinner. Is that okay?"

"Sure." Nellie bobbed her chin in agreement as she gripped her books to her chest.

"Okay. Bye. Bye, Jonesy." She fluttered her fingers in a goodbye wave as she walked away.

"You're friends with a cheerleader?" Jonesy raised an eyebrow.

She raised her hand flippantly. "Yeah, I guess I am now."

His stare grew warm again, and she shuffled her feet under his gaze.

"Like I was saying, do you think we could go out—"

"Jonesy!" Boone hollered before he and half the baseball team came over and surrounded Nellie and Jonesy.

Fuck, fuck, fuck!

"What are you doing with my little sister?" asked Boone.

"Like it's any of your business," Nellie spat.

"Whoa, come on now." Boone eyed Jonesy suspiciously. "I know my best friend isn't going after my little sister. Right?"

All eyes were trained on Jonesy as he shifted, giving Nellie a brief sideways glance, careful not to linger, before turning back to Boone and the team.

"Of course not." Jonesy's hand found its way back into his pocket. "I was just checking on her, that's all."

Nellie's insides flipped as she rounded on her brother, who grabbed her by the shoulders and guided her away from the pack.

"We need to talk," Boone whispered, pulling her farther away.

"What about, you jerk?" She tried unsuccessfully to tug away from him.

"You know what." He gave Jonesy a nod to come over. "About Grayson."

Nellie shook away from Boone's grip as Jonesy walked up. All three of them peered up at the clock as the late bell for class rang, then back to each other.

Nellie rocked back. "You told Jonesy?"

"Of course."

"I wanna help." Jonesy caught her eyes with his and held the stare just a little too wonderfully long.

Tearing her eyes away and trying to focus on the subject at hand, she said, "Well, I believe Grayson is a good guy."

"Nellie, he's crazy," Boone said, keeping an eye out for teachers as the remaining students rushed to their classes. "And I don't trust him."

Genuine concern flashed across Jonesy's face. "I don't either."

Surprised, Nellie stopped and considered his position. But after a moment, she dismissed the idea in favor of her gut feelings about Grayson, Fin, and Dawson.

She crossed her arms tightly around her books. "Well, none of us knows what's really going on here, right? And whether you like it or not, Grayson is family."

"Yeah, but, Nellie—" Boone started.

"No, don't 'Nellie me'," she said sternly. "He's our brother."

"Half-brother," Boone corrected.

"I say brother. Like it or not, he needs our help. And I believe him."

Boone and Jonesy exchanged a pointed look. Nellie could tell they were considering trying to change her mind but recognized that it was useless.

"Fine," Boone said.

Jonesy nodded. "But you gotta admit, this is all pretty strange."

Nellie said, "Yeah, I don't think it's a coincidence that all these people showed up at the same time lookin' for something behind our house." She directed her next comment at her brother. "And don't tell me you didn't notice the"—she floundered, throwing her hand up—"*something* about Fin."

"Yeah, I know." Air left Boone's lungs like he was a punctured tire. "I get a real strange feeling about Dawson too."

"What kind of feeling?" Jonesy asked.

The siblings shifted awkwardly.

Nellie squirmed a little under Jonesy's stare and scoured her brain for the best way to verbalize it.

After a moment, she said, "I can't describe it other than saying that they feel like Grayson. They feel like family."

Boone nodded, but his mind seemed miles away.

Jonesy said, "Okay, so now that we all agree this shit is weird, what's the plan for our summer vacation, ladies and gents?"

"We're goin' on a treasure hunt," Boone said with a sly grin. "Whether they want us to come or not."

The other teenagers grinned back in agreement.

"You know what this means?" she whispered. The two boys leaned in. "We gotta make a pact. A blood pact." She straightened her shoulders and raised an eyebrow. "Whatever happens, we don't tell anyone. It stays between us."

Boone chuckled. "Come on, we're too old for that sort of stuff." He rolled his eyes.

Jonesy initially laughed too but stopped when he saw Nellie's face.

Her cheeks burned with embarrassment.

"Come on, Boone," he said. "It's just a little blood pact. Won't do us no harm."

Boone shrugged one non-committal shoulder. "All right." He herded them toward the boys' bathroom, pulling out his pocketknife once they were inside.

Nellie wrinkled her nose at the smell and mess inside. "Ugh, this is disgusting. Don't you all wash when you're in here?"

Taking the knife from Boone, Jonesy turned to Nellie. "Finger." When she reluctantly stuck her index finger out, he said, "Now hold still."

Nellie obliged, squeezing her eyes shut, as a small prick lanced her finger. When she opened her eyes, a small cut on her finger oozed blood.

Jonesy did the same thing to his finger and Boone's.

"All right, what's the pact?" Jonesy asked.

"It stays between us." Nellie put her finger in the middle of the group.

"Nobody gets hurt." Jonesy looked right at Nellie, extending his finger.

"We all stay until it's done." Boone presented his finger. "Loyalty. No matter what this is."

Peering at each other, they nodded in agreement and merged their fingertips together. The blood mingled from one finger to another. After a solemn moment, they pulled their hands back.

Perking up, Jonesy asked, "Cut the last day of school?"

Nellie tried for casual but knew her face lit up. "I'm in."

"Let's go." Boone headed to the door and peeked out to make sure the hallway was clear.

They snuck through the corridors and down the stairs. As they ran out the back entrance, Nellie dumped her books into the trash can with a wide grin. Jumping into Boone's truck, Nellie sat herself firmly between the two boys before Boone fired up the engine and drove off.

They had only gone about ten feet when Marci McKenna ran in front of the truck. She jumped as though the large vehicle had appeared out of thin air.

Boone yelled, "Fuck!" and slammed on the brakes.

She looks like a deer in headlights.

"Marci?" Nellie questioned. Strangely, the ends of her hair were wet, and her face was flushed. Nellie's forehead crinkled. *What's that look on her face?*

"You know her?" Boone asked.

"Yeah, they're friends." Jonesy laughed. "If you can believe that."

"What? You? You're friends with a hot cheerleader?" Boone nudged her lightly with his elbow. "I thought you hated cheerleaders?"

I do hate cheerleaders. "I don't hate cheerleaders."

Smiling, Boone rolled down his window. "Hey, Marci!"

"Boone!" Nellie elbowed him hard in the rib cage.

"Ow!" He gave her a dirty look before leaning out the door toward Marci, who had come around to the driver's side. "Wanna skip with us?"

Marci's face displayed an odd mix of emotions before she answered. "You skippin' the rest of the day?"

"Yep." Boone gave her an encouraging grin that showed off his perfect teeth. "Come on. It ain't no tea party. It'll be fun." He winked at her.

Good grief. But her embarrassment about her brother's flirtation was trumped by the strange expression on Marci's face. *What is that? Almost like she's scared or somethin'.*

"Ignore him, Marci," Nellie said. "Come with us. It'll be fun."

She didn't really want the cheerleader to come, but Marci had an air about her. *Maybe she needs to come.*

After a beat, Marci said, "Yeah, okay. That'd be great."

She seems relieved. Nellie was confused by her own behavior but also Marci's. How could a cheerleader that pretty with a sexy reputation be relieved to be invited to skip school by a group of misfits like them? *She must get offers like this all the time from more popular kids.*

"Hop in," Nellie said.

"Here," Boone said, opening his door and getting out. "You can hop in here. Want me to put your book bag in the back?"

"Thank you." Marci handed it to Boone, who placed it in the bed of the truck. She got in and scooted close to Nellie.

Boone looked at the ground and bent down.

"What is it?" Nellie asked.

Standing, he held up a steak knife and glanced at Marci. "This yours?"

Marci blushed and squirmed a little. "No, why would I have a knife?"

"Huh. Well, this could puncture a tire." He shrugged and tossed it near her bag. "I'll get rid of it later."

"Fine, let's go already." Nellie rolled her hand in a get-on-with-it gesture.

Boone slid into the driver's seat as he gave Marci a little nudge with his shoulder. The four of them were squished in tight.

Nellie asked, "Why are the ends of your hair wet?" She reached out and touched them, but Marci jerked away and pulled her hair behind her back. She smiled at Nellie, but it didn't reach her eyes. *What's goin' on with her?*

"Where should we go?" Jonesy asked.

"Blue Falls." Boone bounced his eyebrows, and everyone laughed.

"It's supposed to be haunted you know." Marci shrugged. "Weird stuff happens there."

"I'll protect you." Puffing up, Boone laughed as he glanced at Marci.

Nellie leaned forward and shot an eye roll at him.

Boone reached his arm across the back of the bench seat and smacked his little sister in the head.

"Ow!"

Marci turned to Nellie. "What?"

"Nothing." Nellie flipped off Boone behind Marci's back. "Let's go to the waterfall."

Nellie smiled at Marci to prove everything was okay. When Marci's returning glow seemed almost grateful, Nellie felt an unexpected pull on her heartstrings.

Marci faced forward and gazed out the windshield for a moment before closing her eyes and tipping her head back against the seat.

Hmmm. I may just like her.

Realizing that Marci didn't want to talk anymore, Nellie also faced the windshield and glanced at Jonesy out of the corner of her eye.

He put his arm around the back of the seat, touching her shoulder with his fingertips.

Her insides tingled. She wanted to believe that Jonesy was the man she would love someday. The man she'd marry. The man she'd have a child with. Suppressing a dopey grin, she couldn't help imagining what their child would look like. If it was a boy, she'd name him after Jonesy. And if it was a girl, she'd name her after the woman who was making her think differently about her life.

She'd name her Fin.

16

It's Called a Groin Kick

Marci closed her eyes, basking in the warm wind blowing through the open windows of the truck as they headed to the haunted waterfall. The breeze carried Nellie's fresh powder scent. Their bare arms bumped together as they bounced over the gravel roads. She thought of Nellie's long, tan legs and silky, dark hair. *Stop thinking that.*

She opened her eyes and gazed at Boone, who glanced back at her. He gave a warm grin and returned his eyes to the road. Most teenage boys would have been revving the engine, driving fast, and trying to impress her. Boone, though, was trying to drive carefully. *Like he wants us to feel safe.*

Her eyes brightened as she peered at him even though he was concentrating on the road. *He's cute.*

Taking in their surroundings, she realized they were through town now and maybe ten minutes from Blue Falls. She was grateful they found her when they did. Rubbing her wrists, she pushed her bangle bracelets over the red marks the football player's hands had left behind. The steak knife lying in the bed of the truck had a different story to tell about how her day was going to end. She hadn't really planned it, but after he pulled her into the janitor's closet and forced her to . . . *Don't.*

Shaking her head and closing her eyes, she pushed the horrible memory away and let the warm air caress her face.

The assault was the third in as many days. It followed a year of the football team passing her around until it just got easier to stop fighting. Her brother could fix it, but Tommy would probably kill them. Her mom would probably kill them. But for them to help, they'd have to know. *I don't want anyone to know.*

She took a steadying breath as the wind whipped her hair around, drying the wet ends. After this morning's incident, she'd run to the bathroom and stared at her flushed, sweaty face in the mirror. She pumped soap out of the dispenser and shoveled the powder into her mouth followed by a handful of water. Swishing and spitting multiple times until the chemicals were all she could taste.

Dazed, she wandered around for a bit, eventually finding herself in the school cafeteria. When the cooks weren't looking, she stole a steak knife and ran outside to find a quiet place she could let herself bleed out and pass peacefully.

And then Boone almost hit her.

She gulped down the fresh air, smelling the flowers and smiling. *I would've missed this smell.*

"So why do you think it's haunted?" Boone had to shout over the noise of the truck.

Opening her eyes, she saw that he was looking at her. "I don't really know if it is. My mom just always said it was. But maybe she said that so I'd stay away?"

"That's something our mom would do, too." Nellie tilted her chin up at her.

Marci felt her whole face brighten. *She's so pretty.*

"I mean, it's the seventies, what's the big deal?" Nellie continued. "People do worse things than hanging out by a waterfall. Like that murderer guy you were talkin' about? Bundt cake."

Marci laughed, bumping against Boone. *He feels so safe.*

"Who's Bundt cake?" He laughed.

"Bundy!" Marci laughed. "Not Bundt cake."

They all laughed as Jonesy chimed in, "I'd rather have Bundt cake."

"Mmm, me too," said Boone. "Nellie, are there still cupcakes left from your birthday?"

"Yeah." Her tone darkened. "The ones Russell didn't mess up."

"Who's Russell?" Marci asked.

An irritated eye roll passed between Boone and Nellie as Jonesy squeezed Nellie's shoulder to comfort her.

Touchy subject.

"I s'pose you'd call him our dad," Boone answered dryly.

"He's a sperm donor not a dad," Jonesy said.

"Exactly, my man." Boone pointed at Jonesy and banged the steering wheel, jerking it a little and swerving the truck.

Marci reached out and touched the dashboard for balance, tossing him a whoa glance.

"Sorry," he said.

A little breath of surprise escaped her mouth. "It's okay." *Did he just apologize?* She leaned back into the seat, letting her body relax.

"Teach me the stuff at Blue Falls." Nellie's big dark eyes peered at her as Nellie's graceful fingers tucked her flying hair behind her ears. "I need to be able to kick Russell's ass."

I know how to fight. Why didn't I fight back this morning? "Does it make him mad that you call him Russell?"

Nellie shrugged. "He's always too drunk to notice."

Boone grinned at his little sister. "You need to pull out your bow and arrows. Scare the shit out of him."

"He'd be too drunk to even know what he was lookin' at," Nellie countered.

"You can shoot arrows?" Marci asked.

Nellie tucked her hair behind her ears again and gave her a sly grin.

"She's good, too," Boone hollered. "I put 'em in the back of the truck if you wanna shoot by the falls."

"You did? Oh, so you and Jonesy were already plannin' to cut school, weren't you?" Nellie reached across Marci and slapped his arm as a mischievous smirk crossed his face.

"We brought beer, too," said Jonesy.

Boone pumped his fist in the air. "Let the good times roll."

Chuckling, Marci turned to her right, but Nellie's attention was on Jonesy. Nellie leaned her body into his and spread her legs just a little so her knee was touching his.

I wonder what it would feel like to touch the inside of her knee?

Marci trained her eyes back on the road. *What's wrong with me?*

They started onto the back road that led to the waterfall. Boone was handling the truck well and driving slower now because the bumps and divots were bigger. But like everyone else, she still had to put one hand on the roof and one hand on the dash to steady her body.

Marci said, "You're a good driver." When Nellie cackled, Marci swiveled to see what was so funny. "What? He is."

Nellie rolled her eyes. "Don't give him a big head about it."

"Hush, Nellie, I think I wanna hear what Marci has to say." He beamed at her in a way that made her giggle. "Go on, girl. Tell me how great I am." They all laughed as Boone puffed up like he was something special. But he couldn't hold the pose and deflated, chuckling at himself. "I'm just kiddin'. I like to drive. I like cars."

"Any kind in particular?" *Boy, I really like him.*

"Oh no, here we go." Nellie rolled her eyes.

136

Jonesy said, "Oh Lord, don't get him started."

"Go on," she said.

He seemed to be asking for permission when he peered at Nellie and Jonesy who shouted, "Go on!"

His face lit up.

He's so cute when he smiles.

"All right, listen, the 1975 Pontiac Firebird Trans Am is my girl, okay? Fire red on the outside, white upholstery inside. Tops out around one hundred and eighteen miles per hour. That's my baby."

"That's your baby, huh?" Marci teased.

"Not unless you wanna be?" He winked at her.

Nellie snorted in disgust. "Gross. Don't hit on my friends."

Warmth bloomed in Marci's chest. *She said I'm her friend.*

"Oh, like you're hittin' on my friends?" Boone shouted back.

As they started to bicker, Marci leaned back to get out of the line of fire. Jonesy yanked his arm out from behind Nellie's back and stared straight ahead at the road.

Nellie shouted, "I'm gonna do what I wanna do. You can't stop me."

"Watch me." He slammed on the brakes, jerking the truck to a halt. "You ain't datin' my best friend. Ain't that right, Jonesy?"

Their eyes pinned Jonesy to the door.

Better speak up, Jonesy. She bit her lip to keep from smirking at all the emotions crossing his face. *Fight for her or lose her. Come on. Be better than Hubbell! Love your Katie!*

"Fine!" Jonesy splayed his hands in front of him in a stop motion as he eyed Boone. "I wanna date your sister."

"Oh my God!" Boone yelled. "Get out!"

"What?" Jonesy shouted.

"Get out! You can walk the rest of the way, you traitor."

"Don't yell at him!" Nellie screeched.

Boone pointed a menacing finger at her. "You stay outta this."

"Stay out of it? Stay out of it? It's about me, you jerk!"

"Yeah? Then you get out, too!"

"Oh, I am so telling Mom."

Marci had to cover her mouth to hold back her laughter.

"Fine!" Boone shouted. "Get out!"

"Fine!" Nellie started pushing Jonesy toward the door. "We'll meet you there."

"Fine!" Boone hollered.

Marci couldn't hold it in anymore. She let out a laugh as Jonesy and Nellie scrambled out and walked ahead of the truck.

Boone's first reaction to her mirth was giving her a dirty look. But the more she laughed, the more he started to loosen up, and within seconds, he was laughing, too.

What a great family.

"You got a brother?" Boone asked.

They sat calmly, watching Nellie stomp away. Every now and again, she'd turn and shoot Boone a dirty look.

"Tommy. He's older than me." Her heart squeezed when she thought of him. "He was drafted."

Boone's face went from curiosity to apprehension to concern. "I heard them boys weren't the same when they came back," he said quietly. "What they saw. Changed 'em for the worse." He gazed out the windshield.

She twisted her fingers together. "It did."

Tommy was the best brother. Funny, charismatic. He'd been headed to college when he got his draft notice. He wanted to be a history teacher and coach football. Maybe get married, have a few kids. Now he sat at home, watching the news, chain-smoking cigarettes, and drinking so much beer that her parents couldn't keep it in the house. But she never doubted for a second that he loved her. And if she needed her big brother, he'd step up and out of the fog of his own mind.

"He's still the best brother," she said, defending him like she'd spoken her thoughts and now needed to take them back. "Like how he's teaching me how to defend myself. And now I'm teachin' Nellie. So, some good things came of it, I s'pose."

"Nothin' good came out of Vietnam."

They sat in silence for a moment before Boone cleared his throat. "Where's your dad?"

She scrunched her nose as she thought for a second. "Right now? Not sure. Him and my mom work together. And they travel a lot. They're great parents, just not around a lot. I mean, they're not great, but they love us. We know that."

He snorted. "I wish Russell wasn't around."

"He sounds pretty terrible."

Boone shifted, the leather seat crinkling under his jeans. "He is terrible. But it's okay. Me and Nellie will be outta there soon and Mama can—" He shifted again. "Well, she can be who she wants to be. We'll all be free."

Who does she want to be?

When he looked at her, she smiled reassuringly, but he glanced out the window and winced. She followed his stare to Jonesy and Nellie holding hands. She winced, too.

"None of us can help who we love." She felt his eyes on her, so she glanced at him.

"I guess that's true." His eyes devoured her features, looking at her lips a little too long.

She didn't mind that his eyes flicked to her breasts as she took a deep breath. It wasn't the first time a boy had looked at her like that. But it was the first time that she, maybe, wanted to return the look. That maybe she wanted to feel Boone's chest brush against hers before he kissed her.

"We should go," he said.

"Okay."

They gazed at each other for a moment.

The back of his hand brushed the outside of her thigh when he went to put the truck in gear and start down the road.

It sent electricity into her belly. *Maybe I am normal.*

After a moment, the view opened up, and she said, "Oh my."

"Beautiful, right?"

The waterfall and the lake it tumbled into were crystal clear and surrounded by lush foliage and oak trees that went for miles. The colorful mushrooms looked almost magical.

I've never seen anything like it. She exhaled slowly, noticing that Nellie and Jonesy were already perched on a rock that was front row to the splendor.

Boone brought the truck to an easy stop. "Doesn't seem haunted to me."

"Nope. Doesn't seem like there are any ghosts hangin' around." She sighed. "It's beautiful."

"It is," he said.

In her peripheral vision, she could see that he was looking at her when he said it. Heat prickled at her neck.

"Let's go." He opened his door and climbed out before turning around and offering his hand to her.

Wow, that's a real thing? She slowly reached out, and he took her hand gently, helping her out. She fought down an absurdly girlish giggle.

After closing the door, he grabbed the beer and Nellie's bow and arrows from the back of the truck and nodded for her to walk with him.

As they approached, Nellie and Jonesy glanced to them.

"Wanna teach me those moves?" Nellie hollered.

Marci bounced excitedly. "If you'll teach me." She grabbed the bow and arrows from Boone and held them in the air.

"Okay." Nellie jumped up and ran to her, ignoring Boone as he walked by and sat on a rock about twenty feet away from Jonesy.

He cracked open a beer and took a swig while hiding the other five beers so Jonesy couldn't see them.

Marci chuckled as the guys shot annoyed glances at each other. "Think they'll get over it?" she said as Nellie bounded up.

"Yeah, they're boys. By the time we leave, they'll be best friends again and I'll have a boyfriend."

She had to laugh at the younger girl's confidence.

Nellie cocked her head to the side. "So, how come you're hangin' out with us misfits, anyway? You're a cheerleader. Don't you, like, hang out with other cheerleaders and the football players?"

Marci tried to cover her grimace with a smile and glanced at her toes. "They're not as great as you might think."

Nellie must have sensed something because she quickly spoke in a voice that was a little too high. "Oh, okay." Nellie gave her a little tap on the arm. "So, teach me how to kick balls, and I'll show how to shoot an arrow. We'll use that tree over there as the target." She pointed to one about ten feet away.

Relieved at the subject change, Marci chuckled and said, "It's called a groin kick."

"Whatever." Nellie shrugged with a chuckle. "Just show me how to defend myself."

~~~

It only took about an hour for Marci to teach Nellie some key moves, and for her to learn just how bad she was at shooting a bow and arrow. When they were done, everyone stripped down to their skivvies and swam in the lake at the bottom of the waterfall.
~~~

In the midst of all the fun they were having, Marci realized that this was the best day she'd ever had. *After we leave, I have to go back. It'll happen again. And again.* She jumped out of the water.

Boone surfaced and wiped the water from his eyes. "Where are you going?"

Nellie interrupted her conversation with Jonesy and asked, "Marci?"

Ignoring them, she walked barefoot to the side of the lake near the rushing water and peered up. She quickly plotted out crevices and jutting rocks that would make good handholds and footholds. Impulsively, she started climbing. As she grabbed her third rock, her hand slipped and she started to fall. But she caught herself just before she went backward.

"Marci, this is crazy. Stop, come back!" Boone yelled.

"Marci, please stop!" Panic laced her new friend's voice.

But she just kept going. Up and up until she was twenty feet in the air looking down at them. *It would be better to fall than go back.* She climbed to the top, hoisted herself up onto the peak, and gazed down at them.

"Marci!" Boone had gotten out of the water and was at the base of the rock wall, where she'd started. Nellie and Jonesy weren't far behind. They were all watching her like she was crazy.

I can't go back.

When Boone started to climb, fear seized her gut at the thought of him falling. "No!" she shouted. "I'm coming down." He stopped, but she couldn't. Instead of heading back the way she came, she walked into the rushing water at the top of the falls.

"No! Stop!" Boone yelled.

She waded into the middle and peeked over the rushing falls. The water crashed into the rocks below but was calm not far beyond that and deep enough to swim without touching the bottom. The water pummeled her ankles and calves, urging her on.

Straight down, I'll be fish food.

"Don't!" Nellie screamed.

It was the last thing she heard as she jumped.

Her feet hit the water first before she sunk down, down, down. Her heels smacked the rocks at the bottom hard enough to make her wince as her red hair swirled around her face. She forced the air out of her lungs and sat there for a minute.

Peaceful.

In a flash, Boone's strong arms were around her chest, hauling her up until the quietness at the bottom turned into shouting.

"Bring her over here, Boone!"

Marci coughed as he pulled her to the shore, and Jonesy helped Boone haul her out. She laid on the ground, her coughing changing to laughing. "You should see your face." She pointed to Nellie.

"That's not funny!" Nellie huffed and slapped her thigh.

She laughed harder because if she didn't laugh, she would cry. *I can't go back.*

"Damn you, Marci." Boone walked away, and Jonesy followed him. They grabbed their clothes and put them back on.

Nellie started tentatively laughing as Marci calmed down.

"You're crazy." Nellie shoved Marci's shoulder. "Don't do anything like that again."

Boone called out, "Let's go." He'd gathered his stuff and was on his way to the truck. "Nellie, get your bow."

"Boone!" Hurrying, Marci stood up, grabbed her clothes, and yanked them on as she chased him to the truck. "Don't be mad." She nudged him, trying to catch his eyes, as she pulled up her shorts and buttoned them.

He gave her a hard look. "You could'a killed yourself."

"I'm sorry." She shifted her weight from one foot to the other, watching her toes.

His voice softened. "Just don't do it again, okay?"

She flashed a toothy grin up at him.

Relenting, he let out a half sigh, half laugh. "C'mon. Let's get outta here."

Everyone piled into the truck as Nellie put the last of her clothes back on and they got back on the road. Marci leaned her head on Boone's shoulder as the warm air from the open windows dried their wet hair and clothes. Each of them were sun kissed and sleepy.

"Do you wanna spend the night tonight?" Nellie asked. "Since you were comin' over anyway, you might as well stay."

Startled, Boone looked at his sister. "What? I don't think you've ever had anyone spend the night."

Nellie snapped at her brother. "Well, Russell's never been in jail this long, so I never could." Marci glanced at her as Nellie waited for an answer. "Well, do you wanna?"

Marci bounced her head with excitement. "I need to let my mom know. Can I call her from your house?"

"Yeah." They started bouncing a little in their seats as they slapped their hands together. "Sleepover!"

I have a friend.

"Do we know your mom?" Nellie asked.

"Probably not. She travels a lot."

"What does she do?" Boone asked.

"Honestly, I don't know. She just comes and goes. I think she does stuff with books. She's into history."

"What's her name?" Nellie asked. "Maybe our mom knows her."

"Can't miss her. Tall redhead," Marci said. "Her name is Sophie. Sophie O'Sullivan."

17

Trust Me

Fin shifted her hips awkwardly on the hay bale as she sneezed. Finishing up the last of the chief's case files, she wiped her nose on her sleeve. She reached into her backpack, pulled out a Zyrtec, popped it into her mouth, and swallowed it dry. *Ugh.*

After making sure Dawson wasn't looking, she pulled out the old letter she got with her bracelet from her back pocket and looked at the note inside. *I need to see Nellie's handwriting so I know if she wrote this or not.* When footsteps approached, she tucked the note into the envelope and stuffed it inside her bag.

She glanced up to see Dawson walking around the Cutlass pretending to look it over.

"You know, it's totally fine if you don't know what you're doing," said Fin. "I'm pretty sure Boone put in the last part before he left for school, so it should be good to go."

"Yeah, I know." Dawson grabbed the keys and did one final look-see before swaggering over to the driver's side.

When he yanked on the locked door and the handle smacked his fingers, she tried to hold back a grin.

"Ouch." He shook out his hurt hand.

This time she couldn't suppress her chuckle.

He reached through the open window and unlocked the door before glaring at her and opening it. As he slid into the seat, the keys jingled before he tried to start it, but nothing was happening.

Just give him a second.

Nothing.

"Push in the clutch," she said.

"I know!"

After a brief pause, the car started.

Grinning, Fin shook her head as she dropped the files beside her and pulled out Auci's now-clean handkerchief. *Thank goodness Clara Belle let us throw in a few things with the laundry.*

The Cutlass stalled and jerked to a stop. The driver's side door swung open, and Dawson stepped out with the green book and stone pen in hand.

"Car works," he said. "Mostly."

She grinned. "You did a great job." As he walked over and sat down on a bale of hay in front of her, she eyed the green book. "Did you, uh, did you use the book there to help you?"

"No."

"You sure?"

He said nothing, and she reached for the book. Before she could grab it, he smacked her hand.

"Hey now. Let me see!"

"No!" He whacked her hand away again.

She flared her eyes in an imitation of terror and shouted, "It's Bigfoot!" When he whipped around, she grabbed the notebook and ran away, quickly flipping through the pages.

"Fin!" He chased her around the barn as she read.

"How do you fix water damage in a 1970s Cutlass? How do you drive a stick shift? How do you start a stick shift? Why is Fin a know-it-all? Hey!" She threw the green book at him.

It flipped through his hands before he finally caught it. "Well, you're quite annoying sometimes."

"Oh, *I'm* annoying?"

"At least I don't act like I'm always right."

She laughed from deep in her chest as he sat down again in a huff.

Sighing dramatically, she said, "Well, it is really hard being this right and this good-looking all the time." She plopped down onto the hay bale across from him and tried not to laugh.

But neither could hold it in, and they cracked up.

"I'm sorry." He poked at his glasses.

"No, I'm sorry if I come off like that."

"You don't." He bent the soft cover of the green book back and forth in a nervous gesture. "Not on purpose, anyway. You're usually right. It's just hard sometimes. You're so special and I'm so—"

"What?"

"Average."

"You're powerful," she said. "You just don't know it, yet."

He let out a deep, heartfelt sigh.

"You're a truly good guy." She crossed her legs under her. "You remind me of Boone. His core, who he is on the inside, is a solid dude."

A tenderness spread across Dawson's face. "Thank you," he murmured. "I wonder who my mother is."

"Whoever she is, I'm sure she's equally kind."

He tilted his head in agreement as a slight blush highlighted his cheeks. "You see what you got from your mother, don't you?"

She cocked her head. "What do you mean?"

"Nellie can read people. She's got an emotional sensibility. You have that, too."

The idea flooded Fin with so many emotions she wasn't sure how to respond.

"It's why I think you could be right about Grayson." He leaned back on his elbows. "You and your mom. Good gut instincts about people."

She smiled at him. "Thank you, Dawson."

He gave her one quick nod. "Right then. We should get back to business." He leaned forward, took off his glasses, and used his shirt to clean the lenses. "We leave first thing in the morning?"

"Correct."

"Now, here's what we know." He put on his glasses, opened his little book, and ran his finger across the page as he spoke. "Asshole Russell is married to Clara Belle, and they have Nellie, fifteen—"

"Just turned," Fin interrupted.

"Yes. And Boone, seventeen."

"Uh huh." Fin stretched her back. "And the same time Boone was conceived, Asshole Russell had an affair with Rose down in Kentucky."

"Yup. Are we just gonna call him Asshole Russell now?"

"Feels right."

"Asshole Russell it is. Okay, so Rose had twins. Grayson and Lily, both seventeen."

Fin rubbed her neck. "And we believe the girl you saw and the girl I fought with are the same person. Lily. The one who attacked Nellie."

"That's where we're at, yeah."

"Okay, then Rose died. Breast cancer."

"Grayson dropped out of school to take care of her." Dawson rested his elbows on his knees.

"And Lily just dropped out for whatever reason. Got angry. Thefts. Violence. Bad seed."

"But Grayson had similar charges."

"Yeah. Doesn't seem trustworthy, does he?"

Dawson shook his head. "Not in the least. Think they're working together?"

"I don't know. When he was here last night, he seemed genuine. Like he wanted to help. And also, I don't know, scared."

"Of what?"

"More like who. What if Lily is the actual bad seed. And Grayson's along for the ride?"

A guffaw burst out of Dawson. "You really think a tiny girl like that can get a huge guy like Grayson to do her bidding?"

"Manipulation, coercion, and intimidation don't have to be physical."

"I don't know . . ."

Fin leaned forward. "Did you see how Nellie responded to him?"

"Yeah. So?"

"Look, Nellie lives in a house of drunken violence. She'd be able to spot a lunatic at a hundred yards, but that's not how she treated him. I have to think that means something."

Dawson waggled his head from side to side. "Okay, fair enough. But I don't think we should break out the welcome mat for him, either. I mean, he split as soon as the cops showed up. He's got to be hiding something, right?"

"Absolutely. It's just a matter of what he's hiding. Maybe he's protecting his sister."

"Hmm." Lost in thought, Dawson's eyes glazed over. "So, Lily and Grayson, they're from Gunnar's line? Team Gunnar?"

"Yeah, well, Lily is Team Gunnar. We don't know about Grayson. Or even if he has the same abilities. All we know is she's strong and fast."

"Right. And you are Auci's daughter, so . . ." One side of his lips quirked up. "Team Auci."

They both chuckled.

Fin tossed her hands up. "I mean, I'm on the side of no one getting killed and getting weapons off the street. But, yeah, I'm Team Auctioneer."

"But what about Nellie? And Boone? And Clara Belle?" He checked his notes.

Of course he's been taking notes.

"They're just human." He peeked over his glasses at Fin. "Which means Russell isn't anything, either. Which means, whatever powers they have must've come through Rose to Lily and Grayson?"

"That seems right to me."

They sat in silence for a minute.

Fin touched the papers next to her and said, "Lily is angry. Reading these files, I can see why. You saw it, right?"

"The attempted rape?"

Rage flared inside Fin. "Asshole Russell. Her own father. And after all that, they come to find out that they have half-siblings? Who have led, I mean not fairy tale lives . . ."

"Asshole Russell," they said at the same time.

Fin raked her hands through her hair. "But from Lily and Grayson's perspective, Nellie and Boone at least have two parents and a decent house and food and each other. Lily and Grayson have absolutely nothing. They have to feel that. Her maybe more than him."

"So, she maybe has enough anger toward them to hurt them. That's what you think?"

"I think it's one of many theories that makes sense."

He held her stare a little longer than usual as though he was considering something.

"What?" she asked.

"Well," he said, squirming a little. "I just, I'm a bit curious."

"About what?"

Apparently making a decision, he leaned forward with excitement. "The healing thing."

"What? My healing thing?" She poked her chest.

"Um, you and Auci talked about it, but I'm dying to see it." He pushed his glasses up his nose.

"You want me to show you?"

"Would you? I mean, it's not like you're a circus freak or anything, but kind of." Face flushing, he dropped his eyes. "If that's too much, I apologize. But as someone who loves knowledge, I'm dying over here." He peeked at her earnestly.

She laughed a little as she shook her head. "Dawson, you've earned the right to see it, trust me."

Fin reached for the knife strapped to her thigh. She pulled it out, held the tip of the blade to the fat part of her palm, and winced as she cut herself. Blood seeped lightly from the fresh wound.

Dawson gasped as the wound healed immediately. "Astonishing." He scribbled furiously in his book before snapping it closed. "Thank you."

"Of course."

At the sound of tires crunching up the driveway, their heads turned.

"The kids?" Dawson asked.

"Stay here." She grabbed her gun and put it behind her back as she stepped to the open door and peered out. Smiling, she holstered her gun. "They're back. And they've got friends."

"Oh, well," he shoved his book into his back pocket. "Let's meet these new kids."

They walked into the late afternoon sunlight as four teenagers climbed out of Boone's truck. Nellie and Boone's friends included a red-haired girl who was sticking close to Boone and an athletic boy whose eyes never left Nellie.

As the group approached, Boone hollered, "What are you two wearing?"

For the first time, Fin realized what they must look like to the kids. Dawson's joggers and Fin's skinny jeans and boots with their relaxed T-shirts bearing unknown brands must be weird.

Nellie said, "Yeah, you guys dress kinda strange. Where do you shop?"

"Uh." Dawson gawked at Fin.

She quickly said, "New designer in New York. Up and coming."

Apparently satisfied with their answer, the kids resumed their conversation. The boy, who Fin had seen when the auctioneer first showed them this timeline, spun Nellie in a slow waltz. With mushy expressions, they grinned at each other.

They're in love.

Nellie waved her over. "Fin, come meet Jonesy."

Fin walked over to them.

Jonesy offered his hand. "Nice to meet you."

"You too," she said. He had a solid handshake and a confident stare. *I can see why she'd like him.*

"And this is Marci." Nellie gestured to their other companion.

Fin shook the redhead's hand.

Although the girl seemed surprised by the handshake, she smiled brightly. "Nice to meet you."

"You too."

Nellie waved at Dawson. "And this is Dawson."

They said another round of hellos.

Dawson pointed to his dry hair and then their semi-wet hair. "So, where were you guys? Swimming?"

"Yeah, up at Blue Falls," Boone answered.

"Oh, we've seen it," Dawson said.

"You have?" asked Nellie. "I thought you just got here yesterday?"

"Oh, right." Dawson shot Fin a look.

She glanced at the kids. "Uh, while we were researching the area, we saw a picture of it in a travel book. It looks really beautiful."

Nellie nodded. "A lot of kids go swimming there."

As they started to discuss the positive properties of Blue Falls, Fin noticed a large figure emerging from the woods across from the property. She put her hand on her gun and started walking. "Keep the kids back."

Startled by her cop voice, Dawson stuttered, "O-oh okay."

Grayson crossed the road into the driveway. His massive body seemed to change the gravity around him.

She drew her gun. "Hands up."

He sputtered, "I, I'm not . . ."

"Hands. Up." Fin aimed the gun at his chest.

This time he listened, raising his hands and stopping about ten feet away.

Nellie ran to Fin's side and pulled on her arm. "No. Please stop."

Fin's super strength meant her mom might as well have been pulling on a flagpole. Not budging, she kept her eyes on Grayson. "Do you have the dagger?"

He shook his head.

"Do you have it?" She leaned the gun forward for emphasis.

"No, I swear," he said.

Without taking her eyes off him, she called over her shoulder, "Dawson, search him. Check his waistband, pockets, and pat down his legs to the boots. Be careful not to touch it. Just pat over the clothing."

"Uh, okay." Dawson did as he was told.

Grayson didn't move or act put out, stoically enduring the pat down.

When Dawson finished, he shook his head at Fin.

"Fin, he won't hurt us," Nellie pleaded.

Fin narrowed her eyes at Grayson. He seemed sincere, but there was something in his eyes that she was reacting to. Whatever kind of bad he was, he wasn't here to do bad to them. She lowered her weapon but didn't put it away.

150

"You mentioned the dagger last night. What do you know about it?" she asked.

He slowly put his hands down. "The Grim. Made from Death's bones. Will kill anyone it's inserted into, no matter what part of the body it touches or how deep it goes."

"Are you working with your sister to find it and kill the auctioneer?"

"She thinks I am."

"A double agent?" Fin huffed out a held breath. "I don't buy it."

"Lily wants to hurt Nellie. Real bad. She wants to hurt lots of people real bad. That's why I'm here."

"But she's been doing that for a while. I saw her records. And yours. Why a change of heart now?"

Surprised, he rocked back a step. "There's even worse stuff than you know about. Stuff I can't control anymore. I can't stop her. But you can. You gotta get the dagger before she does and destroy it."

Fin stared at him, weighing his words. *Wait a minute.* His face was perfectly clear. Like nothing and no one had touched it. *But last night, he fought with Russell.* She remembered the cuts and bruising. None of it was there anymore.

"Cut yourself," she said to him.

"Fin!" Nellie shouted, horrified.

"It's okay." Grayson eyed Nellie. "It won't hurt me." Grayson searched for a sharp object, finding a piece of metal from Russell's busted truck and holding it up. He sliced his arm with it, blood oozing out of the wound.

The kids gasped but gasped even louder a few seconds later when the cut healed. They all talked at once.

"H-How did you—"

"No way—"

"What the hell—"

"Whoa—"

Fin held up a hand to quiet the peanut gallery. "Can Lily do that, too?"

He nodded.

Fin holstered her gun. "Do you know where the Grim's at?"

"Only that the entrance is behind the house at a tree line."

They stared at each other for a second.

"I know you don't believe me, but I am on your side." Grayson's face was a picture of sincerity. "And I bought you some time. She and her two goons aren't gonna leave for the dagger until tomorrow morning. So, if you go tonight, you'll have a jump on her."

"Wait." Nellie held up her hands. "I don't understand. What's happening right now?"

Fin dragged her eyes away from Grayson and looked at Nellie. "The dagger isn't just a knife." She shook her head. "It's—"

"Dark magic," Grayson said.

A laugh exploded out of Boone. "Oh, come on, dark magic? Gim'me a break."

"It is." Fin locked eyes with Nellie.

"That sounds scary." Nellie squirmed a little and tucked her hair behind her ears.

"It'll be okay." Fin put a reassuring hand on her mom's shoulder before facing Dawson. "We need to go now."

"Agreed," Dawson said.

"Grayson, you're coming with us so you can't pull anything with them"—she tilted her head toward to the kids—"while we're gone."

"No." Grayson looked alarmed. "You can't leave them here."

"We can't take them with us. It's too dangerous," Fin said.

"No, you don't understand." His voice sounded more and more desperate. "As soon as she knows I've betrayed her, she'll kill all of them."

Fin pursed her lips. "Look, she's dangerous, I get it. But you're suggesting a teenage girl would murder multiple people?"

"I'm not suggesting," Grayson said, his eyes looking haunted. "I'm telling you what she's planning. And what she's capable of."

Fin raised a skeptical eyebrow. "There's a big difference between beating up people and slaughtering people."

"I know." He clenched his jaw and flung his arm out at the group. "And I'm telling you, if you leave them here, they'll all be dead by morning." Getting increasingly agitated, he took a deep breath, visibly trying to calm himself. "Please. You have to listen to me." He shook his head like he was arguing with himself before finally saying, "I seen what she can do."

Something about the look in his eyes or maybe the way he spoke sent a chill down Fin's spine.

But before she could reply, Boone said, "We're going with you."

"Yep," said Jonesy while Marci nodded emphatically.

"Where's Mama?" Nellie asked, fear saturating her voice.

"A woman came by earlier and picked her up," said Dawson. "Her name was—"

"Annie," Boone said.

"Yeah." Dawson pointed at his dad. "She said she'd be back around dinner time."

"You should probably go home," Fin said to Marci. She turned to Jonesy, "You, too."

"Oh, I'm not going anywhere." Jonesy stepped to Nellie and put his arm around her.

"Yeah, me either." Marci squared her shoulders. "Besides, I already told my mom I'm spending the night. Now she's gone, so I'm stuck here."

"Fin, we're going to need gear," said Dawson. "With this late start, we'll probably have to pitch a tent. Horses or four-wheelers might help us get there faster . . ." He trailed off, lost in thought.

The teenagers gave him a confused look.

"What's a four-wheeler?" asked Jonesy.

Fin quickly said, "He means a three-wheeler."

"Three-wheeler?" Nellie was as puzzled as the other two.

"You mean an ATC? An All-Terrain Cycle?" Grayson asked.

"Yeah, exactly," said Fin.

Saving them from further explanations, a woman drove a Volkswagen bug up the driveway with Clara Belle in the passenger seat.

Must be Annie.

Fin's grandmother stepped out of the car wearing leather boots and flared jeans. Her hair was pulled back into a ponytail. The bruises from the night before and the night before that were no longer covered with makeup.

Interesting. She doesn't hide them from Annie.

"What's going on?" Clara Belle asked as everyone waved.

"Nothing," they all said at once.

"We're gonna go find the dagger," said Boone. "You should come, too. Like a camping trip."

"No," Clara Belle grabbed a bag of groceries from the car. She hugged Annie goodbye before her friend drove off. "I'm tired. And I've got dinner to make."

"Clara Belle, could I have a moment?" Fin nodded for Clara Belle to come talk to her in private. "Dawson, keep an eye on him." She glanced at Grayson.

"Me?" Dawson looked Grayson up and down dubiously.

"What the hell?" Clara Belle started, finally noticing Grayson standing there. "Have you been there the whole time?"

"Yes, ma'am," Grayson said.

"Why's he here?" She looked at Fin in confusion.

Fin walked her away from the kids as she whispered, "Clara Belle, I can't explain every nuance of this situation right now. But what I can tell you is that Grayson is here because he's worried Lily is planning to come to your house tonight and hurt all of you."

"What?"

"Hurt all of you. Badly. Worse than what she did to Nellie before."

Clara Belle's mouth dropped open as she blinked at Fin.

"We have to go get this dagger before Lily finds it. And I can't be in two places at once. I can protect you. But only if you come with us."

"We can go to Annie's."

"She'll kill her, too." Clara Belle jumped when Grayson spoke so close to them. Fin threw Dawson a questioning smirk as he shrugged with fear at Grayson's back.

Exuding determination, Grayson continued, "I seen Lily and Fin in action. Fin's the only one who can stop her."

"We'll go to the police—"

"They can't stop her, either," Grayson said. "She's too strong. Too fast."

Fin took in his face and knew that was true. The police wouldn't stand a chance against Lily's supernatural abilities. "He's right," Fin said.

Clara Belle whispered, "I don't know what to say."

Fin softened her voice. "I know this is sudden. And trust me, I don't feel good about bringing everyone along, but Lily is dangerous. And if what Grayson is saying is true, then I can protect you better if you come with us."

Clara Belle speared Grayson with her eyes. "How do we know you ain't lyin'?"

"I guess you don't," said Grayson. "All I can tell you is she's worse than Russell's ever been. You saw what I did to him, but I can't do that to Lily. I need help."

Clara Belle's eyes widened with surprise and concern. She put her hands on her hips. "She's the one who beat Nellie the other night."

"Yes," said Grayson.

"You were the one who yelled out to stop her, weren't you?"

"Yes, ma'am."

"Harumph," Clara Belle grunted. She let out a long sigh and looked at Fin. "Doesn't seem like I have much choice, does it?"

"Nope," Boone said from where he'd been eavesdropping. "We're going. We need ATCs then? Is that what you said?"

"The police chief bought a couple ATCs," said Clara Belle. "You're a cop, right? I'm sure he'd do you a favor."

"I have no doubt."

"And Annie's got horses who can handle that terrain. I can go get them, because honestly, I don't know how far you'll even get with an ATC in those woods."

"I can help you get the horses." Grayson gave Clara Belle a tentative smile.

"Oh, then I'll come, too." Boone walked over to his mother and puffed up. "Marci, you should come with us."

Marci ran to Boone.

Dawson said, "I can come with you guys, too."

"Okay," said Clara Belle. "We'll go get the horses and some supplies."

"Nellie, why don't you come with me to see the chief?" Fin was hoping to spend some much-needed time with her mom. "Jonesy, you can come, too."

"Okay."

Even though Nellie still looked a little worried, Jonesy seemed to make her feel better. "Yeah, okay." Nellie glanced at her mama for reassurance.

"You're safe with Fin, Nellie," Clara Belle said.

"Okay." Nellie relaxed a little.

"All right then," Fin said. "We'll meet back here in an hour with supplies and gear. Then get ready to go."

They all reluctantly agreed and went their separate ways.

18

Too Twilight Zone

No one spoke as the gravel road crunched underfoot on their way to Annie's farm. Walking next to Marci, Dawson was grateful that he wasn't Clara Belle, who was clearly trying to be a buffer between Boone and Grayson. The boys kept glaring at each other.

To cut the tension, Dawson asked, "So, how do you know Annie?"

Clara Belle looked back at him, beaming. "We met years ago, just before I met Russell. We've been close ever since."

Given how his grandmother's face lit up when she talked about the woman, he couldn't help but wonder if there was something else there.

"She seems like a good friend, then," said Dawson. *Or perhaps more.* "Nice of her to lend us the horses."

"That's her. Kind to a fault." Clara Belle swung her hands behind her back, interlocked her fingers, and walked a little faster.

"I see." Dawson grabbed his green book and made a note as they all walked in silence for a moment. *Annie more than a friend? Lesbian in the 1970s? Covering with marriage? Could explain why she stays with Russell.*

When Dawson glanced up from his book, he noticed Grayson and Boone stealing iron glimpses at each other. *Classic young man territorial aggression.* Boone was a good guy, but Dawson suspected that he may also have a Russell-sized temper when he wasn't happy about something. Grayson certainly did, as demonstrated at Nellie's birthday party. Together they were a match and a powder keg.

"Why are you really here?" Boone threw down the verbal gauntlet at Grayson.

Here we go. "Uh, gentlemen, maybe not the time or place," Dawson squeaked out.

Clara Belle shot her son a warning look. "Boone, settle down."

Dawson put his book away and shoved his glasses up his nose. Although he trusted Fin's gut about Grayson, he also knew that the last thing Grayson needed or would put up with was a version of Russell getting in his face.

Grayson shot Boone a murderous stare. "I told you why."

"I don't believe you." Boone squared up on his half-brother.

"Enough, you two," Clara Belle said. "Whether you like it or not, you're brothers. And Grayson seems to be here to help. Not just us but also our guests. So, let's help them get the dagger, help Grayson get Lily under control, and then we can all move on. But until then, knock it off." Clara Belle eyed Grayson and Boone.

Please listen to her. He was Fin's cousin, but he wasn't like Fin, much to his chagrin. If Grayson and Boone started to fight, he wouldn't know what to do. That was Fin's area of expertise. His was books.

Marci looked over at him, and they smiled awkwardly at each other.

Clara Belle said, "I really think you should head home, Marci."

"Oh, no, it's okay. My parents are out of town, and my brother . . ." Marci and Boone exchanged a quick glance. "He's got plans. Plus, I love treasure hunts. I'm good at finding things."

"Oh, I didn't realize they were out of town," said Clara Belle. "Okay, then."

Boone slowed down and walked with Marci.

The look they gave each other made Dawson's heart tingle. *Wait, is Marci—is she my . . . No, can't be. Can it?*

Ahead of them, Clara Belle said to Grayson, "We never did thank you for taking care of Russell the other night."

Why isn't she more afraid of him? She should be given he's Russell's son.

But when she looked at Grayson, it was almost a cross between guilt and motherly affection. He wouldn't say her body language indicated she trusted him. But like Fin, she didn't distrust him either, which was confusing.

Clara Belle asked Grayson, "Did you always know he was your father?"

Rather than answering, Grayson just focused intently on the road in front of him, not speaking or looking at anyone.

He's an interesting puzzle. And he's my blood, through Russell. Oh my God, I'm related to Russell. Dawson tripped on his own feet and crashed to the ground, his glasses flying.

"Oh, my goodness." Marci rushed to his aid, trying to help him up.

Embarrassed, he smiled but waved her away as he pushed himself to his knees. Grayson handed him his glasses. He put them on and saw Grayson clearly.

"Thank you." Dawson said to Grayson, who nodded back at him. Feeling self-conscious, Dawson peered at Marci. "Thank you, too."

"You're welcome," she said lightly.

A pair of strong hands gripped under his armpits, and his body was lifted off the ground. As he got his sea legs under him, he realized Boone was the one who had picked him up.

Boone slapped Dawson's back before resting his hand on Dawson's shoulder. "You okay?"

Dawson dusted himself off. "I, yes, I am, thank you."

He looked at the four faces staring back at him, which brought unexpected tears to his eyes.

Her face creased with concern, Marci swooped in and asked gently, "You sure you're okay?"

"Yes," Dawson croaked. He ducked his head and grabbed his shoulder, pretending it hurt. "Just a little pain. I'll be fine."

He started walking and everyone quietly followed suit. The surging emotion of seeing his family looking at him with such care was overwhelming. *And none of them even know who I am.* He squeezed his own shoulder for comfort.

Grayson began to speak to Clara Belle. "We found out when we were five. About Russell. He came back for our mom. For sex."

Clara Belle winced.

"He did that a lot. She tried to make him stop, but . . ." Grayson shrugged.

"I know," Clara Belle said. A look of understanding passed between them.

"He quit when she got the cancer," he continued. "Told her she was disgusting."

"That son of a bitch." Clara Belle took a second and got her emotions under control, then said. "I'm sorry, Grayson." She reached out to lightly touch his arm.

At first, he flinched away, then slowly relaxed into her hand.

Dawson said, "I'm sorry, too. That's terrible." He looked at Boone, hoping his father would show compassion, but Boone just glared even more intently. *Come on, Dad, let it go.*

"Your mom passed?" Clara Belle asked.

Grayson nodded and kept his eyes on the ground.

"How long ago?"

"Five months." He kicked a rock.

"I see," said Clara Belle. "Were you taking care of her?"

Grayson gave a quick upward tilt of his chin, affirming the question.

"Do you visit her grave often?" she asked.

"Not anymore," Grayson said.

"How come?"

Grayson didn't say anything for a long time.

Compassion radiated from her when she asked, "Grayson?"

"We don't live there anymore."

"Live there?" The cruelty of Boone's laughter cut through the air. "You lived at a cemetery?"

Clara Belle shot him a dirty look as Marci slapped his arm.

"Shut up!" Grayson whirled on Boone, but Clara Belle moved to intercept him.

When Boone started forward, Dawson jumped in front of him and held up placating hands. "Whoa, whoa."

"Boone, no." Clara Belle stared hard at each one in turn. "Grayson, stop."

The teenagers hesitated but didn't stand down.

"Enough," she said with more force.

Grayson grunted and turned away.

Boone took a step back.

Dawson waved the group forward and said, "Come on, let's go."

Cooling down, they started to walk again.

A touch of pride swelled in his gut. In Fin's absence, Dawson stepped up between two young men who could probably kill him. *That's new. I've always wanted to do something brave like that.* He grinned to himself and glanced at his father.

Boone kicked a rock.

It's probably a good thing he doesn't trust Grayson. One of us should keep our heads about us. Might as well be Boone.

Clara Belle asked Grayson, "So, you lost the home where your mama is buried?"

"After she died, we didn't have no money." He was quiet as he continued to speak. "But sometimes I go back at night. I planted roses because her name was Rose. But they ain't never grown. I think I did it wrong."

"Maybe sometime I could come and help you fix that," said Clara Belle. "I'm pretty good with roses."

Although only the corner of Grayson's lip tilted up, the glowing gratitude in his eyes reflected his love for his mother.

"Oh, there's the farm." Clara Belle pointed to a large pasture with several horses and a charming little house.

Annie walked out of the house and waved.

Clara Belle happily waved back. "That's Annie."

"Beautiful here," Dawson said.

"Yes." Clara Belle stared at Annie. "It is."

~~~

Fin started the Cutlass with a roar of the engine. She gave it a little extra gas just to hear its powerful purr, grinning at Nellie in the passenger seat.

"I can't wait to drive." Nellie caressed the dashboard.

"It's fun, for sure." Fin waggled her eyebrows, making Nellie laugh.

Returning her attention to the console, she clicked on the radio, and the opening bars of "American Pie" floated across the air waves.

Fin and Nellie said simultaneously, "I love this song!"

"What?" Fin asked. "Really?"

"Yeah, Mama had to buy me another record 'cause I wore the first one out." Nellie hummed along with the hit tune.

Is it my favorite song because it was hers? "We ready?"

"Heck yes!" Nellie bounced on the passenger seat as Jonesy made an affirmative sound from the backseat.

Fin reached down under the driver's side and made sure the small paper bag with the cupcake was still there. *Check.* Touched her badge on her hip. *Check.* Holstered gun. *Check.* Newcross map for directions. *Check.* She checked all the mirrors and put on her seatbelt before saying, "Seatbelts, everyone."

They gawked at her like she had three heads.

Nellie tilted her head at Fin. "Uh, what?"

Jonesy snorted. "No one wears seatbelts."

Come on, Fin. There're no seatbelt laws in the seventies. Hell, drunk driving laws aren't even enforced yet. "Right, of course. I'm just a cop, so I do. It's cool though if you don't want to."

Shaking their heads, they settled into their seats with a laugh.

She pulled the car out of the barn and took it slowly down the dirt road toward the police station. She'd been to traffic accident scenes. If they weren't going to wear seatbelts, she was going to drive slow.
~~~

"Nice job fixing this, Jonesy." She peeked in her rearview mirror.

"No problem," he said quickly before turning his adorning attention back to Nellie.

Fin snuck glances at Nellie in the passenger seat. *We both have dark hair. Her eyes are more hazel than brown, but the shape is similar. She walks with my confidence, too. Or wait, maybe I walk like her?*

Her eyes flicked up to Jonesy in the rearview mirror. *I wonder why they don't last?* She was initially struck by how much love existed between the two high school sweethearts. But he wasn't Fin's father, so something must happen. *And how does she meet Auci? And when?*

Growing up in a foster home she'd always wondered why she'd been abandoned. It led her to think the worst of her real parents. Assuming that she was better off in a foster home because her parents were reckless vagabonds was easier. If her mother was a drug addict or a pregnant teen and her father was a criminal, then she'd gotten the better end of the deal. But seeing her mother now, she couldn't imagine that she had been anything but wanted.

How did I end up at a foster home, Mom?

Nellie asked, "So, what do you think of Newcross?"

"It's an interesting little town," Fin said. "Seems like there are some good people here. Most of them."

Nellie squirmed a little. "Russell isn't always that bad."

Fin infused her voice with compassion when she said, "He must not be good if you don't even call him Dad."

Nellie played with the ends of her hair for a moment. "What's it like being a girl detective? Is it like being Wonder Woman? You know they're turning the comic book into a television show."

"I've heard about that." Fin tamped down a knowing smile. *And movies. And a bunch of other stuff you don't know about yet.* "Yeah, being a cop is kind of like that. But with worse uniforms."

They laughed together, and Fin noticed how similar their voices were. Her mother was so young and free. *What happens to you?*

"You know what else is coming?" Jonesy's voice vibrated with excitement as he slid forward and popped his head in between the front seats. "Mobile. Phones. They won't even have to be attached to a wall. We'll be able to walk around and still talk on the phone. Like, anywhere. It's crazy."

Nellie tossed an incredulous look over her shoulder. "Oh, you've been watching too much TV."

"I haven't, I swear," he replied. "And soon, you'll be able to have it in a car."

"Stop that, it's too *Twilight Zone* for me." She examined Fin. "What do you think?"

"I mean, you may as well say a phone could become a computer, right?" She glanced at them as they tilted their heads at her, confused.

"What's a computer?" Nellie asked.

"I've heard of that." Jonesy said excitedly. "They're huge though. You'd never be able to put one in a phone. That'd be impossible." He laughed as he slid back in his seat. "Now that's crazy!"

"Sorry, bad joke." Fin smiled to herself as they came upon the edge of town. *He's gonna like the future. The little tech ninja.* "We're here."

Fin pulled into the police station parking lot, kicking up some dust. The three of them climbed out of the Cutlass and walked toward the front door just as a new police cruiser pulled up. A tall, familiar man stepped out. It was the chief, only thirty years younger. Lost in his own world, he picked his teeth with his fingernail.

"Chief!" Fin waved at him.

He swiveled around, looking for his boss.

"Ah, crap," Fin said under her breath. *He's still a patrolman, dummy. And he hasn't met you yet.* "Yeah, hi, my name is Fin. I'm a detective from New York."

With her badge visible on her hip, she trotted up to him and extended her hand.

He shook it warmly as a grin spread across his face. "Hello Fin, detective from New York. I'm Officer Quincy J. Booker, but people just call me Booker. How can I help you today?" He kept trying to get something out of his tooth with his tongue. "Excuse me, corn on the cob for lunch."

Smiling, Fin said, "You should just carry toothpicks in your pocket," and pointed to his shirt.

"I think you're right," he said. "I'm new, so I'm still learning what I need to carry with me and where to carry it. My mama always said a pack rat like me needed more pockets than I had."

Chuckling at his most recent mama-ism, she was happy to see that his huge smile was part of his younger version, too.

"Now." He smacked his hands together. "How can I help you, Fin from New York?"

"Oh, right. Well, that's my . . ." She turned and pointed at the kids, who were flirting with each other and laughing as they leaned against the car. *What do I call her?* "That's my friend, Nellie, and her friend, Jonesy. We're headed out to find a stolen artifact that could help me solve a crime back in New York. I think it's been tossed in the deep woods behind the Ellis house. But I've heard that it's rough terrain, so I was hoping for a bit of professional courtesy. Could I borrow one of your ATCs?"

"The deep woods, huh?" He wrapped his big hands around his duty belt, which had a bright and shiny gold key dangling from it. "How deep?"

"Past Blue Falls," she said.

"Ahh, Blue Falls." He glanced toward that area as though he could see it from where they stood. "Pretty daunting environment back there. Why would someone toss it there?" He tilted his head at her.

She tried to look congenial. "Well, your guess is as good as mine." She smiled through gritted teeth. *Boy, young Chief is a pain.*

"Lots of stories about that area." He tilted his head the other way.

"So I've heard." Being a cop, she could tell that he wasn't buying what she was selling. "Look, I'm not going down there for fun, Officer Booker. I'm on a case. I need that artifact."

"What is it?"

She narrowed her eyes at him, weighing whether to loop him in. "A dagger."

His eyes got big. "Hoo-eey, that's something. Daggers are dangerous. Small, too. How ya gonna find it in that brush back there?"

Starting to lose her patience, she said, "I'm good at my job."

"New York streets are different than woods with foliage from your ankles to your ass."

They eyed each other for a second.

Fin looked pointedly at his belt and asked, "What's that gold key for?"

"The ATC."

She raised an eyebrow at him.

"You got a badge?"

She pointed with a sarcastic flare to the badge clearly visible on her hip.

"That from a Cracker Jack box?"

She sucked her teeth, took her badge off, and handed it to him.

He eyed it and tapped it with his finger. "Well, it's metal, so it's not from a Cracker Jack box." He beamed sarcastically at her. "You get a point, Detective Fin Baker."

I wanna strangle you.

He started to return it to her but pulled it back quickly and took another gander, peering at her, then the badge, then back to her before finally handing it to her. His eyes looked her over. "The chief has to approve interagency loans. Sorry, can't help you." He abruptly spun around and started toward the station.

"What?" Fin sputtered for a moment before realizing what he'd seen. On one side, was her badge. On the other, was her police identification that listed the date the badge was issued: 2012.

"Shit." She chased him, calling out. "But, wait, I really need your help."

"Can't help," he said. "Doubt those ATCs could get very far in the woods anyway."

"But—"

"Sorry," he said.

She stopped as he kept going and yelled, "I've got a cupcake!"

He stopped in his tracks.

You've got to be kidding me.

He twisted back to her with an appraising look. "What kind?"

"Chocolate. With peanut butter icing," she said.

"Hooeey!" He smacked his hands together. "My mama always said peanut butter cupcakes were—"

"Sweet like you?" She put her hands on her hips as he cocked his head at her.

"Now, how'd you know that Detective Fin Baker?"

"Lucky guess." She walked a few steps toward him. "You actually read my badge?"

He nodded slowly. "I keep hearin' strange stuff happens 'round these parts."

"You're tellin' me."

He gave her a once over. "Yeah, okay. You go get the cupcake; I'll go get the ATC."

She gave him the stink eye. "I thought the chief had to approve it."

Shut up, Fin. You're getting what you want.

He chuckled and walked into the station.

She shook her head. "Unbelievable." She dropped her hands to her sides as she strolled back to the car.

"We copacetic?" Jonesy asked.

She gave him a thumbs up and went to the driver's side door, opening it and grabbing the small sack under the seat.

"What's in there?" Nellie whispered.

Fin jumped. She looked over her shoulder at Nellie, who was suddenly standing right beside her with an odd expression on her face.

"A cupcake." Fin tried to step back, but Nellie wasn't moving. Fin searched her face. *She wants something.* "What is it? What do you want?"

"Can Jonesy drive the car and you drive the ATC back to the house?" Her mischievous grin paired nicely with her double eyebrow raise.

"Uh." Her mother asking her for permission to be alone with a boy made Fin uncomfortable.

"Pleeease?" Nellie made a sad face and blinked her eyes like a doe-eyed toddler.

This could not get any weirder.

"I might get kissed for the first time!" She squealed quietly.

Annnnnd weirder. "If I say yes, and you wear seatbelts, can we quit talking about this?"

"Uh-huh." Nellie's face lit with hope.

"Then, yes."

"Thank you, thank you, thank you!" Nellie pulled her into a hug.

It felt like the whole world got quiet and slid into slow motion. Fin closed her eyes and let the sensation of her mother's hug fill her senses. *Please don't let go.*

The rumbling of an ATC engine filled the air.

Nellie released her and ran to Jonesy grinning from ear to ear.

The young version of the chief rode up to Fin on the ATC. He parked, shut the engine off, and walked up to her. Holding out his hand, his eyes glimmered with anticipation. "I believe you have something for me."

She handed over the bag, not sure what the big deal was about a chocolate cupcake with peanut butter frosting but happy to have the leverage.

He pulled out the cupcake, sniffed it, licked the icing, put it back in, rolled up the bag, and tipped his hat at her. Opening his other hand in a dramatic fashion, the gold key shined brightly in the late afternoon sun.

As soon as she took it from his hand, he whipped around and started toward the police station. "Have it back in two days, Fin from New York!" He threw a hand in the air with a backward wave.

She shook her head and glanced over at Nellie and Jonesy. The teenagers were already piled in the car with Nellie leaning on the console almost in his lap. *She is definitely not wearing a seatbelt.*

Fin got on the ATC and started it up. *Son of a bitch, my mom's a teenager.*

19

Sometimes You Buy an Apple

On the way back to Clara Belle's house, Dawson rode his horse next to Boone. On the other side of Boone was Marci. Every now and again, Dawson looked at the two of them, noticing how similar his nose was to Boone's and how Marci had an attached earlobe like him. He seemed to have the pieces of the puzzle, but they hadn't been fully put together. Marci could be his mom, but he couldn't be 100 percent sure just yet.

Wonderful and frustrating all at the same time.

Boone asked, "So, how do you and Fin know each other? Just because of the case you're working on?"

"Uh, yes and no," he said. "Fin and I are also family. Cousins."

"No way?" said Marci. "That's so cool you get to work together."

"Yeah, it's been"—when he saw their expectant smiles, he changed direction—"a lot of fun."

"You got a wife? Kids?" Boone asked.

"Not yet." Dawson adjusted his grip on the reins.

"How come?" Marci asked.

This feels like I'm twenty and my parents are hammering me about who I'm dating. He grinned so hard that the muscles on the back of his head tightened.

Well, Marci, who-could-be-my-mom . . . "I haven't met the right girl yet." *And listen, Dad . . .* "I really want to focus on my career."

"Is there a lot to being a librarian?" Boone asked a little sarcastically.

Dawson pushed his glasses up higher, feeling compelled to please his father. "Well, you might be surprised. There's lots of things I can do. Get hired at bigger libraries—like the ones at universities—and run library systems."

Even as he was saying what his future could hold, Dawson was skeptical. He'd spent his whole life acquiring knowledge, trying to quench a thirst that he knew now was only going to be satiated once he understood where he came from. Knowing that, he was at a crossroads. *What do I want to do next? Because I don't think it's being a librarian anymore.*

Mentally changing direction, he brightened up a bit. "You know, I always wanted to be Indiana Jones. Like in *Raiders of the Lost Ark*."

He expected them to laugh or think it was cool or interesting, but instead their faces were blank. *Oh shit.*

"Who's Indiana Jones?" Marci asked.

"Is he a superhero or something?"

"Uh." He shifted nervously in his saddle. *Think, Dawson, think.*

"Sometimes, at the library, we get screenplays or movie scripts." He sat up straight, proud of himself for thinking so quickly. "We just got one about a professor named Indiana Jones, who does stuff like this. Goes and finds treasure and has adventures. I'd like to do that." *And create the stories of my life instead of reading about everyone else's.*

"Right on, man. I like that." Boone flicked Dawson's arm with the back of his hand.

Dawson's chest expanded. *My dad likes me.*

Marci said, "Just be careful. Make sure you're safe and you know stuff. Like how to get fresh water, how to fight, how to build a tent. My brother says it can be dangerous if you don't have skills."

If you're my mom, thanks for wanting me to be safe. Honestly, he thought his chest might burst. "And how about you two? Dating anyone?"

They flashed googly-eyes at each other and looked away, both blushing a little.

"Sorry, I didn't mean to pry." He absolutely meant to pry so he could see what was between them. And, happily, something was.

"Well, maybe." Boone cast a boyish grin at Marci.

Dawson played dumb to stir the pot. "Is she nice?"

"Yeah." Boone sat up in the saddle a little. "She's smart and kind and beautiful and brave." Marci blushed and Boone grinned at her, saying, "I'm hopin' to spend some time with her this summer."

"Nice," Dawson said. "And what about you, Marci?"

She twisted happily in her saddle. "I think this might be the summer I actually find a boy I want to date."

"Well, then I hope you both get what you want." As they traded shy smiles with each other, his whole chest warmed. Not wanting to make things too awkward for the teenagers, he nodded ahead at Grayson and Clara Belle. "So, what do you guys think they're talking about?"

~~~
~~~

Although they had been riding in silence, Grayson could feel Clara Belle stealing glances at him.

Finally, she spoke. "Why should we trust you?"

He'd been expecting the question and would have been disappointed if she hadn't asked it. If she was anything like his mother, she'd want to protect her kids. Especially since he was Russell's son.

Eventually, Grayson said, "You know how sometimes you buy an apple, but on the drive home it gets all beat up and bruised? It don't look so good." He waited for her acknowledging nod. "But you go ahead and cut the bruises off, and you find out the inside is, well, it ain't as bad as you thought?"

"Yeah." She pulled on the reins to slow her horse next to his.

"I guess I'm kinda like that."

Clara Belle searched his eyes for a moment. "I bet your mama didn't see you as bruised or broken. Mamas always see the best in our children and push them to be that best version of themselves."

Emotion surged inside of Grayson. He tried his best to keep it under wraps, but he couldn't help his eyes from glistening. *I guess we're both hiding things from the world.*

"Tell me the truth," he said.

"Okay." She seemed a little nervous that he was turning the tables on her.

"You stayin' with Russell 'cause you love that girl back there?" he asked.

A small breath escaped her chest. "What? I mean, that would make me—"

"A dyke?"

"Jesus, don't say that out loud." She glanced behind her and tossed a pretend smile back at Dawson, Boone, and Marci.

He followed her example, giving them a nod.

She shot him a look of death. "Don't talk like that." She resolutely faced forward, and they trotted in silence.

"It don't mean anything's wrong with you," he said quietly. "I seen people who got actual things wrong inside them. And I seen people who have a bright light in them, like you. Who you kiss goodnight don't matter. Just matters how you treat people."

Clara Belle closed her eyes like it could make the world go away.

His stomach clenched at the thought that he'd hurt her. He just wanted her to know he wasn't one of those idiots who believed she was a bad person for who she loved. But he knew why she hid it. A woman who loved another woman wasn't worse than anyone else, but try telling the world that. Or Newcross, at least.

She couldn't win that war. Hell, up until a couple years ago, doctors would've said she had a mental disorder and cops would've arrested her. If she ever said it out loud, she could lose her part-time job as a cashier at Gilbert's Grocery. But he wanted her to know that if anybody tried anything like that in front of him, he'd have something to say about it.

"Let's just forget we had this conversation," she said.

He waited a moment, then said, "I'm just sorry you had to marry that son of a bitch. That's all."

"Me, too," she said, her voice wavering.

An understanding passed between them, and they rode quietly for a bit.

Eventually, she asked, "How bad did he beat you?"

He winced. "He wasn't there much. But when he was . . ."

Grayson shifted in his saddle, taking a deep breath. He'd never told anyone about the things Russell did, and wasn't sure he wanted to now. But he had to trust someone with his secrets since Lily was no longer an option. And it was important to him that Clara Belle liked him. Trusted him even.

"One time, I was about ten, he gave me a dollar to go get him a soda. When I walked outside, the wind whipped it out of my hand. I thought about just going on to the store, you know? Just stealin' it. I wasn't nearly as scared of the cops as I was of him. But I knew if I got caught, he'd take it out on Mama. It'd be me or her. So, I went back in and told him what happened. He acted like it was no big deal, got up, walked away. I had a few seconds of relief. I thought maybe he'd changed. He came back a few minutes later and told me to put my hand on the table palm up. He put another dollar in it and told me to close my eyes."

Pure dread infused Clara Belle's face.

She knows how this ends. "Next thing I know, I'm screaming in pain. He'd nailed my hand and that dollar bill to the table. He told me I better never lose his money again."

Clara Belle's eyes filled with tears. "How long did he leave you there?"

"A few hours. Beat Mama every time she came near me. When he finally left, she pulled the nail out and took me to a doctor. Said I'd had an accident building a bird house."

"The lies we tell," she said quietly.

"He pulled shit like that over the years. When I was fifteen, he came in drunk looking for sex, and Mama tried to kick him out. He wouldn't go, so I got in his face. He tried to beat me down."

"What happened?"

"Like I said, he tried." Grayson held Clara Belle's stare. "Then he tried to hurt my sister. Real bad. I almost killed him. We never saw him again after that. Mama was sick by then anyway and no good to him."

Grayson knew he had an intense look on his face, so he wasn't surprised when Clara Belle looked away. He couldn't talk about Russell without feeling a surge of anger that threatened to overcome him. *Probably the same anger that fuels Lily.*

She asked, "He talk about us?"

"Not really. He'd just say, 'I'm goin' back to my real family,' or somethin' like that. Russell don't mess with me no more. You saw."

A touch of joy tugged at the corner of Clara Belle's mouth.

"What?" he asked.

She pursed her lips but was having a hard time suppressing her glee. "It was nice to see Russell get a taste of his own medicine." She chuckled a little. "You and Fin both put him down pretty hard."

Grayson let a small laugh escape. "Fin's pretty tough."

"You're right," she said.

"You can trust her with Nellie."

"I know. Somethin' about her . . ." She drifted off into some other thought and then came right back. "But I agree with Nellie. You don't need to kill Russell, you understand? Don't become a murderer because of that asshole. You deserve better."

He pulled at the reins to keep the horse on track as he glanced at her. "Yes, ma'am."

A comfortable silence fell between them.

Clara Belle said, "I try to protect my kids. Step in and take the beatings. He'd never laid a hand on them until recently." Her posture went rigid. "Boone. He's older now. Decided he's not gonna take it, you know? Not without hittin' back. Boone's smaller than you, but he's scrappy."

"He seems like it."

Their eyes met again before flicking away. A few moments passed. He whispered, "Russell raped Mama."

"What?" Clara Belle's head snapped around to Grayson.

"That's how me and Lily came to be." The familiar rage bubbled up inside him. "He bragged about it. He tried to hurt Lily, too. I didn't let him."

"Oh, Grayson . . ." Clara Belle whispered, tears pooling in her eyes.

After a moment of quiet, he asked, "Is that how it happened to you?"

"No." A beat later, she added, "Not with Boone. And anyway, you can't rape your wife, right?"

His stare connected with hers and then flinched away. Theirs was a communion of pain, and at times, silence seemed like the best way to honor it.

As they neared the house, she said, "I'm so sorry about your mama. And I'm so sorry about what Russell did to her and to you and to Lily."

Grayson frowned. "It's okay, it's not like you knew."

"I did know."

A confusing cocktail of emotions flooded his body. "What?"

Eyes going wide, she shook her head. "Oh, not all that. I mean, I knew your family existed because I followed Russell one night after he talked about you all. I even confronted him about it. He almost killed me."

"He beat you?"

"Almost to death," she whispered, tears in her eyes. "I thought about your mama and you kids every day since then. I did what I could when I could. Wish I could'a done more."

He searched her face as the horses trotted up to the house. "What kinds of things did you do—"

"Mama!" Nellie jumped out of the Cutlass and ran toward them.

"We can talk more later." Clara Belle jumped off her horse and started to lead it to the barn. "And Grayson." She turned and waited until they locked eyes before continuing. "You're family, son. So long as you don't hurt mine."

He nodded as Nellie and Fin walked up.

"Hey girls," Clara Belle said. "Only one ATC?"

"Yeah, just the one." Fin caught Grayson's eyes, and they gave each other a look of mutual cease fire.

"Jonesy took the Cutlass back into town to grab the last few supplies," said Nellie. "He'll be here in the next hour, and then we can go."

"Sounds good," said Clara Belle. "We got the horses. And Annie gave us some camping supplies."

"Okay," said Fin. "I'm gonna grab Dawson and get the rest of our stuff. We'll head out once Jonesy gets back. You good with that, Grayson?"

He hopped off his horse and nodded. His chest clenched when he looked at Clara Belle and Nellie. This was his family. The only one he had left.

I'll die before I let anything happen to them.

20

Who's the Idiot Now?

Lily used her knife to slice off a piece of red delicious apple before shoving it in her mouth. Crunching loudly, she sat on the cabin's porch as Luke and Carl gathered the final supplies: rope, hunting knives, a couple guns, water, food, flashlights, and binoculars.

Morons. She sniffed the air. *What's that stench?*

"We got everythin' you asked for," Carl said.

Rather than responding to that, she asked, "Why are you two idiots wearing camo?"

Luke clapped back, "Ain't you never been huntin' before?"

With a razor-edged smile, she said, "You seen my freezer, haven't you?"

She took great pride in his reaction. A little fear, a touch of "forgot about that," mixed with "let's shut up now."

"I don't need to wear camo to get the job done." She finished the apple, tossed the rotten core into the grass, and stabbed her knife into the porch plank.

"You say we're leaving in the mornin'?" Carl adjusted his balls.

"Touch your nuts again and I'll cut them off." She narrowed her eyes at him and yanked her knife from the wood. The slow thump in her chest was, for the moment, easy to ignore. But she knew that if he kept that up, it wouldn't be. It would become a deep pulsing in her brain. The compulsion would erupt, a life would end, and she'd go back to normal.

He snorted. "Fuckin' women." But he relented and pivoted toward the woods. "I'mma take a piss," he hollered over his shoulder.

She placed all her attention on Luke, who did his best to ignore her stare before finally glancing, wide-eyed, her direction.

"Have something you wanna to say to me?" Her lip twitched as he shook his head nervously. *Pussy.* "Where are the horses?"

"That's where we're headed next." Luke's voice wavered a little.

He's scared. Good.

He cleared his throat. "Carl's got friends."

174

She eyed him for a second. "Get all this packed up so we're ready to go first thing."

"Yes, ma'am." He hopped to it.

She sniffed the air again and frowned. *Grayson must not have buried my collection deep enough.* She scanned the woods around her. *He should'a been back by now.*

She used to love her brother. Grayson had been her hero, protecting her from Russell, from herself, and from other people. When she started with the animals, he thought he could just shame her into feeling guilty about breaking a cat's leg here or shooting a dog with a BB gun there. She acted like it bothered her, but it didn't.

Who gives a shit about a fuckin' cat?

At ten years old, she was petting the neighbor's cat gently, but something about the fur made her twitch. It was the first time she felt the thump in her chest. She started to hate the cat, thinking about how easy life was for it. Being fed, taken care of, and loved all without having to ask. The thumping grew until her entire body was pulsing. When the cat's neck bones cracked, the pulsing went away and she felt better. For a while.

Sitting on the porch, she propped her elbows on her knees. As she rested her chin in her palm, her gaze went hazy at the fond memories. *I've gotten so much better since then.*

When she was thirteen years old, Grayson had taken her swimming at Blue Falls. While they were there, two boys showed up and started making fun of them. When the six-year-old boy got in, Grayson waved Lily out of the water.

With an understated fear in his eyes of what Lily might do, he said, "Come on, Lily. Get outta there."

Sneering, the ten-year-old boy walked over to Grayson. "Where you going? Are you chicken?" He tucked his hands in his armpits and flapped his elbows like they were wings while making *bok-bok* sounds.

Grayson ignored him and went to find his towel.

Frustration and rage started bubbling up inside her like lava, but she didn't want to fight with her brother. As Lily swam past the younger one, he spit water in her face. The thumping grew into pulsing. She pushed him under the water and held him there with a strength that surprised her until his body went limp. A shiver of relief cascaded down her spine. She walked away from the waterfall and put on her clothes as though nothing had happened.

Eventually growing bored with a target that wouldn't fight back, the boy looked around for his sibling. At the sight of the floating body, he screamed the boy's name. He almost tripped dashing over to save his little brother. But it was too late.

As the surviving sibling wailed, Grayson whispered, "What did you do?"

Lily didn't say anything. Admiring her handiwork, she felt like she was floating. Her entire body was electrified. Feeling powerful, invincible, and deliciously dangerous.

The police reported it as an accidental drowning because no evidence of foul play was found. Miraculously, the scratches the boy had left all her over arms had healed almost as soon as she left the water.

But Grayson knew the truth.

After that, he tried to never leave her alone with anyone. Later on, she would find ways to relieve the thumping beyond his watchful eye.

Lily smashed her fist down on a cricket crawling across the wooden floorboards of the porch before rubbing the bug goo off on her pants. Smirking, she thought, *It's funny. I don't even remember that little boy's name anymore.*

Two years ago when she was fifteen, she killed the first girl. Lily ran into town, to get away from Russell. He'd tried to rape her that night, but Grayson stopped it.

Her body was pulsing, and she couldn't control it. The young woman was leaving work at the local newspaper. She was alone, so Lily ran up to her. Her second victim clearly thought Lily needed help until it was too late. Once the stranger realized she was in trouble, she scrambled to get into her car but dropped her keys. Lily slammed the woman's head through the car window with an unusual strength that was growing by the day.

The woman tumbled to the ground with blood oozing from her forehead, face, and neck. Lily jumped on top of her and squeezed her soft throat until the trachea cracked. Once she crushed that windpipe, relief washed over her.

She floated back to the house and calmly told Grayson what she'd done. Without asking him to, he went to the newspaper, put the body in the trunk of the car, stole the car, and hid all the evidence. She was still listed as a missing person.

Lily snorted and shook her head. *Police are so stupid.*

Luke finished packing the gear, and Carl came back from the woods.

Her lip curled. *God, I hate Carl.* A slow thumping started in her gut. *I'd love to carve him up.*

Over the last year, she'd learned the carving was the real pleasure. She always carried the switchblade with her just in case, never knowing when the thumping would start or stop. Carving used to carry her longer between episodes, but even that pleasure was starting to wane. Her cravings were coming faster now. She needed to do more to make the pulsing go away. The ultimate prize would be Nellie.

"Yes." She closed her eyes and savored the thought. The thumping ticked up a notch at the memory of chasing Nellie down that dirt road and beating her. Lily's fists clenched in short pulses.

Back when she and Grayson had found out about Nellie and Boone, they both wanted revenge. Grayson was angry and wanted a confrontation, but she wanted to carve the other family from stem to stern. The two of them had started watching Nellie and Boone and traveling to Newcross to plan how they were going to do it.

But that was before Oliver appeared and explained why they were so strong and why they healed quickly. He told them the story of the Grim.

Oh, God, the Grim. She shivered in anticipation. *What I could do with that . . . Maybe it will make the pulsing stop.* Taking deep, peaceful breaths, she frowned. *God, that stench is strong.*

She opened her eyes to see Luke and Carl staring at her. "Why don't you two clowns go and finish Grayson's job. Bury them pieces deeper so they don't smell."

As she stood up to go back in the cabin, Carl started laughing. She spun around, giving him a death glare. "What're you laughing at, hick?"

"You think that stench is from a shallow grave?" He squinted at Luke, whose smile quickly faltered before he looked at the ground. "Girlie, that stench is from the freezer. Your brother didn't bury those body parts. He's still at that girl's house."

No!

She ran into the cabin and swung open the freezer door. The stench overwhelmed her. The remnants of her last rampage, from torsos to hands, filled three-quarters of the freezer.

"Grayson!" she screamed.

Just outside the door, Carl chuckled. "Who's the idiot now?"

21

Lucky You

Lily stormed up to the front door of the shabby bar.

I'll make Grayson do what I want. Even if it means working with this asshole.

She flung open the faded door to the dimly lit watering hole with the worn pool table and sticky floors. The smell of stale cigarettes and old whiskey hung heavy in the air.

The bartender yanked an empty glass from Russell's hand.

Mother fucker. The thumping started almost immediately and seemed to keep time with the loudly ticking clock behind the bar.

The man behind the counter flipped a towel over his shoulder. "You're done, man."

"Fuck yoooou." Russell, the man responsible for half her genetics, flipped him off.

But the barkeep didn't seem to notice because he was looking at her. When she curled her lip at him, his eyes flicked away with fear.

Russell started to grab his things before noticing the man's frightened expression. Russell scoffed as he lobbed a glance over his shoulder toward the door. "What are you scared of, asshole?" He froze as his eyes met hers.

Good.

"Hello, Daddy," she said in a syrupy sweet voice as she started to move toward him. "Happy to be out of jail? You can thank my men, Carl and Luke, for bailing you out."

"Who the fuck are they?" He shivered and his chest heaved with thick breaths at her approach. He glanced anxiously at the door behind her.

Asshole. "Grayson isn't here." He let out a sigh of relief, which pissed her off even more. She unleashed her boiling anger in a slap that knocked him off his stool. "It's me you should be scared of not Grayson."

He tried to right himself from the ground, but she forced him to strain away from her as she knelt and leaned into him. Russell started to squirm away from her, so she wrapped her hand around his throat to hold him still. His eyes flew open at her strength.

"Pl-ea-se," he eked out.

This is fun.

It made the thumping slow down. She let go of him, and he sagged in relief. As he coughed and rubbed his throat, she pulled the knife from her pocket and stabbed his thigh. He screamed and writhed in pain.

"You crazy bitch!"

When she twisted the blade, he screamed again. She pulled it out, held it near his face so he could see his own blood dripping from the blade, and lifted the knife again to strike.

"No, don't! Stop!"

She flexed her chest and shoulders as she stood and stepped away, putting the knife back in her pocket.

He put pressure on the wound to stop the bleeding and sent a pleading look up at the man behind the counter.

She followed his eyes to the barkeep, who quietly put a phone back down on the receiver and scurried away. "I guess I only have a few minutes before the cops get here. Lucky you."

"You're insane."

"You would know." She leaned down and grabbed his face, briefly considering jamming her thumbs into his eyes. "You made me this way."

"You were born this way."

She sneered as sweat dripped down his face. "I'd kill you, but I'm going to use you first."

"What do you want?"

She let go of his face and put her hand over his wound, slowly pushing down until he winced.

"I know you heard that idiot Oliver tell me and Grayson about the Grim. I saw your drunk ass behind the dumpster. So, you know what I want." She pushed down a little harder. "And you know the woods behind your house better than anyone. Now, I know where I need to go, but I don't know how to get there. So, you're going to follow Grayson and plant these yellow flags every twenty to thirty feet or so." She reached into her jacket and pulled out a small sack, dropping it in front of him. "Then I can follow the flags to the entrance. I don't give a shit what you do after that."

He said through clenched teeth, "Why don't you just go with him?"

She cocked her head as though she was just considering the situation. "Why don't you do what you're told, and I won't kill you."

"Follow Grayson?" He scoffed. "You're fuckin' crazy. He'll kill me."

She yanked her knife out of her pocket and stabbed him again in the same leg.

He leaned forward and retched.

"Stop calling me crazy," she whispered.

"Dammit!" Russell screamed as she pulled the blade out. "Fine. I'll do it." He glared at her. "But why can't you just follow him yourself?"

"I can't be in two places at once, now can I?" She straightened, giving him a beauty pageant smile. "And I've got a family to kill while Grayson's gone. I think you know them. It's the other one you have up the road."

"You psychotic—"

"Tsk, tsk." She raised her knife again, and his mouth snapped shut. "You better get going. I think Grayson's already headed out with some dark-haired woman. A cop, I think. They started right behind your other family's house." She leaned down and patted his shoulder. "But don't worry, I'll make sure you're gone before I get started on them." Her hand went from patting to a vice-like squeeze. "And don't get any ideas about going to the cops. If you do, I'll pin everything on you. And trust me, I know how to do it."

She let go of his shoulder and patted his head like he was a dog before turning and walking toward the door.

Before it swung closed behind her, he yelled, "Crazy bitch!"

She beamed with pride, knowing it was true. But more importantly, now he knew it was true, too.

22

Wanna See Who's Stronger?

Fin slapped a bug on her arm. "Well, this isn't as bad as we thought."

The group picked their way through the heavily wooded area, lush and green with the vibrancy of spring ready to burst into the heat of summer. The ATC had lasted a mile before the dense foliage was only passable by horse or foot.

"Any idea how close we might be?"

Dawson pulled out the map and pointed at their possible location. "Let's see, Blue Falls is over to our right a mile or so. The house is behind us by a couple miles. Maybe two or three more miles. But it's getting dark. We should probably find a place to set up camp. Head out at first light."

"I agree," said Clara Belle. "In about a half mile, it gets difficult to travel. Not anything you want to attempt at night. I can't even get through it when I'm out riding horses. And wouldn't want to, honestly."

"Why's that?" Fin asked.

"Something very strange is past it. I don't know. You can feel it. During the summer, I come out here and pick berries, mushrooms, and flowers. But I don't ever go past that tree line."

"Then we're going the right way," said Fin.

Grayson said, "This is a good spot." They all locked eyes on him. "It's flat here, for the tents. Fire in the middle. Trees surrounding us for protection. Stream just over there for water."

Everyone reacted with identical looks of surprise, and no one moved for a second.

On the one hand, Fin was glad Grayson was there. *He knows the woods. Lived in and around them his whole life.* On the other hand, if he was working with Lily, he could have pre-picked this spot, and they would be sitting ducks.

"Fine, but we'll take shifts keeping watch." She zeroed in on Grayson. "Just in case."

He gave a slight nod at her stare.

Clara Belle clapped her hands. "Let's set up camp then, shall we?" Being an experienced camper and a mom, she got everyone organized and delegated tasks.

As twilight started to darken the day, Fin helped the group stand up tents while she kept an eye on Grayson building a fire.

After everything was set up, Nellie grabbed her bow and arrows. "I'm gonna go shoot a few before it gets dark, Mama."

"Okay, honey," said Clara Belle. "Take Jonesy or Boone with you."

Nellie winked at Jonesy, and he followed her.

"You can really shoot that thing?" Fin asked.

With a cocky smile, Nellie said, "Pick a tree."

"What?" Fin asked.

"Pick a tree. Any tree."

Raising her eyebrows, Fin searched the area. She spotted a skinny birch about fifty feet out and pointed to it. "That baby birch between the two big maples."

Nellie huffed in faux offense. "Too easy." She nocked an arrow, pulled back the string, aimed, and fired. The shaft *thunked,* slamming an inch into the middle of the tree. "Bullseye," she whispered with a wicked grin.

"Wow," Fin said, genuinely impressed. She noted the faces of Dawson and Grayson, whose expressions echoed her own.

Nellie gave a "told you" eyebrow raise to Fin, then waved Jonesy toward her. "Come on." They disappeared into the woods.

Fin felt deep roots of pride take hold of her insides. *My mom is a badass.*

She turned at the sounds of banging and rustling as Clara Belle pulled out the food and started putting together a dinner. "Unbelievable, right?"

"Honestly, yeah," Fin said.

"If only she carried that confidence with her in everything," Clara Belle said. "She will. Someday."

"I believe it," Fin said as her eye caught an empty pot sitting off to the side. "Do you want me to fetch some water for you?"

"That'd be great, thank you."

Fin grabbed the pot on her way to the stream. When she got there, she knelt and noticed that the bed of it was glowing similar to the lake.

"Interesting." She smacked a bug on her other arm.

"What?"

She started a little as Grayson walked up beside her. He bent down and rinsed his hands in the bubbling water.

"Oh, uh, nothing," she shrugged. *I wonder how extensive his abilities are.* "So, what else can you and your sister do? Besides the healing?"

He wiped his wet hands on his pants. "We're both real strong."

"Like throw a car strong?"

He shook his head. "No. But I could lift a car if someone was stuck under it."

She shot him an impressed glance.

"You?"

Fin gave him a questioning side-eye.

"I felt your kick. And you knew about the healing thing. And the Grim. So, I know you're like me and Lily. Somehow."

She nodded her head a few times as she thought. *Bond, but don't tell him everything.*

"Yeah, the strength thing." She watched his face carefully. "How do you keep it in check? You know, not show people how strong you are so they don't freak out."

"It used to be real hard." He flicked a rock into the bubbling stream. "But once I was grown, I started knowin' my limits without thinkin'. Except when I come to Newcross."

"You're stronger in Newcross?"

He sunk his hand into the water and pulled out a bigger rock before tossing it back in with a *plunk*. "There's somethin' here."

"Yeah." She wanted to tell him why, but she still didn't trust him. He was hiding something. And until she knew what it was, it was better to keep some things to herself.

"My mama had the healing thing, too," he said.

"Your mom?" She frowned. "But she—"

"Died of cancer? Cuts are one thing. But cancer or being mortally wounded, I don't think we can heal from that. We ain't immu-mortal."

She repressed a smile so he wouldn't think she was laughing at him. "I think you mean im-mortal. No u."

"Oh." Looking a little self-conscious, he stood up. "Thank you."

"Do you ever hear any buzzing? See anything glowing? See, uh, ghosts or . . ." She knew she sounded crazy. "Never mind."

"I can see a glow. It's real faint, though. I have a little bag of things I've collected that glow. Er, well, I had."

"Really?"

A touch of a smile snuck out before quickly disappearing as he dried his hands again on his pants.

She cocked her head. "Wait, what do you mean had?"

"Well, I wanted to make sure we could get back fast if we needed to, but I didn't want Lily to find us. And she can't see the glow. So, I used the glowing stones I been collectin' like breadcrumbs. That way, I can see the way back, but she can't see the way here."

Smart.

"I did keep this little guy though." He pulled a stone from his pocket and squeezed it. Glowing water came out and left a trail. "I call it a water stone. You can see the trail, right?"

Excited, she stood up. "I can, yeah."

"I'll use this the rest of the way to mark the trail. I don't know if rain would wash it away though."

"May I?"

He nodded.

She took the stone from his hand and examined it. When she squeezed it, a much larger, thicker, brighter stream of water came out.

Grayson's eyes went round as saucers. "Wow."

They peered at each other as she handed it back.

He eyed it. Then her. As he put the stone in his pocket he said, "It helps at night, too."

"What do you mean?"

"Oh, I, uh, I like having a little bit of light. You know, for protection. Just being cautious."

She eyed him for a second. "I'm not fond of the dark either."

"I didn't say—"

"It's okay," she interrupted, wiping her hands on her pants. "I used to demand a night light as a kid. Even now, there's a diner sign outside my bedroom window. It's comforting."

He relaxed a little. "Yeah."

"So, where did you get them?" She pointed at the stone.

"I just see them lying around in different places, mostly in the backwoods of Newcross." He shrugged. "This one was on Main Street, though."

"Do any of the other stones do things?"

"One of them catches fire when you tap it."

"What?" she exclaimed as he let out the first full grin she'd seen on him.

"Yeah," he puffed up with pride at her excitement. "Another turns weeds into flowers. Simple stuff like that."

"Hmm, I'd like that fire one," Fin murmured, inspecting the river and the huge boulders along the sides. She checked to make sure everyone was still busy and elbowed Grayson with a half-smile. "Hey."

"What?"

"Wanna see who's stronger?" She bounced her eyebrows at him. *Let's just see how extensive his abilities are.*

The corners of his lips slid up. "Hell, yeah."

Fin took the lead as they walked out of view and down the side of the river.

"That one." She pointed to a one-foot boulder. "That's probably, what? Ninety pounds."

"So, just pick it up?"

"Sure." She shrugged one shoulder. "Maybe give it a toss? Downstream, away from everyone. See who can throw them further." She grinned.

"Okay." He walked over to the boulder, easily picking it up. "Too easy."

He walked over to a three-foot boulder. "How much is this one?"

She squinted at it. "Maybe eight hundred to one thousand pounds."

He bent over and picked it up, only struggling a little, before tossing it maybe five feet with a big thud.

"Not bad." She gave him a quiet golf clap.

"Your turn." His eyes held a hint of a challenge.

Oh, he's competitive. She walked the few feet to the boulder. The truth was, she didn't know how strong she was after hiding it her whole life. She'd always tried to prevent her strength from hurting others, but in Newcross, her strength had almost quadrupled. *Okay, let's see how strong I really am.*

She squatted down, put her hands under the huge rock, and prepared herself for the strain. Before she knew it, she was standing, holding the boulder as though it was a pebble.

"Holy shit." The boulder was over her head. *This is unreal.* She looked at Grayson whose face said it all: surprise, shock, and awe.

"Whoa," he said.

She swallowed hard, took a deep breath, and threw. Grayson walked up beside her as they both watched the boulder fly over the trees and land over a mile away with a loud thud that they could feel.

Grayson said, "Holy—" and she finished with, "—shit."

Clara Belle ran down to the stream and hollered, "What was that noise?"

Fin and Grayson shot glances at each other.

He faced Clara Belle. "They're cutttin' trees over yonder. Prob'ly one just fell."

"Oh." Her posture relaxed. "Okay." She started back to camp but stopped by the empty pot at the stream's edge. "Don't forget the water."

"Right, we're coming," Fin shouted. As Clara Belle walked away, they grinned at each other like two truant students. *He doesn't seem as powerful as I am.*

"You know you were that strong?" he asked.

"I do now."

"I guess you win." He clapped her on the back before walking away.

She followed and said, "Yeah, I guess so."

As she began to move back towards camp, satisfied that he didn't seem like a threat to her, he stopped and faced her with a quizzical look.

She asked, "What?"

He shifted his weight as the grass crunched under his feet. "Nellie and Boone. They like us?"

Fin shook her head.

"Oh." Disappointment saturated the word. "I was hopin' we had somethin' in common other than Russell."

"Ah." Fin eyed his sagging shoulders. "He doesn't define you, Grayson. None of you."

He grunted. "You don't know Russell."

Bowing his head and staring at the grass, he stopped to snap a daisy from its stem and twist it in his fingers as he headed toward camp. Fin felt bad for him, all of them, as she went back to kneel at the river and fill the pot with water.

When she rejoined the group, the fire was roaring with life. Clara Bell already had beans and franks cooking in a pot while Grayson tended the fire.

Fin set down the sloshing water next to Clara Belle. "What's this for then?"

"Drinking water and dishwashing water," Clara Belle said. "Not my first camping trip."

Fin swelled with pride at her grandmother, who complimented Grayson's work. "Good fire."

"Thanks." He relaxed a little bit.

Clara Belle stuck her fingers in her mouth and whistled before calling out, "Dinner! Let's eat."

Within a few minutes, Nellie and Jonesy walked in from the woods looking innocently happy, while Marci and Boone came back to camp looking a little flushed. They all gathered around the campfire with paper plates and plastic forks. Clara Belle dished out beans and franks with some Wonder bread to sop it up.

"I got s'mores, too." Clara Belle beamed.

"Oh my God, s'mores." Dawson groaned in anticipation.

"Right?" Fin said.

"I love s'mores!" Marci smiled at Boone, who slid next to her and said, "Me too."

Nellie said, "Mama, I should get the first s'more. It's my birthday this week after all."

"Happy birthday to Nellie!" Jonesy shouted.

"Happy birthday!" they all shouted at varying intervals.

"What's a s'more?" Grayson asked.

Like everyone else, Fin turned to him in shock.

"Of course you don't know," Boone said under his breath.

"Shut up, Boone," Nellie said through clenched teeth before peering at Grayson. "It's a piece of chocolate and a marshmallow smashed between two graham crackers."

His eyes softened.

"And you roast the marshmallows over the campfire so they melt the chocolate," Marci added. "They're dyn-o-mite!"

Everyone laughed at her impression of J.J. from *Good Times*, which dissolved any lingering tension.

"Okay." Grayson accepted his plate of food from Clara Belle. "They sound good." But when he faced the group, all the lawn chairs and stumps were taken except the one by Boone.

Boone stuck his hand across the stump. "That's for Mama."

Fin's heart squeezed in sympathy at the all-too-familiar scene of the new student getting frozen out in the cafeteria.

"Grayson, sit here." Fin scooted over and gave him half her stump.

Obviously relieved, he walked over and sat down, his big body forcing hers over a bit. He ate his food quietly and slapped at a couple bugs.

She didn't blame Boone for being suspicious. She felt that, too. They would be stupid not to at least keep an eye on Grayson until they knew him better.

For a few minutes, there was barely a peep as everyone chowed down their food.

Fin broke the silence with a laugh. "I haven't eaten like this since . . . I've never eaten like this."

Dawson smiled broadly at Clara Belle. "We did. In Ireland. Lots of campfires and beers and s'mores."

"Is that where you studied to be a librarian?" she asked.

"Yeah." He studied her face more intently than was strictly necessary.

Fin was doing that, too. Their grandmother was so young and strong. Fin wanted to know everything about her.

"And is there a pretty girl back in Ireland?" Boone asked with a goofy, romantic squirm of his body. Everyone laughed as he made kissing noises.

"Hey now!" Dawson laughed and threw a small piece of his bread at Boone.

Boone picked it up and threw it back.

"Careful. We don't want wildlife over here while we sleep." Grayson's face was so earnest everyone stopped laughing.

"Don't be so serious, Grayson." Nellie threw a slice of bread at him.

It bounced off his face, and he sat stunned for a moment.

Nellie's giggle set everyone off.

Grayson gave that elusive, small grin, which was basically the corners of his mouth turning up.

It's like he's never really laughed in his life.

Grayson looked around a little sheepishly.

Clara Belle smiled at him. "We're just teasing you, Grayson."

Nellie asked, "What about you, Fin?"

"What about me?" A little happy thrill went through her that her mother was taking an interest in her instead of Jonesy. *Good grief, I'm jealous of a teenage boy.*

"Do you have a boyfriend?"

Everyone looked at her expectantly.

"Ha ha, uh." *It's like Hodge has talked to them.* She remembered Riggs, from the crime scene. *I felt so drawn to him.* "No, nothing, uh, serious, no. But maybe. Someday, someone. I don't know."

"Ooo, I'll bet he'll be cute," Nellie said in a singsongy way.

They all laughed, tossing pieces of bread at Fin.

Grayson threw one a few seconds too late. And because he was sitting right next to her, his piece hit her a little harder than the others.

They all stared at him.

After looking around, he asked Clara Belle. "Did I do it wrong?"

Laughter erupted again as Fin patted his shoulder. "No, you're fine."

"Who wants s'mores?" Clara Belle stood, grabbing a trash bag.

Everyone's hands went up with a syncopated chorus of excited replies as they took turns throwing away their plates.

Clara Belle tossed the bag aside and gathered the ingredients to make the dessert. "Grayson, can you grab some sticks and use a knife to sharpen the ends? We need to roast marshmallows."

"Sure." He walked toward the darkened woods.

Nellie asked Fin, "So, what kind of music do you like?"

Fin pulled out her cell phone and opened her music app. "I'll play you a few songs."

"Fin," Dawson said in a strange tone of voice.

She looked up at his panicked expression. *Shit.* Her cell wasn't from their time. And even if she could explain the phone, her apps didn't work in 1975. She swallowed hard and took in the curious faces staring at her.

"What's that?" Jonesy stood up, squinting at the object in her hand.

"It's nothing." She quickly put the phone away. "Sometimes, on the force, they ask us to test new technology. It's just a prototype of police equipment, that's all."

No one said anything for a moment.

Grayson came back with the sticks but stopped mid-stride when they all turned to look at him. "What?"

"Nothin'." Boone said with a smirk as Marci elbowed him.

Nellie mouthed, "Do it," at her brother.

What are those girls up to?

Sighing, Boone stood up and walked toward Grayson. "I can help you sharpen those."

"Okay," Grayson said with obvious surprise. He handed half of them to Boone. They went about the task while casting silent and cautious glances at each other.

That was nice of the girls. Fin was proud of her mom. *I wonder how Dawson's feeling.*

He beamed at his dad, stood up, and walked toward the boys. "I can help, too."

Together, they made quick work of it. Before long, they handed out the sticks to everyone.

As the group roasted marshmallows, an incredible warmth spread through Fin's body.

This is my family.

~~~

After dessert, Boone was the first to head to bed, followed by Dawson, then Jonesy. Grayson, on the other hand, kept watch at the edge of the woods. Marci disappeared into the girl's tent while Clara Belle cleaned up and Nellie walked over to Fin and sat down.

"Hey." The fire gave a warm glow to Nellie's skin.

"Hey." Gratitude warmed Fin's chest as she looked at the young girl. *If I'd grown up with her, I might've wasted most of my life hating or resenting her. Thinking of her as only a mom. But seeing her like this, young and on fire, is so much better.*

"I always wanted a big sister," Nellie said. "I mean, Boone is great and all. But sisters are different, you know?"

"I get it."

"I know you're not my sister, but I thought maybe we could be, like, friends or somethin'? And you could give me boy advice and tell me how to line my eyes or stuff like that?"

Fin chuckled as she looked at Nellie's delicate features, which didn't need makeup at all. "Of course. I always wanted a sister, too."

"You don't have siblings?"

"No siblings. I don't think. I'm not even sure what happened to my father. Or my mother. I grew up in a foster home."

In a deep part of her heart, Fin desperately hoped that maybe her mother might recognize her own soul inside of Fin's, but of course she didn't. She was too young. Having a baby wasn't even on her radar yet.

"I'm sorry," Nellie said.

"It's okay. It's not your fault." *At least I don't think so.*
~~~

Nellie's face lit up as she reached into her pants pocket and pulled out a ring that had a mood band through its middle. It matched the one that Nellie was wearing from the auction.

Nellie offered the ring to Fin. "Maybe I can be part of your family?"

Fin had a hard time keeping the tears back as she took the ring and slipped it on. Blinking rapidly, she looked down at the band, which was turning bright blue. "It's perfect."

Nellie smiled proudly as she held up her hand. "I've got one, too. Boone gave it to me for my birthday. It had a matching one with it."

"I couldn't love anything more," Fin said.

Nellie squealed with delight and hugged her.

Fin could barely contain her emotions as she gripped her mother, reveling in her vanilla scent.

"I'm so glad we met." Nellie pulled out of the hug, her eyes glimmering.

She has no idea I'm her daughter.

"Goodnight." Nellie hopped up.

"Wait," Fin said.

"Yeah?" Nellie tilted her head.

Fin held up one finger. "I have something for you, too." She got up, grabbed her backpack, pulled out the compass bracelet, and showed it to Nellie.

"Pretty," Nellie said as her eyes widened with joy.

Fin held up her other wrist so her mother could see they looked the same. She pointed at Nellie's wrist. "May I?"

Nellie nodded, flushed with excitement.

Fin put the twin compass bracelet on her. When the latch clicked together, Fin could feel the bracelets connect. She searched Nellie's face, but her mother didn't react to the magic.

"I love it!" Nellie caressed the stone. "We really are family now."

"Yeah." Fin's throat choked with emotion. "We're family."

"Cool." Nellie grinned and ran to her tent.

Through a haze of tears, Fin watched her mother go.

23

You Got a Shotgun, Don't Ya?

Fin stirred awake at the sound of Clara Belle's voice.

"Fin?"

"I'm up." Fin sat up from the rock she was leaning against. The blanket between her back and boulder slipped to the ground as she twisted her neck and shoulders. She sneezed almost immediately. "Everything okay?"

"Yep," Clara Belle said. "It's just your shift. We're about an hour away from dawn."

"Oh, okay, great," Fin whispered. She grabbed her backpack and started digging in it. "You get some sleep?"

"Yeah, Dawson came out a few hours ago and relieved me. We're all gettin' a little shut eye."

"Good." Fin stood up and stretched before grabbing her water bottle and reaching into her backpack for another antihistamine. She popped the pill and swallowed it with some water. "You doing okay? I'm sure all this has been pretty strange for you."

"Used to that 'round here." Her grandmother grabbed a blanket and wrapped it around her shoulders as she sat on a boulder nearby and investigated Fin's face for a moment. "Who are you really?"

Fin took another long sip of water before she answered. "I don't know what you mean?"

"Well, besides the fact you look a little bit like my daughter and Dawson looks a little bit like my son, I have the feelin' you're someone we should know." Clara Belle stared a hole through Fin's head. "I ain't much of a trusting person. I don't let people in easily. But for some reason, I trust you and Dawson. Even Grayson. So, I know somethin' else is goin' on for me to take to all of you so quickly. I'd be lyin' if I said it wasn't part of the reason that I'm on this little trip right now."

I want to tell you so bad. "I—"

"Mornin'," Grayson interrupted. He sluggishly walked up from behind a tree on the other side of the fire.

Excellent timing. "Grayson. You sleep okay?"

"I guess. Trees aren't comfortable."

Fin huffed in agreement. "Neither are rocks. Have a seat."

As Grayson sat on a boulder, Clara Belle stood up. "I'll make some coffee." She grabbed supplies, put the coffee on, and sat back down.

The three of them sat quietly for a moment.

Grayson peered at Fin. "So, you're a cop?"

"Yep."

The flames glinted in his eyes. "I thought about doing that. When I was little."

They locked eyes across the fire.

"Why didn't you?" she asked.

Grayson avoided her stare. "Couldn't leave Lily."

A thud into the brush followed by a man chirping, "Fuck!" sounded loudly just outside the tree line. Fin jumped, her hand on her gun.

"What the hell?" Clara Belle said as she and Grayson stood.

Fin grasped the butt of her gun as Grayson held his knife at the ready. She gave him a sideways glance. *Is this something he planned?*

Clara Belle grabbed her small, iron skillet from her supply bag, and they listened intently for a moment until they heard more mumbling and rustling of the brush. Fin narrowed her eyes at Grayson, evaluating everything about him. *He genuinely doesn't seem like he knows what's going on.*

"Stay here." Fin drew her gun and moved stealthily away from the bright campfire and into the cool early morning air of the darkened woods. Grayson followed close behind as Clara Belle stood her ground.

As Fin made her way, she strained to hear every little sound. *Who the hell could that possibly be?* She kept her eyes peeled as they adjusted to the darkness.

A pale-looking Russell limped out from the shadows, holding his hands in the air. "Don't shoot. Don't shoot."

Grayson rushed at his father.

Clara Belle shouted, "Grayson, stop!"

Fin reached out her arm and glared at him. "Don't."

Grayson stopped at her piercing stare.

Russell wheezed a laugh. "Got yourself a new bimbo to order you around, boy?"

"Don't you fuckin' call me boy." Grayson's body coiled, ready to attack.

"Ain't she a little older than your normal sluts?"

Grayson moved toward Russell as Fin stepped in front of him.

"Stop, Grayson. Both of you shut up," Fin said as Russell choked out a laugh. "Clara Belle?"

"Yeah?"

"Get my cuffs out of my bag."

"Okay," she said and rustled around.

"Down on your knees." Fin trained her gun on him as he obeyed her order. "Hands behind your head."

He complied as Fin walked behind him, and Clara Belle ran up with the cuffs. Russell didn't resist as Fin ratcheted the cuffs around his wrists and patted him down. She found a knife in his waistband.

"What's this for?"

"Protection."

"From?"

"That crazy bitch, Lily."

When Grayson lurched forward, Fin spoke in a hard tone that left no room for argument. "Grayson, back."

After a moment's hesitation, he backed off but said, "You made her that way, you son of a bitch."

"That's the second time today I been accused o' that." Russell scoffed. His pale skin and struggle to keep his eyes open seemed off. "I got news for you and e'ryone else. She came out that way."

"Enough, Russell," Fin ordered. "Why are you here? Are you following us?"

"I told you." His jaw clenched. "I need protectin'."

"What happened to your leg?" She pulled out her phone and turned on the flashlight, shining it over his thigh.

"What the hell's that?" Russell squinted at her iPhone.

"Answer the question," Fin said.

"Lily." He nodded to the wound. "She sent me to track Grayson and leave a trail of yellow flags she could follow. Said she was gonna kill my whole family while I was out here."

"You were gonna let her?" Clara Belle whispered. "You came out here instead of trying to save us?"

Russell spit onto the ground. "You got a shotgun, don't ya? You could'a used it."

When Clara Belle moved toward him with murder in her eyes, Fin held up a hand and said, "Stay there." She studied his injuries. "That leg wound is bleeding pretty bad. I'm surprised you made it this far."

194

"I passed out for a bit." Russell swayed.

He's getting weaker. "He needs a hospital."

Through a locked jaw, Grayson asked, "Did you use the flags?"

"I ain't stupid." Russell sneered. "She'd kill us all, me included."

Clara Belle spoke up. "Me and Grayson can take him."

Fin swiveled toward her.

"We'll take him to the hospital. Everyone would expect me to take him. And Grayson can hold off Lily on the way." Clara Belle gave Fin a pointed look. "You can stop this and protect the kids."

"No—"

"With all due respect, Fin, this isn't your decision." Clara Belle gave her a flinty stare. "These are my kids. As long as Russell's here, he could lead Lily right to us. Once we get back to the house, I can call the chief and get help. Send it your way. Hold Lily back."

"But—"

"Grayson?" Clara Belle asked.

Grayson's hateful gaze never left Russell's face, but he nodded. "I'll do everythin' I can to keep Lily as far away from all of you as possible."

Fin warred with herself as an awkward silence fell.

"You know I'm right," Clara Belle said. "She could be on her way here right now."

"Nah, she'll wait 'til daybreak," said Grayson. "She ain't stupid. These woods is too dangerous to be out at night. And she don't know where she's going." A spiteful huff burst out of him. "Hell, she probably hoped you'd die out here."

Russell lifted his chin. "I'm like a cockroach. You can't—"

"All right, enough," Fin said. "Take him back. Find Lily and keep her back as long as you can. Give us time to find the dagger and get it in the right hands."

Clara Belle said, "If we take two horses, they'll get us back faster."

Even though she didn't like it, Fin said, "Okay. Clara Belle, are you sure?"

"Yeah. Get the dagger and keep my kids safe."

Clara Belle and Grayson walked back to camp and readied the horses while Fin tied a torniquet above Russell's wound to slow the bleeding.

A few minutes later when they came back, Grayson and Fin hoisted Russell onto one of the horses and tied him to the saddle.

Clara Belle said, "We should be able to get back to the house in an hour, maybe two."

"Be safe," Fin said.

"You too." Clara Belle reached over and hugged Fin tightly. "Keep my babies safe."

"I promise." She squeezed her grandmother tightly.

As Clara Belle got on her horse, Grayson walked back toward Fin.

"You need to know that Lily is dangerous," Grayson said. "I mean it. She ain't right in the head. I'll do what I can to keep her back, she may even be at the house when we get there, but she ain't dumb. And she knows by now I'm not on her side. So, she'll do whatever she thinks she has to do."

"I got it." Fin flicked a meaningful glance at Clara Belle. "Protect her with your life."

"I will." Grayson walked over and climbed on the horse, sitting just behind Russell.

They started off into the darkness.

Anxiety coiled in Fin's stomach as she returned to camp. They had less than thirty minutes before the morning would start to push the night to the other side of the world. She needed to get everyone up before then so they could get moving.

I don't know what's gonna happen next, but it's gonna be a long and dangerous day.

24

We've Got Some Hunting to Do

Grayson and Clara Belle made their way back to the house through the dark predawn. Every now and then they'd hear the rustle of a nocturnal animal, and Grayson would always look twice, just in case. *Can't be too careful.*

Russell glared at his wife. "What the fuck are you doing with Grayson?"

"Shut up." Grayson slammed his fist into Russell's lower back.

"Fuck you!"

"Shut up, Russell," Clara Belle spoke through clenched teeth. "He told me what you did."

Grayson couldn't clearly see her expression in the dark, but her voice caught like she was about to cry or kill. "How could you?" she asked with a thinly veiled rage. "You sick bastard. To Rose. To Lily. To Grayson."

"Me?" Russell's lip curled in disgust. "You're the sick one. God don't like dykes. You and that lesbo up the road better get ready for hell."

Grayson punched him in the back again. "Shut up!"

"Ugh, you mother fucker." Russell was breathing hard and nearly falling off the horse.

I hope he falls and the fuckin' horse tramples him.

They rode in silence for a moment before Clara Belle spoke again.

"You know what, you evil bastard, I ain't scared of you and your nonsense no more." After a humorless chuckle, she continued. "Remember when you got sick last week? That wasn't the flu, you idiot. I put laxatives in your breakfast, lunch, and dinner for three days after you beat me!"

"You dumb bitch!" he hollered.

Grayson snickered. *I wish I'd thought of doing something like that.*

"Good thing I beat you again yesterday mornin' then," Russell clapped back.

But Clara Belle cackled again. "Oh, and your tolerance for whiskey in the evening ain't droppin'. I've been grindin' sleepin' pills into your bottle so you pass out at night and you and your whiskey dick leave me alone!"

"I'm gonna kill you!" he screamed.

Grayson chuckled but made sure his dad couldn't move.

Clara Belle continued, "And by the way, you piece o' shit, you might've beat me to keep me away from Rose and those kids, but it didn't work. All those years, you thought you were paying off a debt with part of your paycheck." She leaned in and leered at him. "You're so stupid. I put that money in a bank account for Rose. I typed up a letter sayin' it was a dead relative left her money. She never knew. And neither did you."

"Bitch, you stole my money!" he shouted.

Grayson's whole chest warmed up. He'd always wondered how his mother, who only worked part-time as a secretary, could afford what little they had. Now he knew. It was Clara Belle.

"I hope you rot in hell!" she shrieked.

"I'll meet you there, dyke!"

"You're a drunk idiot."

"I have to be drunk to be married to you."

Alarmed, Grayson halted his horse. "Shut up, both of you."

He scanned around the darkened house. The woods were quiet as the morning light showed itself in the eastern sky.

Clara Belle whispered, "I left the porch light on when we left."

Chills ran down Grayson's spine as he surveyed the area, focusing on shadows and hidden crevices. It seemed as though even the animals knew something was afoot. They watched and waited. *She's here.*

An arrow whistled through the air and ripped through Russell's neck. He toppled off the horse, which reared into the air.

"Grayson!" Clara Belle screamed. Her horse reared, too.

They both fell to the ground as the horses bucked and ran away.

A shadowy figure emerged from the side of the house.

"Lily." Grayson grimaced in pain as he twisted toward his sister, who stormed over with Luke and Carl flanking her.

She radiated rage. "You traitor!"

Grayson winced as she screamed. He rolled to his knees, grabbing his side. *Broken rib.*

"How could you? Mama would roll over in her grave. She told you to take care of me!"

"Lily, wait." He tried to stand but realized he couldn't. Looking down, he could almost see his ankle swelling.

"Pathetic." Lily made a bee line for Clara Belle.

The older woman was trying to crawl away, but she was holding her arm to her chest and not getting very far.

"And you." Lily grabbed the back of Clara Belle's hair and yanked her onto her back.

Clara Belle screamed.

"Lily, stop it!" Grayson yelled. *My rib is healed.* He tentatively moved his ankle. *Ankle is healed.*

But before he could jump up, Luke and Carl marched toward him, one with a crossbow and one with a gun aimed right at him.

"Oh, shut up." Lily scoffed at him, then nodded toward her minions. "They know your little secret about healing fast. So, they won't take any chances letting you get too close."

Lily grabbed Clara Bell's shoulder and spun her so that Lily could keep an eye on Grayson while focusing on Clara Belle at the same time. Lily straddled Clara Belle's chest, pulled out her knife, and ran it lightly across the woman's throat. "Why are you still alive?"

Clara Belle stuttered, "P-please, if you—"

Lily slapped her. "Shut your mouth."

Grayson yelled, "Leave her alone. She's got nothin' to do with this. You're mad at me."

"You're right, I am mad at you." Lily flicked a glance at him before raising her knife in the air and stabbing Clara Belle's left arm.

Clara Belle screamed.

"No!" Grayson screamed. "Lily, stop, please!"

Lily's eyes sparked with hate. "I'll let her live if you promise to protect us on the way to the dagger and make sure I get it no matter what." She yanked the knife back into the air. "Swear on mama's grave!"

"I swear." Grayson stumbled toward Clara Belle as Luke and Carl raised their weapons. He stopped in his tracks. "I'll take you. I'll make sure you get it."

Lily held the knife to Clara Belle's throat. "Swear."

Forgive me, Mama. "I swear on Mama's grave."

"Good boy." She wiped the blade off on Clara Belle's pants and signaled to Luke and Carl.

Luke kept the bolt in his crossbow trained on Grayson while Carl walked toward Clara Belle.

Lily said, "Keep this bitch here 'til I get back."

"No." Grayson stepped toward Carl but looked at Lily. "Let her get help for her arm. You've got me."

After looking him up and down, Lily relented. "Fine. For now."

I hope you're movin', Fin.

Lily stood triumphantly. "We better get going. We've got some hunting to do."

25

Common Enchantments

Newcross, May 23, 1975

As the eastern sky lightened, Fin walked over to the boys' tent to wake everybody up.

Dawson stepped out of the tent and looked taken aback as he almost ran into her. "Oh, good morning?"

"We have to leave now."

"What's happening?" He looked around at the cleaned-up campground. "Where's Clara Belle? And Grayson?"

"Russell showed up last night." Fin went back to packing up.

"What?"

"Lily sent him. To leave a trail for her to follow."

He sputtered and poked his glasses. "Did he leave one?"

"Not that we know of. Grayson and Clara Belle took Russell to the hospital. But I'm not sure he'll make it. Lily hurt him pretty bad."

"Oh my. This all happened in the last few hours?"

"Yeah. And Grayson is supposed to keep Lily at bay when they get back." Fin finished up and stood to look at him.

"Do you think he actually will?"

Fin tossed her hands up. "That's the great puzzle, isn't it? I don't know. And not because of him but because of Lily. Look, we need to assume that they're on their way right now." She swept her arm in an arc at the sky. "We've got light. So, we need to move. Amon is hiding the Grim as we speak."

"Oh, right. What do we tell the kids about Clara Belle and Grayson?"

"The truth."

When Fin started to walk away, he blocked her path. "Okay." He pulled out his green book and thumbed through the pages. "But I've been thinking."

"Yeah?"

"So, I think once we cross that tree line, things are going to get weird."

"*Get* weird?" She raised one eyebrow. "I'm not sure they can get any weirder."

"I'm just saying, let's think about it. The auctioneer, the master of all mystical objects, can't touch the Grim. We're not going to just be able to breeze through to wherever this protected place is and pick up the Grim, right? I mean, Auci is unbelievably powerful which means Gunnar and Amon are too. No way Amon hid it without traps."

"I think the word Auci used was enchantments."

He poked at his journal. "Right. So, I used the magic pencil and consulted the green book about common enchantments."

"It told you what they are?"

"Not exactly. I've discovered the book doesn't quite work like that. Facts, yes. But choices, as in whatever enchantment Amon chose to use in this place, no. Choices change. Facts don't."

Fin rested her hands on her hips. "Okay, so what did you find?"

"Nothing." He slapped the book against his hand. "All it says about the first trial is 'weakness'."

"What kind of weakness?" She crossed her arms with an irritated shift of her hips.

He mirrored her attitude with a shake of the book. "This thing is a pain in the ass."

Why is my bracelet cold? Her forehead crinkled in concern as she peered around.

Auci said, "Or maybe, Dawson, it's operator error?"

Fin and Dawson jumped, swiveling toward Auci, who was sitting on a stump.

"Auci." Fin was a little surprised at how relieved she was to see him.

"I really hate when you do that." Dawson grimaced and scribbled in his notebook.

"I was wondering when you might pop up again," Fin said.

He inclined his head. "I told you I'd be watching."

"You did." She held up her arm. "I've felt the bracelet go cold a few times."

His chest swelled with pride. "Very good."

Tamping down her emotions at his reaction, she said, "Listen, Auci, you can't expect us to take the kids with us to get the Grim."

Dawson sheepishly raised his hand like they were in a classroom. "I actually disagree."

"Dawson." Fin glared at him.

"I mean it. We keep trying to ditch them, but they keep ending up with us despite our best efforts. I think the whole reason they're here with us is because we can't get through without them."

Fin shot Auci a questioning look.

He raised his eyebrow. "Agreed."

She shook her head. "If something happens to them, to my mother . . ."

"Your mother is stronger than you think," the auctioneer said. "You need them. And they need this training, too."

Fin narrowed her eyes at her father. "Why do you say that?"

"I need you to trust me," he said. "And I know it's not fair for me to ask it of you. But I am asking anyway. Please."

"What do you know, Auci?" Fin asked. "What do you know about the future?"

He gave her an enigmatic look. "You know I can't tell you that. Please trust me."

She relented. "Well, how are we supposed to get through these enchantments? We don't know anything. What if we can't figure them out? What if we're wrong?"

"Trust me," he said. "Together, you will make it."

Fin glared at the ground, knowing that glaring at Auci wouldn't help.

"But that's not why I'm here," Auci said. "I've brought something for your journey. This time, it's for Boone." He handed Dawson a long, wooden whistle hanging from a leather strap. "In times of need, it calls forth help to assist the wearer."

Dawson brought it to his lips.

"No." Auci held up a hand.

But it was too late. He'd already blown on it, however no sound came out.

"I think it's broken." Dawson shook it.

"It's not broken," Auci said dryly.

A loud flapping sound approached, and the air gusted around them. A huge blue phoenix crossed over the sky before landing just outside their campground.

No one moved as Fin asked, "What. The hell. Is that?"

Dawson whispered, "A phoenix."

"What?" she asked.

The bird stepped forward, towering over them. It bowed down and bumped Dawson's head with its beak. After a moment, it repeated the gesture.

"I think he likes you," Fin whispered.

The next time it bent down, Dawson slowly reached up and touched its head. The bird leaned into his hand, and Dawson petted it like an old friend.

"Incredible," Dawson said.

Auci wandered over to Nellie's bow and arrow before waving his hand over them. The turquoise ring on his hand briefly glowed.

"What are you doing?" she asked as Dawson bonded with the bird.

Auci made his way back toward them. "Just giving them a bit of a boost."

"What kind of boost?" she asked suspiciously.

"You've heard of heat-seeking missiles?" He gave her a sly grin.

She huffed a laugh. "So, she won't miss anything?"

"I didn't say that. But as long as her aim is true, she'll hit her target. It won't be able to hide from her arrows."

"Humph." Fin slowly approached the phoenix. It nudged her, so she petted its head. "You're so lovely." The phoenix made a trilling sound as they touched foreheads.

Auci clapped his hands. "I think it's time to go." He bowed to the bird, who returned the gesture. "Stay ready."

The bird dipped its head once in acknowledgement, stepped back, launched into the air, and flew away into the western sky.

Dazed, Fin and Dawson faced Auci with awed expressions.

"Cool, right?" Auci asked. "Is cool the correct word? I'm never quite sure of the time's lexicon."

Dawson started, "Well, technically—"

"Cool works," Fin interrupted.

Auci gave her a grateful nod. "I have to go. And so do you." A weighted silence hung in the air as Auci beamed at Fin. "I'm really quite proud of you."

She sucked in air at the swirl of feelings inside her.

The *whoosh* of the tents opening distracted Fin, and she glanced over at the kids walking out of their tents one by one. They sat down around the fire pit, rubbing their eyes and stretching. Fin panicked as she looked back toward Auci, but he was already gone.

Boone asked, "Who were you talkin' to? I didn't recognize the voice."

"Uh." Dawson gave Fin a wide-eyed shrug. "Anybody feel like breakfast?" Dawson stashed his book, threw the whistle around his neck, and got up. He pulled out a box of Pop Tarts from Clara Belle's food bag and waved it at the kids.

"I'll have some." Boone held up his hand.

Dawson tossed a foil package first to him, then Nellie, then Jonesy, and finally Marci before opening up one for himself. He munched on the pastry as he hauled a jug of water around and poured cups for everyone.

"What's that?" Nellie pointed at the whistle around Dawson's neck.

"It's actually for Boone." Dawson headed in the boy's direction. "Quite useful. In a time of need, just blow into the whistle."

"And then what?" Boone took it from Dawson and placed it around his neck.

Dawson glanced at Fin and said, "Uh—"

"Wait," Nellie interrupted. "Where's Mama?"

They all looked around.

"And where the hell is Grayson?" Boone stood, suddenly concerned.

"I can explain that." Fin patted the air like she was pumping the brakes on a car. "But we need to get out of camp in the next ten minutes. Once we're on our way, I'll tell you where they went."

26

The Entry Point

Fin took in the richly dense foliage alive with small animals and bugs. She stood before the same glowing tree line she'd visited only a day ago with Auci.

"It's just a bunch of trees," said Boone.

"Shut up, Boone," said Nellie.

"You shut up."

"No, you shut—"

"Enough," said Marci. "If you quit bickering this would go faster."

Fin ignored them and stepped up to the knotted tree where one particular spot in the center was glowing brightly. She tentatively pushed her hand through the portal to the other side, then pulled it back out and observed her uninjured hand. "Come here," she said to Dawson.

He walked up to her. "Yeah?"

"Try putting your hand through this knot." She pointed to the right spot.

He tried, but his hand stopped at the tree bark.

"What does it look like when I do it?" She pushed her hand in and out.

"Do what?" he asked. "Is something happening?"

"Yeah, my hand goes through it. You can't see that?"

Shaking his head, he cast a glance over his shoulder at the kids, who were talking among themselves, and lowered his voice. "But magic just comes naturally to you. Not us."

Fin thought for a moment before remembering the words Auci spoke during her training. *Blood.*

"Cut your finger," she said as she pulled out her knife.

"What?" He yanked his hands back as he grimaced.

"Cut your finger." She impatiently held out the blade with the handle pointed toward him. "Auci said ordinary humans may need blood to activate magic."

She could see his brain working as his expression moved from incredulousness to consideration to understanding that he was going to have to do this.

In a gentler tone, she asked, "Do you want to do it, or do you want me to?"

"You do it." He thrust his hand at her and squinched his eyes shut.

She grabbed Dawson's hand and held the tip of the blade to his index finger. "Ready?"

"As I'll ever be."

She pressed the knife into his finger, drawing blood.

He winced and opened his eyes to see the damage. "Oh," he murmured. "That wasn't bad."

"Okay, put your finger on the knot."

They held their breath as Dawson reached forward. When his bloody finger touched the magical bark, it poked through the illusion.

She let out her breath with a clap of her hands. *OMG, it works.* At Dawson's delighted expression, she asked, "What?"

"I can see it. Oh my God, this is so cool. There's a blue-green glow."

"Yes!" *Thank goodness.* "Oh, you have no idea how good it feels for you to see it."

"You have no idea how good it feels to finally see what you've been talking about!" They shared a grin. "Okay, now what?"

"Can you put your hand through?"

His hand easily disappeared into the portal. His face lit up with a mixture of excitement and fear before he jerked it back out. "Oh my God, oh my God, oh my God. Amazing."

From behind them, Boone called out, "Umm, what's happening?"

"Oh." Fin peered at Dawson. "What if we just leave them here."

"And what if Lily shows up and slaughters them?" Dawson whispered.

"Well, what do you expect me to say to that?" She was flummoxed.

Before she could say anything else, Nellie's bloody thumb touched the knot. Her eyes flared wide at what she saw.

"Nellie!" Fin exclaimed.

"You guys gotta see this," Nellie said.

Seconds later, three more bloody thumbs slid through the portal.

"Enough!" Fin backed them up. Taking in their excited, fearful, adrenaline-filled faces, she tucked a hair behind her ear and put her hands on her hips. *Trust Auci.*

Boone asked her, "Is this that dark magic stuff you were talking about?"

"This isn't black magic. It's regular magic." *I think.* "Listen, I don't really know what's beyond this portal entrance. All I know is that it's filled with spells that are like challenges or riddles or puzzles, maybe? Things we'll have to deal with to get the dagger. Dawson and I think the first hurdle has something to do with weakness."

"Like an Achilles heel?" Jonesy asked.

"Oh, good guess, could be." Dawson poked at his glasses.

Nellie said, "Well, somebody's gotta stick their head through and see."

Boone stepped forward. "I'll do it."

"No!" Dawson yelled. After everyone shot him surprised glances, he moderated his tone. "I mean, no."

"Nice," Fin whispered sarcastically. *He tries to be cool, but he's a book guy who wants to be an action guy.* "I'm—"

"Marci!" Nellie pointed and yelled.

They turned in time to see the redhead walk through the hazy turquoise portal.

"Shit!" Fin headed for the portal.

Marci popped her head and shoulders back through. "It's just a grassy area with a small stream and a bridge. There's nothing weird over here."

Marci stepped back, disappearing, before Fin pushed her head through. The scene was exactly as Marci described. It mimicked what they had just come from, but it was different somehow. Plus, the bridge was glowing like blue wildfire. "The bridge. . ."

Cocking her head, Marci looked at it. "What about it?"

"Marci," Fin shouted, "don't do that again."

"Okay." Marci had the decency to look abashed.

But Fin was pretty sure it was just that: a look. "Don't go near the bridge. Let's get everybody through first."

"Okay."

Fin gave the girl her best cop stare.

Marci put her hands up. "I swear."

Yeah, right. Fin held her eyes for a moment longer before stepping back through the portal and addressing the others. "I think the bridge is where the enchantment is located. And I think we may have to deal with it individually because it's only wide enough to cross one at a time."

A variety of looks bounced around the group.

"Dawson, you first." Fin waved him forward. "And don't let anyone set foot on that bridge until we're all through this portal."

"Got it." He finished scribbling in his little book, put it away, and gingerly approached the portal. He looked back at her and swallowed.

"It's going to be okay. You got this."

He took a deep breath and slowly stepped through. They all waited a second, and he popped his head back out. "All good. Marci's still here."

"Keep her there." Fin glanced at the others. "Jonesy?"

"Yep." He sauntered up to the portal and breezed through it. They waited a moment before his hand poked out with a thumbs up.

Fin pointed at her uncle. "Boone?"

He said to his sister, "I'll put my hand back through and bring you over, okay?"

"Okay." Nellie nodded, clearly nervous.

Boone confidently entered the portal. As promised, his hand reappeared.

Nellie looked sheepishly at Fin. "You know, I don't need him to hold my hand anymore. I'm not a kid."

I don't want her to feel embarrassed because she's nervous. "I get that."

Nellie flushed a little. "But do you ever get scared?"

"All the time."

"You never look scared."

Fin started to answer as Boone's head poked through. "You comin' or what?"

"Just gimme a second." Nellie glared at him.

"Fine!" Boone yanked his head and hand back through.

"Sorry," Nellie said.

Fin squeezed Nellie's arms. "Just don't focus on the fear. Focus on taking the next step. And then the next one. You'll get stronger every time you move forward, even if it's just a little bit."

Nellie nodded. "Okay."

"And listen, if it helps, this bracelet . . ." Fin touched the compass bracelet on Nellie's wrist. "It's a good kind of magic. Like a tracker. I can find you anywhere, anytime. Just don't take it off."

"Wow. Okay." Nellie touched it, too, then gripped Fin in a fierce hug.

God, please, keep her safe.

"Get going." Fin gave her a gentle push towards the portal. "I'm right behind you."

Boone's head popped back through. "Let's go!"

"Fine!" Nellie took hold of Boone's hand before glancing back to Fin. "You promise? You'll be right behind me?"

"I promise."

"Okay." Nellie gave Fin one final glance before entering another world.

Fin took one last look around, listening intently. *No Lily. No anyone.* She took a deep breath and followed the others.

27

More Than One Enemy

When Fin got to the other side of the portal, everyone's expressions ranged from concerned to panicked. "What's happening?"

She walked through the group as they slowly separated until she came to Dawson and Marci at a spot near the bridge. "Dawson, what's going—"

He moved out of her way, revealing at least five dead bodies on either side of the bridge, and a few underneath, in varying stages of decay.

"Oh my God," she whispered.

"We're not the first to try to get the dagger," Dawson said.

"But how could they possibly know about it?" Fin asked. "Let alone have time? Amon just hid it. I saw it happen in the timeline."

"I've been considering that." Dawson pulled out his little book. "Think about what the Siblings do. These artifacts have value in the real world. There must be treasure hunters or pirates or thieves hunting them, right? Like a magical, black-market network. Maybe they know about this place because of gossip or maybe some of them use magic to let them know when something valuable is created? And maybe they have ways of time traveling too?"

"So, you're thinking there's more than one enemy. Like Halo." They exchanged a knowing look, and she scanned the area for movement. "And they're already here. I wonder if anyone's actually made it to the Grim?"

"Just based on statistical probability, some must have." Dawson put his book back in his pocket. "But more will come. Who knows how many could be behind us? Or in front of us."

Fin said, "We can't stand around. We need to go."

"Like, now," Dawson said.

"But we need to be smart about how we cross the bridge," Fin said. "Either you or me has to go first and the other last."

His face paled.

"Someone has to face the trial first. And someone has to make sure everyone gets through, battling anything that might come up behind us."

Visibly collecting himself, Dawson said, "Right, I'm first."

Boone stepped forward. "I'll go first."

Fin turned to him. "Not happening."

Quick as a whip, Marci ran past them. As soon as she planted both feet on the wooden planks, a light flashed.

"Marci!" Fin yelled.

Several menacing football players materialized and strode toward Marci, who was frozen in fear as the bridge morphed into a football field.

"Shit." Fin ran forward, but when she was about to cross the threshold, an invisible force knocked her to the ground. "What the hell?" She stood up and touched the air in front of her. It felt like solid glass.

Thinking fast, she pulled out her knife, cut her finger, and touched the barrier. Nothing happened. "Fuck." She glanced at the group. "Can you all see this, too?"

Everyone nodded, fear written all over their faces.

Dawson winced. "All of it."

The football players had morphed into monstrous versions of humans with distorted features and skin that had different tones and textures.

"Dawson, your book."

The attackers groped Marci. Sobbing, she tried to cover herself but couldn't fend them off.

Dawson pulled out his green book but looked confused. "I don't know what to ask. It'll only give facts."

Fin said, "This is a fact now, not a choice. Ask what this enchantment is."

He quickly wrote in the book, waiting for its answer and twisting his face in dread when it came. "It's an Agony enchantment. The thing that makes you suffer the most. It's designed to either kill you or make you kill yourself. Unless you can overcome it."

Fin ran her hands through her hair. "Amon wasn't messing around, was he?"

Dawson shook his head. "She has to figure out how to stop them from hurting her. If she can't . . ."

Nellie, Boone, and Jonesy were listening closely.

With tears in her eyes, Nellie ran up to the invisible glass. "Come on, Marci." She banged on the magical barrier. "Fight! Do something!"

Boone's face was a tornado of rage and helplessness. He walked over and stood next to Nellie. "Do you think the knife was hers? Yesterday. Outside the truck."

Fin gently pulled Boone and Nellie away from the horror playing out in front of them. "Don't look. Turn around. All of you." As they did, Fin whispered, "Come on, Marci. Fight."

~~~

Marci shivered at the revolting drool on her body. At least in this place, they appeared the way they really were. If she'd told anyone what the kings of the high school had done, she'd lose everything.

I was supposed to be Homecoming Queen. I was supposed to be happy.

Their hands plundered her body.

She squeezed her eyes shut. *Just let it happen. It'll be over soon.* But the harder she cried, the harder they laughed. *I'm their entertainment.*

An image of Boone made her slap one of their hands away. *Boone would never do this to me.* Her eyes snapped open.

The monster stared at her with rage in his bright red eyes. He let loose a flurry of slaps that pushed her to the ground as she screamed. They laughed as she writhed in pain.

A vision of Nellie bubbled up in her mind. *She would protect me with her bow and arrow. A real friend. Why haven't I been fighting back?*

Marci grabbed Red Eye's wrists, squeezing as hard as she could. When she let out a blood-curdling scream, they stopped the assault and stared. One of the monsters backed up and vanished.

I could fight like Fin. A brave girl cop.

Rage filled her body as she took a deep breath and screamed an ear-splitting, "No!"

Two more monsters melted into the air. But Red Eyes remained. And so did his buddy, Fang Face.

Get up. Get the fuck up!

She shoved Red Eyes backward as she jumped up, but Fang Face grabbed her.

Remember what Tommy taught you.

Letting her body go limp, she slid down and out of his grip. Turning as she hit the ground, she punched him in the balls.

Again. Again!
~~~

He doubled over in pain as Red Eyes grabbed her by the hair and dragged her to him. He wailed on her chest and stomach from above as she squirmed under the intense beating.

Use your legs!

Kicking straight up at his head, she broke his nose. He tipped backward and dropped to the ground. She jumped up, but Fang Face was back. This time, her brother's moves flowed out of her. A palm strike to the nose, breaking it. A throat punch, sending him staggering to the ground.

Fang Face rolled to his knees and tried to lunge toward her, but she kicked him in the stomach and the face, throwing his head back. Before she could deliver the final blow, he disappeared.

Red Eyes.

She squared up as her last attacker approached her. "I'm not scared of you anymore."

His monstrous appearance dissolved, and he transformed into the football player who had assaulted her yesterday. She lowered her fists and glared at him as he gave her a wicked grin.

"That was the last time you'll ever touch me. I promise you that."

As the last word left her mouth, he dissipated into nothingness.

The sky brightened, and sunlight streamed down onto a rocky, steeply slanted area. At the bottom of the mini mountain was a boulder bigger than she was. At the top, rocks formed what looked like thick goal posts.

But more importantly, multiple dead bodies lay on the hill, looking like pin cushions with arrows sticking out of them.

"Oh no," she whispered.

Worried about the others, she glanced behind her, but the bridge she had just crossed was gone. *Alone, again.* She gripped her aching rib cage, wiped the blood from her broken face, and turned back to the gruesome tableau.

"Please hurry, Boone."

~~~

"She made it!" Fin yelled.

The teenagers spun around.

Fin pumped her fist with relief. "She crossed the bridge."

Boone rushed up to Fin. "How'd she do it?"

"She fought back," said Fin.

Jonesy rubbed his jaw. "So, this bridge, we have to battle our worst fear?"

214
~~~

Fin looked at Dawson, hoping he'd explain it.

Dawson obliged. "It's whatever makes you suffer the most physically or mentally. Real or imagined."

Nellie's eyes were still pink from crying. "Was it real? I mean, what they did to her. Will she have bruises or pain?"

Fin said, "I'm not sure."

"I think we should proceed as though it will hurt us for real," said Dawson. "Better to be careful."

"I'm going next," Nellie said.

"No!" Fin grabbed Nellie's arm. "Are you crazy? After what we just saw? You're going back home."

"How?" Nellie pointed. "The portal is gone."

Fin whipped her head around and discovered that Nellie was right. The only way back was through. *Fuck, fuck, fuck.*

"I can't leave Marci alone wherever she is." Nellie moved toward the portal, but Boone beat her to it.

Before anyone could stop him, Boone was separated from them by the enchanted partition.

"Dammit." Fin pulled at her hair before saying to Dawson, "You have to go next. I have to stay if anyone comes through."

He swallowed but said, "I know."

"Okay." She fixed her attention on Boone. *Please, God, don't let him die.*

~~~

Darkness overtook the bridge until Boone could barely see a few feet in front of him. He collapsed from the pain gnawing on his stomach that spread to his chest, arms, and face.

"What's happening?" he screamed.

The agonizing pain stopped as quickly as it started.

He rolled to his knees and started to push himself up but got distracted by the strange appearance of his hands. *These aren't my hands. They're old. Dirty.* He looked down at his shirt and pants. *Whose clothes are these?*

A small sound brought his attention up. An empty, oval room with mirrored walls that reflected forever greeted him. *What is this? Where am I?* He stood and his heart stopped as he looked in the mirror.

"No," he whispered.

Boone touched his cheeks and stared at Russell's face in the mirror.
~~~

"No!" he screamed as he punched the first mirror and pivoted to the next one. But he couldn't break the panel no matter how hard he tried. He staggered back, rejecting his reflection and refusing to believe he had become Russell.

"You mother fucker!" Boone yelled.

Mirror Russell said, "Yeah, boy, feel that anger."

Boone jumped back like he'd been stung. "I'm not you. I'll never be you."

"Ya think? I seen your temper, boy. You're only a few years away from living my life, you pathetic piece of shit."

Boone's rage erupted as he raced to the mirror and broke that one, too.

Wicked laughter ricocheted around the room. "See, you are me, son," said Russell's reflection.

Boone raced across the room and broke that mirror.

More laughter. "Keep breakin' 'em, boy, until you destroy everything around you. Just like me."

Boone skidded to a stop in front of the next mirror. He took a second to catch his breath before stepping back.

"Oh, you think you won 'cause you didn't break one?" Russell peered behind him, so he followed his gaze.

One of the monstrous football players who'd hurt Marci leered at him.

"I'll kill you," Boone said through clenched teeth.

He rushed the monster, and they traded punches. The jock got in three quick jabs to the gut, dropping Boone to the ground before kicking him in the face.

Russell kneeled down, offering Boone a knife. "Need a little help?"

Boone snatched it and scrambled to his feet before crouching into a fighting stance.

As the monster charged him, he remembered Nellie telling Grayson not to kill Russell. He heard his sister's voice in his mind, *Don't do it.*

Boone dropped the knife and let his attacker knock him to the ground.

The jock vanished.

"You're such a pussy!" Russell's twisted face flushed red.

"I'm not gonna be like you," Boone shouted. "I'm not gonna beat people."

"Coward." Russel sneered. "No wonder your best friend went after your little sister."

Jonesy appeared at Boone's side, kneeling beside him. "I'm totally gonna do it with your sister."

"You asshole."

Boone tackled Jonesy to the ground. But as he cocked his fist back, scenes from the years of his friendship with Jonesy flashed through his head.

He looked at his best friend and offered his hand. "I'm sorry."

As he pulled Jonesy up, his friend faded away.

"God, you make me sick," said Russell's disembodied voice.

Getting his bearings, Boone looked around and realized every mirror held an image of Russell.

All of the Russells jumped out and ganged up on Boone, who dropped to the ground under the weight of their attack.

Something grew out of Boone, ripping his skin. "Oh my God," he screamed.

A bone-jarring snap sounded in his ears before another version of Boone formed on the ground.

The real Boone rolled over, jumped up, and stared in the mirror. He was so relieved to see his true face that he didn't pay much attention to his doppelganger at first.

His second self stood with all the swagger and cruelty of the real Russell. "You're pathetic." Second Boone sneered and ran to the mirrors. He jumped inside, shattering them.

Boone ducked down to shield himself from the shards. When he stood back up and opened his eyes, the sky was bright. Out of the corner of his eye, he saw a wisp of long auburn hair. He shouted, "Marci!"

"Boone!"

He raced to her as she raced to him. They met in the middle and embraced.

"Boone!" She gripped him, and his whole body warmed at the feeling of being wrapped up with her.

"I'm so sorry about what happened to you."

His eyes watered as Marci's tears wet the back of his T-shirt. But his heart swelled knowing that whatever he was, whatever they were going to be together, he would never be Russell.

When he let go of her, his stomach dropped at the apprehension on her face. "What?" He followed her gaze to the scattered human remains and swallowed. "Oh, that's not good."

He peered back to the bridge, but it was gone now. "Please, hurry," he whispered.

~~~

"He's through." Fin gave Dawson a sportsman's slap on the arm. "You're up."

He swallowed hard.

"Dawson?" she asked.

"I don't think I can do this." He poked his glasses.

She reached out and gripped his shoulders, giving them a reassuring squeeze. "Whatever it is, you'll be able to face it."

"I don't want to die, Fin," he whispered.

"You're not going to die," she said as she gripped his shoulders and shook before letting go. "You're stronger than you think, Dawson. You can do this."

He peered over her shoulder at the bridge and nodded before grabbing his gear and slowly walking toward it. After a brief pause, he made his way to the bridge and stepped on.

~~~

Dawson found himself in a hospital setting without all the equipment and people. Just clean, white walls. The murmurs of a man beyond the walls broke the silence. Dawson followed the sound to see where it was coming from. As he entered an intersection of hallways, the murmuring man came out of nowhere and ran into him.

Dawson jumped back. "I'm sorry, sir."

The old man had unkempt graying hair and eyes wild with fear. "Who are you?"

"I'm Dawson. Nice to meet you." But the longer he stared, the wider his eyes got. *He looks like an older version of me.*

"Who am I?" Without waiting for an answer, the man continued walking down the hallway and disappeared.

Baffled, Dawson stared after the man. A moment later, someone bumped into his back.

The same old man asked, "Who are you?"

"I just told you." Dawson's heart took off like a racehorse.

"I would've remembered that." He pulled out a worn, faded green notebook and looked at its pages. "This might have an answer." But the old man just stared without reading before looking up. "I didn't know anyone was here. Who are you?"

Fear prickled down Dawson's spine as he nervously walked the other way. But the hallway looked the same as the one he'd just come from. As he glanced back over his shoulder, someone collided with him again.

"Who the hell am I?" The man shook with terrified anger. "I don't know who I am. Where am I?"

"I-I don't . . ." Dawson shook his head.

The man grabbed him and shook him. "Tell me what my name is!" His face went blank like someone had flipped a switch. He let go and ran off only to reappear again.

"Hello." He gripped his green book to his chest. "I used to know this place. Where am I?"

Dawson peered around at the uniform white walls. "I don't know this place, either."

"I'm trapped here, Dawson."

Surprised that the man remembered his name, Dawson gaped at him.

"I'm trapped by my own mind," the man said.

Dawson rocked back a step as the man started screaming.

Two bigfoot-like orderlies tore down the hallway and grabbed the old man.

Fear plastered Dawson against the smooth wall.

"No," the elderly man screamed as they dragged him down the hallway. "It's me, Dawson, it's me!"

Panting, Dawson turned to run but fell onto a hard stretcher. He tried to move, but he was strapped down. The Sasquatches circled him with needles and knives, jamming an IV into his arm. He screamed under the tape over his mouth.

One of the monstrous orderlies jumped on him with a butcher knife. As the blade started to come down, the old man rushed into the room and knocked the creature off. After ripping the tape off Dawson's mouth, he removed the restraints.

"Hurry!" He grabbed Dawson's arm, and they ran back to the intersection where they met. "There's not much time before they find us again."

"Who are they?" Dawson looked around. "Where are we?"

"Your mind. After it's left you."

Dawson's knees went weak. "My mind is gone?" He frantically shook his head. *No, no, no . . .*

"It comes and goes." He tapped his temple.

A rumbling noise down the hallway made them jump.

Dawson asked, "How do I make it through this?"

The thunderous pounding of heavy footsteps was getting louder.

"Let go of it," said the old man as he tapped his head again. "Don't just think. Live."

The monstrous orderlies grabbed them and pushed them down onto stretchers. They struggled but they were outnumbered. A beast grabbed Dawson's throat with one paw-like hand and yanked the notebook out of his pocket with the other. He lunged for his green book, but the creature side-stepped him easily and whooped.

An overwhelming anger and frustration propelled Dawson forward. He burst through the bigfoots holding him, raced to the thief, punched it in the face, and grabbed his green book. As he shoved it in his pocket, all the orderlies aimed their rageful glares at him.

"Oh shit," Dawson whispered.

"Run!" the old man hollered.

"I'm not leaving you."

"I'll be fine. Go!"

Dawson ran through the twisted hallways as the Sasquatches chased him. One hallway after another led to more orderlies. Eventually, they surrounded him. Dawson grabbed the green book and wrote one word on its magical page: Help.

Dozens of orderlies tackled him, piling on him and beating him. He dropped the book but held on to the turquoise pencil. The kicks and punches had him curling into a ball. Through the barrage of blows, he could feel something pulsing near his chest. He peeked down as the pencil became a sword. The stone handle and turquoise blade glowed from his hip to his toes.

What would a hero do?

Dawson screamed, thrusting the blade into the air. An invisible power radiated out and blew the orderlies off him. Every creature that touched the blade disappeared into a burst of turquoise powder. Dawson stood, squared up to the orderlies, nudged his cracked glasses higher, and raised his sword.

He grinned. "As Indiana Jones would say, fortune and glory."

Giving a warrior's cry, he rushed the monsters, taking out wide swaths of them with each swing. Eventually, all that was left of them was the turquoise dust settling to the ground.

The old man walked down the hallway, holding his worn green book. He stooped to pick up Dawson's notebook and handed it to him. "I think this is yours."

Dawson gently took it from him. "Thank you."

"Who are you?" asked the old man.

"Someone you used to know."

"Oh, okay." He walked away for a few steps then glanced back to Dawson. "Thank you for getting rid of them. I really hate bigfoots."

Dawson laughed. "Me too."

The man strolled away in a pleasant mood, disappearing around a corner as the room got painfully bright. Shielding his eyes with his hand, Dawson turned away. When the light dimmed, his environment had changed from the hospital halls to the great outdoors, and his sword had transformed back into a pen.

Boone called out, "Dawson?"

Dawson dropped his hand from his face as Boone and Marci rushed over.

"Ah, you're alive." Marci hugged him. "Was it bad? Oh, your glasses are cracked."

She touched them gently.

"It, uh . . .yes, they're broken. They'll be fine." Dawson reflexively pulled out his green book and went to write in it, but he stopped, looked at the kids, and put it away.

When Marci stepped back, Boone embraced him. After a moment, they pulled away from each other with buddy slaps to the arms.

"I'm glad you're both okay." Dawson looked at Marci. "I'm so sorry about what you went through."

She blushed a little but nodded. "Thank you."

"You too," he gave a supportive smile to Boone.

"Thank you," Boone said.

Dawson glanced around at the bodies sprinkled across the landscape. "So, this looks nightmarish." There seemed to be a pattern to their deaths, but he couldn't quite put his finger on it.

"Yeah," said Boone. "Any ideas?"

Dawson used his stone pencil to ask the green book what enchantment they were dealing with.

Oh no. He looked at the boulder, then at Boone and Marci.

"What?" Marci asked.

"What's wrong?" Boone asked.

Dawson shoved his glasses back up his nose. "It's called a Sisyphus enchantment."

Marci's face crinkled into a puzzled expression. "What does that mean?"

Dawson's shoulders drooped. "It means we need Fin."

~~~

"Okay, Jonesy, you're up," said Fin.

Jonesy took a deep breath and looked at Nellie. "Whatever you see, don't think less of me, okay?"

"That's crazy," she said. "Don't worry about that."

"Just promise."

"I promise."

He turned away, then quickly stepped back and drew Nellie into a hug, before dropping his eyes to the ground and stepping onto the bridge.

Fin said, "What, uh, was—"

"I have no idea," Nellie said.

~~~

As soon as Jonesy crossed the bridge, he closed his eyes and begged whoever might be listening. "Please don't be clowns. Please don't be clowns. Please don't be clowns."

Rough breathing tickled his ear.

Jumping, Jonesy squealed and cracked open one eye.

Standing behind him was a towering clown with bright red lips, fangs for teeth, makeup that was melting off, a big red nose, and a blue wig of curly hair. The jester costume cinched tight at his throat, and oversized shoes splayed out in front of the huge man.

The clown leaned in and whispered, "Hi ya, Jonesy."

"Ahh!" Jonesy screamed and bolted into the shrub maze that appeared in front of him. As he skidded around a corner, a different clown with a purple wig jumped out at him.

"No!" He chose the other route.

At the next intersection, a clown jumped from the left and pelted him with a water balloon. "Who's afraid of clowns?" It threw another and another. Each one hit harder and harder, leaving welts on Jonesy's body.

"Stop!" Jonesy ran to the right.

But before he reached the next turn, the original clown stepped into his path and walked toward him.

Jonesy spun around but the other two clowns were coming at him. "No!"

A small hand grabbed Jonesy from behind and pulled him through the wall of shrubbery.

He landed on his back and looked up at his small rescuer.

"Don't be scared," said a little boy. "You're safe here."

The panting teenager sat up taking in the dark cellar with junk stashed everywhere. A slapping sound filtered down the stairs followed by a scream. "What is that?"

"Don't you remember?" The boy played with toy cars.

Jonesy stood up and stared at the kid for a second before walking to him and kneeling in front of him. "Is your name Peter Joseph Jones?"

The little boy nodded. "But everybody calls me Jonesy."

"I know." Tears pricked at his eyes. "That's my name, too."

The boy whispered, "This is a good hiding place when the bad man comes."

"I remember now." He stood and listened to the beating, then glanced down. "You don't have to hide anymore, okay?"

"Are you sure?" Huge, scared eyes stared up at him.

"I'm positive. Close your eyes and count to ten real slow. When you open them, the bad man will be gone. And you'll never have to hide down here again."

"Okay."

"Go on. Close your eyes." When he obeyed, Jonesy strode to the cellar steps. "Now start countin'."

"One."

Jonesy took the cellar stairs two at a time before opening the door into a small, poor house with barely any furniture.

"Two."

As he walked down a dark hallway, the screaming and the beating got louder. He stopped in front of a closed door that vibrated from the violence on the other side.

"Three." He could hear the boy counting over everything else, as though the voice was inside him.

Kicking open the door revealed his mother being choked to death while lying bloody and half-naked on the bed.

"Four."

The bastard's costume was pulled halfway down, exposing his bare chest. His makeup ran down his face in a gruesome mockery of joy. The murderer was one of the entertainers from a traveling circus.

Jonesy's mother was a waitress at the local bar, and she made herself entertainment for travelers. Every asshole that gave her extra cash for rent or food looked different, but they were all the same.

"Five."

Jonesy's hands tightened into fists.

"Get the fuck off my mother," said Jonesy through gritted teeth.

"Who's gonna make me?" The twisted bastard leered at him.

"Six."

"I am." Jonesy pounced like a panther, tackling the clown.

"Seven."

They traded punches as his mother screamed in the background. Jonesy picked up the man and threw him through the window.

"Eight."

Jonesy looked for his mother, who was now fully dressed, her face clean and bright, almost luminous.

"It wasn't your fault, Peter." She pressed a loving hand against his face. "I love you. Take care of your brothers and sisters."

As her image dissipated, he leaned into her hand to extend the contact as long as possible. After she was gone, he wiped a tear away and headed down the hall to the cellar door.

"Nine."

He went down the stairs and finally stood looking down at his childhood self.

The boy said, "Ten."

The world around him changed into a bright sky over an expansive nature scene.

"Jonesy!" Boone yelled, relief tinging his words. "Over here."

Jonesy glanced at Boone, who was standing next to Marci. Boone waved him over.

"You okay?" Boone asked as Jonesy walked up to them.

"I will be." Jonesy gave a quick nod as Boone reciprocated. "What the hell is this?"

"Nothin' good," Marci said.

Boone pointed at a steep hill. "We have to push this boulder up there."

Jonesy followed his best friend's finger to where Dawson stood at the top. Dawson picked up a stick and threw it between two rocky columns near him. The wood exploded into blue flames, which then disintegrated into turquoise dust.

"Well, this just keeps getting better." Jonesy looked back to where he came from. "Come on, Nellie, you got this."

~~~

Nellie looked aghast. "I didn't know that's how his mom died."

"That's awful," said Fin. *But not unusual.* She'd seen more women killed like that than she cared to admit to her mother. "But you have to focus. You're up next."

Nellie nodded. "I'm ready."

"Are you sure?"

Nellie shook her head.

"Okay, I need to tell you something else about that compass bracelet."

Nellie lifted her wrist and admired the gift. "What about it?"

"Well, besides me being able to track you, it's also a shield." Fin unsheathed her knife from its thigh holster and held it out to Nellie. "Try and stab me."

"What?" Surprise widened her delicate features as she took the knife.

"Do it. Hurry. But don't swing too hard. It smarts the wrist."

Looking skeptical, Nellie did as she was told.

As the knife arced toward her, Fin swung the bracelet in front of her and the glowing blue shield blazed to life. The knife struck it with a hollow tinging sound and glanced off the surface.

"Wow." Nellie looked at the bracelet with a new appreciation.

"Give me your finger." Fin retrieved the knife and held out her hand. "I know it might seem a little gross, but the magic needs blood to activate the shield. Like the portal entrance."

Hesitantly, Nellie presented it.

After giving it a quick jab, Fin directed, "Dab it onto the bracelet."
~~~

As soon as Nellie touched it, it glowed brighter to Fin, but she knew it was the first time Nellie could see it glow.

Transfixed, Nellie said, "It's so pretty. Why is it pulsing?"

"Because the bracelets are connected."

"Oh, wow," Nellie said.

"Okay, hurry, now, you try," Fin took the knife as Nellie stepped back. "Just hold the bracelet in front of you like you're protecting yourself. It'll do the rest." Fin made a stabbing motion at her mother.

Nellie swung her forearm around, and the shield popped up just before Fin's knife banged against it.

Fin was surprised by the powerful corresponding burst she felt in her bracelet as Nellie's shield popped out.

"That's amazing." Nellie's eyes sparkled.

"Yeah, it is." She rubbed away the leftover tingles from her wrist. "And last thing."

"Yeah?"

"When you need help but you don't where to go or what to do, you can call on it to guide you. A sort of, I don't know, spirit guide or animal or something will appear and take you where you need to go."

"So, I just follow it?"

"Yeah, it'll lead you to the place or thing that will help you the most in that moment."

Nellie's face scrunched up in thought. "How does it come out?"

"I'm not sure, actually," said Fin. "When it happened for me, I threw my arm up to protect myself and it appeared. I think it's like the shield. It'll show up if you're in imminent danger."

"Okay." Nellie stroked the bracelet again.

A silence stretched out between them.

"You're going to be okay, Nellie. I promise you. Plus, you have your bow and arrows. And with an aim as true as yours, you'll never miss."

"Thank you," Nellie said.

Her mother took a deep breath and faced the bridge. After tossing one last glance at Fin over her shoulder, she started her trial.

As her mother was engulfed in the magical glass, Fin whispered, "Please make it through."

<p style="text-align:center">~~~</p>

As Nellie crossed over the bridge her foot landed in her living room. Her ears rang from Russell screaming at her mama down the hallway. Something caught her eye in the corner of the room.

Are those mine? She glanced at the shoes on her feet, then at the pair of cream-colored shoes sticking out from underneath the velvet curtain.

Oh no. As the yelling got louder and the hitting began, Nellie raced to the corner, dropped her bow and arrows to the floor, and pulled back the fabric.

A small, scared version of herself was pressed against the wall.

"Get up," Nellie whispered to the sobbing girl in the corner. "Can't you hear she needs help? Get up!"

Her former self didn't seem to hear or care.

Nellie knelt and gently touched the girl's arm. "I'll take care of this."

She stood and closed the curtain. *I can do this.* She walked slowly toward her parents as her heart beat faster and faster. The shadow of Russell beating her mother arched against the wall like a Hitchcock film and her breath caught in her chest. When the silhouette of her mother's body fell to the ground, Nellie halted and leaned against the wall, her chest heaving for air. She started to leave, stopped, and faced the lumbering shadow of her father. The wall steadied her as she forced her body down the hall.

Don't run away. Don't run away. Don't run away.

She kept walking, and as she reached the door, her mother screamed. Her heart felt like it was going to burst through her chest.

Go! Get in there!

Nellie took a deep breath and jumped around the corner of the room, but no one was there.

"Surprise."

Nellie spun around. Russell squeezed her throat like a python, picking her up and throwing her on the ground, knocking the wind out of her. With a cruel laugh, he shouted, "I'm finishing this once and for all." Russell's face was mottled with rage as he yanked out a knife and lunged at Clara Belle.

"Mama, run!" Nellie yelled.

Russell charged, slashing his knife down. But Nellie stepped in front of her mother and brought up her arm. Russell's blade clinked off her shield, and he fell backward, exploding into turquoise dust. Nellie scrambled to help her mother, but Clara Belle was gone, and in her place was the field outside her house.

Nellie stood like a warrior as she searched the fields. She heard screaming and beating through the weeds.

"Lily," she whispered.

She dashed toward the danger as the screaming intensified. The tall weeds cut her skin as she charged through them. When she burst through the foliage, Lily was on top of the old her, relentlessly beating her.

You can do this. Marci taught you how to fight.

"Get off me!" Nellie screamed and tackled Lily.

The other version of her disappeared.

They rolled together, then stood and circled each other. Lily raced forward, throwing a fist that Nellie blocked before bringing another fist around into Nellie's gut. After Nellie landed a few blows, Lily pulled her knife. She swung it at Nellie, who threw up her compass bracelet. A bright seafoam green force exploded from the bracelet, launching them apart.

Whoa. She admired the bracelet's power as she readied herself for the next attack.

In front of her, a transparent jade-colored wolf appeared. It shook itself and ran past Lily's prone body, stopping a couple of times to look back at Nellie. Nellie hurried to follow it as Lily staggered to her feet. Nellie ran after the wolf back to the house as Lily's heavy footsteps were once again closing in quickly.

After dashing into the house, she grabbed her bow and arrow. Lily's footsteps echoed from the porch. Nellie nocked an arrow, turned, and aimed as Lily crashed through the entrance. Buying herself more time, Nellie jogged backwards and fired.

Lily jerked to a stop and looked down at the shaft protruding from her chest before bursting into a bright turquoise powder that twinkled down to the ground.

Nellie sagged in relief until the whole world shifted. She clamped her eyes shut, swaying and dizzy. When she opened her eyes, she saw Boone running toward her.

"Nellie!" He grabbed her into a tight hug. "Oh my gosh, you're okay."

She gripped him back. "Yeah." They let go of each other as Nellie looked at her bracelet. "Thanks to Fin."

Marci ran up and hugged her, too. Nellie whispered in her ear, "I'm sorry what happened to you."

"You helped me while I was there," Marci whispered. "Thinking about being your fiend." Releasing her, Marci smiled gratefully as Nellie returned her affection.

"Friends," Nellie whispered.

"Yeah," Marci smiled before her expression contorted with worry. "But you should see what's next."

"What do you mean?" Nellie looked at the scene around her, rearing back at the human remains with tiny arrows sticking from them. "What happened to them?"

"No idea. Dawson's theory is arrows start firing from somewhere magical. Boone thinks it's some kind of freakish army of monsters. Jonesy has no clue." Panic was plastered all over Marci's face.

"Fin will make it. I know she will." Nellie turned to where the bridge used to be. *Please hurry.*

~~~

Fin sighed with relief as Nellie disappeared and hopefully joined the others wherever they were. She started toward the bridge, but someone tripped her as she landed flat on her stomach. She felt whomever it was sit on her lower back, pinning her down. Twisting her head to see who was crushing her pelvis, she came face-to-face with a blue-eyed, blond-haired woman with a sinister smile.

The woman's tone was triumphant when she said, "Halo made it seem like you'd be a lot harder to take down."

"Halo?" *Does everybody know this guy?*

The woman pushed down on Fin with all her weight as she leaned towards Fin's face. "Mm-hmm. And I'm Ice."

"You really should have listened to him, Ice." Fin brought her elbow up and into Ice's nose, throwing her off her game, before pulling her gun and firing near Ice's foot.

The woman screamed and tumbled off Fin to inspect her boot.

Fin stood and aimed her gun at the woman's chest.

"You tried to shoot me!" She looked up at Fin in shock before laughing. "Oh, you don't know, do you?"

"Know what?" Fin backed toward the bridge as Ice gingerly stood up.

"About the Bounty Hunter Council." She wiped herself off before lifting the bottom of her shirt and pulling down the waistband of her blue leather pants to reveal a light glow beneath her skin.
~~~

"What is that?"

"Ask Auci." She gave Fin a shit-eating grin. "Better yet, ask the council. I'm sure before this is all over, you'll have to answer to them for one thing or another."

"Wait, what?"

But before Fin could ask another question, the woman touched the blue light on her hip and disappeared.

"Holy shit," Fin whispered. *Can she travel just like Auci? How does she know him?*

Two strange-looking men appeared in the place where the portal entrance had been.

"Shit," she said.

"Hey." One man tapped the other on the shoulder and pointed at her. "That's that Fin girl."

"No, that's ten-thousand-blood coins for us." The other one laughed.

"You'll have to catch me first." Fin ran onto the bridge.

~~~

Standing in the middle of the bridge, Fin could see Nellie, Dawson, Boone, Jonesy, and Marci on the other side. "Hey!" She waved, but they didn't react. *They can't see me.*

Nellie kept looking in Fin's direction, worry and disappointment flitting across her face.

Fin walked forward but bumped into another invisible wall. "I don't understand." She backed up and looked behind her at the empty bridge.

When she faced forward, a woman who looked like an older version of Nellie stood between her and the others.

She looks about my age. "Who are you?"

"You know who I am."

From behind her, Auci said, "Fin?"

But when she turned around, he wasn't there. She glanced back at her mother, who was joined by Auci. They stood, blocking her path.

"You want answers," said adult Nellie.

Fin marveled at how beautiful her mother had become. "I want to know why you left me. Both of you."

Nellie's eyes softened with tenderness. "You must realize by now how this constant need to know, to search, has taken a toll on you. Don't you?"

"You're agonizing over something you can't change," said Auci.

230
~~~

Fin's eyes filled with tears. "But now that I can move in time, maybe I can go back and—"

"No," said Auci firmly. "You can't."

Through her choking emotions, Fin said, "But if I just knew why. Just tell me why."

"Make peace with not knowing," said Nellie. "Before it destroys you. It's making you suffer. It's driving everything you do."

Auci said, "It's ruining your relationships. Look at what you're doing to Hodge."

"I'm not . . ." Fin paused, stepping back. "I'm not doing anything to him."

Nellie's expression was loving but reproachful. "You're leading him on, like he has a chance. He deserves better."

Auci nodded. "And what about your career? Are you a cop because you really want to be one? Or is it because solving cases allows you get closure on something, unlike your past."

Nellie said, "Maybe the people involved in your cases deserve someone who's there for the right reasons. Someone who isn't searching for their own answers but is focused on finding answers for the victims."

Fin whispered, "That's not true."

"What about being here now?" asked Auci. "You said it's not for me, it's for you."

"Everything you do is all about you and your search for your answers," said Nellie. "What are you going to do when you run out of questions? When you can't save everyone, including yourself? What then?"

Hot tears slid down Fin's cool skin as she stepped back from her parents. "No. It's not true." She skirted away and was stopped by a muscular, familiar body. "Hodge?"

He said, "You never loved me. Not really. You can't love anyone. And you know it." A painful blend of hurt and resentment mixed on his face. "This obsession for answers, to save people, overshadows everything you do. Everything you are."

"Hodge, please   "

"You led me on. You knew you couldn't love me, but you kept me around anyway."

She swiveled away and collided with the chief.

He shook his head with disappointment. "Nobody should be doing this job for themselves. You shouldn't be a cop just because you're searching for your own answers. People deserve better."

"I deserve better." Hodge was right behind her as she turned in a circle.

"You need to let go," said Nellie.

"You can't change what happens," said Auci.

She sunk down into a ball. "Stop, please stop."

"Let go…can't change…I deserve better…you shouldn't be a cop." The voices spoke over each other until Fin couldn't tell them apart anymore. "You're never going to know."

She cried as the voices got louder and louder. "Stop," she yelled, shooting up to her feet and facing the chief. "I did start as a cop because I needed my own answers. You're right. But that became the thing that drives me to work so hard for these victims. I know their pain. I did start for me, but I stayed for them."

The chief disappeared.

Fin faced her boyfriend. "I'm so sorry, Hodge."

She considered the pain etched in the lines of his face. *I caused that.*

She relented. "You're right. I've known for a while that you loved me more. I just kept thinking that I could get to where you are. Good intentions, you know? But there was just always something . . . missing."

"For you," he said dryly. "But not for me. You knew that."

She nodded shamefully and stared at her shoes. *No, look him in the eyes.*

The hurt in his stare made her want to fold into herself. "I did know that. You caring for me, it was comforting. I didn't want to lose it. And I gave you just enough to keep you."

She reached up to touch his face, but he knocked her hand away.

"I'm sorry," she said quietly.

Leaning into her, he said, "You need to tell me that."

"I promise."

He gave her a quick, pained nod and vanished.

She looked at her parents. "I'll never be able to change it, will I?" Tears streamed from her eyes. "No matter what I do or how often I move through time. This gift. It won't ever change what happens, will it?"

Her mom shook her head as she moved to comfort Fin. "You can't let it be the only thing in your life anymore. It can't be your only purpose. You have so much more to give."

"It's time to let people in," said Auci. "It's time to move forward. To move past this. Not every question has an answer."

Fin wiped her eyes with his handkerchief. "I understand. But it doesn't mean I won't try."

As they started to dissolve, Fin lunged at them. "Wait, no, please don't go yet."

A blinding light forced her eyes shut. When she opened them, she blinked away tears. She was so relieved that everyone was alive, but especially Nellie, who ran to her and hugged her tightly.

"Fin." Fear saturated Nellie's voice.

"What's wrong?" Fin wiped her eyes, noticing the fear on everyone's faces, the human remains, and Dawson scribbling in his book. "Oh, wow. This is . . . what is this?"

Dawson poked his cracked glasses and looked at her. "Nothing good."

"I can see that," Fin said. "What're we dealing with?"

He gave a dejected shake of his head. "A boulder, arrows, portal, and who knows what else."

Everyone exchanged nervous glances.

"We can do it," said Fin. "Together. So, fill me in, and let's get moving."

28

Nom, Nom, Nom

As Luke and Carl escorted Grayson to the supposed tree line portal, he glared at them. He was stronger and could take them, but he couldn't outrun a bullet to the heart or an arrow through the throat. Seeing his mother die from cancer, he knew the healing power they had only went so far. He and Lily weren't going to live forever.

Though Lily seems to think she will.

The group stopped at the trees that formed a clear barrier between the woods and whatever lay beyond. They looked around. Grayson could see a light glow, especially around the knot in the large oak tree. He'd always been able to see it. Fin could see it, too. But Lily couldn't. When he'd take out his special stones she'd just ask, "Why do you have a bag of rocks?"

While the others argued about what to do, he squinted at the knot and used his thumb to dab at some liquid.

Blood. Hmmm.

Lily interrupted his thoughts and said, "Well, brother, how do we get in?"

He took a deep breath and stepped back toward the knot as he turned to face her. "How would I know? I ain't the one who got taken here like you did. What'd Oliver tell you?"

"He didn't tell me anything." She let out a yell and kicked a rock that soared like a pro baseball player had hit it with a bat.

"Hey, he messed with that knot," Carl said, pointing at Grayson and the tree right behind him. "On that tree right there."

Grayson tried to look confused. "What're you talkin' about?"

"Move." Lily rushed over, pushed him aside, and investigated it.

Fuckin' Carl. Grayson gave him the look of death, and Carl leered back.

"There's blood on it," Lily said.

He winced when she grabbed his hands and searched his skin. He had tried to wipe them on his jeans, but he couldn't be sure he'd gotten all the blood off. *Don't see it. Don't see it.*

"Goddammit, Grayson."

Lily screamed at the sky, yanked her knife from her pocket, and slashed it across his face before shoving it into his thigh.

He screamed in pain, dropping to his knee.

"You're not my brother," she said.

Grayson peered up into her frigid green eyes. *Nothing's left.*

Carl laughed. "She told you."

"Swallowed you up and spit you out." Luke's eyes twinkled as he made a chomping face at Grayson, like he was taking a bite out of him. "Nom, nom, nom."

Pride unfurled across Lily's face. "All these years, everyone was always scared of you and how big you are and how scary you look." She jabbed her index finger at her chest. "Everyone's gonna know my name. And you're just gonna be one of the bodies I left in the dust."

"Lily, please, Mama wouldn't want this."

She backhanded him so fast he didn't realize what had happened until he hit the ground.

"Don't you take her name in vain." She walked over to where he'd fallen and put her knife to his throat. "Get up."

"Lily," he pleaded.

"Get up!" She led him by his throat to the tree, seized his thumb, pushed it into the blood on his thigh, and pressed it on the knot.

Grayson could see the knot and the area surrounding it light up.

"Why isn't it working?" She shoved Grayson, and he flew through the portal.

Grayson rolled onto the other side and was greeted by trees, a bridge, and two guys staring at him. He stood up as his wounds finished healing and ran toward them. "Get outta the way."

The two men broke apart as Grayson ran between them and onto the bridge. As soon as his foot touched the worn wood plank, everything went dark and snow started to fall. As his surroundings lightened, he realized he was standing in a five-foot drift. He glanced up as a little girl ran by. The snowflakes fell harder and harder, obscuring his vision.

"Hello?" *Where is she?* He waded through drifts that were getting higher and higher as sleet pelted his face. "Little girl!"

She appeared and struggled to push through the wet, piercing snow. His heart squeezed at how small, frightened, and alone she was. He could barely see through the raging blizzard, but he trudged toward her. She reached out her small hand, and Grayson valiantly tried to grasp it. He wanted to keep her safe, to pull her out of the depths, to hold her until the storm passed.

But she sunk too quickly into the snow.

"Hey, girl!" he shouted.

He dug through the drifts for her hand even as he started to sink into it like it was quicksand. Pushed down by the heavy weight of the ever-increasing blanket of snow, now he needed help. He held up his hand, and she appeared in front of him.

"Help me!" he said, spitting out the snow that was pouring into his mouth like a rising tide.

When she reached out her hand, he grasped it, relieved.

But the girl laughed. "The difference between you and me is I don't care if you die." She jerked her hand away before grabbing a shovel and hastening his burial.

"No! Stop, stop!" he croaked, choking on the snow. As his lungs burned, a bright light appeared in front of him that took the shape of a woman. "Mama!"

"Son." Rose's face suffused with love, and her dark blond hair flowed around her as though she was submerged in water. Her pale skin looked translucent and glowing. She was dressed all in white, the cancer gone, her body healthy. "You've done everything I asked. But it's time to let go. Lily isn't yours to watch over anymore. Save yourself."

He desperately wanted to burn this image of her in his mind. "You're an angel."

She smiled and reached out to him.

He wanted to stay with her forever, but he knew he couldn't. She patted his head like she did when he was five years old. He leaned into her touch and grasped the moment for all it was worth.

"It's time to let go," she said. "Now, breathe."

Her hands on his chest were like a defibrillator, jerking his body to life. His eyes shot open. He shoved his hands above him, clearing the fluffy ice crystals from around his head, and taking a deep breath of fresh air. He choked to life as he cleared the snow away from his body until he could climb out.

The little girl walked away from him through the swirling blizzard.

"Hey!" he yelled.

Whipping around, she transformed into Lily. She stared back at him with an emptiness he recognized and a coldness he could feel. He bowed his

236

head and realized he'd done everything he could to save her. There was nothing left of his little sister. Collapsing against the gale force wind, he reached out his hand one more time. He reached and reached and reached, but she was gone.

His mother's musical voice floated through his mind, "You can't save her, son. Accept it."

Grayson's body shook as the tears fell from his face. As he let go of the sister he used to know, the snow began to melt. He looked up at a bright, cloudy sky. Hearing screams and a loud rolling sound, he stood slowly and wiped his eyes.

A girl's voice yelled, "Grayson!"

He checked out the group as a boulder bigger than Nellie rolled down a hill. They looked surprised to see him as they caught their breath.

Nellie ran to him and gave him a hug. "I knew you'd come to help us." She searched his face. "Were you crying?"

"I—" Grayson's reply caught in his throat at the concern in her eyes. *I think she cares.*

"Where's our mama?" Boone raced up to them as the group followed. "Where is she, damn you?"

"She's hurt pretty bad," said Grayson.

Fin held Boone back as he lunged for Grayson and demanded, "What happened?"

Grayson shifted his weight and rubbed the back of his neck. "Lily went to the house. To hurt you all."

Nellie asked, "She was really gonna kill us?"

He nodded. "I stopped Lily from hurting Clara Belle too bad. I promise you I did. Clara Belle should be able to call for help, but we need to get back."

Dawson asked, "What about Russell?"

Grayson aimed a questioning glance at the kids.

"We told them about what happened at the campsite," said Fin. "They know what's happening."

"Uh, well . . ." Grayson wasn't sure what to say.

Boone stepped toward Grayson. "Did you kill him?"

Nellie looked horrified. "Grayson?"

Grayson shook his head. "No, I didn't. I swear. But, uh, he's gone. One of Lily's men killed him. I'm sorry."

"I'm not." Boone spit.

"Boone!" Nellie started to cry, and Marci hugged her.

Grayson melted at how tender her heart was even after everything. "I'm really sorry, Nellie. I couldn't help him. Lily had already hurt him pretty bad."

"That's true," said Fin. "He'd already lost a lot of blood. You guys knew that."

The group was quiet for a moment.

"I know you wanna know more," Grayson said. "But right now, we got bigger problems."

"Besides pushin' that fuckin' boulder up the hill?" asked Boone.

Grayson let out a deep sigh. "Lily's right behind me. We've been on your tail since early this morning. So, if we gotta move that boulder, we gotta do it right now."

29

Ladies First

After they touched the knot with their bloodied fingers, Lily shoved Luke then Carl through the portal. *Idiots.* Lily sauntered forward, her knife at the ready in case one of those hick morons decided to cross her. *Fuckin' Carl.*

Stepping through the tree, she entered a lush landscape. Her minions were looking at something near a bridge. Two unknown guys, who looked frightened, were standing across from them. They all slowly twisted toward her when she appeared.

Instantly annoyed, she asked, "What? Who the fuck are you two?"

Grumbling, the strangers moved off to the side as Lily walked up to Luke and Carl.

"Bodies," Carl said.

"What is this place?" Luke asked, trying and failing to hide his fear.

Fear makes people weak. And Luke is a weak mother fucker. "You're a disgusting excuse for a man."

Hatred burned in his eyes, but she didn't care. He was like an insect to her. Lily looked between the bridge and him.

She said, "You go first."

He shook his head, and Carl stepped between them.

"No, make them boys go." Carl poked his chin toward the two men.

Lily gave them her sweetest smile as she waved them forward. "Go."

With an indignant rod through his spine, one guy said, "I don't know who you think—"

She shoved them. But once the first man was on the bridge, an invisible barrier wouldn't let the second man on.

"One at a time," she said under her breath.

They watched as the first man was magically transported inside a bank. A robber burst in and shot two people right off the bat before making any demands. The man she'd pushed onto the bridge cowered in the corner next to a child. As the robber came near, the man shoved the kid forward. The gunman shot the little boy before shooting and killing the man. The indoor scene dissolved back into the picturesque bridge.

Lily laughed. "Guy was a coward."

"He deserved to die." Carl agreed.

Lily stared at the bridge for a moment, then pointed at the other stranger. "You, go next."

He held up his hands and backed away. "Listen, no dagger is worth dying for."

Quick as a rattlesnake strike, Lily grabbed him and threw him onto the bridge.

The scared man scrambled to his feet and banged on the glass-like wall. Terror etched into his face as a scene of children teasing a younger kid materialized around him. They were jeering and kicking a little boy. One of the tormentors looked like a younger version of the scared man. With a wicked grin, the familiar bully swung a bat and knocked down a wasp's nest on top of the child they were teasing. The boy screamed, writhing in agony from hundreds of stings. The shrieking seemed to last forever, but eventually death stilled his blotchy, bloated body. When the bully kicked the wasp's nest at the man, a fresh swarm flew out and attacked. The man thrashed in pain, screaming until he died a swollen mess of thickened, grotesque skin and blotches. His body sank into the magical underground.

The bridge returned to normal.

Lily cocked her head, considering their predicament. "Were those things from their pasts? Like a memory. Or fear. Something that makes you feel pain." Lily flicked her stare to Luke. "You're up."

He paled. "I had a terrible experience with a rattlesnake. Been scared of them ever since. I can't go in there."

"Go." Carl grabbed him by the shoulders and threw him toward the bridge.

"No!" Luke slipped out of Carl's grip and tried to run back to the portal, which had disappeared.

But before he took his second step, Lily pulled her knife and shoved it through his throat.

"Dammit!" Carl jumped back before sneering at Lily. "You got blood on my boots."

Desperate tears sprang to Luke's eyes as he began to gargle on his own blood, the life draining from his body.

"Lived like a pussy, and died like one, too." Lily snorted and yanked the knife out of Luke before his body hit the ground. She peered back to the bridge. "So, if you die on the bridge, you get pulled down into the ravine. If you die outside the bridge, the body stays here."

She peered around her at the carnage then down to Luke's carcass. "We're not the only ones huntin' this thing."

She kneeled down, inspected the various ways the people had been killed, and grinned. "This is my kind o' magic."

Carl's gleeful expression mirrored hers. "Mine, too."

Lily stood slowly and tilted her head at Carl. "Go on through, and we'll see what's gonna kill you."

"Same thing that's gonna kill you." He adjusted his crotch. "Nothin'. I ain't scared o' nothing."

"Not even me?"

She held his gaze for a second as he snorted with disgust.

Waving her hand toward the bridge, she said, "Ladies first." As he swaggered toward the wooden planks, she added, "Try not to die."

"Same to you." He spit on the ground and crossed onto the bridge.

Goosebumps danced up her arms in delicious anticipation, but when Carl went into the magic shell of glass, he simply walked across the wooden planks. Before his last step off the bridge, he turned to give her the malicious grin of someone with no conscience. She twisted her neck with a small crack.

"I don't believe it," she said.

"Believe it," a light voice said from behind her.

Lily whipped out her knife and faced the unknown woman behind her. The tall drink of water had wickedly cool blue eyes and lightning blonde hair. She felt electric.

"Who are you?"

"I'm Ice. You're Lily. Now let's move on because you've got somewhere to go, and I need you to get there." She stepped closer.

Lily brandished her knife. "I've killed for less."

Ice raised an eyebrow of approval. "You'll fit in nicely with us."

"Us?"

"We'll get to that later. For now, I need you to get to the other side and beat Fin to the dagger."

Fin must be the dark-haired woman with Grayson.

"How do you know about that?" Lily narrowed her eyes .

"Do you want the dagger or not?"

"Better question is why you want it?"

"Because once we have it, we'll be more powerful than the bounty hunters. You don't know them yet, but they work with the Siblings, who you kind of know."

"But if I get the dagger, I can keep all that power myself."

"You don't get it." Ice shook her head. "This is bigger than you. There's a whole world for you to play in, Lily. And there's people who will love you for exactly the blood-thirsty psychopath you are."

Lily defended herself. "I'm misunderstood, not crazy."

Still, she pondered the notion, and Ice took advantage of the silence to take a step toward her. This time, Lily let her.

"Imagine a family," Ice said with some pathos, "who accepts you and loves you and appreciates everything you bring to the table. You have always been the smart one. Not Grayson."

"How do you know my brother?"

"I know many, many things. For example, unlike Carl, who is a true psychopath with absolutely no conscience, you do have something you're scared of."

Lily's pulse ticked up a notch as her skin began to tingle. "I'm not—"

"Scared of anything?" Ice interrupted as she took a step closer. "You're lying. You're scared of what you might meet on that bridge. The thing that bubbles under your skin. The thing that pulses in your head and won't let go until your freezer is full."

Lily felt the awful thing beginning to gurgle in her belly.

Ice gently placed her hand on Lily's knife and lowered it. "I know you don't want to meet that thing on the bridge. Because you know and I know, you will lose to its power over you."

Ice backed away as Lily's shallow breathing quickened.

"What do you want?" Lily asked.

"I want to help you, which helps us."

The slinky blonde pulled a necklace out of her pocket. It had a skinny leather band with a small piece of flat bone hanging from it.

Lily leaned forward. "Is that from an animal?"

"A wolf."

Ice closed her eyes and began chanting nonsensically, moving her hand slowly back and forth over the bone. Lily gaped as every wave of the woman's hand created a new line on the bone, culminating in a symbol.

Lily asked, "What is that?"

Ice opened her eyes and handed Lily the necklace. Lily took it, surprised by how warm it felt in her hands. The etched symbol was a straight line with a series of three x's down its stem.

"Beautiful," Lily whispered.

"It's a rune of protection."

"A rune?"

"Norse magic. Powerful. But specific. You can only use it for its intended purpose. I created it to get you through this trial, but when you do, you bring us the dagger."

"And if I don't?"

Ice's piercing eyes thinned to slits. "Then you'll die. Either on that bridge or once I find you again on the outside." Relaxing a little, she said, "Of course, if you take my help, and bring us the dagger, you'll be part of our family. A hero, even. Beloved."

Lily thumbed the symbol. *A family.* She bobbed her chin in agreement.

Ice said, "Good. Put it on."

Lily looped the leather strap around her neck. The bone felt warm against her chest, and the pulsing that had started in Lily's gut retreated. *Maybe there is another way to make it stop.*

Lily considered her situation for a moment. "How can I trust you?"

"How can you afford not to?" Ice stepped away from Lily, slid her index finger under the waistband of her leather pants, and vanished into the air.

She has powers—real ones. If I work with her, I can figure out how to get them, too. Lily felt deliciously deadly as she marched onto the bridge.

When the magical boundaries went up around her, the murderous urge inside her began to pulse and move. Gripping her stomach, she bent forward as the thing slithered from her gut and worked its way up her throat. Retching, she grabbed her neck as it crossed into her mouth. She coughed out a kitten-sized black lizard-looking thing with sharp fangs and slits for eyes.

"Oh my God." Lily lurched away in fear, tumbling onto her back and scurrying in a crabwalk away from the creature.

It hissed as it clawed the planks, coming toward her. Without warning, it veered off the side of the bridge and splashed into the water below. Lily jumped up and cautiously peered over the edge. The inky water was still.

Too still.

She pulled her knife and crept toward the other side of the bridge. Breathing fast, her wide eyes were vigilant. Her other hand slowly reached up to her neck and grabbed the bone, which warmed at her touch.

The creature sprang from the water. It was now as big as a house with dripping fangs and glowing green eyes.

"No!" Lily screamed.

As the monster with razor-sharp claws came down on her, she squeezed the necklace and was blinded by a light. When she blinked her eyes open, Carl's smug smile greeted her.

In response, her lips stretched into a Cheshire-cat grin.

She let go of the necklace and flexed her body with a new sense of pride. "Nothing can stop me."

30

I'm Gonna Go to Hell

As the group stood around the boulder, Fin considered the bright blue glow between the rock formations at the top of the hill that only she and Grayson could see. She glanced his way.

Grayson said, "So, anything that passes through the rock goal posts before the boulder—"

"Bursts into flames." Dawson pushed his glasses higher on his nose.

Grayson tossed a questioning look to Fin. "And our strength doesn't work?"

"It works on everything but the boulder."

Grayson walked up to the giant rock and tried to pick it up, but it wouldn't budge. He tried pushing it but could only move it a little before it spun in place. Stepping out of the way, he let it roll back and said, "That's no good."

Dawson said, "It's like this place cancels out our strength against the boulder. Like, however strong we are collectively, the boulder is equally heavy, so it's always a struggle to push it."

Grayson walked around the stone obstacle. He peered up at the rock pillars and back to the boulder before asking Fin, "What if we pull it?"

They looked at him like he'd sprouted a second head that looked like Einstein.

Dawson plucked his chin. "Actually, that's a good thought. Amon may not have anticipated a group versus one or two people. That could mean there's a magical loophole?"

"But if we pull it, we'd reach the top before the boulder and burst into flames." Fin sighed.

"We could just jump aside," said Marci.

The group turned to her and considered her proposition.

"She's right," said Boone. "We can pull it almost all the way, get the momentum—"

"And jump to the sides at the last minute," said Jonesy.

"Let it roll past the posts," said Grayson.

"And we'll follow right behind," said Dawson.

Fin could feel their eyes boring into her for affirmation. *Just like Auci said. The only way through is together.*

"Yeah," said Fin. "Sounds like the right plan."

"Hang on." Dawson ran over to the bodies on the sides of the hill and studied them for a moment. Eventually he said, "Okay, I think I might understand the arrows. The boulder must be the trigger for everything. So, maybe, once the boulder crosses a certain place, arrows start shooting from the sides. Look at the patterns on their bodies, Fin, and where the arrows start. About two feet past where we've gotten."

Fin studied the bodies. "I see that." She inspected the sides of the hill and noticed an intermittent blue glow tingeing the rocks that lined either side of the hill all the way to the top. "You walked up there and nothing happened, right?"

Dawson nodded.

Fin stared at the bloody proposition. "So, the only way to survive getting to the top is to be in front of the boulder, use the momentum to roll it through, then cross immediately after it. Virtually impossible."

"Impossible if you were alone," Dawson said before a pensive look crossed his face.

Fin gave a nod and turned to the group. "Alright. We pull, jump, and cross."

"We need rope then," said Boone. "Dawson?" When the librarian didn't react, Boone called out, "Dawson?"

They turned to Dawson, who was investigating the scene and murmuring, "It's too easy."

Stepping toward him, Fin asked, "How so?"

"You really think it'll be that simple? Just pull it? It's a Sisyphus curse. Sisyphus pushed. Plus, everything we've done so far has required blood or sacrifice of some sort. If we only pulled, we're not Sisyphus, and what would be sacrificed? Nothing."

Frustrated, Fin asked, "So, what are you saying? Someone has to push?"

"I think that's what activates it," said Dawson. "And since the magic seems to only counteract the strength of the person pushing it, then pulling it is what will get it up the hill and keep us alive."

An eerie quiet descended on the group as they all contemplated what it would mean for only one person to push.

The arrows. Fin looked at Grayson and could see that he understood the implication.

His eyes glistened as he said, "I'll do it. I'll push it."

Nellie gasped. "But, no, that would mean . . ."

Fin raised a cautionary hand and took a step toward him. "That's a death sentence. If we get a mortal wound, we won't heal. You know that from your mom's death."

Grayson swept his hand in an arc, indicating everyone. "Ain't none of you got the body size or strength to push that thing alone, 'cept me, once it gets moving. And it'll cancel me out anyway, which will help you." He waved a hand at Fin.

"Grayson," Fin said quietly.

"You gotta live," Grayson said softly. "You're the only one who can stop Lily. We all know it."

"Grayson, no." Nellie's eyes welled with tears.

As Grayson walked up to Dawson, he said, "I know you brought rope, adventure man. Give it to me."

Dawson looked wide-eyed at Fin.

Shit. "Grayson . . ." she said gently.

"You know it's true," he murmured and held out his hand. "Rope."

Dawson cast a stricken look at Fin, who reluctantly bobbed her head once. He dug through his bag for the rope before handing it to Grayson.

"No!" Nellie yelled. "Please don't do this." She tried to run to her half-brother, but Jonesy held her back.

Jonesy said, "Let him do it, Nellie. He can heal. You can't."

Nellie's body sagged as she relented. Grayson didn't look at her or anyone else as he tied one end of the rope around the boulder and the other end around Fin's waist.

"Hang on, we don't even know if this will work," said Fin. "Let's just, uh, test it, okay?"

Grayson shrugged. "Okay."

As Grayson stepped back, Fin noticed everyone exchanging worried glances as she turned and walked up the hill. When the rope was taut, she hunched down and pulled. Her body tightened and she used her legs, but it wouldn't budge.

Oh, shit. "Let me try again," she yelled without looking back, not wanting to see the disappointment on their faces.

She assumed the position, tightened her body, and pulled. This time she moved easily. Cackling in relief, she stopped and turned back to the group, but their faces were grim.

"What? It worked."

Grayson stepped out from behind the boulder. "I was pushing."

Fin deflated.

Boone gave Grayson a thoughtful side glance, then jumped into action with a clap of his hands. "We need to protect your lungs, Grayson. Neck. Head."

Grayson's eyebrows shot up in surprise. "Oh, okay. How?"

Nellie whimpered. "Fin?"

Fin untied the rope around her waist and ran down the hill to her bag. She pulled her bulletproof vest out and walked over to Grayson. To protect his sides, she shimmied it around his chest so that the head part of the vest was at his back and the bottom of it was at the front, giving him thick protection on the sides. She did her best to maneuver the Velcro straps to make it stay. "It won't stop every arrow, unfortunately. It's made for bullets. But it's better than nothing."

Grayson's eyes, gentle now, scanned Fin's face. "Thank you."

She gave one last tug at the straps and gave him a crisp nod, which he returned.

"His head." After looking around, Dawson ran to a rock that was about the right size. "Fin, can you hollow this out to make a helmet?"

"Maybe. But I'd need a tool or something."

"Your knife?"

Staring off into the distance, Fin absentmindedly spun her bracelet. "No, that would break the blade." She stiffened as a thought struck her. Peering down at her bracelet, she whispered, "Help."

A bright blue force exploded from the bracelet and knocked everyone to the ground as the caterpillar popped out and wriggled in front of her.

"Whoa," she said as she slowly picked herself up. *It wasn't that powerful last time.*

"Is it stronger?" Dawson asked as he stood. Intrigued, he walked over and inspected it. "It's not green anymore, either."

The caterpillar was now orange and slightly bigger. Its other markings and double eyes remained the same.

Marci peered at it as she stood and inched closer. "Wow. What is that?"

"Is that a caterpillar?" Jonesy chuckled, getting up along with everyone else.

"Yeah, so?" She looked at Dawson and lowered her voice. "It doesn't look the same. Is it a different caterpillar? If it's a representation of what's inside me, why would it be different?"

He studied it more closely. "I think it's the same caterpillar. It's just changing." He gave Fin a cheeky grin. "Becoming a butterfly?"

She straightened her shoulders as a smile tugged at the corners of her lips.

The caterpillar took off.

"Wait!" Fin followed as it dove toward one of the corpses, and she groaned. "Oh, come on."

The orange spirit animal hovered over a dead man's worn leather bag. She grabbed it and opened it. *Cigarettes, lighter, cash, beans, knife, more survival gear. Aha!* She yanked out a pry bar. "This should work."

As she stood, the caterpillar dissolved into a cloud of turquoise dust that was sucked back into her bracelet. "Thank you." She ran back to the group and made quick work of the rock with the metal bar. When she was done, she handed the mishappen stone helmet to Grayson.

She said, "I mean, it's really stupid, but it'll help."

Grayson took it with a lopsided smirk and put it over his head.

"You look like a video game football player," said Marci.

They all chuckled, cutting the tension.

Grayson grinned but said, "If I don't make—"

"We'll see you at the top," Fin interrupted as she slapped his shoulders like a determined hockey coach. "Keep your shoulders up around your neck. We're gonna fucking do this. Everybody to the front of the boulder."

Fin grabbed her gear, then led the charge as she tied the rope around her waist and Grayson got into position. Everyone else grabbed the rope, faced the boulder, and prepared to pull.

Fin shouted, "Listen up. Nobody stop. Keep going until we get through those stone columns. We may only get one shot. And with Lily right behind us, it's now or never. Everybody get it?"

The group gave a chorus of agreement.

"All right, here we go. On the count of three," Fin yelled. "One." As she lined up like a football player on the field, she glanced over at the bridge portal. It flickered blue as a grim-looking man with unkempt, curly, red hair stepped through.

"Two."

Everybody dug their feet into the ground except Jonesy, who stepped away. He stared at the freckle-faced man with the evil grin. "I hate clowns."

Fin said, "Jonesy, leave him. We need you to pull."

"Don't go," Nellie said. "The arrows!"

The intruder pulled a knife and started toward them, before coming to a sudden stop. He cocked his head as he took in the situation and slid the knife back into his pocket.

Jonesy returned to his place on the rope.

"Three!" Fin yelled.

The group moved much faster now with Grayson pushing while they pulled.

Keep going, Grayson. "Faster!" Fin yelled as the first magical arrows whistled through the air. "Grayson, watch out!"

The sounds of flying arrows, grinding stone, and grunting people filled Fin's ears for several difficult moments. When they were more than halfway up, she peered over her shoulder at the red-haired man, who was watching them intensely.

Shit. We're teaching him how to do it. "Go! Faster!" Fin shouted.

A few seconds later, Jonesy slipped, dropped to the ground, and an arrow caught his thigh. Swearing, he jumped up, grabbed the rope, and gritted his teeth in pain as he kept pulling.

Eyes wide, Fin asked, "Jonesy, are you—"

"Help!" Nellie screamed.

Fin whipped her head around as a zombie hand protruding from the ground pulled Nellie down.

"Nellie!" Fin shouted.

The boulder slid backward unexpectedly, forcing everyone pulling the rope to stumble. Taking advantage of the group's setback, mottled hands shot from the earth, grabbed each of them, and dragged them to the ground.

"Grayson!" Fin pushed with her legs, feeling the whole weight of the boulder. It sat stubbornly in place, refusing to move forward but willing to roll backwards if Fin didn't hold on for dear life. *What happened to Grayson?* "Dawson!"

Although the zombie hands were jerking him down, he yanked the stone pen from his pocket.

What the fuck is he doing?

Dawson let out a primal yell as he swung the pen into the air. It transformed into a glowing blue-green sword.

Surprised relief surged through Fin. *Auci's got a gift for tools.* "Kick their asses, Dawson!"

Dawson cut off the hand that was holding his ankle, and it burst into turquoise dust. He freed everyone from their undead attackers like a warrior with a chip on his shoulder.

He yelled to the kids, "The boulder!"

They ran, grabbed the rope, and hauled on it with all their might. The boulder started to roll up the hill again.

"Keep going!" *Grayson must be okay.*

Collectively, they pulled it higher and higher.

Fin bellowed, "Get ready to jump to the side!"

They picked up the pace near the goal posts.

"Almost there . . ." Fin shouted.

Coming dangerously close to the blue field, she yelled, "Now!"

The pullers jumped to the side as Grayson shoved it through the rock formations. As they tumbled through after him, a bright white light blinded them.

Everyone tumbled onto soft grass into what felt like a sauna. Fin blinked her eyes open as she stood up and looked around her. They had been transported to a rainforest with trees taller than New York office buildings.

Fin sighed. "Oh, come on. I'm so much better with urban jungles." She slapped away a bug bigger than her thumb before peering back at the group. Everyone stood up, bruised and battered, but okay with the exception of Jonesy.

When she rushed over to him, he said, "I'll be okay." Although clearly in pain, he held up his hands for her to stop. He slowly pulled the arrow out of his thigh, wincing as his flesh released it.

Nellie helped him by slapping away more bugs.

"It's okay, Fin. Find Grayson," Jonesy said as he laid back in pain.

"All right, but once I get him squared away, I'll be back to bandage that leg."

Nellie gave Fin a haunted look. "I know how to do it."

Fucking Russell. "Oh, okay." *I hate that you know how, Mom.*

Fin untied the rope around her waist and investigated the area behind them. She found a trail of blood and followed it through the grass and trees to a bloody and barely breathing Grayson. As footsteps followed her, she turned and said, "No. Stay there."

"What is it?" Boone asked.

"It's okay, just stay there. Dawson, grab the first aid kit from my bag and bring it over."

Dawson nodded and pulled Boone back.

Fin walked to Grayson, who had collapsed onto his stomach. She knelt by his right side, knocking away a slimy centipede that had made its way onto his back. *He looks like a pin cushion.* His wheezing meant the arrow lodged under his armpit had penetrated in his lung. *Can he survive that?*

His stone helmet lay beside him in the grass. She gingerly pulled out the arrows stuck in the bulletproof vest. A couple of them had punched their way through the material at the lower part of his sides. He turned his head to face her, laying it back on the ground as he struggled to breathe.

"It's," he wheezed, "healing."

"But—" She stopped, not knowing how much she should say.

They locked eyes for a moment.

"It'll . . . heal . . . enough."

Dawson appeared with the first aid kit but skidded to a halt behind Fin. "My God." He cleared his throat as he wiped sweat from his face with his forearm.

Fin took the first aid gear. "Let's take the arrows out, except for this one." She pointed to the bolt under his arm.

Together, they removed the arrows from Grayson's body one by one. The projectiles were lodged in the vest and all along his arms and legs. One was near his neck in the meat of his upper back, and another was in his lower back where the vest didn't cover. But the one lodged in his lung seemed to be the most perilous. Fin snapped that arrow's shaft near the entry point. She and Dawson rolled Grayson over onto his back before sitting back on their haunches to wipe the sweat from their eyes.

"Give me that rag there. The large one." Fin pointed at it. "Then, can you go find something that will protect this from being pushed in any further. Like a cover. Maybe something metal?"

"On it." Dawson ran back to the others.

Fin carefully slung Grayson's right arm up and away from the wound. "So, you don't accidentally bang it into your own chest."

"Thank you," he said.

She surveyed his wounds and was relieved that most of them were almost completely healed. Plus, his breathing had improved.

She asked, "How do you know your lung is healing?"

"I don't know how to describe it." He was still a little short of breath but able to speak in complete sentences now. "I can just tell. It's healed as much as it can."

A wave a gratitude brought a sheen of tears to her eyes. "What you just did for us was—"

"Don't," he interrupted. He took a moment as his breathing caught, then evened out. He struggled for enough air to say, "I done some bad things. Now…I'm just tryin' to be the person…Nellie thinks I am. Be better…than Boone thinks I am."

"He's just an angry kid."

"Ain't we all?" He gave her a guilty grin.

She huffed a laugh and wiped the perspiration from his forehead.

"Fin?"

"Yeah?"

"I'm scared…I'm gonna go to hell," he gasped with a tremble of fear in his voice.

"Yeah, well. Ain't we all?"

They shared an easy laugh.

Dawson ran up with a small metal bowl. "Clara Belle left this with the cooking gear." He held up duct tape. "And this fixes everything."

After taking the supplies, Fin wrapped most of tape around Grayson's chest to hold the bowl in place.

Dawson admired her work. "We should get moving. That ginger saw how we got up the hill."

"I saw that," said Fin.

"Yeah. He'll be right behind us." He tapped on the metal bowl. "Feel like it won't move?"

Grayson gave a nod. "Thanks." Fin and Dawson gently helped Grayson roll to the side, get on his knees, and stand with a wince. Once he caught his breath and balance, Grayson asked, "What'd the guy look like?"

Dawson answered, "Wild red hair. Freckles."

"Evil grin," Fin added.

"That's probably Carl, Lily's guy," said Grayson.

"Great." Fin scrubbed her dirty hands on her pants. "So, he's with Lily. And they're right behind us."

Boone walked over to them. "All right, we're ready. And Jonesy's all fixed up. Which way do we go?"

Fin glanced at the kids, impressed how sturdy and capable they were becoming on this journey. *Auci said this was for their benefit. Why? Why do they need to know these things?*

Boone walked up to Grayson's left side and slid a shoulder under his armpit. "I'll help ya."

"A'ight," Grayson said, accepting the truce.

Jonesy ran over to the other side of Grayson and grabbed hold of his belt. "I'll help steady you."

"Thanks." Grayson gratefully leaned into their help.

Fin said, "Dawson, take the front. I'll stay behind."

"Okay," said Dawson. "Let's move then."

The group started walking. Marci walked up ahead with Dawson while Jonesy, Boone, and Grayson were sandwiched in the middle, and Nellie fell back to Fin's side.

Fin said, "I'm so glad you're okay. I was worried when I saw your trial."

"I know. I was worried, too." Nellie gave Fin a side glance. "What was your trial?"

Fin stared forward, managing a bittersweet smile. "I had to face down some inner demons."

Nellie eyed her with an air of patient expectation.

Fin caved, "I've been obsessively searching for answers about why my parents abandoned me. It's, uh, it's poisoned my life in some ways, I guess. I suppose I need to learn to be okay with not having all the answers."

Nellie snorted as she slapped at a creepy crawler on her leg. "It seems like you have all the answers."

Fin shook her head. "I don't."

They were quiet for a moment as they moved through the jungle.

"If it helps at all," Nellie said, "I'm sure your mama wanted you."

Fin's eyes pricked with tears as she looked at her mother. "Why would you say that?"

"Because." Nellie shrugged. "You're awesome. You're exactly the kind of daughter any mama would want."

Fin's eyes misted over. "Thank you," she whispered.

"I mean, if it's okay with you, someday—and I mean a long way away 'cause I got stuff I wanna do—but someday, if I have a daughter, I'd love to name her Fin. If that's okay with you."

Fin stopped and yanked Nellie into a hug, holding her tight.

Nellie hugged her back. "Wow. I guess it's okay then."

"It's more than okay." Fin gave one more squeeze and pulled away to quickly wipe her eyes. "Uh, yeah, we should get moving. Like, faster."

"Okay."

Nellie gave her a strange stare, but Fin kept her eyes forward.

As they picked up their speed, Nellie said, "What a weird couple of days. This family is somethin' else. I swear they'll be the death of me." Nellie shook her head with a snarky laugh and jogged up next to Jonesy.

Fin had a sinking feeling that perhaps she was exactly right.

31

What Did You Give Me?

As the group walked through the jungle along the river's edge, snakes slithered nearby, staring at them but not approaching them. Several large spiders crept out from the foliage, their hundreds of eyes keeping watch.

Marci walked with Dawson, leading the way through the treacherous terrain. She peered at him. *What is it about him? There's something so familiar.*

"You don't seem scared of much," Dawson said.

"No, just curious. Adventurous, I guess. That's what my mom says. She's like that, too."

"What does she do?" asked Dawson.

"I don't know for sure." Marci frowned. "They seem to travel a lot. Historical stuff. She goes to Ireland a lot."

"Ireland?" His face brightened. "Whereabouts?"

"Not sure. She just brought me back a book though. A couple days ago, before breakfast. From a library there."

As she glanced at Dawson, his face turned pale. "Dawson? Are you okay?"

He gave a favorable grunt as he adjusted his glasses. "Was, uh, the book . . . I mean, what was the book?"

"I didn't really look at it before I left. But I think it was green. Old. Dusty." She grinned at Dawson, but he gave her the strangest look.

"What's your mom's name?" he asked.

"Sophie O'Sullivan."

Dawson stopped in his tracks as she kept going.

After a few steps, she stopped and turned to him. "Really, are you okay?"

He nodded vigorously, glanced back at Fin, and started walking again.

He's so strange but kind. I like him. Marci also glanced behind them. Boone gave a side-eye glance to Jonesy, who had one hand on Grayson's belt to steady him, and the other wrapped in Nellie's hand. *He's starting to let go. Good.*

As if on cue, Boone looked at her and grinned from under the weight of Grayson's left arm.

She tucked back a sheepish smile before facing forward. Dawson kept glancing at his feet, so she looked down, too.

Hundreds of centipedes slithered around the group's feet as they walked. The insects' dark maroon bodies artfully dodged the group's heavy steps as their cream-colored legs pushed them along.

Almost like they're walking with us.

"Anyone else sweating profusely? Thirsty?" Dawson wiped away the sweat as he glanced at everyone.

Boone repeatedly tugged on his shirt, creating his own breeze. "It feels like it keeps getting hotter."

"That's because it is." Fin wiped her forehead with her arm. "Dawson, this feels like more than just a hot jungle. It feels oppressive. Like magic. Any thoughts?"

He pulled out his green notebook and wrote something.

How many notes can you make? Marci leaned over to see what he was scribbling.

But he snapped the book closed and adjusted his cracked glasses, which immediately slid back down his slick nose. He cocked his head as he examined her. "Your face is quite red."

"Yours, too."

They looked at each other before checking out the others. Sweat poured from all of them, their clothing soaked, their skin glistening.

Dawson addressed Fin, waving the book at her. "It's not a trial. It's just an added element. Like the arrows. Something to make it harder. A heat spell."

Marci reached into her bag. "I've got some water for us." She grabbed the bottle, opened it, and peered in. "Oh no."

"What?" Dawson asked.

Marci tipped the bottle upside down, but nothing came out. "The water's gone. But, how? It's a thermos."

Everyone grabbed their water canteens and thermoses from their bags. All of them were empty.

"Grayson!" Boone yelled.

They spun around as Grayson fell over unconscious, taking Boone down with him.

The river. Marci ran to the crystal clear stream, kneeled, and dipped her bottle into it.

Boone yelled, "Hurry, Marci!"

"Coming." *Almost full.*

Nellie screamed, "Marci, look out!"

A spray of water hit Marci's face as a thirty-foot reticulated python lunged from the river. Its fangs sunk into her right shoulder, and she let out a blood-curdling scream. The snake's diamond-painted body wrapped around her chest and squeezed.

"Oh my God," she gasped.

Dawson and Fin sprinted to her and tried to pry it off.

Dawson said in a rush, "Nellie, get rubbing alcohol from the first aid kit. Hurry."

Marci gasped for air. Her lips and fingertips tingled. Her head felt like it might explode from the pressure. *Boone.*

"Grab the tail!" Fin yelled.

She sounds like she's one hundred miles away.

Fin, Boone, and Jonesy worked together to uncoil the tail.

Nellie screamed, "Move!"

Everything was blurry. She could just make out Nellie's shape. Then something brown appeared. *Fin's hair.* She felt herself slipping away from this world. *I'm dying.*

Just as she was about to pass out, the sharp odor of alcohol hit her nose the second before it stung her shoulder. The snake released its grip and uncoiled rapidly. As her body hit the ground, she heard the python slosh back into the river.

"Marci!"

Marci couldn't tell who was shouting at her as hands grabbed her wrists.

"Is there a pulse?"

I'm alive, you guys. I swear.

Finally, Marci sucked in a lungful of air, and the world around her came into focus.

"Thank God," Boone said.

Marci's lips turned up at the corners. *He cares about me.* "That was a bummer," she whispered.

"Yeah, it was." Relief replaced the worry on Boone's face. "Are you okay?"

"Yeah." Marci tried to move, but it was painful. "Uh."

Fin placed a gentle but restraining hand on her. "Just hang on a second." Fin peered under Marci's shirt and checked her injuries.

"How bad is it?" Boone asked.

"Pretty bad bruising on the chest." Fin pulled the shirt off Marci's shoulder area and she and Boone both winced. "Ooo, shoulder is . . . Yeah, that's no good."

Nellie shuddered as she walked up and caught a look at Marci's shoulder. She handed Fin the first aid kit.

Fin took it with a nod of thanks. "We can sling her shoulder. Get some antiseptic on it and stop the bleeding. Chest is—yeah—beat up. Let's wrap it and get going. As soon as we're outta here, she needs to go straight to a hospital."

Marci glanced around as Fin started working on her. "Is Grayson—"

"He'll be fine," said Fin. "We found water."

"From the river?" Marci asked.

Nellie's eyes twinkled like she knew a secret. "Not exactly."

Trying to focus on something besides the pain, Marci asked, "What do you mean?"

"It came from a rock." Jonesy chuckled as he stepped up. It was quickly replaced by a grimace when he saw Marci's shoulder.

Dawson walked up and handed a stone to Boone, who held it over Marci's mouth and said, "Open up."

She did. Cold water hit her throat, and she drank. It was the best thing she had ever tasted. "That's incredible." Marci sucked in air from the pain as Fin worked on her shoulder.

"Hold still, we're almost done," said Fin.

By the time everyone had a drink, Marci was wrapped up and standing.

"We need to get going." Fin reached out to steady her. "Marci, can you walk?"

"I'll be okay." She leaned against Boone as Grayson leaned against Jonesy.

"We, uh . . ." Fin tapered off as she glanced behind them. "We need to go."

Marci glanced over Boone's shoulder at the outline of what looked like two people in the distance.

"Let's go, everybody," said Fin. "Now. Quickly. Stay together."

The pack hurried through the woods parallel to the river as a slow drizzle began to coat them with raindrops. When they rounded the next river bend, a gorgeous ravine with a sparkling waterfall on the other side came into view. By the time they got close, the rain had become a storm and had picked up to the point that the large drops felt like enemy gunfire. It pelted down on the coattails of a gusting wind.

"Shit," said Boone and Dawson at the same time as the storm began to roar around them.

The group hunched and tightened their bodies against the onslaught.

As they pushed forward, Marci could tell that the river went over a waterfall just ahead. Its water plunged down into what sounded like a rushing river. The face of the farthest side of the ravine was rocky and dangerous with an opposing waterfall that looked like it was at least as high as the tall skyscrapers she'd seen in her mom's travel books.

Fin pointed at the opposing waterfall. "That's it. That's where we need to go."

How does she know that? God my chest hurts.

The rain attacked from every side, and lightning struck near them with a thunderous bang, causing them to jump.

Fin shouted over the deluge, "The dagger is there. Behind the waterfall on the other side. There's a cave dug into the rock wall. Can you see it?"

They all squinted through the onslaught to the other side and nodded. It was barely visible, but Marci could see there was some kind of opening.

"How do you know it's there?" Boone yelled over the storm.

"I just know."

Grayson hollered as best as he could, "I see it, too, Fin."

Marci eyed them. *See what?*

As if on cue, Nellie hollered, "See what?"

The banging skies unleashed a riotous downpour as Fin yelled, "Remember when you put your thumbs on the knot and it glowed?"

Heads bobbed as the group tried to keep moving a little at a time.

"I can always see that whenever there's magic around," Fin shouted. "That's how I know. The cave. It's glowing. Super bright."

"How the hell do we get over there?" Boone yelled.

After checking behind her, Fin spun around. "We have to go. Now!"

Everyone glanced back to see Lily approaching like a lion with Carl in tow.

But as Fin, Dawson, and Nellie jumped forward, the rest hesitated. Jonesy was hindered by helping Grayson, who was struggling to breathe. And Boone was slowed down by Marci, who could barely stand because of the pain in her chest.

I need a hospital. Marci looked behind her at Lily, who seemed to be advancing at a pace that didn't seem human. *Oh my God, what is she?*

Thunder shook the skies as they arrived at the point where the river tumbled over the edge of the waterfall. Unfortunately, the woods also ended in a cliff, so they couldn't go any further without falling over the rocky rim. The storm's gale-force winds almost pushed them backward as small chunks of hail left red splotches on their exposed skin.

What the hell are we going to do?

"Your whistle," Fin yelled at Boone. She pointed to her own neck to get Boone to look at his. "Your whistle. Blow it."

Boone fought the wind for the rain-slick whistle, finally grabbing it and blowing into it as hard he could. But no sound came out.

Shit.

"It's broken," Boone shouted.

"It's not," Dawson yelled. "Just wait."

Although it didn't seem possible, the storm grew even more intense.

"Grab something!" Fin clutched a thick branch with one hand and Nellie's hand with the other.

Slipping, Jonesy landed on his back with Grayson alongside him. Marci sympathized with Grayson's pained expression. Her injuries from the python stabbed her nerves as Boone grabbed her and pinned her against the nearest tree, his body pushing her back painfully into the bark. She glanced at Fin, who was shielding Nellie and Dawson with her body. Miraculously, she was able to hold both of them steady despite the torrential forces fighting against her.

"Hang on," Boone yelled.

Lily arrived before Carl and grabbed Boone by the throat.

A flapping of wings drowned out the storm as a bright burst of blue fluttered through the air. Marci gaped at the enormous, majestic bird hovering vertically in midair as its red and blue wings flapped at its sides. The storm combined with the massive gusts from the bird's wings, with a few punches from Boone, forced Carl and Lily back down to the river and out of sight once more.

Marci's eyes bulged with awe at the creature, sensing its power. *Beautiful.*

The bird landed in front of Boone but was almost twice his size. It bent its head to Boone. He arched away at first, protecting Marci, but after a slight hesitation, he allowed their foreheads to touch. It cooed and closed its eyes. A moment later, it turned to Marci and slowly opened its mouth repeatedly.

Does it want to eat me? She rocked back on her heels and cast a nervous glance at Boone. "I don't understand," she choked out past the pain in her chest.

The huge bird repeated the action again and scooped its head forward like it was pushing something toward her.

Marci shook her head in confusion. *Wait, does it want me to open my mouth?* Feeling a little silly under Boone's curious stare, she slowly opened her mouth.

The creature bowed its head over Marci's mouth and shed a tear into it.

Oh God, that's salty. Marci swallowed and squinched her face as Boone reflected her own disgust.

The bird waited, then pointed its beak toward Marci's chest.

As the cold wind and rain whipped her face, a warmth spread across Marci's chest as her breathing improved. *I feel better.* She peeked down her shirt and gasped. The wound was almost gone.

"I'm healing!"

"What?" Boone yelled.

She tugged a little at her shirt exposing a portion of her shoulder to Boone, who gasped in surprise. They both looked at the bird with fresh awe. "H-How did . . ." she stuttered.

Fin spoke to the animal. "Blue! The cave!" She pointed to the other side of the canyon.

The phoenix bobbed its head, settled down on the ground, and extended its wing like a ramp.

"Get on!" Fin waved frantically at the teenagers.

Marci and Boone climbed aboard, straddling its shoulders above its wings, and grabbed onto the feathers for dear life. The huge bird lifted them into the air and soared across the ravine. Marci gripped the creature with a fierce panic and tried not to think about falling hundreds of feet to the racing river below. It flew down to the opening of the cave and hovered in the air as it lowered its neck and head like a ramp to the ledge that was thick by the entrance but tapered outward. Boone and Marci looked down at the river below.

"Oh my God." Marci clutched the animal tighter.

Boone said, "We have to, Marci. We can't leave them alone with Lily over there. Hurry!"

He nudged her with his body. "You can do this, Marci! You're the bravest girl I know. Come on! I'm right behind you."

Somehow when he said it, she believed it. Focusing on his body against hers, she began to crawl down the bird's thick neck, holding on with her thighs and arms as Boone kept her steady at the back. When she got to the head, she extended her hands to the ledge and begin to slowly walk them outward as her body followed. *Don't look down.* When she was more than halfway onto the ledge, she rolled onto the rocky surface and let out a held breath as Boone rolled next to her, grasping her into a hug as the bird lifted into the storm and headed back for the rest of the group.

When she held onto him like he was a life preserver, he said, "You're okay. I got you."

A warmth tingled across her body in a way that made her want to look at his lips. She pulled back, surveying their soft texture, and they parted at her stare. Memories of how her body came alive when he'd kissed her at the campsite crashed through her.

If I'm gonna die, I wanna kiss him again first.

She quickly pressed her lips to his until he kissed her back.

Once they pulled away from each other, Boone said, "I'm never gonna wanna stop doing that."

"Yeah." She pressed into him.

But a gust of wind broke the spell. They glanced up to see Jonesy and Dawson sandwiching Grayson.

Dawson cried out, "A little help!"

Boone and Marci carefully stood together on the ledge and shimmied over to help Jonesy off first. With Dawson helping from behind, they carefully slid Grayson off the bird in a coordinated effort that rivaled any gameday cheerleading routine. Once Grayson was stabilized on the ledge, the bird leapt into the air to retrieve Fin and Nellie. They gingerly navigated themselves and

Grayson the few feet into the cave and lay him down to rest as the four of them caught their breath.

"Nellie." Jonesy ran back out onto the ledge, followed by Boone.

Dawson walked up to Marci. "May I look at your shoulder?"

"Okay," she said, knowing he wanted to write about the magic in his little book.

"Remarkable," he said as he scribbled. "And your chest and back?"

"Completely healed."

"What did that feel like? To be healed?"

"Warm," she said as Fin and Nellie stepped into the cave followed by Jonesy and Boone.

Marci let out a relieved, "Nellie!"

Nellie ran over and embraced her friend as Fin plopped down on a rock. Everyone peered at each other. Without warning, laughter spread like wild fire through the group, disrupting the tension of the moment and ushering in a well-deserved breather. When the laughter died down, Marci listened to the heavy rush of the falls. The sound blotted out the torrential downpour just outside the quiet, dark cave, which was barely lit at the entrance by the sunlight seeping through the storm clouds.

Boone held up the whistle. "Dawson, what did you give me?"

"Help." Dawson puffed out his chest a little.

Apparently realizing Dawson wasn't going to elaborate, Boone asked, "So, what was that thing?"

Dawson answered, "A phoenix."

"Wait, aren't those mythical creatures?" Jonesy asked. "I mean, they don't actually exist."

"Apparently, they do," Marci said.

Dawson changed the subject. "Fin, you're sure the dagger is here?"

"Positive." She glanced at Grayson, who nodded.

Jonesy asked, "Do you think there are more traps?"

Dawson and Fin traded meaningful glances.

"Probably," Dawson said. "I don't know."

"I guess we're going to find out," Fin said, standing up and pulling out a rectangular, thin, shiny black device from her pocket. She tapped it a few times, and a beam of light shot out of it.

"What is that?" Marci asked.

Jonesy followed that up with his own excited question. "Yeah, is that a flashlight or something?"

Fin answered, "Yeah, a flashlight."

She walked away from the subject, and everyone followed.

In the back of the group, Marci turned around and glanced out the entrance, across the river, and to the opposite twin falls. Although it looked a little blurry through the rain, she could just make out Lily, Carl, and what looked like a giant winged scorpion standing behind them in the trees.

She shook her head and looked again, but they were gone. Shrugging, she walked into the cave with the others and prayed they had already found the dagger.

32

I'll Take That

Fin knew that Grayson was the only other person who could see the beautiful glow in the cave. Although admittedly her ability to see it was much more powerful. When she had first entered the cave, it was like an electric blue neon sign lit the walls and intensified towards the back. The magic had a bit of a pulse to it, almost a hum. But because everyone else didn't have her special vision, she turned on her cell phone's light. Thankfully, they didn't press her about the advanced technology.

They already know so much. Except for the time traveling. I don't think they're ready for that just yet.

As they moved further into the cave, Fin was dazzled by the color intensifying into varying shades of sapphire and turquoise. It felt like she was underwater with waves of cerulean light pushing in and pulling out like the tides. The rhythm echoed in her heart like a second beat luring her toward the dagger.

She couldn't help but glance at Grayson as the peacefulness of the cave wrapped around her. He was already staring at her, and they shared a moment of reverence.

Facing forward again, Fin pulled up short. "What the hell?"

Just ahead were piles of human bones. Skulls, ribs, feet, hands. All glowing with a turquoise light only she and Grayson could detect.

Nellie skidded to a halt. "Oh, no, no, no."

Everybody stopped and stared.

Jonesy said, "This feels like a bad sign."

"Another trick," said Boone.

Dawson searched the walls, the ceiling, the floor, and near the bones. "I don't see traps or anything."

Fin said, "It's the bones."

She waved at them to follow. They inched forward in wary silence. As they got closer to the pile, it started to move.

"You see that right?" Fin asked.

"Uh, yeah," Dawson replied.

The pile shook as the bones hopped around, but the seven of them kept advancing forward like soldiers on a mission.

"What's happening?" Nellie eyes were wide with fear.

One bony hand shot from the pile and latched on to Dawson's throat, squeezing hard.

"Help . . . me . . ."

Fin tried to pry the phalanges off him, but they were firmly attached. Dawson collapsed as his attempts to yank the hand away failed.

All the bones lurched from the pile and attacked the group. Two hands pinned Nellie to a wall while several feet kicked Boone in the guts. Three skulls chased Jonesy into a corner and started chomping on him as rib bones shackled Grayson's wrists and ankles painfully to the wall. Various bones formed a pinching cage around Marci.

But Fin was spared.

Suddenly, the assault stopped and the bones held each person in their place. Everyone watched in frozen horror as one of the skulls floated slowly through the air and stopped just inches from Fin's nose. She held her breath as the hollow eyes stared at her. The glow illuminating the skull almost glittered with power.

I should feel scared.

She checked in with her emotions and confirmed it wasn't fear she felt; it was power.

The skull tilted down toward her necklace. Reflexively, she reached up and touched it.

Its deep, rumbling voice was laced with intense curiosity as it asked, "Who are you?"

"I'm Fin."

After observing her for a few more seconds, the skull said, "How curious."

The bones gripping the weary travelers disengaged and slowly floated back into a pile.

"You are not of Amon," the skull said as the other bones settled.

Fin said, "No. Well, not exactly."

The skull tilted in approval. "You are more powerful than Amon."

"Wait, what?" Fin asked. "That's impossible."

"Auci is your father." The disembodied head turned to look at Nellie. Fin's heart ticked up as she slowly shook her head. *Don't tell her.* The skull turned back to Fin. "She doesn't know."

The group looked at Nellie before going back to Fin and the skull.

The reanimated skeleton cocked its head. "A life sacrificed has imbued you with a greater power than even Auci could have imagined."

Dread pooled in Fin's stomach. "What does that mean?"

Ignoring her, the skull said, "Despite Amon's spell, I must let you pass. I cannot deny a demi-God with more power than the one who created me."

The severed head bowed to her and floated back to its pile. Once it came to rest on the top, it and the pile of bones shattered into ivory dust.

"Holy shit," she whispered. *How powerful am I?*

The group faced Fin, utter fascination writ large on their faces.

Boone was the first to find his voice. "A demi-God?"

She peered at their curious faces. "Uh…"

Nellie said, "Wait, what did he mean when he looked at me? What don't I know?"

"I—"

"We should keep going." Dawson interrupted, adjusting his glasses. "Lily and Carl may be right behind us."

Jonesy scoffed. "How would they get over the river?"

"I might be able to answer that." Marci squirmed sheepishly.

"How?" Fin asked.

"I took a quick peek across the river before we started in. I don't know what I saw exactly, but it could have been Lily and Carl at the edge of the ravine. And…" Marci paused.

"And?" Fin asked.

"This is gonna sound crazy, but…" She flipped her hands in the air as if she was exasperated with knowing how crazy she sounded. "It looked like there was a scorpion with wings with them."

Fin put her hands on her hips and shook her head. "Not crazy. We need to go right now."

Fin forged ahead going deeper into the cave as the group followed closely behind her. The cavern brightened into the most beautifully ornate room with jewel-colored markings on the walls and golden swirls across the ceiling and stone steps that led down into a small room. The area was lit by a sea of blues emanating from the dagger which floated above a stone podium.

Not far behind Fin, Nellie gasped. "Is that it?"

Dawson walked toward it, slowly reaching out. But his hand was still several inches away when he yelped and jerked it back with a shake. "Right, should have expected that."

Grayson wheezed around his injury and said, "It's Fin's to take."

Dawson stepped away, still shaking out his hand.

Fin approached the stone podium but stopped when she realized the dagger was moving toward her.

"Whoa." Boone stepped back, taking Grayson with him, as the dagger passed by.

Everyone watched with wide eyes as it stopped in front of Fin.

She scrutinized its details. The handle had intricately woven swirls of 14-karat gold that protected what looked like a piece of magical rock from Blue Falls. The stone glowed a rich, deep cobalt with speckles of sea green that had a rust-colored shine.

"Beautiful." Mesmerized by its power, she considered its strange markings. *Might as well be chicken scratch.*

"Take it." Dawson scribbled furiously in his green book.

Fin glanced down at his detailed drawing of the object.

She reached up and gave the handle a tentative touch before fully grasping it. "It's warm." Fin held it for only a moment before confusion burbled up inside her. "Grayson, touch it."

Grayson's brow furrowed as he reached out and laid a gentle finger against the handle. "Hmm."

"You can feel it, right?" she asked. "Like it has—"

"A pulse?"

She nodded. "There's power inside it."

Boone asked, "What does the blade look like?"

Fin stepped away from the hovering group and carefully removed the sheath, revealing a blade made of thick bone streaked with age and rot. Connecting the handle to the blade was a larger, single stone with the same color as the blue-green rock in the handle. When Fin tilted it, the speckled material inside the stone flashed.

"Wow," Dawson said as he continued to sketch.

Fin gave him a moment to finish and then replaced the sheath. She put the dagger inside a small burlap, drawstring pouch that was in the bag slung around her chest.

"We need to get out of here," said Fin.

"Do we go back?" Boone asked.

A shadow crossed the wall, and everyone spun toward the front of the cave.

Standing between them and the exit, Lily said, "I'll take that dagger."

Carl filed in behind her.

She swaggered their way. "You must've forgotten to send that bird back for us."

The group retreated as Lily and Carl stepped down into the room with them.

Lily waved the subject away. "We got our own ride, thanks." She smirked at Fin. "I think your friend Ice sent it to us. Remember her?"

Fin squared her stance, dropping her weight into her knees. "She's no friend of mine."

"She said that, too." Lily flicked a look of disgust at Grayson. "I don't need you anymore, brother. I'm getting a new family. As soon as I get that dagger."

Grayson said, "It belongs to Fin."

"Wrong!" Lily yelled so loud they all jumped. "It belongs to our family line. Gunnar told me that dagger is as much mine as it hers."

Trying to draw Lily's attention away from her injured brother, Fin said, "Only one of us is going to leave with that dagger, Lily."

Rage flushed Lily's face. "You're right. And it's gonna be me."

33

Much Different Circumstances

Nellie's breathing picked up as her palms began to sweat. Everyone eyed each other in the cramped cave. It was only big enough to hold four or five people, let alone nine. Although some light from the entrance seeped in around their enemies, the back of the cave was black as night except for one spot with a faint glow.

Please be a way out.

Lily asked, "Quite a family reunion, isn't it?"

Nellie caught Lily's gaze and held it. *I'm not scared of you anymore.*

Lily twisted her neck until it cracked. "Nellie. You slipped away from me before. It won't happen again."

"Stop it, Lily," Grayson croaked.

"Shut up, Grayson!" Clenching her hands into fists, she faced Nellie again. "He used to protect me, too. It'll pass."

When Lily started forward, Fin stepped in front of Nellie and pushed her backward further into the cave.

What's she doing?

Then Grayson pushed her even further.

What's going on?

"Not a chance," Fin said to Lily.

Lily grunted. "Careful now. We're related, too. I don't know how though. You're my aunt? Cousin? What are you to me?"

Wait, what? If they're related, then is Fin related to me? How? Is that what the skull meant? Impossible. Isn't it?

Her heart beat a little faster and her breath felt shallow as she stepped back.

It's so cramped in here.

She glanced at the soft light behind her, which was a little brighter now. To not attract attention, she slowly bent down to check out the area and noticed a small tunnel.

It is a way out!

She stayed low but returned her focus to the group, catching her brother and Dawson's nonverbal conversation. Boone used his eyes to point to Fin's backpack and made a slight stabbing motion. Dawson dipped his chin an inch in understanding.

Boone stepped up next to Fin and said, "You gotta know we're gonna win. Seven against two."

As Jonesy moved in front of Grayson and pushed him back toward Nellie, Dawson slipped his hand into Fin's bag and stealthily retrieved the small burlap sack with the dagger. He tucked it behind his back and gave it to Grayson, who put it around his back to Nellie. Grayson flared his eyes, encouraging her to take it, and looked pointedly toward the light.

She grabbed the pouch with the Grim and tucked it into the back pocket of her jeans.

Already low to the ground, she simply rotated on her heels and ducked into the tunnel. The ceiling wasn't high enough for her to stand, but she could stay on her feet without crawling. Because it was roomy widthwise, she tilted her quiver of arrows slightly sideways to keep them from scraping the ceiling. Dashing toward the light that was getting brighter by the second, she slipped on a few wayward pebbles.

"Ouch." She froze, pausing to see if anyone heard.

Fin's voice echoed through the tunnel. "You've got to be crazy to think we'd hand over the dagger to you."

"Don't call me crazy." Lily's voice was barely audible.

Nellie quietly transitioned from the tunnel into a small cave with a large opening to the outside. Relieved, she paused to catch her breath before dropping to her knees and crawling to the edge. She peered over.

"Oh no," she whispered.

Her perch was almost as high as the top of her high school and overlooked a large field of tall prairie grass and graceful flowers surrounding a house.

Squinting, she leaned forward. "That's our house."

"Nellie?" a female voice said from below.

Startled, Nellie leaned farther over the edge. "Mama? Mama! You're okay? How are you here?"

"I'm fine, Nellie girl." She smiled up at her daughter. "Come on down now."

"I can't. I don't have a rope or anything."

"There's one right next to you," Clara Belle said.

Nellie craned her neck to the right, and her gaze landed on a pile of rope.

"Where did that come from?" she whispered. She touched it lightly as a hint of fear tingled down her spine. She peered back over the edge. *Is that really my mama?* She wasn't sure what she was looking for, but she took note of the woman's stance, clothing, hair, and skin. Everything looked right, but something seemed off about her.

The woman called up to her, "Tie it to the boulder. It'll hold your weight, and you can climb down."

With her intuition poking her, Nellie weighed her options. She considered the scene in front of her and noticed that it vibrated the way air does on a hot day. *That house is almost exactly like ours. Almost.*

Her head jerked up at the sound of commotion in the cave and the scuttle of feet moving her direction. She grabbed the rope, tied it to the boulder, and leaned over the edge for more instructions.

"Tie it around your waist, then slowly step backward over the ledge. Holding your body stiff as a board, keep your feet against the rock wall, and walk down. Play leap frog with your hands rather than letting the rope slide through them."

"Yeah, okay," Nellie said tentatively.

Another round of commotion reached her ears. *No time to think about it now.*

After tying the rope around her waist, Nellie crawled to the edge of the hole and peered over at the sharp rocks could easily slice her skin open or crush her skull if she fell. She jerked back as her breath came fast and hard. The sound of someone coming through the tunnel got closer and closer.

Go!

She turned her body so her back faced the open air, grabbed the rope near the boulder, and pulled it taut. After slowly put one foot over the edge, she eased out her other foot. Holding her body as straight as a steel rod, she took a couple steps down the wall and moved hand over hand as she descended. She was now half-inside, half-outside.

Boone's shoes appeared just above her head, and she lurched backwards in surprise, losing her footing.

She screamed as she swung in the air, gripping the rope for dear life.

A dusting of pebbles hit her in the face, and she waited for it to stop before peering up into Boone's face.

He said, "Put your feet against the wall and lean back."

I can do this! I can do this!

She swung toward the wall, found spots for her feet, and pushed her weight into them.

"Don't look down," he ordered.

You think I'm gonna look down? She wished she had the extra breath to yell at him.

"Nellie, you have to go! Walk your feet down."

"Okay." She stared at the wall in front of her. *Just take it one step at a time.* Slowly, she started to walk down the rocky wall. *Don't look down. Don't look down.*

Nellie worked her way down faster, gripping the rope hand over hand. When she landed on the ground, she wanted to cry in relief but looked triumphantly up at Boone instead.

Fin stood next to him and yelled, "Run to the house, Nellie! We're right behind you."

"Okay!"

Nellie untied the rope from her waist and took off for the house. The tall grass and flowers around her whipped her relentlessly as she ran for the porch. She glanced over her shoulder in time to see Lily push Fin off the cliff.

"No!" Nellie screamed, coming to a sudden stop.

Fin grabbed Nellie's rope and swung in the air.

"She's okay," said Clara Belle, who had materialized beside Nellie.

Nellie gasped, backing away from the woman who was clearly not her mother. "Who are you?"

"Run, Nellie."

"Wha—"

The imposter yelled, "Run!"

Startled, Nellie sprinted toward the porch. While she ran, she stabilized the bow over her shoulder with one hand and held fast to the quiver's strap with the other. She glanced over in time to watch the woman running beside her morph into the black cat.

"Sylvester?"

Sylvester took off toward the house, pulling ahead and changing into a panther as Nellie followed. She and Sylvester raced up the porch and through the door. Slamming the door behind her, she locked it and glanced around, surprised that the house was empty.

"Sylvester?" Her voice echoed in the silence as she took in the rooms.

They looked exactly like her house, minus any furniture or photos or anything that would make it feel like home. Its emptiness made it seem bigger, which made her feel smaller. Sunlight shone through the window, turning dust particles into glitter. Mesmerized by the dancing dust motes, she slowly walked to the window.

"Weird."

She reached her hand out to touch the sparkling flecks, but their movements slowed then froze in mid-air like time had stopped.

"Hello," said a male voice.

Nellie jerked around to face a tall man wearing an oddly formal outfit. He was handsome and inviting. She approached him, tilting her head to one side. A magnetic power emanated from him.

I feel like I know him. But how?

"Hello, Nellie."

"Who are you?"

He adjusted the tie at his neck and said, "That is a complicated question."

She gave him a lopsided grin. "What's your name, then?"

"Auci."

She said, "What a weird name."

"What a pointed tongue." One side of his lips quirked up.

She crossed her arms behind her back and intertwined her fingers as delight tickled her belly. His quick wit was entertaining.

A moment passed between them. Her mother had always told her she had a sensibility about people. A surprising sensibility that didn't always make sense. *That's certainly true now.*

"Have we met before?" She took another step forward, releasing her hidden arms.

"No."

"You're lying." She tilted her head.

"I'm not."

"I know liars."

"I'm not a liar." He took a step backward as his eyes smiled. "I know better than to lie to you."

Noticing his retreat, she paused her feet. "You know me. I can tell."

He seemed to be fighting a smile. "This is the first time we meet."

Nellie's ears perked up at the word "first."

Auci continued, "But we will meet again, under much different circumstances."

"How could you possibly know that?" Her feet brought her closer to him like they had a mind of their own. She was drawn to him in a way she couldn't describe.

As she crossed into another beam of sunlight, she realized that the dust motes were moving again. When she looked at Auci, urgency infused everything about him .

"Do you have the dagger?" He held out his hand.

She took a step back. "Wait, how do you know about that?"

Someone banged on the door, and Nellie jumped, retreating another step. She looked anxiously at the door.

"Nellie, wait, please." He presented his palms in a placating gesture. "You need to give me the dagger."

The door crashed down, revealing Lily standing in the doorway. "You bitch!"

Lily ran and tackled Nellie to the floor. The bag with the dagger fell from Nellie's back pocket.

"No!" Nellie yelled, reaching for it.

The girls wrestled for the bag as it slid across the floor. Lily slammed Nellie's head into the floor, dazing her, as Auci raced for the dagger. But Lily was too fast, grabbing the bag before he could. Pulling the Grim from the bag brought a triumphant gleam to her face. She glared at Auci, and he stepped back.

"You must be the auctioneer." Lily smirked. "Gunnar said I'd know you by your weird clothes and that ring."

Nellie shook the fog from her head and got up. She dashed toward Lily, who yanked off the sheath of the dagger and swung it at her.

"No!" Auci ran over and slammed his fist down on Lily's wrist.

The blade dropped to the ground, and Nellie grabbed it by the handle.

Auci yelled, "Nellie, give it to me!"

I don't know what to do. She backed toward the door.

Someone tackled her from behind, sending the dagger flying from her hand and landing on the stairs. Auci extended his hand and did something to summon the dagger. It came to life, floating into the air and soaring toward him.

Nellie elbowed Carl in the ribs and squirmed away from him. She frantically reached for her bow and arrow.

276

"That's mine." Lily snatched the dagger out of the air and brandished it at Auci, backing him into a corner.

A vicious glee lit Lily's face as she plunged the Grim toward Auci until an arrow shot into her hand. Lily screamed and dropped the dagger to the ground.

"Bullseye," Nellie whispered as Carl rushed to Lily's side.

A woman in leather appeared from nowhere and grabbed Lily, Carl, and the dagger. The three of them disappeared from the house just as Fin and Dawson burst through the door.

"No!" Auci yelled.

"Auci?" Fin's gaze bounced around but landed on Nellie. "Are you okay?"

Nellie nodded as Boone and Marci charged through the door, followed by Grayson leaning on Jonesy.

"What happened?" Boone asked before noticing Auci. "Who are you?"

Fin radiated tension. "Where's the Grim?"

Nellie felt like her whole body was collapsing in on itself. "I didn't know what to do."

All the color drained from Grayson's face. "Oh no."

Auci's voice was laced with defeat as he said, "Gunnar has Lily and the Grim."

"I'm sorry." Hot tears spilled out of Nellie's eyes. She peered up at Auci, expecting disappointment.

"You have nothing to be sorry for," Auci said with surprising tenderness. He turned to Fin. "I'll take you back, but then the council will put me in hiding until the Grim is found and secured."

Fin nodded as her shoulders slumped. "I'm so sorry."

Auci walked up to Fin and whispered something in her ear. Nellie tried to listen but couldn't hear anything. He turned around and held out a cane Nellie didn't remember him having.

He said to the group, "Gather round and grab this cane. Fin will explain later."

Everyone obliged. Suddenly, they were standing in the real Ellis house. The familiar furniture, photos, and everything else let her know she was home.

"What just happened?" Boone asked as red and blue lights strobed across his face.

Cold dread settled in Nellie's stomach. "Mama." She ran out the front door and shouted, "Mama!"

The group followed her out as she raced toward Officer Booker, who was standing outside the ambulance.

A confused expression crossed his face when he saw her. "Where the hell did ya'll come from? I was just in that house, and there wasn't no one in there."

Fin said, "I'll explain later."

"Oh my God." Nellie reached Clara Belle, who was lying on a stretcher, ready to be loaded into the ambulance. Nellie bent down and hugged her mother, who was barely conscious.

"Nellie," Clara Belle said, struggling to focus. "I'm so glad you're okay."

"Mama, what happened?"

"Grayson saved my life," she whispered.

Boone patted the sheet over her leg. "We'll follow you to the hospital."

Clara Belle managed a slight smile before her eyes drooped shut. "My good boy."

Boone, Jonesy, Marci, and Nellie hopped in Boone's truck. Although it only took a minute for the EMTs to secure Clara Belle inside the rig, it felt like forever. Finally, they were able to pull up behind the ambulance.

Nellie checked out the back window of the truck to see if Dawson and Fin were coming too. She slid open the back window to invite them as they hopped in the Cutlass. Fin hollered at Grayson to get in. He shook his head and said something quietly. Fin looked a little confused, but she nodded and pulled up behind the truck.

Officer Booker and Grayson turned and looked back at the house.

Nellie's jaw dropped as a tall man appeared from thin air on the porch. A moment later he was joined by the woman she'd seen talking to Marci in the grocery store.

Officer Booker threw up his hands. "Now, who the hell're you?"

Nellie didn't catch much more of the conversation before Boone put the truck in drive and followed the ambulance onto the road. She pinched her brows together as she faced forward.

Who the hell are Riggs and Sophie? And what the hell is really going on?

34

Don't Ever Come Back

Nellie held Jonesy's hand in the brightly lit waiting room of Newcross Memorial Hospital. The group sat slumped with various degrees of bruising, bloodiness, and fatigue while waiting for word on Clara Belle and Marci. Nellie studied Fin and Dawson, sitting across from her with a white coffee table loaded with random magazines between them. Every time they moved, she felt a tinge of irritation.

She shot a barbed glance at Boone, who was pacing behind them. "Stop it. You're driving me crazy."

Boone said, "I'll do what I want."

He continued his march to nowhere.

"They'll be okay, right?" Nellie's eyes misted over.

Boone stopped his feet just long enough to answer. "Mom's tough. She'll be fine. And they're just checking Marci to make sure there's no permanent damage. That snake had a good hold on her."

Jonesy asked, "Do you think they believed us? Our story about Marci?"

"Why wouldn't they?" Boone said in a lowered voice. "She's a cheerleader. A fall that could have injured her insides is something they'd expect."

"Okay," Jonesy said. He squeezed Nellie's hand. "Don't worry, Nellie. The doctors here are pretty good. They've been real good to me and my brothers and sisters since my mom died."

"Okay." She wiped her eyes. "You should really get looked at, too." She pointed to his thigh wound from the arrow.

He waved the idea off and gave her a weak smile. "I've had worse."

"No, you haven't," she shot back.

Nellie snatched a magazine from the table and sat back in a huff. Feeling everyone's eyes on her, she peered over the edge of the magazine at Fin's curious stare before slamming the magazine down.

She lurched forward in her seat and asked, "Why are you even here?" Fin seemed hurt by her question. "Who are you? Really?"

Fin said, "I don't—"

"No," Nellie interrupted. "Everything and everyone was fine until you showed up."

"Everything was fine?" Boone asked sarcastically. "Are we livin' in the same house?"

Nellie jumped up and glared at her brother. "Shut up, Boone!"

Fin's voice was gentle. "Nellie, I'm—"

"No," Nellie interrupted her again. "We were happy. Everything was fine. Mama was fine, and now all of these things are happening. Why are you even here? That skull said I didn't know something. What don't I know?" She threw her hands up. "Now you're related to Lily? And Grayson? And maybe to us? How? And who is Auci? And how did we get from the fake house to our real house in the blink of an eye?" Flinging her arm in an arc, she gestured to Fin. "And your strange clothes, and strange tools, and the way you can heal. And Grayson can heal. What is it? How is any of this possible?"

Fin started again. "Nellie—"

"No." Anger flared through her body as Boone and Jonesy both turned curious faces to Fin and Dawson. "You brought all this into our lives. Why?"

Nellie tried to understand the strange combination of emotions that raked through Fin's eyes and body, but she could glean nothing from it. Switching to Dawson, she saw a similar set of feelings cascading across his face as he stared at Boone. It made no sense.

Finally, Fin said, "I know. You're right." She looked down and spun the mood ring on her finger. "I'm sorry. I truly am."

Nellie blinked back the burgeoning tears preparing to fall. "I don't want you here anymore."

Jonesy stood to face Nellie and gently touched her arm. "Hey, come on, we all went along willingly with this thing. You don't mean that."

"Don't tell me what I mean," Nellie yelled at him before whirling on Fin. "I want you to leave, and don't ever come back."

Dawson stood and touched Fin's arm. "We'll go."

Nellie didn't care about the tears in Fin's eyes. Her mama, her new friend, and her new brother almost died tonight. And it was Fin's fault. *She can go to hell.*

Fin dipped her head at Dawson and stood as she wiped her eyes and glanced at Jonesy. "Let us know everyone is okay?"

Jonesy nodded as Dawson stepped toward the doors to leave. Fin followed but stopped and glanced back. Nellie gave her a fierce stare, defiance pouring from every inch of her body. *I'm not giving you even a little bit on this.*

"Okay." Fin hesitated for a second. "Thank you. For everything."

Nellie relented for a moment, catching something in Fin's eyes. *Is that pride?* But before she could figure it out, Fin followed Dawson out the door. *That was so strange.*

A doctor walked over. "Are you Nellie?"

"I am," she said without looking at him. She watched Fin and Dawson disappear instead before turning to him.

"You can see your mother and Marci now."

Boone stepped up next to Nellie and asked, "Are they gonna be okay?"

"Their prognosis is good. Your mom will need to stay here for the next few days so we can watch for an infection in her arm. And Marci's x-rays were clear, but if she really took a fall as hard as you say, we'd like to keep her overnight for observation. But yes, they should recover nicely. We've contacted Marci's family as well. Her brother, Tommy, is on his way."

"Thank you," said Nellie.

"Yeah, thanks," said Boone. "Can we see them now?"

"Go right in." The doctor gestured down the hall and walked away.

Nellie turned to her brother. "I'm gonna see Mama. Will you check on Marci?"

"Yeah," said Boone. "Sounds good. Then we can switch."

Jonesy sat back down with a weary sigh of relief, tipping his head back and closing his eyes. "I'll wait out here."

"Okay." Nellie peered sheepishly at Boone. "Was I too hard on Fin?"

"No." He half-grinned and tilted his head side to side. "Maybe a little."

They shared a sigh, then a relieved laugh.

Boone chuckled. "You're kind of a rebel now."

She stood a little taller. "I think I am."

Boone hesitated before he said, "You know, Fin's like that, too."

"We are a little alike," Nellie said quietly.

A silence took hold as they got lost in their own thoughts.

Boone pointed his thumb down one hallway. "I'm gonna check on Marci."

"Yeah."

"Tell Mama I'll be down in a minute."

"Okay."

As Boone walked away, Nellie glanced back at Jonesy, who was asleep on the waiting room chair. The sight of him made her stomach flip. She smiled as she turned to head toward her mama's room.

Walking along, she realized something in her was different. After everything they'd seen and been through, she could feel that something had changed. But what exactly that was, she didn't know.

As she strolled deeper into the hospital, she felt a new bounce in her step.

I think I am a rebel.

35

Everything I've Done

Fin twisted her necklace in her fingers as she wiped away a tear. She swept her gaze around the barn at the random piles of junk, a wall of collected keys, and dirty tools.

"You can't blame yourself." Dawson sat down on the hay bale next to her. "She's scared. She was just lashing out."

"But we lost the dagger, too." Fin tucked her dark hair behind her ears. "And we don't know where Auci is. Or where Lily is."

Dawson didn't say anything.

He knows I'm right.

"I don't know what to say." He poked at his cracked glasses.

They sat quietly listening to the hum of crickets outside as a soft breeze jangled the nearby windchimes.

A moment later, the sound of noisy engines and yelling outside made them jump up.

"What the hell." Fin grabbed her gun and held it at the ready as she crept forward in cop mode. She nodded to the door the way she would signal to Hodge if they were entering a dangerous situation. For a second, she missed him.

Dawson hopped to the door and seemed to understand her body language. He opened it wide but stayed back so she had room to aim. After peeking outside, she lowered her weapon.

"Don't shoot." The chief held his hands up.

"Officer Booker." She relaxed as she holstered her weapon.

"So, hell of a lot of trouble up here tonight." He took a toothpick out of his pocket and toasted her with it. "Good idea to put it in my pocket."

She grinned at him as he put it in his mouth and started to chew.

Dawson said, "I'm so glad to see you again."

"Again?" Officer Booker sent Fin a confused look. "We've never met."

"Oh, uh . . ." Dawson rubbed the back of his neck. "Fin mentioned you, so I feel like I know you already."

"That's all, huh?" Suspicious humor twinkled in his eyes as they bounced between the two out-of-towners. He shook his head. "All right, well, two people in the hospital and one dead body since you two showed up in town. And now this guy."

Grayson shuffled into the barn with one hand cuffed behind his back to his belt loop. His other arm was still in the sling to accommodate the bowl covering the arrow.

"Grayson?" Fin shot Dawson a surprised look.

"What's happening right now?" Dawson asked.

The chief poked his thumb at Grayson. "So, he says you need help to find Lily and that dagger thing she stole from you."

"We do, yeah," Fin said.

"I can help with that." Officer Booker crooked his finger for them to follow him and walked out the door.

Fin and Dawson glanced at each other before looking at Grayson, who refused to meet their eyes, so they followed the chief outside. Upon stepping into the cool, country air, Fin saw four police cruisers, one ATC, two horses, and the manpower to operate each of them.

"Think this'll be enough?" Booker asked.

Fin threw her arms around Booker, staggering him back a step.

"Whoa, now, don't thank me too much." The chief patted her back a couple of times before disengaging from the hug as Grayson walked up to them. "Grayson here talked me into it. He gave us some real damning information on several missing persons cases."

Booker gave Grayson one crisp nod. "Say your goodbyes."

"Goodbye?" Dawson asked.

"I'll leave you to it." Officer Booker touched the brim of his hat and walked away.

Grayson gave Fin a sorrowful glance. "I don't want Lily to hurt no one else. So, I got Booker to help you by turning myself in. I told him everything Lily's done. And everything I've done to help her."

Fin had long suspected this moment was coming. For all the good things about him, Grayson was still dangerous in his own way. She knew he had likely done things that went beyond what she'd read in his file. Her chest squeezed with empathy. She had grown to care about her uncle.

"What did you tell him, Grayson?"

"The truth. You'll see." He couldn't quite look her in the eye at first, but eventually he managed. "I tried to help my sister. I tried . . . to save her, but I can't."

Her heart cracked a little when his eyes misted over.

He cleared his throat. "I hurt a lot o' people. But I won't never hurt Clara Belle or Nellie or you."

Looking at Grayson, Fin felt torn. She had seen the best of him and knew him to be a gentle giant. But as a cop, her job was to protect victims and stop their predators. Lily was a predator, and Grayson had helped her.

She finally said, "I believe you."

After a moment of silence, Grayson said, "She's in a cabin." He pointed with his chin toward the driveway and winced. "Go to where Nellie was attacked. About a half mile down the road toward town, take a left into the woods. Go down the hill, and you'll come to a stream. Follow the stream north. You'll run right into it. She'll be there."

Fin nodded, and for a moment she wanted to go back in time and change things for Grayson. She could do that now. She could go back and change lives, save them even. But Auci's rules echoed in her head as she studied Grayson's pained face and body. She wasn't allowed to materially change anything, without changing everything.

I have all this power and I can't use it.

The weight of that dichotomy suddenly felt like a heavy piece of steel on Fin's chest.

She said, "Grayson—"

"I done real bad things," Grayson said softly. "And Lily, she's a murderer. A real one. I helped her. I didn't kill 'em, but I knew. And I buried the bodies. Now that she has the Grim . . . It'll be like nothing you ever seen."

She was struggling to reconcile the dueling emotions swirling in her chest.

"Why did you do it?" Fin asked.

The sadness in his eyes broke her heart into pieces.

"I promised my mama I'd watch out for her. I just kept tellin' myself that's what I was doin' until I couldn't tell myself that no more. I'm real sorry for what I done."

Not knowing what else to do, Fin walked up to Grayson and hugged him on his good side. He didn't make a sound as she gripped him tight, but warm tears dripped onto her shoulder. It was almost more than she could take. Eventually, she let go.

He walked away, drying his eyes with his good shoulder.

"Grayson," she called after him with a catch in her voice. He stopped but didn't turn around, and she swallowed hard to keep her emotions at bay. "Clara Belle is going to be fine. So is Nellie."

Grayson nodded and trudged over to Officer Booker, who put him in the backseat of the police car.

The chief lifted his ten-gallon hat, smoothed his hair back, and repositioned it on his head. "All right, I'mma take him to the hospital first, then to jail. We'll start patrolling the area now and let you know as soon as we have something."

"Thank you," said Fin, pulling herself together.

They watched in silence as the calvary left to search for Lily.

As the dust settled, Dawson asked, "So, how bad do you think it is? What he did?"

"I don't know. But I suppose we'll find out." Facing Dawson, she went into cop mode. She couldn't change the past, but she had absolute control over her policing skills, and she was ready to use them. *Time to work.* "We've got to find Auci. The cops'll be helpful, but they're no match for Lily, especially with the Grim. We need to find her first. And Auci's the only one who might have something to help us fight her."

"Great." Dawson gnawed on his lower lip. "Now, where is he? And who is this Council that's hiding him?"

36

The Things You Can't Put into Words

Nellie walked into Clara Belle's hospital room, and the smell of bleach flared her nostrils. Tears sprang to her eyes at her mother's pale, drawn face. Her visible heartbeat beeped on the monitor, and the IV in her arm dangled like a new piece of jewelry. Nellie must not have been as quiet as she thought because her mother opened her eyes.

"Baby girl." She smiled groggily and held out her hand. "Don't worry. It looks worse than it feels."

Nellie grabbed her mother's hand. She sat down in the chair next to the bed, dropped her head into her mother's lap, and let the tears flow. "I'm so sorry, Mama."

"You didn't do nothin' wrong." She patted Nellie's hair. "I'm so glad to see you. What happened? Did you get the dagger?"

Nellie lifted her head, shaking it. "It was so scary, Mama, but—"

"What was scary? Were you hurt?" Alarm sharpened her dark eyes.

"No, not hurt." Nellie would never be able to explain what happened to her, the changes she felt inside of her. "I'm okay, Mama, I swear."

"But?"

"What?"

"You said it was scary, but . . ." Clara Belle nudged the air with her head.

"Oh, right." *It was scary, but also wonderful somehow.* "I don't know how to describe it."

Clara Belle's smile said she understood. "Sometimes the things you can't put into words are like that because there are no words for it. Just a feeling. A wonderful, scary feeling."

Nellie exhaled in relief. *Exactly.*

"My girl. I forget sometimes you're only fifteen…you've had to be so strong." Clara Belle offered a weak smile as she touched Nellie's arm. "Where's Boone? Is he okay?"

"He's good. He's visiting Marci. He'll come see you after."

"Is Marci okay?"

"She will be." *We all will.*

"And Jonesy?" The glint in her mama's eyes said she knew how Nellie felt about him.

"He's good, too." Nellie blushed a little, looking away from her mother's knowing stare.

"Okay." Clara Belle shifted in the bed to get comfortable. "Where's Grayson? Is he okay?"

Nellie shook her head. "He got hurt pretty bad. I'm not sure why he stayed with Officer Booker back at the house. He should be in the hospital."

"Hmm," Clara Belle murmured. "I've known for a while about Grayson and Lily."

"What?" Nellie rocked back in her chair. "You knew?"

"Your father, when he found out I knew . . ."

Nellie understood. He'd beaten her over it. *That'll never happen again.*

"I helped as much as I could," said Clara Belle. "But I had no idea about the terrible things they've been through. I would've done more if I'd known. I'm sorry if me not doing more made Lily want revenge on you. Maybe she would've been different if I'd done more."

Nellie frowned. She wanted to be mad at her mom for not doing more, but she couldn't. Nellie knew how awful Russell had been. He made other people worse. *And now he's dead.*

Nellie whispered, "Grayson told us Russell's gone."

Silence stretched between them.

"I'm sorry," her mama said. "I know he wasn't the father you wanted or needed. But losing a father is still losing a father."

Emotions swirled inside Nellie, and she didn't know what to do with them. She was glad Russell would never beat her mother again. Glad that she'd never feel the panic of not knowing if something she said or did might cost her mother or brother a bloody nose or broken lip. As much as she disliked Lily, she was a little bit grateful to the rotten seed for freeing them from that monster.

On the other hand, Lily also stole Nellie's hope that her father could change and be the dad she so desperately wanted. Dead men can't change. And the last memory she'd ever have of him would be when he tried to cross a room to kill her on her birthday.

Tears stung Nellie's eyes at the realization. She took a deep breath and expelled her frustration.

Clara Belle looked at the ceiling. "I'm so grateful Fin's here. And Dawson. I'm not sure we would have survived without them."

"What do you mean? They caused all this." She waved her hand at her mother's body.

"Caused it? No, honey, they stopped it from getting worse. You heard Grayson. He couldn't handle Lily anymore. That's why he warned us. Fin is maybe the only one who can handle Lily. We're lucky she's here."

"Oh," Nellie said quietly.

"Where are Fin and Dawson?"

Nellie shifted uncomfortably, looking away. *I shouldn't have yelled at them.* "Umm, they left. They're probably back at the barn." She felt Clara Belle eyeing her.

"And they didn't get the dagger?"

"Well, we had it. I had it, actually. But Lily found us and stole the dagger from me." *It's my fault we lost it.*

"Oh dear." Concern pinched Clara Belle's face. "Fin and Dawson must be worried, then." She sucked in a breath, her eyes flaring. "That means you're not safe. None of you are if Lily has that dagger."

Nellie started, looking at her mama in surprise. *Shit. None of us are safe, and I sent everyone away.* "I should get going." She stood up.

"It's too dangerous." Clara Belle grabbed Nellie's arm with surprising strength.

"I'm safer with Fin right now. And you're gonna be okay, too. I promise. There's a guard outside your room."

Her iron grip held firm.

"Mama, please, trust me." She stroked Clara Belle's hand, trying to reassure her.

Her mother relented and let her daughter go. "I'll never forgive myself if anything happens to you or Boone."

"Fin, Dawson, and Grayson won't let anything happen to us."

The combination of pain medicine and left over anesthesia made Clara Belle's eye lids droop again. "There's something about them. Fin and Dawson. You can feel it, can't you?"

Nellie bobbed her head and said quietly, "Get some sleep. It's all gonna be okay." As her mama drifted off, Nellie kissed her forehead. After watching the slow rise and fall of her chest for a minute, Nellie snuck out of the room.

Jonesy walked toward her in the hallway.

"Where's Boone?" Nellie asked.

"I dunno," said Jonesy. "I went to check on Marci and say hello, but when I got there, she said Boone never came in. He's not with you?"

"What? No." Apprehension shivered down her back. "Wait, where did he go? He would never have gone anywhere else, he wanted to see Marci."

Jonesy peered around, worry etching lines into his forehead. "I don't know, but I think we need to go find Fin and Dawson. Now."

"Do you think they're back at the house?"

"That's what I'm thinkin'." He put his hands on his hips. "They'd need to get more supplies if they're gonna try and find Lily. I'm guessing that's their plan."

"True. And there's something else, Jonesy."

"What?"

"That man at the weird version of our house said his name was Auci and the dagger was for him."

"The guy who brought us home with the cane?"

Nellie gave a shy nod. *Still figuring that guy out.*

"What was that anyway?" Jonesy asked. "We, like, traveled." His face darkened as he sank into deep thought. "We moved locations without moving. How?"

Her heart fluttered a little. *It was weird.* "I don't know."

A silence crashed between them as they pondered the strangeness of it all. Nellie couldn't take being trapped in that oddness any longer, so she spoke up.

"Yeah, so, what if Fin and Dawson were getting the dagger for him and not themselves? But why?"

Jonesy puffed his cheeks out and let the air escape all at once as he splayed his hands. "I don't know. But there's only one way to find out."

"Right, let's go."

As they walked out of the hospital, Nellie had two thoughts on loop. *Who is Auci? And where the hell is Boone?*

37

Explained and Unexplained

Fin grabbed the dulled, gold handle of Clara Belle's front door and threw it open as she and Dawson raced inside the cozy living room. It still carried several reminders of the ruined birthday party that Russell crashed. *Literally.*

"Auci!" Fin yelled with an urgency she hoped he sensed. She frantically cast about and gripped her necklace, hoping it might summon him. "Auci, where are you?"

A smooth bass voice said, "Hi, Fin."

She whipped around to the open door. Rather than Auci, she faced a man with a leather jacket, scruffy face, and a Taser instead of a gun.

Dawson jumped forward. "Who are you?"

Fin hoped they couldn't see the emotions bubbling up inside her. His presence made her pulse start thumping inside her ears.

Collecting herself, she said, "You're the guy. From the crime scene. But that was—"

"In the future?" he interrupted. His eyes bored into hers as he strode confidently into the living room, closing the distance to her in a way that tightened something delicious in her belly.

She said, "Riggs. Right? That's what Hodge said your name was."

A warmth lit his face, but before he could respond, a woman with long auburn hair appeared from thin air behind Riggs and stepped beside him.

"Sophie?" Dawson and Fin both asked at the same time.

"How do you know her?" Fin asked Dawson as he stepped forward.

He said, "She's my friend. She's always at the library where I work. How do you know her?" He spoke to Fin but stared in disbelief at Sophie.

Fin's voice softened when she spoke to Sophie. "You were my counselor when I was in the system. When I turned eighteen, you gave me the envelope with the letter from my mother."

Fin absentmindedly rubbed the stone on her compass bracelet. Her chest tightened as she realized that whatever this was, Sophie's presence in her life was no accident.

With a catch in her throat, Fin asked, "You know what happens to my mother, don't you?"

Sophie tilted her head. "I know a great deal about both of you. Especially you, Dawson."

"So, you're . . ." Dawson paused. "I need to sit down."

He grabbed a chair at the table and unloaded the weight of his new knowledge on the hard wood.

Sophie walked over and sat down with him. With a light Irish accent, she said, "You had a sense about me, right? I saw you studying me like the books your nose is so often glued to. By now, I think you've put together who I am."

Dawson took out his green book and Sophie put her hand on it before he could open it.

"No," she said softly. "Look at me."

He did and she poked his chest. "Heart, not your head."

Dawson's eyes misted as he shifted in his seat. "You're my grandmother."

She beamed at him. "And a proud one at that."

Joy radiated from Dawson's eyes even as his voice broke. "You're Marci's mother, and Marci is my mother."

"Well, she doesn't know that yet. Nor should she." Sophie reached out and patted Dawson's hand. "But yes. We're your family."

Dawson grabbed her hand as fully grown tears emerged from his eyes. "I had hoped—"

"I know," she said softly.

She scooted forward on her chair and opened her arms. Dawson hugged her as his tears wet her green jacket.

Fin's heart burst with happiness for Dawson. *I hope I can have that someday with Clara Belle.* An odd sense of relief washed over her from the guilt she'd been feeling at being able to form a relationship with her father while Dawson stood by and watched.

"Auci," whispered Fin. As her chest filled with a deep concern for her father, she faced Riggs. "Where is he?"

"Safe."

Sophie said, "But unavailable."

Dawson sat back from the hug and wiped his eyes as he rejoined the conversation, "So, we have no access to him?"

"None." Riggs turned his attention to Fin, cop to cop. "Protective custody. With the Grim, we can't risk him being out in the open."

She gave him her best detective nod, but underneath her professionalism, she noticed his rich, brown eyes had flecks of hazel in them.

"We don't need him anyway, we've got you." Sophie slapped her hand on the table and stood. "And you've got us."

Dawson's chest puffed up a little as he gazed at his grandmother.

The woman's got moxie. Fin grinned before asking pointedly, "And what exactly are you? Are you like Auci? Like me?"

"We're just humans." Riggs tossed her a playful look as he leaned her way. "Not everyone can be a demi-God."

Heat surged inside her as his stare lingered on her face. She squirmed a little, suddenly very aware of her body.

Dragging her mind back to the subject at hand, she said, "Well, you can time travel, so you're not just human."

Riggs said, "Nope, sorry, just human. But you're right, we can time travel."

Dawson pushed his cracked glasses higher on his nose, opening his green book and scribbling notes down.

Sophie said, "Hold that thought." She disappeared and reappeared a moment later with a new pair of glasses, which she handed to Dawson. "Try these."

"Oh!" Dawson took off the old glasses and ushered on the new ones. He looked around the room, grinning. "Perfect. Thank you."

Sophie tousled the hair on top of his head. "Only the best for my grandson."

Dawson beamed as he sat up straighter, responding to her love like a flower to sunlight.

Fin hated to break into their moment but said, "How do you do it? The time travel?"

As if on cue, Riggs and Sophie pulled up the bottom of their shirts. A small spot glowed on their right hips.

"Holy shit." *Ice had one of those.*

When Fin leaned in to see it better, Riggs's freshly showered scent tickled her nose. The way his tan skin stretched over his muscles was hard to ignore. She quickly stepped back and tucked her hair behind her ear. When she glanced at his face, he tilted his head in a playful way that made her bite the inside of her lip to keep from grinning.

Riggs dropped his shirt with a touch of swagger, and said, "Auci made them from the stones at Blue Falls. They allow us to travel, but they're also trackers. So, we can't go rogue."

Frowning, Dawson leaned in too to stare at Sophie's hip. "I don't see anything."

"Give it a poke." Sophie pointed to a place high on her hip. "Right here. You can feel it."

Dawson reached over and touched the spot. "Oh, wow." He stepped back and wrote in his book.

"Wait, you said the chips track you?" Dawson pointed at their hips. "Why?"

Sophie explained, "Auci and the council—"

"Who's the council?" Fin interrupted.

"The Bounty Hunter Council." Riggs leaned his back against the staircase with a casual, confident stance that Fin appreciated. "That's who we report to."

Ice said I'd have to answer to the council. Concerned, she asked, "What do they do exactly?"

Riggs and Sophie had a silent conversation with their eyes.

"Don't worry about that right now," said Sophie. "Right now, we need to focus on finding Lily and getting the Grim back."

Crossing her arms, Fin glared at Riggs, quietly demanding a better answer.

Sighing, Riggs said, "Big picture? There are lots of different systems—human ones, mystical ones, and ones we still don't quite understand—that are always at play on this planet. There's explained and unexplained phenomena, right?"

Fin and Dawson nodded.

Sophie pointed back and forth between her and Riggs. "Bounty hunters like us and the council are one of those systems."

Riggs continued, "Gunnar was already working with people here on earth since she's in human form. She had a whole network. They were the original bounty hunters. Their purpose was to step in when things like the Grim fell into the wrong hands."

Sophie took over. "But over time, bounty hunters took on other purposes, especially as more and more of them came from law enforcement, the military, and protection services. Basically, they organized themselves. Separating from the siblings and all other magical systems, especially once they learned how to time travel. Which brings us back to what I was saying earlier about why the chips track us."

Riggs picked up the loose thread and put his foot against the banister and said, "The council has placed locks and gates, so to speak, on certain times in the past and future. We can only go so far back. And we can only move forward with assistance from the Mystic. And if we violate those rules—"

"You get called to the council," interrupted Fin.

"Yeah," said Riggs.

Fin put her hands on her hips. "It must be tempting to go back and change all the bad things in history."

"Well, first of all, we can't access those timelines." Sophie walked into the kitchen and came back with a cupcake. "They're gated by the council." After licking off some frosting, she said, "And second, our only objective is monitoring mystical objects and keeping them out of the wrong hands. That's it. Anything outside that scope, we can't get involved in."

When she took a huge bite of the cupcake, Dawson asked, "So, what can you do?"

Sophie sent a pleading look at Riggs and pointed at her full mouth.

Taking the hint, he replied, "As Fin knows from her police work, the good guys aren't the only ones who know about these objects and can time travel."

Sophie walked back into the kitchen and banged around while Riggs talked.

"Think dark web and black markets." Riggs's hands became animated puppets helping to tell the story. "These objects and the ability to time travel are worth a lot to people. The auctioneer and Gunnar manage most of it. But when humans get out of line or they start selling powerful things on the black market for blood coins, we get involved."

"Wait, blood coins?" She stood a little straighter. "In the trials, there were two men. One said I was worth tenthousand blood coins."

"There's a bounty on your head," said Riggs.

"Yeah, I figured," she said.

"Okay, Fin, we promise, that's all going to be explained later," said Sophie, trying to focus the conversation. "For now, Lily and the Grim."

She shifted her weight uncomfortably. *You don't need answers to every question. Trust them.* She nodded. "Okay." Then it hit her. "Oh, wait.

That's why you carry a Taser instead of a gun. You have the same rules as Auci. You can't kill anyone or change things."

Riggs looked impressed. "Right. But we do have to fix things when they go awry. Most of the time, we restore balance to the timeline and secure the object. Then we hand the object and the criminal off to the council."

"What does the council do with them?" Dawson asked as Sophie reappeared with another cupcake and a glass of milk.

She placed them down on the table in front of Dawson and squeezed his cheek.

"You need to eat." She sat down and eyed him until he started eating. She patted his hand as he cast an embarrassed but happy look at Fin.

With a look of satisfaction at her grandson, Sophie said, "It's just like our court system. The criminals are held accountable, and the objects are held as evidence before being secured or returned to Auci."

Riggs jumped in, "Our work is surgical. In and out. We work without disturbing anything. And if we do disturb something in a way that changes it, we report it to the council and the Mystic."

"Who is this Mystic you keep talking about?" Fin asked.

Riggs smiled. "She's a fancy demi-God like you. Her name is Tally."

Fin rolled her eyes to keep from grinning as a hint of his shampoo smell wafted her direction.

Undeterred, he said, "Tally can see every possible path forward, backward, and sideways in time. If there are problems, she warns the council. Then they assign hunters to fix it."

When Fin looked at him, he added, "And if there are good things, sometimes she'll tell us that, too."

Fin's heart jumped as he searched her eyes.

Breaking the spell, Sophie said, "She helps us because as humans, we don't know the infinite number of possibilities or realities that exist in the timelines. Every time a human makes a different choice, or one of these interruptions happens, a new timeline is created."

Fin had another lightbulb moment. "Oh, that's why the evidence techs were different." Riggs gave her a nod.

Dawson's pen hovered over his notebook as he asked, "So, wait, after we get the dagger back and the council has it, you'll go away?"

Dawson shot a pained expression at Sophie as the front door creaked, and Nellie and Jonesy walked in.

"Nellie." Fin reflexively smiled at her mother before schooling her expression. *She hates me right now.* "What are you doing here?"

To Fin's surprise, Nellie rushed over and hugged her. "I'm sorry."

Fin held onto her for dear life. *Oh, thank God.* "It's okay. You weren't wrong. I'm so sorry we put you in danger."

"Yeah, but you helped us with Lily and Russell." Nellie let go and stepped back.

"This is all so complicated." Fin tucked a hair behind her ear. "I just, I want to keep you safe."

"I know," Nellie whispered, looking sheepish.

Not wanting to belabor the point, Fin glanced at Jonesy. "Hey, Jonesy."

"Hey, everyone." He cast curious glances at the newcomers.

Nellie cocked her head at Sophie. "I've seen you before. Talking to Marci."

Sophie beamed with pride. "I'm her mother."

A shadow of worry passed across Nellie's face. "Oh, did you know she's—"

"At the hospital?" Sophie interrupted. "Yes, I know. My husband, Tom, and I have already been there. Her brother, Tommy, is with her now."

Visibly relieved, Nellie said, "Oh good."

"She had nothing but good things to say about you," said Sophie. "And Boone. And Fin. All of you."

As Sophie beamed at Fin, she felt a surge of guilt. *Should I tell her about the assaults on Marci?* She wasn't sure what knowledge she was or was not allowed to share.

If I tell her, am I materially changing the past? The future? If I lived in this timeline and it was reported to the police, of course I would tell her. Hell, I'd be obligated to. But I'm not part of this timeline, and the only reason I know about this is because of magic.

After a pause that was probably too long, Fin said to Sophie, "Marci is, uh . . .She's one of the bravest girls I know. Beyond her years, even."

Sophie puffed up with pride. "I think so, too."

An uncomfortable weight settled on Fin's shoulders. *What good is time travel if we can't fix people's problems?*

Riggs inserted himself into the conversation. "Hey, I'm Riggs." He reached out his hand.

Jonesy shook it briefly. "Jonesy."

"I'm Nellie." Standing tall, she extended her hand, which Riggs shook.

"Nice to meet you," said Riggs. "We're friends of Fin's. We're here to help."

"Good." Nellie looked around, seeming a little antsy. "So, where's Boone?"

"What do you mean?" asked Fin.

"We hoped he might be here," said Jonesy. "He said he was going to Marci's hospital room, but Marci said he never showed up. And he's not at the house. Have you seen him?"

Fin's internal cop alarm went off. "He's not here."

Dawson stiffened as he stood. "We have to find him."

Fin patted the air in Dawson's direction, not wanting him to panic the kids. "We will."

"So, he is missing, then." Nellie's voice raised a notch and her eyes widened.

"It's okay." Fin clasped Nellie's arms and gave them a reassuring squeeze. "We'll find him."

"And what about Grayson?" Nellie's eyes went wide and watery. "I saw him refuse to come with you to the hospital. Where is he?"

How do I answer that? Let's see, they're both of this time. He turned himself in. I'm not changing anything by telling her what's already happened.

Fin said, "Grayson is . . . he's a good guy inside. And he would never, ever hurt you or me or any of us. But he did do some bad stuff. To protect Lily."

"Did he . . ." Nellie swallowed hard. "Did he kill?" she whispered the last word.

"No, Nellie, he didn't. But he knew that Lily did, and he didn't report it. He helped her cover it up. Do you understand?"

A tear spilled down Nellie's cheek as her upper lip quivered. She nodded but pulled herself together. "We need to find my brother."

Atta girl. "Grayson told us about a cabin he and Lily use in the woods. If Lily is involved with Boone's disappearance, it's possible he's there."

Nellie dropped her head into her hands.

Fin kept going. "The cabin isn't that far into the forest, so we should be able to get there pretty quickly."

"That's Old Man Owen's cabin," said Jonesy.

"It's been abandoned for years." Nellie wiped her face and squared her shoulders. "Teenagers used to go there to make-out and stuff. But then, they said bad things started happening. It was haunted. So, people quit going."

"Do you know where it is?" asked Fin.

"I don't," said Nellie.

Jonesy raised his hand like he was in class. "I do."

Fin repressed an urge to grin as Nellie shot him a who-have-you-been-making-out-with look.

Jonesy shoved his hands in his pockets and studied the floor.

Dawson walked up to them and pulled out a folded piece of paper from his back pocket. "Can you mark it on this map?"

"Sure. Got a pen?" Jonesy seemed relieved to move away from Nellie's questioning stare.

As Jonesy and Dawson looked over the map, Fin left to get her gear together. After checking her supplies, she reloaded and holstered her gun and donned her bulletproof vest marked with a few holes and stained with Grayson's blood.

Riggs walked over to her, and her breathing ticked up a notch. Her body tingled in response to his proximity.

He said quietly, "I'm glad we're here to help."

He held her gaze a moment too long.

"I'm glad you're here, too," she said.

He lightly touched her hand before turning away.

The contact sent a zing of pleasure up her arm. *I wonder what he knows about me.* Shaking her head, she aggressively zipped her bag closed. *We've gotta find Lily…and we'll probably find Boone.*

38

I Like Trouble

In the tiny cabin, Lily circled Boone, admiring how well she'd tied him to the chair. Every now and then she'd glance at Gunnar, who was nervously looking out the bedroom window. Although bedroom was a strong word for a room with a cot and a chair.

Lily said to Boone, "Snatching you from the hospital was one of my better ideas." She twisted the blade of her favorite knife against her finger. "Eventually, everyone you love will come for you. And when they do . . ."

She stabbed his thigh.

He screamed and writhed in pain, tipping forward and yelling, "Go to hell!"

She yanked the knife out, eliciting a yelp, and wiped it on his pants.

Gunnar spun around to face Lily. "This wasn't our deal. You were supposed to steal the Grim and kill Auci since I can't, then hand it over. That's it. Not all this." She flapped a hand at Boone in revulsion. "And where's Oliver?"

"He's coming." Lily repressed her delight, not wanting to tip her hand. "Where's the auctioneer?"

"I'll find him." Gunnar faced the window. "What is that stench?"

"Rotten meat," Lily said as casually as she could.

Courtesy of the window's reflection, Lily saw Gunnar grimace and wrap her arms around her body. A maybe-I-shouldn't-have-done-this expression crossed her face.

You shouldn't have done this. A smile toyed with Lily's lips.

Since it wasn't Gunnar's turn yet, Lily went back to playing with Boone. "You know, at first, I just wanted to get even with you and your sister." She licked her blood off the blade and her finger. "I just wanted to punish your stupid family for all the pain me and Grayson went through. Then, out of the blue, Oliver shows up and tells me I actually am the warrior I always thought I was. And there's a dagger that can unleash hell if I just kill the auctioneer."

She walked over to Boone and leaned close to him before aiming her stare at Gunnar. "But I can't take all the credit. Gunnar here is the one who started all this."

At the mention of her name, Gunnar's reflection looked at Lily with a cold disregard.

"She wanted to cause some trouble." Lily smirked at Gunnar. "And I like trouble."

Lily stood up straight and eyed the small bag draped across Gunnar's chest. She'd seen the witch pull a couple of fancy things from it that looked like they belonged in a Halloween shop.

If I could just get hold of that bag, too.

Taunting Boone, she lifted her shirt and patted the sheathed dagger at her waist. "Now, I've got the Grim and all the power."

In the window, a flash of alarm crossed Gunnar's face, sending a thrill up Lily's spine.

"Oliver." Gunnar's pensive reflection transformed into relief as Oliver arrived.

Facing Boone, Lily dropped her shirt back in place, nodded toward the window, and held a shushing finger up to her lips before drawing the same finger across her throat.

"Gunnar!" Boone called out a warning.

Gunnar banged her hand against the window and yelled, "Oliver!"

Lily reveled in the horrified look on Gunnar's face as Carl slit Oliver's throat outside.

"No!" Gunnar screamed.

Lily watched out the window as Oliver gripped his throat. Choking on his own blood, he fell to his knees and collapsed to the ground.

The thumping in Lily's chest reached a crescendo of joy as she used her supernatural speed to jam the Grim into Gunnar's back. But the blade arced toward an empty windowpane.

Gunnar had vanished.

"Dammit!" Lily whirled around in a blind rage, needing to kill something. She slammed the Grim into a mouse running across the floor. Its body evaporating into a fine, white powder that crackled and popped with blue fire before disappearing completely.

"Ahh." Lily shuddered with relief.

Killing with the Grim was different than a regular knife. Since it was made from bone, it was lighter. But the main difference was the strength required. Stabbing a human body was normally hard work. She really had to push to get a blade through skin and muscle and fat. And she had to do it a few times to get them to die. The Grim, on the other hand, slid in like a hot knife through butter. And it only took one jab.

But that wasn't all.

When the Grim went into the mouse, she immediately felt a rush. As she returned the magic blade to its sheath, her whole body vibrated with power. Intrigued, she looked in the mirror behind Boone's head, staring in wonder at her eyes. They now had a bright blue ring around the iris. She felt euphoric. Like she could do anything.

Boone leaned away from her. "What's wrong with your eyes?"

"Wow," she said, amazed that her new look reflected her new power. *I'm beautiful.*

She strutted out of the bedroom, through the kitchen, out the cabin's back door, across a small tuft of grass, and into the modest shed that sat behind the cabin.

Inside, Grayson sat on a chair on the brink of death. He squinted up at Lily and winced. "What happened to your eyes?"

"Now everyone can see that I'm the powerful one. I'm the strong one. Me, not you. Me!"

She yanked out her favorite knife to stab him again but stopped. At least thirty minutes had passed since she'd beaten him last. "Why aren't you healing?"

He coughed up blood. "I'm not gonna heal."

"That's impossible." *He's not allowed to die yet.*

"We ain't immortal, Lily." He hung his head and spit blood onto the floor.

Looking at the crimson glob, the same helplessness burbled up inside her that she felt when her mama told them she was dying of cancer. Cold terror coursed through her veins as she stared at her dying brother.

A moment later, boiling anger burned away the cold.

"So, you're going to leave me, too, huh? You're gonna go out a quitter. Just like mama."

"I tried—"

"You never tried!"

She screamed, spun around to the other chair, and punched the man sitting there. One hit was so hard it catapulted him and his chair across the shed. The deep crack of a bone breaking preceded his squeal of pain. She exhaled and rolled her shoulders with relief.

Turning back to Grayson, she said, "Go ahead and die. I don't need you anyway. I have a new family waitin' on me." Stepping back, she glowered at her other prisoner. "But you. I'm not done with you yet."

Unconscious, Officer Booker didn't reply.

39

Every Horror Movie in the World

Fin and Riggs led the group down the road from Nellie's house toward town.

"Grayson said a half mile or so," Fin said, glancing behind her.

Sophie walked beside Dawson with her hand tucked around his elbow. It looked like she was relaying stories to Dawson, who ate them up with bright eyes and grateful chuckles. Nellie and Jonesy were a few feet behind them, walking quietly, lost in thought.

"Everything okay?" Riggs asked.

She peeked at him, which was dangerous. He captured her attention in a way that was demanding, forcing himself into her brain in ways she wasn't quite comfortable with but deeply craved.

So many feelings. "Yeah."

Pointing at her face, he said, "Your eyebrows say differently. When you're thinking, your eyebrows come together and your eyes squint." He imitated the expression.

"Very observant, bounty hunter." *I can't believe he's watching me that closely.* Thrilled by the idea, she smiled as she tucked her thumbs in her back pockets.

"It's cute, is all." He smiled with a shrug.

A warm blush crept up her chest and neck. *See, distracted. Again.* She shook her head.

Fin whispered, "I don't think Nellie should come with us. I keep thinking I can protect her. But the more I think about it, it seems like taking her is delivering her right to Lily."

"I get that," said Riggs. "But how can you be sure Lily wouldn't come for her if you left her behind?"

Fin shook her head. "Lily has the Grim, and Gunnar is with her. We're assuming it's all about Auci right now."

Approaching the half mile mark, they rounded a turn. A police cruiser with a smashed front had crashed into a tree.

"Stay here," she yelled over her shoulder as she drew her weapon.

Riggs pulled out his Taser, and they approached the scene together. Sophie moved behind them and off to their right, providing wider support.

With her left hand, Fin snatched her small flashlight from her pocket, clicked it on, and held it underneath her right wrist to support her gun hand. Its bright cone of light let her search the woods as they approached.

Fin moved in to inspect the vehicle but kept her head on a swivel. As she approached the car, she could see no one was in or near it. She holstered her gun and swept her flashlight around the cruiser, investigating every detail. Blood stained the steering wheel. She shined the light on the passenger's side floor. Toothpicks. A familiar cupcake bag.

"This is Booker's car," Fin said.

"Grayson was in it too, then." Riggs shined his light across the road, went over to something, knelt down for a moment, and stood back up.

"What is it?" she asked.

"Needle," said Riggs. "Probably something to subdue Grayson."

Sophie walked up to them. "He's a big boy. How'd they move him?"

Fin checked the area. Her flashlight illuminated ATC tracks, so she followed them off the road and over to another tree.

"Shit." Fin ran down the hill to the officer lying on the ground with a bloody head. "Hey, buddy. Hey. You okay? Come on, man."

She felt his wrist for a pulse. *Nothing.* She started CPR as Riggs ran to other side of the downed officer.

Fin said, "Sophie, get on the radio and call for an ambulance. Riggs, we'll switch off breathing and compressions."

Neither of them moved.

Looking up, she did a double take as he shook his head.

"Riggs, help me," she ordered.

"I can't," he said. "You shouldn't be, either. If it weren't for time travel, you wouldn't be here."

"Fuck you!" She turned pleading eyes onto Sophie. "Help me."

Sophie's face drooped with sadness as she also shook her head.

"He's gone," said Riggs.

Fin's eyes filled with angry tears. "Where I come from, we don't leave officers down."

"Exactly." Riggs squatted down and softened his voice. "Where you're from. You don't know what it would change if you saved his life."

She glared at him. "And what if the next time it's Nellie? Or Boone? Or Grayson?"

Riggs's dark eyes pooled sympathy and regret, but he still didn't help.

Sophie touched her arm. "Fin . . ."

It made her skin crawl. "Don't touch me."

She jerked her arm away and stomped up the hill. Storming over to Dawson, who stood somberly with Nellie and Jonesy, she pulled the Cutlass's keys out of her pocket and tossed them at him.

"Take them back to the house, call the police, and ask for one of the patrol cars in the search party to come back and protect you. Then pack them in the car and wait for me to come back. If anything happens, leave. Get the hell out of Newcross as fast as you can."

Dawson nodded but worry furrowed his brow. "What about my d—I mean, what about Boone?"

"I'm not gonna let anything happen to him, okay?"

He swallowed hard. "Okay, but take this." He pulled out the map that Jonesy had marked. "You'll need it."

"Thank you." Fin faced Nellie. "You need to stay here."

Jonesy stood tall. "I'll stay with her."

Nellie looked at them like they were crazy. "I'm not staying. I'm going with you."

"What?" Jonesy's head reared back. "You need to stay."

"Don't tell me what to do," she said. "You're not my keeper. I'm going with Fin."

"Okay." Fin put up her hands, surrendering and walking over to Nellie. "Okay."

As Fin went in for a hug, she slid her handcuffs from their pouch at her side and cuffed Nellie to Jonesy.

"Fin!" Nellie screamed.

"Keep her here." Fin gave Jonesy the key to the cuffs, which he put in his pocket.

"Dammit!" Nellie pried at the restraint with her other hand.

Her back rigid, Fin walked down the hill into the woods with Riggs and Sophie.

~~~

Thankfully, by the time they hit the stream, they couldn't hear Nellie yelling anymore. Fin compared the map to their surroundings. They were at a point where a large rock formation and trees caused a small river bifurcation.

We're in the right place. "The arms of the river are going the same direction. One is just slightly north of the other. We can split up."
~~~

Sophie snorted. "Every horror movie in the world would predict that's a terrible idea."

"I agree," said Riggs.

Fin refrained from rolling her eyes. "Look, I'm a cop, in case anyone has forgotten that. I'm perfectly capable of going it alone."

She consulted the map again. "It looks like the left arm goes behind the property, and the right arm goes in front of it. We can hit them from two directions." She refolded the map and tucked it into her back pocket. "Sophie, why don't you go up behind the property. And Riggs, why don't you go to hell. I'll go in front."

She hiked off by herself as Riggs told Sophie to go without him. His boots scuffled quickly through the forest floor as he caught up to her.

"You've got to get a handle on how this works," Riggs said. "Especially before anything happens to someone you care about."

She didn't slow down or look at him. "I'm not going to let anyone die on my watch. Especially not a fellow officer. And most especially not my family."

"Then I'll take your ass to jail," Riggs said pragmatically.

She huffed and rolled her eyes. "Bounty hunter jail?"

Fuming, she continued following the stream but hesitated at the sudden silence behind her. She swung around to face Riggs, but he was gone.

"What the hell?" When she turned back around, he was standing in front of her. "Holy shit, what are you doing?"

Oozing impatience, he said, "Proving a point."

"Oh," she said, remembering who she was and what she could do. "We don't have to walk, do we?"

"Nope. And you don't need that map, either. Hell, Sophie's probably already there."

"Why didn't you just say something?"

Riggs briefly closed his eyes in exasperation. "Like I said, you need to get a handle on this. Know your powers. When you can use them. When you can't."

She repressed the urge to tell him to go to hell again and listened instead. He was right, unfortunately. She was acting like a child.

He said, "Open a portal, and let's see where to land."

Fin didn't love the tone of his voice but she knew she needed to focus. She shook out the tension from her body and concentrated on opening a square.

Okay, I don't know the exact location this time. So, show me the cabin's perimeter five minutes from now?

Her magic obeyed, and the frame revealed Sophie standing behind the cabin.

Riggs nodded but said, "Front of the cabin."

She tried it again. *Show me the front of the cabin's perimeter five minutes from now.*

This time they saw themselves in the frame. "Oh, that's trippy."

"Right?" Riggs said. "Maybe go back a minute."

She did.

"There." He pointed to a place when they suddenly appeared. "That's us."

"Whoa. This is creepy." Her future self looked back through the portal at her past self, which was her present self. Fighting a shudder, she closed the square.

"You okay?"

She squirmed uncomfortably. "I just, uh, got a sense of what you were saying, that's all. Tinkering with time. With people. It feels wrong."

"You'll get used to it." He lightly brushed a loose hair away from her eyes. "You'll figure it out, I promise."

His kindness brought her deeper feelings to the surface, and her eyes watered with emotion. "I don't think I can let someone die."

The chiseled edges of his face softened. "The concept of 'don't kill, don't save' is the hardest one to wrestle with. Being a bounty hunter is hard. We see a lot of things, and we can't do anything about them."

He lightly touched her arm and waited until she looked at him. When she did, he gave her a supportive smile. "Look at it this way, if we didn't do our jobs, it would be much, much worse. Because there are people who don't care what happens to time or anyone else. And if we didn't stop those people, it would be bad. Imagine what would happen if there no bounty hunters right now looking for the Grim? This is why we do it."

She chewed on her lip, not quite able to look him in the eye. *I don't know if I can.*

"Not doing the job would be much worse than doing the job. I promise you that."

She let that sink in for a second before moving on to something that had been bugging her. "Can bounty hunters move other people through time? Like Auci can?"

He effortlessly pivoted with the subject change. "No. No one but the siblings can do that. Even Gunnar has to use a tool. Auci is the only one I've ever seen transport people."

"Do you think I can? I mean, I've got Auci's powers." She cocked her head. "Well, some of them."

"Try it. With me. Right now."

Taking a deep breath, she reopened the square. After grabbing Riggs's arm, she stepped inside and looked around. No Riggs. "Shit."

She went back through the portal. "I guess I can't."

"Uh," Riggs squirmed.

"What?" Fin eyed him. "Was I doing it?"

"Maybe. Try again but don't let any doubt in. Just focus."

She stood tall and grabbed Riggs's arm. *Easy. I'm Auci's daughter. I can do it.* This time, stepping into the square felt like moving through jello. Halfway through, the resistance disappeared, and she landed without Riggs again.

He appeared next to her.

"Why did it feel like that?" she asked.

"Honestly? I've never seen or felt that before," he said with awe. "You were doing it, I think, but then something changed. Maybe talk to Auci about it after we get the Grim. And Lily."

Tucking that idea away for the future, she looked around. If Grayson said Lily was here, then she was here. He knew her better than anyone, and Fin trusted his knowledge. As she took in her surroundings, she realized she could feel the Grim pulsing. It was the same sensation she'd felt when she pulled it from the podium in the cave.

Am I connected to it like the compass bracelet? Why can I feel it?

That was just one more thing she needed to talk to Auci about. She touched the necklace around her throat and followed Riggs toward the cabin.

So many questions, so few answers.

<h1 style="text-align:center">40</h1>

<h2 style="text-align:center">Cook Your Noodle</h2>

Fin was impressed by how well-hidden the cabin was, especially at night. A perfect spot for nefarious activities, it was cloaked by nature as if the weeds themselves were hired specifically to create invisibility. Although it seemed to be only accessible by foot, an ATC was parked out front.

Looking over her shoulder, she remembered that she'd seen herself do that through the portal. She leaned toward Riggs and asked softly, "Did I look because I saw myself do it earlier, or did I make a decision to turn and look?"

"Yeah, those questions'll cook your noodle," Riggs said. "There'll be more, trust me."

She shook her head and turned back to the cabin, listening carefully. Crickets were having a party while woodland creatures raced from tree to tree, unaware of the budding danger. The soothing bubbling of the creek contributed to the peaceful facade. The scene was idyllic if not for the serial killer at the heart of it.

They slowly crept toward the cabin, hiding in the shadows. Oblivious to their approach, Carl stood outside on the porch, scratching his balls and smoking a cigarette. Fin gripped Riggs's arm and jerked to a halt at the macabre scene ahead. When he looked at her, she pointed to where Oliver's corpse lay in his own blood, his throat slit.

This is bad.

Riggs whispered, "Watch out for Gunnar."

Fin whispered back. "Jonesy drew a shed behind the cabin. We should split up."

He nodded at her and unholstered his Taser as she drew her gun.

"I'll take the shed." He glanced down at her Glock. "Don't kill anyone."

She bobbed her head.

He whispered, "Seriously, you need to replace that with a Taser."

"Okay, I'll just pop over to the Taser shop by that tree."

He grimaced sarcastically and headed around back.

She kept an eye on Carl. She picked up a rock and threw it away from her and the cabin. When it landed, Carl's head snapped toward the sound. He pulled out his knife and walked in that direction, investigating as he went. Fin crept the other way to the front window.

The interior was sparse with just a large freezer, probably for deer meat, and some dusty equipment for making moonshine. It was too dark to see much more, but she could tell there wasn't any movement. She went to the front door and quietly tested it. *Unlocked.* The second she cracked the door open, the smell of rotting flesh filled her nostrils.

Oh God.

She covered her nose and shut the door without going in, pausing for a moment as a wave of nausea passed through her. Taking a deep breath, she opened the door again.

As she stepped inside, the stench seeped into her nose and made her eyes sting. The air was thick with dust as she shined her flashlight onto the dirty floor and looked around.

Oh please, God, let that be an animal.

Fin swept her flashlight around, carefully keeping the light below the window to avoid Carl's watchful eye.

Cornmeal.

Sugar.

Moonshine.

Human hand.

"Oh, shit!" Fin clamped her eyes shut but forced herself to open them again. A human hand, severed at the wrist, lay on the floor. It was a woman's left hand. The diamond ring was intact, the nails perfectly polished. It was also just outside the large freezer, which wasn't plugged in.

Oh, hell no.

Fin knew what she'd find, and Christ almighty, she didn't want to find it. But she had an obligation, both professionally and morally, to look inside on the off chance someone might still be alive. Tensing every muscle in her body, she put herself in the right mindset as she pulled the door up. The density of the stench nearly killed her.

The contents of the freezer scrambled her brain.

She'd seen horrible crime scenes. Dead bodies were nothing new to her. But usually, it was one or two intact bodies. When she first started on the force, she would smear VapoRub under her nose. But with experience, she realized she needed the full use of her olfactory system to investigate crimes.

But a freezer full of rotting body parts? After this, she wasn't sure her world could ever be right again.

Fin gently shut the freezer door, then jerked to her left and vomited out everything she'd eaten that day. Unfortunately, it only added to the noxious smells, and Fin felt faint for a moment.

Come on, girl.

Fin spit out the foul taste, wiped her mouth, and got her bearings. Continuing her search, she floated like a ghost to the bathroom and flashed her light in. She immediately wished she hadn't. The acrid smell of iron was like a punch to the gut. The nausea came and went as she collected herself before inspecting the crime scene.

A hand saw and an axe rested on a small table in the tub. Two human torsos, one female and one male lay under the table. The tub and the walls were covered with blood. Pieces of bone fragments and skin were scattered around.

Please God don't let that be Boone. Or Grayson. Or Booker.

She moved to the next room and pushed open the half-closed door. Boone was slumped in a chair, unconscious and bleeding.

Boone! She clicked off her flashlight, dashed into the room, and took his pulse. *Thank God.*

She worked on the knots restraining him, but a commotion in the back stopped her. *Please let that be Riggs.* Too afraid to call out in case it wasn't him, she tiptoed through the cabin and peered out the small window in the back door. The shed door was open, revealing Lily yelling at Grayson.

There's Booker, too. They're alive. Badly beaten but alive.

Lily hit Booker before heading back toward the cabin.

"Fuck me." Fin backed up from the door and cast about for options. Carl on the porch. Bathroom a no. Lily headed for Boone. Time travel? *Not fast enough yet.* Confrontation. *Not yet. Where's the Grim?*

As Lily's voice got closer, Fin looked around, her eyes landing on the worst and only option.

"You've got to be fucking kidding me."

She ran to the freezer as Lily's footsteps closed in.

41

Be Nice to Me

Boone's eyelids fluttered between blackness and the ceiling as the back of his head rested against a man's thick arm.

Fuckin' Carl. He was still tied to the chair as Carl drug it down the hallway. The blood from his face and head trickled into his mouth leaving an iron taste. *So much blood.*

A pounding headache ramped up as his consciousness bloomed. The room he'd been in got farther away as Carl dragged his chair through the cabin. The sound of the two chair legs scraping against the floor was like nails on a chalkboard. He passed a bloody bathroom and a kitchen before Carl tipped the chair forward onto all four legs.

This must be the living tomb. Tomb? Room. Living room.

His head flopped forward and he winced. Everything hurt. He wasn't sure what sound he made, but it helped release some of the pain. The smell was even worse in this room.

What is that?

Carl yanked on the ties that bound Boone's wrists to the arms of the wooden chair, making sure they were tight. Boone lifted his head and cast a hazy gaze around him.

I can't believe I'm still alive.

Lily crossed into his view as she said, "Carl, wait outside."

"No, no, no," Boone mumbled.

"Yes, yes, yes," Lily said in a sing-song fashion as Carl left and the door clicked shut.

Please, God, help me.

Boone looked away as she laughed. He could tell she loved doing this, which was not good news for him. It would be almost impossible to talk her out of torturing him if she enjoyed it.

Even if I could escape, where the hell am I?

From what he'd seen, it was a very small cabin. The front window revealed trees and woods surrounding them. But he couldn't tell if there was a road nearby or not.

Wait, I've been here before. With my last girlfriend. Had sex in the kitchen. He glanced around. *Yeah, that's right. No phone. No nothin' up here.*

He got a sinking feeling in his gut. *I'm gonna die here.* Unwilling to face his tormentor, he looked down. At an amputated human hand.

"Oh my God!" Boone scooted his chair away but stopped with a groan when the world started spinning. He felt like he was going to vomit.

"You worried about a little hand?"

Lily's surprised expression indicated that he should be used to seeing body parts just lying around. Chuckling, she picked up the severed hand and poked him with it. He scooted back in terror as the world spun. Uncontrollable nausea bubbled up. He puked down his clothes and the side of the chair as Lily laughed. She took the hand with her as she sashayed toward the freezer.

"You think this is bad? Don't look in the freezer." Lily slowly opened it, looking at Boone over her shoulder and using the hand to point inside.

Boone could swear he saw something move inside it. *What the hell?*

"Grayson didn't have time to finish burying all of the pieces." Lily casually tossed the hand in and slammed the freezer shut as she smirked at him.

Boone tried scooting back, but he was having some trouble. He couldn't quite get the correct grip with his left hand, which was in a hell of a lot of pain. Looking down at his hand, he almost threw up again. "Oh my God!"

Lily's delighted giggle pierced his ears.

Boone tried to move his pinkie, but it wasn't there anymore. He looked closely—even though he didn't want to—at the layers of his finger. They resembled rings in a tree: the skin, the muscle, the bone, and all the blood that kept everything alive. It was still bleeding a little, but for the most part it had clotted. The more Boone looked at it, the more it hurt.

"I don't understand." Boone panicked and grew faint staring at the stump of his missing digit. "I don't—"

"Yeah, you passed out after that one." Lily eyed Boone with cold disappointment. "So, I had to go play with Grayson and that idiot rookie, Booker. And with my new power, the cop really took a couple hits for the team."

Grayson and Officer Booker are here? He looked around.

Ignoring him, she clenched and unclenched her fists staring in wonder at her hands. "Who knew the Grim could do that? It's like…the life of the thing you kill adds to your life, making you more powerful." She grinned.

"You're crazy." Boone's head tipped forward in pain. *God, just let me puke. Or die. I'll take either one.*

"Aw, Boone, be nice to me." Lily's lifeless eyes bore down on him. "I am your sister after all."

Boone's anger gave him enough energy to raise his head and level a hateful stare at her. "I don't care who Russell was to you, but you are not my family. Not now, not ever." Boone kept his eyes fixed on Lily's blank face.

The blue rings around her irises pulsed like they had a life of their own although they were slightly less blue than before. Lily slowly stepped toward Boone. He sat up a little and eyed her warily. Lily put her hands on her knees and leaned in until she was almost nose-to-nose with Boone.

"The problem is, I'm just so misunderstood," she whispered. "You can understand that, can't you? We both come from Russell. I know you feel that anger. It's impossible not to."

"I'm not Russell."

"Sure you are." She straightened up. "You'll feel so much better when you admit his blood runs through both of us. Come on, they're just words. Say 'em. Say 'You're my sister, Lily.'"

Boone sucked in a breath and held it as sweat dripped down his forehead. The weight of Lily's gaze was like a steel blanket on his chest. He tried to straighten up, but pain exploded through his body, making his head spin. Still, he managed to say, "Never," through clenched teeth.

Lily yowled like an injured beast, picked up the other chair, and threw it out the window, A surprised Carl peeked in but stepped away, an unsettled look on his face. She drew her knife and banged the point into her palm repeatedly as she furiously paced back and forth. Slithering up to him, she pushed her face into his. He tilted his head back as far as he could, but it didn't keep her from touching his nose with hers.

Her volatility was dizzying as she cycled between pleading desperation and explosive wrath. "We can be close like you and Nellie. Like Grayson and Nellie. Come on. Say it. Just say it!" Spit landed on his face with every word.

Boone shook his head, closing his eyes against the nausea and pain searing through him.

"Say it!" She grabbed him by the hair and yanked his head backward. "Say it!"

He nearly vomited from the world spinning. "No." Boone shook his head and saw streaks of light radiating from the pain. "No."

She slapped him again and again. Each time, he refused to acknowledge their bond even though the agony of her blows made him wish for death.

Please, please let me die.

Finally, Lily relented and dropped to the ground like her marionette strings had been cut. Sitting in front of him, she seemed like a small child. And then another sudden and dramatic shift completely changed her again. Like someone had flicked a light switch, she transitioned from a child to a teenager.

"You keep saying no." Lily tilted her head in surprise as she pressed the knife to the top of her left arm and started cutting slices into it, slowly working her way toward her elbow. "But I need you to say it." She gazed at him as she continued to cut herself.

Although witnessing such a drastic change in her was disturbing, he was more disturbed that her wounds were already healed. *She has the same healing power as Grayson and Fin. If we're related, why don't we have that?*

"You know, Clara Belle knew about us all along." Lily's callous eyes quietly absorbed his reaction as Boone snapped his startled stare to her. "She knew about me and Grayson, and she let it happen."

"She would never."

Lily shifted uncomfortably. "Wouldn't she? To protect her precious Nellie and Boone?"

They eyed each other for a second.

"Story time is over." Lily stood up.

Her face transformed again, and a spike of fear lanced through his spine.

"Last chance," she sang. "Tell me I'm your sister."

Boone tried to squirm away, but it was useless. Lily slammed her fist into his broken body. Her strength was so intense that the punch to his gut pushed his chair back a few feet and made him puke.

"Stop!" He couldn't take the pain, but a more agonizing thought hit him. *What if she kills something bigger than a mouse, like me, and gets even stronger? Then Nellie and everybody else will be in even worse trouble.* "All right, I'll tell you what you wanna hear!"

Lily halted her next punch. "Say it."

Don't let her kill you. Don't let her get stronger.

"You're my sister," Boone said breathlessly.

Lily's entire body relaxed as she stepped away from him.

He nearly threw up again from disgust at his words.

Lily sighed. "You can die now."

"What?"

She left the room, went through the kitchen, and out the back door.

"Lily! Wait. Lily!"

Despite the pain it caused, Boone tried to wiggle out of the rope that bound his hands to the chair. Glancing around, he looked for something sharp to cut the rope.

Even if I saw something, how could I get to it?

The freezer door opened and two eyes peered out at him.

"Holy shit!" He nearly pissed his pants.

The lid lifted high enough to expose a familiar face.

"Fin?" Boone whispered. Warm relief spread through his limbs followed immediately by cold fear for her safety. He jerked his head to the right, urging Fin to escape, as he mouthed the word, "Run!"

Lily's heavy boots approached from outside.

His heart kicked into overdrive as Fin put her index finger over her lips and sunk back into the freezer.

Lily came inside with some kind of tool that Boone didn't want anywhere near him. It had a small spinning blade that looked like it could cut through bone.

"I've never done this on someone who was still alive." Lily grabbed Boone's throat and brought the tool up toward his face. "This should be fun. Well, for me."

She turned on the tool, and it buzzed like a dentist drill. Behind her, Fin rose like a phoenix out of the freezer. Lily cackled then paused thoughtfully before shutting it off and dropping the saw to the floor.

"Why am I using this when I can use this?" She pulled out the Grim. "And get even stronger."

As she moved to strike, Fin launched herself onto her feet, almost as if the dead were pushing her out to redeem them. Lily whirled around in surprise as Fin rushed her.

"The Grim," Boone shouted.

When Lily brandished the bone dagger toward Fin, Boone stretched out his foot and tripped her. As Lily fell, Carl charged through the door.

Fin ran for Boone. As she grabbed him, a distant part of him enjoyed Carl's surprised expression.

The next thing he saw was the smashed front porch of his home.

42

Get Off My Side

Nellie gave Jonesy the stink eye. *I could kill him.*

He avoided looking at her, which was difficult given that they were handcuffed to each other.

I need to be helping Fin not sitting here like a little kid.

She huffed out a disgusted breath as she looked away from him. The walk from the patrol car back to Nellie's house was a lesson in patience. She did a lot of yelling, and Jonesy did a lot of nothing. It ended with the two of them sitting on a hay bale in the barn waiting for Dawson to call the police and pack the car.

Why can't he understand I need to help find Boone?

"Jonesy, how could you?" Nellie finally said, sick of waiting for him to say something.

"I didn't do anything wrong," Jonesy said, clearly annoyed with her. "I didn't tell her to handcuff us to each other. If you hadn't acted like a child and insisted on going, even though everyone said you shouldn't, she wouldn't have done it. I know you're a little younger than all of us but come on."

Nellie yanked as hard as she could on the handcuffs, catching him by surprise and pulling him off the hay bale.

"Dammit, Nellie!" Jonesy stood up, dragging Nellie up with him.

"I am not a child." She plopped back down onto the block of hay, tugging him again. *If I could just get that key out of his pocket, I could get outta here.*

"You know, if you were my girlfriend, and that's a big if right now, I'd—"

"You'd what?"

"I'd—"

"What?"

"Get off my side of the hay bale!" Jonesy hauled on the handcuffs, pulling Nellie to the side.

"Oh, you are such a jerk!"

She stood up and smacked the dust off her clothes. A spider flew off her skirt, and she jumped back with a squeal. Stomping at it, she towed Jonesy around while she tried to kill it.

"I'm a jerk?" He whirled her around to face him. "I'm a jerk?"

"Yeah," she yelled. "You're a jerk!"

She closed the gap between them with the intention of screaming some more. But once she came nose to nose with his chiseled features and warm skin, she changed her tune.

Nellie looked at Jonesy's full lips and his stormy eyes. *I wanna kiss him.* She grabbed his face, pulled him to her, and pressed her lips to his.

He kissed her back, and he was much better at it than she was. It was a little wet but not gross. A little warm but in a good way. A little weird but it felt nice.

This is awesome.

His hand moved across the lower part of her back and around to her stomach.

Oh, that's nice.

He finished kissing her, pulled back a little, and gazed into her eyes.

She couldn't hold back the flush that warmed her face. *My first kiss.* "Wow."

He laughed and she laughed back.

"I like you, Nellie Ellis."

"I like you, too, Jonesy Wolfe."

And she really did. Which is why she felt bad about what was going to happen next. She hadn't planned on getting her first kiss and then mugging the boy who gave it to her. But she had to help her brother and Fin.

When Jonesy leaned in for another kiss, Nellie shoved him over the hay bale, flinging him backward and dragging her with him. He landed face down by the car, trapping his free arm, while she landed on top of him with their cuffed arms between them.

The key. She scooted her body weight up and laid on his back so he couldn't move his free arm.

"Dammit, Nellie! What the hell are you doin'?"

She reached into his jean pocket. *Lucky I'm flexible.*

"Hey!" he yelled.

She extracted the key and pulled his arm toward his ankle.

"Stop it!" He fought back, trying to push her off him and bring his arm back up.

I've wrestled Boone a hundred times. I can take you, too. She squashed him down with her body weight and a well-placed elbow. Reaching over, she inserted the key into her handcuff, and unlocked it. Just as Jonesy was scrambling up, she closed the open handcuff around the door handle of the car.

Jonesy's face flushed with rage. "Are you crazy?"

"I'm so sorry, Jonesy." She faced him with a mix of surprise and apology at what she had done. Then she took a deep breath and owned it. "But I gotta help Fin. I have to find my brother. He'd do it for me."

As she ran to her supplies, Jonesy yelled, "No! It's too dangerous."

She spun around and gave him one last tender tilt of her head. "If you decide you wanna ask me to be your girl, I'll say yes."

She snatched her bow and arrows and ran out the barn door as he yelled her name. Her heart was torn, wanting to both stay and go. But she was absolutely determined to save them all, and not even her first love could stop her from doing it.

43

Too Many Wounds

Fin stood in front of Clara Belle's house in shock. She gaped down at her fingers like they belonged to someone else as they gripped the chair Boone was still tied to. "Holy shit. Did I . . ."

Boone winced in pain as he peered up at her, wide-eyed. "How . . ." He glanced around. "How did we do that?"

She just shook her head.

"Hello, Fin."

She whipped around. "Auci!" She pulled him into a hug as tears pricked her eyes. "You're okay."

He held her, his chin leaning against her head, and whispered, "I told you, daughter. You're never alone."

She leaned out of the hug and wiped her eyes on her arm. "It was you? You pulled us through?"

"Sort of," he said. "You started to but couldn't quite hold it, so I helped."

"Thank you," she said as she grasped him again.

"You're welcome," he said before giving her a peck on the top of her head.

My dad. He really is my dad.

She stepped out of the hug and gave him a warm stare as she asked, "Did you know? That I might be able to do it, too?"

"I wasn't sure whether you could or not." He cocked his head at her. "But it appears that you just might."

"Why can't I finish it?"

"My guess is that you haven't fully accepted who you are. What you are. All of this probably still feels impossible."

Considering that, she took a deep steadying breath.

"It will come." Pride beamed from his face.

Boone interrupted their tender moment. "Fin, I need to tell you something."

"Oh!" She hurried over and untied him from the chair while asking Auci, "Will you help me get Grayson and Booker?"

"No," he said. "I trust you can do it."

"But—"

"It's too dangerous for me," he interrupted. "I believe in you. That you know who you are. That you are my daughter."

Her eyes teared up.

"You can do this." He grabbed her arms and squeezed just as two large men appeared behind him. They had Tasers strapped to their hips like old-timey gunslingers. Auci smirked at them before turning back to Fin.

She asked, "Bounty hunters?"

"The Council." He nodded and said, "Please ask Riggs to find my sister. They're protecting her, too. Please tell her . . . tell her I think I've found a way to relieve her pain. To end our centuries long rift."

"Really?" Fin searched his face.

One corner of his lips quirked up. "Someone very smart once told me that when you love someone, there's always a way."

With her throat constricting, all she could do was wipe her eyes and give a slight dip of her chin.

He brought her into another hug and smoothed her hair. After kissing the top of her head once more, he stepped back.

"Know who you are," he said before disappearing with the bounty hunters into the night.

Boone's shrill yell cut through the moment. "Fin!" he shouted. "I have to tell you something."

"Boone, it'll have to wait! I have to get Grayson and Booker."

Fin formed the thought of where and when she wanted to go, and she was there.

Okay, I'm getting faster.

When she appeared in the shed, Grayson and Booker were staring back at her while being untied by Riggs and Sophie in a mad rush.

They, too, turned at her appearance.

"Fin," said Riggs.

"Thank God," said Sophie.

Seeing them flooded Fin's body with relief.

In the cabin, Lily let out a frustrated scream as Carl shouted, "Where the fuck did they go?"

Fin rushed over to her friends. "They'll be here any second."

Riggs helped Grayson up while Sophie helped Booker up. But neither of the badly beaten men could stand, and they immediately dropped back down onto their chairs.

"They can't travel." Riggs dashed to the shed's entrance. "Help me reinforce the door."

Heavy footfalls closed in as Riggs and Fin cast about for something to help them. Fin plucked a thin metal pipe from the corner and slid it through the inner handle, bracing it across the door frame seconds before someone hauled on the door with an undeniable force.

Eyes round with alarm, Riggs said, "Holy shit, she's strong."

The outer handle was no match for Lily, who wrenched it off, splintering the wood around it.

"We won't be able to keep her out," Fin exclaimed.

"How about keepin' her from getting' in then?" Sophie said before she vanished.

Fin gasped. "No, Sophie, the Grim!"

The sounds of struggle stopped outside the shed.

Riggs and Fin shared a quick glance as they held their breath.

After a moment, Riggs said, "We need to get them out of here."

"This is the only way out," said Fin.

"You can take them. Like Auci."

"I can't do it yet," said Fin. "I tried."

"It's all in the mind, Fin. Try again." He cast a nervous glance at the door. "Sophie can't buy us a ton of time. Try now. Pick one."

Fin ran to Booker, who said, "No. Grayson first."

"But—"

"No." Booker glared at her with the eye that wasn't swollen shut. "Civilians first. Go!"

He doesn't know about Grayson's healing power. "Fine."

She went to Grayson, who was bloodied and bruised and touched his hand.

To the house. Right now.

It felt like she was swimming through jello with weights on her feet. She tried to push through, but the magic snapped her and Grayson back like a rubber band. Riggs and now Sophie were leaning back, using all their weight and strength to keep the door pulled closed. Outside, Lily stabbed at the wood, carving off huge splinters each time.

Riggs looked over his shoulder at Fin. "You have to do it. Go!"

"Fin, hurry!" Sophie yelled.

She grabbed Grayson again and entered the portal, still thick with resistance.

I am the daughter of a Greek God, dammit, I can do this!

Adrenaline fueling her, she screamed the mantra in her head and strained against the portal's opposition. With a jarring pop, she appeared in front of Clara Belle's house. Not stopping to celebrate, she commanded her magic to take her back.

Arriving in the shed, she panicked at the sight of the door. It had a hole large enough that Lily had reached through and grabbed hold of Sophie's throat as Riggs tried to hold the door and grab his Taser at the same time.

Fin shouted. "Get her and get out o' here, Riggs!"

Fin heard the distinct sound of a Taser's electricity as she latched on to Booker and launched herself into the portal. This time, when she pushed against the magic, she warred with it only for a moment before she quickly passed through.

Suddenly, she was sprawled on the ground by the Ellis house.

Riggs yelled, "Holy shit!"

Fin rolled over and stared up at Boone. He looked down, blinking at her like a curious owl.

"Holy shit!" Fin echoed with glee. "I did it!"

Grayson and Booker tried to sit up with painful groans and alarmed expressions as they peered around at their new environment.

Booker said, "I must've really got the shit beat of me 'cause this don't make no sense."

"How?" Grayson said, dazed. "D-did we pass out?"

Sophie rubbed her reddened throat, coughing from trauma and surprise as she choked out, "How? How…did you do it?"

As Riggs helped Fin up, he said, "You can move like Auci. Holy shit."

She beamed a proud smile at him.

I did it. I am my father's daughter.

But Fin's smile faded as her eyes fell on Grayson and Booker.

"Help me." Fin hurried over to Grayson and attended to his wounds.

Taking her cue, Sophie and Riggs helped Booker up and onto the chair Boone had been tied to.

The two captives gingerly moved a little, weary from their wounds.

"Fin!" Boone yelled, startling the nearby birds into flight.

She jumped and faced him. "What?"

"Listen to me, dammit!" said Boone. "The Grim does something. When you kill someone with it, you get—I don't know. Power? More life?

Something. Lily tried to kill Gunnar, but Gunnar disappeared. Lily was so mad she killed a mouse. Then she got these blue rings in her eyes, and she was way stronger after that. Like she had more life to her. Or power or something."

"Yeah, her power is intense," Sophie said as she rubbed her throat again.

Fin asked Riggs, "Did you know the Grim would do that?"

"I had no idea." Riggs turned to his partner. "Sophie, go tell the council. Show them your throat. Have them get a message to Auci."

"Wait," said Fin.

"Yeah?"

"Auci was here—"

"What?" asked Riggs. "He's supposed to stay in custody."

"He was here for me. To help me," said Fin. "He said he needs to get a message to Gunnar. He said he has a way to help her. To stop her pain. He needs to see her."

Sophie gave a thumbs up. "Okay, I'll see what I can do."

"Thank you," said Fin.

Sophie disappeared.

Booker gasped at seeing a human vanish into thin air. "What in the Sam Hill is going on around here?"

Fin waved away the chief's question as she stared at Grayson. "I'll explain later, Chief."

Booker said, "Chief?"

"I mean, Booker," she corrected herself.

He muttered an irritated and unintelligible string of words under his breath.

Turning her attention back to Grayson, she examined the three severe stab wounds in his thigh that were slowly bleeding. Touching them gently, she whispered, "You're not healing."

He whispered back, "Too many wounds. Starting with this one." He tapped the metal bowl. "You knew this arrow was gonna kill me. I did, too."

Tears pricked at her eyes as she shook her head.

Refusing to accept that possibility, Fin ran into the house and hauled a kitchen chair outside. She set it down in front of his feet while making sure he was properly prone.

"Fin," Grayson said quietly.

326

"You'll be fine." She lifted his leg onto the chair to slow the bleeding. After ripping off the bloodied leg of his jeans, she tore it into strips and fastened a tourniquet just above the stab wounds. "You're not going to die, okay? Not if I can help it."

He grabbed her arm with a feverish intensity in his eyes. "You need to stop Lily."

"Fin!" someone shouted.

Everyone turned to the barn where the yell came from.

Dawson and Jonesy ran toward them as Fin said, "You were supposed to leave. Where's Nellie?"

"She went to help you," Dawson said breathlessly as he stopped in front of them.

"Oh my God." Fin scrambled to her feet.

Riggs stepped forward. "I'll help you."

Sophie reappeared. "The council is working on the Grim's powers. What it is and why. And they're going to connect Auci and Gunnar."

Fin sprang into action. "Sophie, please stay here until the cops arrive. Riggs, please find Nellie and bring her here. I'm going back for the dagger."

A chaotic mix of emotions washed over Riggs's face. "I can't."

She rounded on him. "What?"

"I'm here for you and the dagger. That's it."

She jerked back like a snake had bitten her. "Fine," she said through clenched teeth.

"I'll find Nellie," said Dawson.

Jonesy chimed in. "I'll go with him."

"Okay," she said. "Dawson, you still have the pen-sword thing?"

He nodded as he yanked it from his pocket.

"Good. Go."

She shot Riggs a nasty look before she vanished.

44

Looking for Me?

The portal trip back to the cabin required more effort than Fin was expecting. *I must be getting tired.* When she finally materialized, a bullet ripped through her shoulder.

"Fuck!" She hit the forest floor with a thud. "Christ!"

Fin gripped her shoulder as she noticed Grayson lay sprawled on the ground next to her.

"Grayson?" *He must've grabbed me right before I traveled. That's why it was harder.* Fin gripped her shoulder as more bullets whizzed by.

Using her good arm, Fin seized the waist of his jeans and dragged him to the nearest tree. A bullet tore into his calf the second before she pulled him behind the thick oak.

"Ah!" he screamed. Fresh blood seeped through his pants even with the torniquet on his thigh.

She pulled her gun and huddled with Grayson as the bullets ripped through the bark, sending fragments of broken wood into their laps and faces. They watched as shot after shot struck all around them in the dirt and the creek.

Fin was surprised to see Riggs behind the tree right next to them. But her focus shifted when a bullet ricocheted off a rock and missed Fin's skull by a fraction of an inch. It embedded deep into the tree, and she stared wide-eyed at it.

"Fuckin' Carl," she said.

She finally noticed that her shoulder was lightly bleeding but working. *A through and through.* It was already almost healed. She glanced over at Riggs, who had been joined by Sophie, as a silence blanketed the woods.

"Stay put," she hissed to Grayson.

His face was getting paler by the minute, but he gave a slight head tilt. Fin scooted her body up the tree until she was in a standing position. She rolled her shoulder as her injury healed completely and spun away from the tree, firing at her attackers. In the muzzle flash from her gun, she saw Carl ducking behind the ATC on Fin's right and Lily running from tree to tree on Fin's left.

As Riggs and Sophie stalked toward Lily, Fin fired in short bursts to keep Carl pinned down while she advanced too. She sprinted to the porch and ducked behind the corner where the porch and house met. Her police training took over as she waited for Carl to pop up like a whack-a-mole, exposing his left side. Her patience rewarded, Fin fired, catching Carl on the side of his chest and dropping him to the ground.

By the time she got to him to check his pulse, he was gone.

"Shit." She wasn't supposed to kill anyone, but she wasn't going to let fuckin' Carl kill her, either. *Add it to the growing list of shit I'm not supposed to do.*

Fin crossed the remaining open grass and dipped behind a large hickory tree. She peeked out to see where Lily had gone.

Nothing. "Fuck," she said under her breath.

She ejected her magazine, loaded another, and centered herself. She sprung from behind the tree into the night, playing a sort of sadistic hide and seek with Lily. A figure popped out from behind a tree and ran to the next, but Fin held her fire, unsure if it was Lily or not.

Fin moved stealthily from tree to tree, trying to spy where Lily was hiding.

"Looking for me?" Lily whispered behind her.

Fin instinctively dodged as she whipped around.

"Fuck!" Fin yelled as she ducked, the dagger just missing her.

A distant part of her mind noticed the crazy blue circles around Lily's irises as Fin fired three times. Lily dropped like a stone as Riggs and Sophie arrived just behind Fin, tasers in hand.

"Check her." Fin kept her gun trained on Lily. "The Grim's in her hand."

Sophie knelt and grabbed the enchanted knife by its handle.

"Got it." Sophie searched Lily's body, found the sheath, and protected the blade before evaluating Lily's injuries. "Barely alive."

Fin lowered her gun but didn't holster it. "We'll see."

Riggs turned concerned eyes on Fin. "Grayson's in bad condition."

Fin swallowed back her emotions and said, "I know. I'll secure Lily, then get him to a hospital."

Riggs gave a quick nod. "Sophie, take the Grim to the council. I'll get Auci out of hiding then come right back."

Sophie nodded and blinked out of existence.

"Go," said Fin. "We'll be okay."

"If she heals, regular beat cops won't be able to handle her," Riggs warned. Fin acknowledged his concern. "When I come back, I'll take her to the council."

"What, do you have, like, bounty hunter jail?" she said off-hand. But when Riggs gave her a serious look, she said, "Of course you have bounty hunter jail."

"Are you okay?" He reached out and lightly touched her lower back.

She twisted away from him. "I don't understand you, Riggs. I don't understand how you can just . . ." But she couldn't finish the sentence.

"You will," he said softly. "Someday."

She sank into his concerned stare, searching for answers as he reached out again. This time she didn't pull away.

He cares about me. "I'm okay."

"I won't be long. I promise."

Fin sucked in a small breath and gave him a nod. He let go and disappeared.

She looked at Lily's unmoving body and holstered her gun. Fin bent to secure her but heard a rustling behind her. Pulling her weapon again, she whipped around and aimed into the darkness.

Oh my God. She lowered the gun immediately. "Nellie, what are you doing here?"

Nellie's happy expression morphed into terror as she grabbed her bow. "Behind you!"

Lily said, "The power from the Grim really helps a girl heal."

Whirling around, Fin raised her weapon. But as she pulled the trigger, Lily smacked Fin's wrist into the air, sending her bullet into the sky.

Lily brought her other arm around and stabbed Fin's shoulder with her trusty knife.

"Ahh!" Fin screamed, reflexively hunching to protect herself.

Pain exploded in Fin's abdomen as Lily kneed her in the stomach, launching her backward.

I can't breathe.

As Fin fell, Lily ripped her handgun away.

No!

With a vicious smile, Lily turned and fired at Nellie's chest just as an arrow landed in her stomach.

Everything went black.

45

It's Too Quiet Here

When Fin opened her eyes, she was standing in the cool woods alone. No evidence existed that anyone had ever been there. No blood, no weapons, no nothing. The stillness was unnerving.

Where's Nellie? "Hello?"

Her voice echoed loud and clear around the trees as an overabundance of fireflies blinked and glowed around her.

Too many fireflies. "Nellie?"

Footsteps cut through the thick silence and crunched the underbrush at a tepid pace.

She grabbed for her gun, but it wasn't there. "What the hell?"

"Fin?" Nellie asked.

They wore identical expressions of shock as a dense layer of fog gathered around the forest floor. It brought with it a cold shock of air that made Nellie shiver.

"I don't understand." Nellie looked down at her chest, which was free from blood and injury. "I got shot. Didn't I?"

Fin shook her head in disbelief. *It can't be.* "Do you remember dying?"

"I don't think so." She rubbed her chest and rested her hand over her heart. "I didn't feel any pain. I just thought, 'bullseye,' and then I collapsed."

"You shot Lily with an arrow."

"Yeah."

"Do you remember anything after that?"

Nellie flicked a glance at Fin but quickly looked away. Instead, she stared at the fireflies as they played peacefully around her head and body, swirling in bursts of warm light as the bitter fog settled at their ankles.

Fin pressed on. "What, Nellie? What did you see?"

"You." Nellie squirmed but looked at her. "You disappeared right in front of me. And then I woke up here."

I disappeared?

Nellie looked around. "It's too quiet here. This can't be heaven."

Fin's mother extended her finger, and a firefly perched there slowly beating its soothing amber wings as its sunrise-colored light pulsed.

"Where are the angels?" Nellie whispered.

Fin began to pace, investigating the strange world they were in. Nellie was right. There were no angels, but there were no devils either. Fin also didn't sense any magic. Nothing was glowing, including her compass bracelet.

With a calmness she didn't feel, Fin said, "I don't think you died."

Nellie peered curiously at her. "What do you mean?"

Fin glanced at their surroundings. "I think we're in between life and death."

Nellie gently blew on the firefly to make it fly off before facing Fin and cocking her head. "But she shot me, so why are you here?"

Should I explain?

She wanted to tell her mom that the reason she was here was because if Nellie died before Fin was born, then Fin would never be born. But there could be another explanation, and it would probably be best to tell Nellie that instead. After all, Fin knew she'd likely have to stand in front of the council for Carl's death—among other things—so maybe it was best to not add any more fuel to the fire by revealing secrets.

"Maybe Lily shot me too, and we just didn't see it." That was plausible. *Plausible deniability, you liar.*

"Huh." Nellie considered that for a moment before her eyes flared as round as saucers. "Did you see her eyes? Why did they look like that?"

"The blue ring is a side effect of the dagger we didn't know about."

"Okay." Nellie bounced on the balls of her feet. "So, how do we get back? Can we?"

Cold fear sent a chill down Fin's back, then she remembered her compass bracelet. "Help," she whispered to her wrist.

But this time, nothing happened. *No magic.*

Cold fear turned to frigid panic as she stared at Nellie. She had no answer and no way of figuring one out.

Oh my God, what if no one comes to help?

46

This is My Stop

Leaning against the tree, Grayson couldn't see what was happening, but he heard Fin yell, "Nellie," before a burst of gunfire.

That's why he latched onto Fin when she came back here. He wanted to help Fin and Nellie. But he could barely move from the pain and the blood loss as he tried to walk his shoulder blades up the tree. It wasn't working.

He rested for a moment, closing his eyes, and tipping his head back against the bark. *Just need a second.* As he struggled to breathe, a bitter cold crept from his feet up his legs and into his hips. He cracked open his eyes as a strange fog rolled across the forest floor, sucking the warmth out of the air. Fireflies with bright amber wings and a warm glow rode the waves of the hazy incoming tide.

"Beautiful," he murmured as he began to fade.

His eyes focused on one firefly that landed on his leg and opened its wings. He watched it for a moment before it launched into the air. Following its ascent, Grayson came face to face with a pair of bright blue eyes staring at him from inside the fog. He was too tired to fight.

Kill me if you have to.

The haunting eyes emerged from the swirling fog. A striking white fox trotted over and sat beside him. Curling its bushy tail around its legs, the creature stared at him, waiting patiently. Grayson could sense its power.

This ain't no ordinary fox. "Are you here for me?"

The fox inclined its head. Grayson's eyes misted over as he sucked in a deep breath and slowly let it out. He deserved to die, but now that he was facing the inevitable, he wanted to fight for his life. His heart was still filled with fire, and he wanted to be a better man than he had been. But he knew his body was failing him.

"Will my mama be there?" he choked out.

The fox inclined its head again.

Grayson shoved down the onslaught of tears waiting for release. "All right then," he choked out. He cleared his throat then exhaled a held breath. "I'm comin'."

He rolled onto his good side, crawled to his knees, and reached out to lean his weight against the tree. Slowly, he walked his hands up to a standing position and put all his weight on his good leg. He faced the fox, who was ten feet ahead of him.

It looked over its shoulder at him, turned, and started walking.

Grayson followed at an agonizingly slow pace, limping from one tree to the next. But the forest around him seemed to be moving faster. Almost like he was on a conveyor belt leading him deeper into the forest as the fog got thicker and the fireflies danced around him.

"What about Nellie, fox?" asked Grayson.

He noticed how quiet it suddenly seemed and how much cooler it was. The animal looked back at him again, giving him a nod before continuing to lead him further into the darkening woods.

Nellie's voice floated over to him. "Grayson?"

He turned to his right, and standing there in shock and surprise were Nellie and Fin.

"Grayson!" Nellie ran up to him and hugged him.

He winced, expecting pain, but it didn't hurt. In fact, nothing hurt. As she pulled away, he looked down at his body. It was completely healed, the metal bowl was gone, and he was back to normal. Incredulous, he looked up at Fin.

"Where are we?" he asked.

"I don't know. Where did you come from?" Fin inspected his healed body with sobering concern. "How did you get here?"

"I-I don't know. I followed the white fox."

"Did you say white fox? Did it have blue eyes?" Fin asked.

Nellie asked, "What fox?"

"That one." He pointed at the animal, but their confused expressions made it clear they couldn't see it. "Yeah, blue eyes. Why?"

"Grayson." Tears pooled in Fin's eyes.

The grief on her face told him he was dying. But he already knew that. The heartbreak in Fin's eyes surprised and touched him.

"I guess this is my stop." Concerned, he asked, "Are you comin' with me?"

Fin shook her head. "I don't think so."

"But how will you get back?"

Fin swiped at her damp cheeks and said, "The fox."

"Oh." Grayson tilted his head in Nellie's direction. "You'll take care of her?"

Fin straightened her shoulders. "I promise."

Nellie jumped into the conversation and said, "I don't understand. What's going on?"

Grayson ambled over to Nellie and hugged her again, whispering in her ear, "I'm so glad you're my sister."

"Me too." Her face was a storm of confusion as he let go.

"I hope someday you can forgive me for the bad things I done."

"I don't understand." Nellie' eyes darted between Fin and Grayson, landing on her half-brother. "Haven't you come to take us back?"

Tears pricked at the back of his eyes. "No, I have to stay. But you . . . you have to live. Go. Follow our new little friend."

Blood spread across Nellie's shirt and Fin's shoulder as the fox slowly faded from Grayson's vision.

"What's happening?" Nellie's eyes went wide in panic as she plucked at her shirt.

Grayson put his hands on her arms, and she looked up at him.

"It's okay, Nellie," he said. "Follow the fox." He tilted his eyes down at the vexing creature who had almost disappeared.

Following his gaze, Nellie gasped. "Oh, she's beautiful." Her eyes followed the retreating fluff ball Grayson could no longer see.

"Hurry." He gave her a gentle push.

"B-but," Nellie stuttered.

Fin came up and took her hand as Fin's eyes followed the fox, too. "We have to go. Now!"

Nellie jerked away and hugged Grayson again. "I don't want to leave you."

Her warmth made him aware of how cold he was. He teetered backward out of Nellie's embrace until he fell on the ground. The icy march crept up his torso and arms, bringing a wave of fear with it.

Fin darted to his side, putting her warm hands on his frosty ones as Nellie hugged herself. The choices of his life sat on his chest like a fifty-pound weight, and the pain of them came out in salty tears down his face.

"I'm scared," he whispered.

Fin squeezed his hands. "You're going to be okay, Grayson."

Fin was always stoic, and he liked that about her. It meant he didn't have to be.

"You don't lie very good." He forced a weak smile through the panic he was feeling as death trudged up his spine.

She said quietly, "Grayson, you can let go. Your mom . . . I believe she'll be on the other side."

Grayson wanted to say more, but it was getting harder to speak.

"She loves you so much," Fin whispered. "She'll be so happy to see you."

Overcome with love and fear, he was barely able to croak out, "Bury me . . . next to . . . Mama."

"And in the light." Fin gave him a hopeful but watery smile. "So, you won't be in the dark."

Grayson's last tear slid down his cheek as the life slipped out of him. "Thank . . . you."

"Thank you, Grayson."

Fin squeezing his hands was the last wonderful thing Grayson felt before seeing his mama.

Rose radiated light, reaching out her hands and smiling for him to join her.

47

I Have You to Thank

Fin realized she was lying on the hard forest floor as she opened her eyes to a dark, starry sky and trees blowing in the breeze. A long piece of grass tickled her cheek, and she twitched her head away from it.

Nellie.

Gasping as she grasped her situation, Fin sat up to movement at her feet.

Lily.

Lily blinked in surprise, but she recovered quickly and aimed Fin's gun at Fin's forehead. Grinning in triumph, she said, "Gotcha."

Fin kicked Lily's hand, knocking the gun up and out of Lily's grip, but it still fired. As the bullet slammed into a tree, the gun landed somewhere in the darkness.

Fin rolled and jumped up just as Lily crashed into her like a linebacker. Lily held on as they tumbled several feet back onto the ground.

My God she's strong.

This time, Fin wasn't worried about what her power might do to Lily. Because of the Grim, Lily had become a near equal enemy.

As Lily slammed Fin's back into a large Oak tree, shaking it to its core, Fin used all her strength to shove Lily away, throwing her into a Birch tree so hard it cracked the bark and rattled the ground.

The air vibrated with their power.

With a shocked expression, Lily stepped away from the tree as Fin positioned herself into a fighting stance.

Lily cracked her neck in a slow manner then pulled her knife. "Who are you? And don't say no one, 'cause only me and Grayson got power like you. You're somebody. Who?"

Fin ignored the question and slyly searched for her gun. She took a few steps to the left, but Lily shadowed her movement.

The blue rings in her eyes are fading. "Why are you doing this?"

Lily barked out a bitter laugh. "Do you know what it's like to not have a real family?"

Where's my damn gun? "I'm sorry, I don't know what you've gone through." Her police negotiation training was coming in handy as she side-stepped again searching with her peripheral vision for her Glock. "I can't relate. But I do know Nellie. If you give her a chance, I'm sure she'd want to know you. To be your family."

Disgust rippled across Lily's face. "I don't want to know her. Or any of 'em. Clara Belle knew what was goin' on, and she didn't do anything. She just kept her precious kids safe, but to hell with me. And Grayson. And my mother."

Lily's expressive hands became more emphatic as she talked. Her arms mimicked a skilled conductor bringing a symphony to its conclusion with her bloody knife.

My gun!

Fin darted toward the gun, but a boot slammed down on it.

Fin jerked back in surprise, looking up at the woman in front of her. "Ice."

"Tsk, tsk, Fin," the blue-eyed vixen sung. "The council will not be happy if you shoot yet another person in the past."

Ice kicked the gun into the night as Fin lurched for it. Missing it by a second, Fin winced as Ice's fingernails scraped her collarbone. Clawing at her neck, she glanced up at Auci's locket dangling from Ice's hand.

The vicious hunter grinned sadistically. "Looks like Daddy's girl is in a wee bit o' trouble."

The magic of Newcross poured into Fin like a dam breaking. Her head hummed with vibrations as she dropped like a stone. Magic pulsed through her body with abandon after Auci's necklace had held it at bay for so long.

Taking advantage of Fin's kneeling position, Ice kicked her in the stomach, launching her backward. Fin sprawled on the ground, struggling to get control of the magic coursing through her and watching her two opponents.

Auci said: Don't fight the magic.

Lily swaggered over to Ice with a delighted smile. "What's wrong with her? Who is she?"

"The auctioneer is her father," Ice said as Fin tried to stand.

Come on, let it in.

"I knew she was somebody." Lily circled Fin like a shark. "What's with the necklace?"

"Protection charm." Ice dropped it onto the ground and crushed it with her boot heel.

The charm's destruction sent a shock wave through Fin's body. But unlike the previous training with Auci, Fin was getting stronger instead of weaker.

I'm doing it. Come on now.

"What do we do with her?" Lily asked as she twisted her knife against her finger.

Almost there, come on. Fin got up on one knee, beginning to stand.

"Now that the Council has the Grim, we don't need her anymore." Ice glanced at Lily. "I should kill you for losing it. But I won't. You might be useful."

"Like you could kill me." Lily scoffed as she approached Fin.

Yeah, get closer, Lily. Time to finish this.

Newcross's magic no longer felt like an electrocution to Fin; now it felt like a defibrillator. She rose to her full height as Lily stepped back in surprise. Fin's muscles tingled with power as she stretched her hands and took a rich, deep breath. Her eyes stabbed at Ice, who also took a startled step back.

Fin said, "You shouldn't have done that."

Harnessing all the power she'd drawn into her body, Fin first punched Lily's chest, knocking her back several feet and into a stream before stalking toward Ice, who tried to run away but tripped over the thick foliage and fell. She landed hard but jammed her fingers into her mouth and whistled.

Fin took a few more steps before a gust of air knocked her onto her butt. She recognized the sound before she saw Halo's winged scorpion. She popped up as it dove at her. Its razor-sharp teeth exposed and dripping with anticipation.

Bracelet.

Fin braced her legs and swung up her arm in front of her. An explosive burst of blue force erupted from the turquoise stone, blasting the beast and Ice back and throwing Fin a few feet backwards to the ground.

Now that's power!

Wings that were twice Fin's height flapped out of the bright blue light. A black butterfly with turquoise spots bowed to Fin.

"Oh, wow," Fin whispered. *Beautiful.*

Ice lay stunned on the ground, gaping at the magical creature. But the angry winged scorpion recovered with a whip of its vicious head. The butterfly launched into the air, spreading its wings with a fierce screech as it raced toward the monster.

Lily emerged from the stream like a dripping wet sea monster and shouted at Fin, "You're mine!" She raced forward, her knife at the ready.

As Fin and Lily charged each other, Fin saw Ice disappear in her peripheral vision. One second before they collided, Fin dropped down and grabbed Lily's wrist, twisting the knife and bringing it down into Lily's thigh.

"Ah!" Lily screamed.

Fin elbowed Lily under the jaw, rocketing her head back. After yanking the knife out, Fin snapped the blade from the handle and threw both pieces as far as she could.

A shrieking sound from above pulled Fin's focus up to the sky. The butterfly fought the scorpion by dissolving into blue powder when the beast attacked, then reforming its body and attacking the monster from the other side.

It's working. The scorpion is getting weaker.

Ice reappeared and whistled for her beast, who fled from battle and flew toward its owner. As Fin went after her, Lily raced from behind and wrapped arms of steel around her chest and squeezed. Fin slammed her head back into Lily's face and hot blood splattered the back of her neck.

"Bitch!" Lily stumbled backward clutching her nose.

The butterfly circled an area over the forest floor, so Fin raced to the spot where it was hovering. Ice met her winged beast on the ground and jumped on. They launched into the air and made a beeline for Lily.

Shit!

Fin slid under the butterfly like a baseball player, grabbed her gun, and turned. The butterfly disintegrated into a cloud of blue sparkles, which obscured her vision. When the blue cloud funneled back into her bracelet, her enemies were gone. For a moment, she didn't move. Holding her gun steady, Fin waited and listened. After a few seconds that felt like hours, she got up and walked over to where Lily had been.

Nothing.

"Fuck." *They're gone.* She holstered her gun. *Mom.* "Nellie!" she yelled. "Nellie!"

She ran to where Nellie had originally been shot and found her unconscious, cradled in Gunnar's arms.

Fin said shocked, "Gunnar!"

Gunnar tipped Nellie's head back and poured a clear liquid from a tiny vile into Nellie's open mouth.

"No!" Fin raced toward her.

Gunnar held up a calming hand. "They're phoenix tears. I'm not hurting her."

"I don't believe you," Fin said as she closed in. "You were trying to kill my father."

Gunnar held out the vile. "See for yourself."

Fin yanked it out of Gunnar's hand and sniffed it.

Doesn't smell like anything. Not that I know what poisons smell like.

Fin put the tip of her finger into the vile. Nothing happened. She touched the tip of her finger to her tongue.

Salty. "Gross." Fin smirked.

Gunnar's green eyes sparkled as they explored Fin's face. "Auci was right. You do look like your mother."

"Auci told you about me?" She tucked a hair behind her ear, her anger receding. "He said he had way to make things right with you."

Ignoring that, she said with pride, "You're very impressive, niece. Powerful."

Fin squirmed a little as she shrugged off the compliment. "Oh, I think that's from Newcross."

"It's not just Newcross."

A moment passed before Gunnar said, "I hear I have you to thank."

"For what?"

"My freedom."

The sincerity in Gunnar's voice caught Fin off-guard. She flicked her eyes to her aunt's face as a range of emotions surged across it.

One side of Fin's lips quirked up. "Auci listened to me?"

"To his only child? Indeed."

A flush of pleasure crept up Fin's chest. *My dad listened to me.*

Nellie began to stir.

Fin leapt forward. "She's moving."

"She is." Gunnar peered down at Nellie fondly, gently moving a hair out of her face. The gesture was surprisingly tender and loving.

But they've only just met. Haven't they?

Fin kneeled into the dirt and leaves with Gunnar.

"You know my mother," Fin whispered. "Really know her."

"Your mother is a rather . . ." Gunnar wiped perspiration from Nellie's forehead. "Extraordinary human."

A surge of warmth and love and confusion spread from Fin's gut into her whole body. "Can you tell me about her?"

"I'm sorry, I can't." Gunnar swung her intense gaze to Fin. "But you are very much like her, if that tells you anything."

A smile toyed with Fin's mouth as she reached out and took her mother's hand. She rubbed her thumb across her mother's soft hand for a moment before turning to Gunnar.

Without looking, Gunnar said, "Ask your question."

Fin tucked another hair behind her ear. "How did the fox come to us in purgatory? Magic didn't work there, so it wasn't my compass bracelet."

Gunnar took a deep breath and exhaled. "Auci bartered with Death for your life."

"What?" Fin exclaimed.

"Auci will tell you more when the time is right."

Fin sputtered, "B-but . . . what does—"

"Fin?" Nellie whispered as she began to wake up.

"Mo—I mean, Nellie."

Fin glanced at Gunnar, who laid Nellie down gently and stepped away. Fin scooted closer as Nellie's eyes flickered open.

"What happened?" Nellie tried to sit up.

Fin put a restraining hand on her shoulder. "Whoa, hang on. Give yourself a minute."

Fin sagged in relief as her mother became fully awake. The blood on her shirt remained, but her injuries were completely healed.

She's alive.

Fin turned to smile at Gunnar, but her aunt had disappeared.

What sort of deal did my father make with Death?

48

Don't Let Go

Fin stretched her legs under the black marbled table of the diner's corner booth making the cherry red leather crinkle loudly. She felt at home here with Dawson and Booker, as they hashed out the last couple days, spilling secrets about some of the more mysterious events.

Booker chuckled. "Mythical creatures, time travel, hooo-eeey." He was full of his typical good spirits. "Strange things 'round these parts, but them phoenix tears sure do make a man feel good."

Fin couldn't help but feel a surge of happiness just looking at the future chief of police. *I wonder if we'll see him again.*

Booker took a long drink of his black coffee—more sugar than coffee, of course—as Dawson flipped through the newspaper he'd bought.

She let out a deep sigh and looked out the window at the WANTED poster on the shop across the street. *Lily.*

Fin asked the chief, "Are you sure you don't need me to stay and help find Lily?"

"We've got it. And with Riggs and Sophie helpin' out, we'll find her."

"What about the victims? Did Grayson's information . . . did it pan out?"

"It did." He sat back with a heavy thud and tipped his hat up. "Gruesome don't even touch what happened to all them victims. But they've been sent back to their families and will be properly laid to rest."

Dawson said, "There's a candlelight vigil announcement in the newspaper."

He kept reading but lifted the paper so Fin could see the back page. She moved her face closer and read that it was scheduled for that night.

Booker set his hat right. "The church folk thought it might be proper since six of them were from around these parts. The rest were from Kentucky."

"It is proper." Dawson flicked the paper and folded it down into a rectangle.

Fin scraped a fry back and forth on her plate as her mind wandered to the horrible things Grayson had done to help Lily. His darkness was equal to his light.

As though he was reading her mind, Booker said, "Grayson was one of them cases that makes your head spin, huh?"

Fin flicked a fry into her puddle of ketchup and fixated on how it sunk into the thick condiment.

"The Grayson we all knew . . ." she trailed off, shaking her head. "I want to believe the best of him, but—"

"Just stop there." Booker wiped his hands on his napkin, crumpled the white square, and tossed it on his empty plate. "Don't say no more. You'll sleep better if you don't."

No one said anything for a moment as the musical notes of a familiar song floated through the air from the pink, fluorescent jukebox.

Fin sang along in her head. *A long, long time ago, I can still remember how that music used to make me smile...*

Sitting up straight, she searched the diner for someone who would know this was her favorite song. An overwhelming sense of being watched flooded her senses, but she didn't see anyone familiar.

Booker asked her, "What?"

She shook her head and cleared her throat as she turned back to him. "Uh, nothing. So, uh, the coroner is keeping Grayson's body until we can move his mother to the cemetery?"

"Yup. We're workin' with the homeowners to find the right spot and dig. We'll let Riggs know. He can get in touch with you. Then we'll do a proper burial. Both at the same time."

"I want to be there," said Fin.

"Of course," he quipped.

The day the music died, so bye, bye Miss American Pie...

Fin glanced around the crowded diner once more, but she again saw no one.

"Well," Booker said loudly, slapping his hands together and looking over their mostly eaten cheeseburgers. He pulled out a toothpick, and popped it into his mouth before saying, "I'll remember your order, and next time—"

"Here ya go, honey." A much younger but still sassy Laverne dropped Fin's change in front of her with a wink.

"Thanks. Did you happen to see who played this song?" Fin asked.

"Sorry, honey. Too busy today to pay much attention." The waitress snapped her gum and walked away.

Booker continued, "As I was sayin', next time, I'll get the bill. You snatched it up too quick this time. Won't happen again."

"I'm positive it won't," Fin said and drained the last of her root beer.

Getting lost in their own thoughts, another silence descended on their booth until Laverne wandered back up to the table.

"Cherry pie for dessert?" She snapped her gum. "On the house. That lady bought it for ya."

They leaned back so they could see around Laverne.

I knew it. Fin smiled at her aunt, who sat at the counter. "If you'll excuse me."

Dawson said, "Sure."

He and Fin shared a smile over the chief dumping sugar into his coffee.

Standing up, Fin said, "Don't know why you put so much sugar in that coffee since your mother says you're so sweet already."

Booker snapped to attention. "Now, how'd you know that, Fin Baker?"

"Lucky guess." She laughed with a wink and walked away.

"I think I'm gonna like this town," Booker said. "Maybe I'll even be the chief of police someday."

Dawson chortled. "I have no doubt."

Their conversation made Fin smile to herself as she headed to the counter. The eight-minute song still drifted through the diner.

Do you believe in rock 'n' roll? Can music save your mortal soul? And can you teach me how to dance real slow?

After sitting down on the shiny red swivel stool next to Gunnar, Fin playfully twisted toward her aunt. "Any particular reason you played this song?"

Gunnar just grinned. "It's your mother's favorite. Stuck in my head."

Fin's smile dropped into surprise. "Oh, right." *It wasn't about me. It was about my mother.*

"You're not going to have any pie? It's the best around." Gunnar took a sip of her coffee before setting it down with a clink on the saucer. "I'd know. I've been around."

"I'll save it for later. You left in a hurry when Nellie woke up."

"Better for her not to meet me just yet." Gunnar lightly traced the rim of her coffee cup with her index finger. She snuck a peek at Fin's face. "Auci and I, we have a long and complicated history."

"I can see that."

Gunnar said quietly, "It's a special kind of hell to be trapped in a life you never wanted and someone else holds the key to your escape."

Fin clasped her hands and rubbed her thumbs together, thinking for a moment, before she said, "I get it."

Gunnar stopped toying with her cup and looked at Fin. She reached over and gently tucked a hair behind Fin's ear just as she had done to Nellie. "Your mother's hair gets in her face, too."

Fin watched Gunnar's hand pull away, noticing a turquoise ring on her middle finger. She grabbed her aunt's hand, bringing it toward her face to investigate it.

"It's just like Auci's," said Fin.

"It's exactly like Auci's."

"I don't understand."

"This is his white flag to our lifelong battle of me trying to escape." She gave a half-hearted twitch of a smile. "We'll see."

Fin released her hand and asked, "What does it do?"

Gunnar tilted her head. "It's a twin of Auci's ring. It allows us to trade places. Six months out of the year I'm the thief. The other six months I'm the auctioneer."

"The one with the most power."

Gunnar shook her head as she went back to tracing the rim on her coffee cup. "No one can be more powerful than Auci." Gunnar snapped her stare back to Fin. "But you're pretty damn close."

Fin shook her head as she leaned back on the stool and twisted in it as she tucked a hair behind her ear. "No, no, no. I'm not—"

"We'll see," Gunnar interrupted quietly.

A realization hit Fin so hard that she reached over and grabbed Gunnar's hand with enough force to knock over her coffee cup. "Oh, sorry…"

Gunnar grabbed a napkin and sopped up the mess as she looked expectantly at Fin.

"When Auci becomes the thief, will he be . . . will he be human?" Fin asked.

"As the thief, he'll be human in body and soul, yes."

Fin's eyes misted with tears as she slowly pulled her hand off Gunnar's and stared at the counter. Her mind whirled and the song marched on to its conclusion.

But I knew I was out of luck, the day the music died . . .

"That's how he becomes my father, isn't it? How he and Nellie come together."

Gunnar's eyes bore into the side of Fin's head as she said, "Their love is one for the ages. Unexplainable, unpredictable, and yet totally inevitable." Gunnar's expression sobered as she righted the coffee cup and stared into its emptiness.

Now it was Fin's turn to bore a hole into the side of Gunnar's head. Her aunt tucked a dark blonde strand of hair behind her ear as a deep sadness spread across her face.

Is that how she felt about Oliver? "You lost Oliver."

Gunnar barely tilted her chin up.

Fin was sincere as she said, "I'm sorry."

Gunnar's eyes drooped with pain. "I've had many great loves over the millennia, as you can imagine. I can say with certainty that you can love more than one person." Gunnar's eyes misted over. "But I can also say with certainty that there may be only one you would die for. Risk…everything for. So, if you find that person, don't let go."

Putting an exclamation point on her last piece of advice, her aunt poked the coffee cup, knocking it down and sending it over the edge of the counter to break loudly on the floor.

"I better get going." Gunnar stood and wiped her eyes. "There are things to steal and Lily to hunt."

Fin spun off the vinyl stool and stood up. "I feel like I should stay and help."

Gunnar pulled her into a quick hug. As she let go, she gripped Fin's arms. "You need to go back home to New York."

"What if I don't want to?"

"We won't leave you again, Fin. Ever." Gunnar squeezed her arms. "But I think there's someone back home you need to talk to. A certain cop?"

Fin shied away from Gunnar's piercing eyes and looked at the floor.

Gunnar touched her cheek. "Don't worry. Auci will know if you need us."

She turned to go, but Fin reached out and pulled her into another, tighter hug. They stayed like that for a few seconds as Fin held back her emotions.

Eventually, they let go.

Gunnar straightened and said with exaggerated cheer, "Now, say goodbye to Auntie Gunnar." She winked as Fin pasted on a heavy smile before Gunnar sashayed out the door.

Fin whispered to herself, "Goodbye," as the last notes of American Pie disappeared into the air.

49

Hello, Fin

Fin considered her situation as she drove the Cutlass down the gravel road with the windows open. She'd always found it easier to keep relationships at bay and avoid the uncomfortable and predictable goodbyes that always came at some point, whether by force or choice. Each mile on the road to Nellie's house added more weight to her chest. Every time she imagined saying goodbye to her mother—to her family—tears sprang to her eyes. Add to that the conversation she was going to have with Hodge, and she was inching dangerously close to sobbing.

"You're deep in thought," Dawson shouted over the noisy engine, pushing his glasses back up on his nose.

The nervous gesture warmed her heart. *I'm going to miss that.*

Clearing her throat, she said, "I'm just . . . I don't like goodbyes. Especially this one."

"I get that," he said as they pulled up to the house.

The four kids were waiting by the barn. Clara Belle opened the screen door on the front porch and stepped out with a wave, her other arm in a sling.

As Fin shut the car off and they rolled up the windows, Dawson nodded at Boone and Marci and said, "They're holding hands,"

Fin followed his gaze. "They look happy."

"Yeah." Dawson sat quietly. "It feels like an eternity since we arrived. But it's only been a few days. Incredible to live that much in such a short time."

Fin noticed his tousled hair, looser clothing, and the fact he didn't have his green book out and said, "You seem different."

"I am different." Dawson returned her stare. "Thank you for that."

"Well, we are family, aren't we?" She playfully shoved his shoulder.

Smiling, he slowly faced the kids, who were staring at them. "We are."

Fin grabbed the door handle. "We better get going."

After they climbed out of the car, Fin tossed the keys to Boone as she walked over to him. "She's all yours."

Dawson added, "Thanks for the loan."

"Thanks for the help fixin' it." Boone grinned at Dawson before giving Fin a sideways glance. "You, too."

Fin nodded to him before slowly moving to Nellie and hugging her. "I'm gonna miss you." She held as tight as she could, taking in everything about her mother. "I'm going to miss you so much." Tears leaped to her eyes as they let go of each other.

"I'm gonna miss you, too." Nellie investigated Fin's face as a myriad of emotions crossed it. "Have you, uh, noticed that we . . . we sort of look alike?"

"Um." Fin shook her head as she looked down at Nellie's shoes. "I'm not sure what you mean."

Fin kept her eyes glued to the ground, worried that she might give away too much if Nellie saw them.

Nellie whispered, "The skull. What don't I—"

"My turn," interrupted Clara Belle as Nellie backed away and turned toward the other kids.

Thank you, Grandma.

Even with her arm in a sling and no makeup, Clara Belle was beautiful. Her one-armed side-hug felt immensely loving and encompassing. "I don't know, Fin Baker, there's somethin' special about you." Her grandmother let go of her. "I'm gonna figure it out one day."

Fin couldn't quite make eye contact when she took Clara Belle's uninjured hand with hers. "Thank you, for letting us—" She stopped and looked around at everyone, the house, the barn, and the car. "Thanks for letting us in."

"Of course." Clara Belle squeezed her hand.

She looked at the fading bruises on Clara Belle's face. *He'll never hurt you again.* "I'm sorry about Russell."

Clara Belle's expression sagged. "I don't ever wish ill on anyone, not even Russell. But I will say, for the first time since he came into my life, I feel free."

"You are free."

Clara Belle's face darkened. "I want you to know, I did help Rose when I could. But—"

"I know," Fin interrupted, putting a reassuring hand on her arm. "You had the kids."

"Russell would'a killed me if he knew what I was doin'. And without me, Nellie and Boone wouldn't have stood a chance."

Fin wished she could tell Clara Belle that it was better for women in the future. It struck a nerve that it wasn't as true as it could be. She put away guys like Russell every day, and then a week later, she'd put them away again. And again. And again.

"Go live your life," Fin said. "Be happy."

A soft smile touched Clara Belle's face as she glanced toward the horses and beyond. "I will."

Clara Belle walked away and sat down tiredly in the porch swing as Marci walked up to Fin with open arms and said, "Thank you for everything."

Fin leaned into the hug, enjoying that Marci really squeezed her. "I'm sorry about what's happened to you," Fin whispered.

"I'm gonna be okay," Marci whispered back. "I told my mom. We reported it. Officer Booker's taking care of 'em."

They let go of each other.

Marci added, "And it's actually helped me decide what I want to do."

"What's that?"

"Me and Nellie," she paused as she caught Nellie's eye. "We're gonna be cops like you."

"Lord help us all," said Clara Belle, slapping her leg as the boys playfully groaned in disapproval and Dawson walked up to Fin.

Boone teased Nellie. "How can you enforce the law when you're such a troublemaker?"

"I think that's what's gonna make me so good." She waggled her eyebrows, and everyone laughed.

Fin said, "Well, you're both brave enough to do it, I'll tell you that."

Marci lifted her chin. "Thank you."

"Yeah, thank you," Nellie said as she linked elbows with Marci. Then a look like she'd just gotten an idea crossed Nellie's face and she ran into the house.

As she did, Boone walked up to Fin and brought her into a hug. "Fin." He let go and faced Dawson, extending his hand. "Dawson."

They shook hands, but one of them pulled the other into a hug.

"It's been great gettin' to know you," Boone said.

They let go and looked at each other.

Dawson blinked back tears. "It really has."

Marci opened her arms for a hug and Dawson obliged. "You're a cool guy."

He wiped the tears from his eyes behind Marci's back before they let go. "Thanks."

"All right, well . . .we have a bus to catch." Fin looked around at everyone, watching the house for Nellie, but she didn't come. *Where is she?* "Well, uh, thank you. All of you."

"Yes, thank you," Dawson added.

Fin and Dawson waved, grabbed their bags, and headed toward the road.

"Come back soon if you can," Boone hollered after them.

Dawson and Fin turned, walking backward for a few steps as they waved again.

"I'm sure we will," Dawson called out.

"We promise," said Fin as Nellie ran out of the house toward her. Her heart jumped inside her chest. *Mom!*

"Here," Nellie said breathlessly as she stopped in front of Fin and handed her a piece of paper. "I wrote down my address. If you ever want to write me."

"Thank you." *Yes! I can finally check the handwriting to see if it's hers.*

As Fin put the paper in her back pocket, Nellie asked, "When will I see you again?"

"I hope soon," Fin squeaked out around the lump in her throat. She took Nellie's wrist and tapped her compass bracelet. "I'm always with you."

Nellie's eyes were shining as she swallowed hard. "And I'm always with you." She held up her hand, wiggling the finger with the mood ring.

Fin raised her hand with the matching jewelry. "Absolutely."

After a final hug between the two, Nellie went back to her family, and Fin watched her go.

Bye, Mom.

The time travelers faced forward again as Dawson gave a quick squeeze to Fin's arm. The gravel crunched loudly as they walked in silence. Once they were around the bend in the road and out of sight, Fin paused and faced him.

"We have a meeting to go to." She extended her bent elbow to him. He gripped it, and they disappeared.

~~~
~~~

When they appeared at Blue Falls, Auci was waiting by the water, staring at the magnificent field of mushrooms dotting the landscape like exotic flowers.

"I'll leave you to it," Dawson said, inspecting the vibrant fungi as Fin walked up to the auctioneer.

"Fin." He removed his hat and tucked it between his elbow and waist. "You are impressive, daughter."

"Thank you." She gave a slight bow with her head then stepped forward and hugged him, reveling in the way he patted her hair down like she was five years old and pecking at her forehead. She stepped away and was buoyed by the glint of happiness in his face.

Fin broached another topic. "I talked to Gunnar."

His brow furrowed with uncertainty as he said, "We will see if this solution might help."

"I'm glad you tried to find a better one."

After a pregnant pause, he said, "I'm afraid I can't be a father in the way you might want."

Fin twitched her nose. "I know."

"But I will do my best."

"You're doing pretty well so far," she said with warmth.

He tucked his chin in appreciation as a smile snuck across his face.

Although touched by his earnestness, she tilted her head and narrowed her eyes at him. "So, what did you do, Auci?"

He looked confused. "What do you mean?"

"The white fox. Gunnar said—"

"I did what I had to do," he interrupted. "To keep you alive."

"To keep *me* alive? What about Nellie? It kept us *both* alive, right?"

Searching her face, he took in a deep breath and slowly exhaled. "Auci?"

He nervously adjusted his tie. "Death had Nellie fair and square."

Fin shook her head. "I don't understand."

"Death is entitled to those who die," said Auci as he stared at the crystal-clear water. "Nellie . . ."

She took in his slumped shoulders and pained expression as she thought about how violent Lily was.

Fin whispered, "Nellie was always going to die, wasn't she? Because of Lily."

Auci nodded. "In all but one timeline."

354

"This one. This timeline."

"We cannot save lives. But there are ways to delay death. Gunnar bargained with Death for the Grim. I bargained with him to delay Nellie's demise in order to save your life."

"At what cost?" She asked helplessly. "Does she know you kept her alive just to have a child? Like livestock, for Christ's sake."

A mysterious expression lit Auci's face. "She knows."

Fin took a stunned step backward, shaking her head in disbelief. "She knows?"

"Hello, Fin," a woman said.

Fin whipped around to face her much older, pregnant mother.

50

There Are Limits

Nellie's heart ached as her daughter broke down in tears amid the spectacular beauty of Blue Falls. She walked as quickly as someone who was six months pregnant could walk and embraced Fin as she cried.

"My goodness." Nellie squeezed Fin in her arms, the crashing sound of the falls against the rocks covering her daughter's heartfelt sobs. "My strong, smart, brave girl."

Nellie leaned back and peered into Fin's hazel eyes. For the first time, she noticed the amber flecks that gave her daughter's eyes a lightness. Fin certainly had Nellie's delicate features and Auci's strong jaw, but that piercing stare was all Fin.

Nellie tucked a piece of Fin's dark hair behind her ear and noticed the simple earrings: one diamond in the front and a gold ball behind it. Functional but classy.

Through a throat choking with love, she said, "I knew, even at fifteen, there was something to you. Of course, I didn't know I was your mother. But it was always easy to see that there was something brilliantly special about you."

They stepped apart as an uncharacteristically bashful smile lit Fin's face. Warmth spread through Nellie as she came face-to-face with the vulnerable side of Fin.

This is my daughter. "I'm so proud of you."

Fin wiped her face and dried her hands on her jeans. "Thanks, Mom."

Nellie let out a rush of tears, and they both laughed as she swatted them away.

"We're a mess," Fin said as she smoothed her hair and settled down.

"We really are." Nellie looked for Auci, but he had disappeared. "Please don't be mad at your father about this whole death business. He loves you. More than you know."

"I have so many questions." Fin swiped at her eyes one last time. "I don't know where to start."

"Start wherever you like, and I'll answer as best I can." Nellie waved them forward, and they walked toward the waterfall whose mist drifted on the wind to cool their faces.

Fin broke the silence. "He said you knew. About—"

"My inevitable demise?" she interrupted. The grass and twigs crunched under their feet as they walked. "I do."

Shaking her head, Fin asked, "Doesn't it bother you?"

Shrugging, she raised her hands. "We're all going to die someday, aren't we? It's the contract we sign the day we're born. It's no different than you knowing that, as a cop, you might never come home."

"I hadn't thought of it that way." Fin kicked at a rock.

"I think what you're really struggling with is the idea that he delayed my death so you could be born."

Fin glanced away and watched Dawson writing in his notebook on the other side of the lake.

Nellie laid a comforting hand on her arm. "Auci told me everything and let me decide whether or not to have you. He gave me the choice to become pregnant in the first place. Or even to die at fifteen."

Fin plucked a colorfully dotted mushroom cap and twisted it delicately in her fingers. "Wow. I don't know what I'd say to that."

"I didn't take it well at first. I slapped him and told him to go right to hell."

Fin's eyebrows launched up as she searched her mom's face before she chuckled.

"There isn't anyone alive who makes me more crazy than that man." She pointed at Fin. "Did he give you the 'I'm a million years old' spiel?"

A laugh burst out of Fin. "I threw my gear down and walked away." She tossed the mushroom cap into the glistening lake.

"Yeah, exactly." Nellie shook her head. "It's such crap that men just get better looking the older they get. Even when they're immortal. Tragically unfair."

Fin's eyes twinkled. "Truly."

Nellie rubbed her swollen belly. "You move a lot."

Fin's face brightened. "I do?"

Nellie stopped, took Fin's hand, and placed it on her stomach.

Feeling a strong kick, Fin's eyes flared before misting over.

"Strong, even in the womb," Nellie said.

Her daughter's face suddenly had a questioning look and Nellie quickly removed Fin's hand as they resumed walking.

Fin asked, "Why did you choose to have me?"

Nellie took a deep breath and exhaled slowly. "Because I couldn't imagine it any other way."

"Then why do you leave me?" Fin's voice broke as raw pain crossed her face.

Nellie stopped and waited for Fin to face her before touching Fin's cheek. "To protect you, of course."

Confused, Fin blinked. "From what?"

"That is a story for another day." Nellie started walking again. When Fin caught up with her, Nellie asked, "Are you tired of everyone telling you they can't tell you things?"

Exasperation colored Fin's laughter. "Completely sick of it."

"That part doesn't get better, unfortunately, and for good reason."

"My head understands that. Making decisions knowing the future would—"

"Change the future," Nellie interrupted with a theatrical gusto that made Fin laugh. "If I have to hear Auci say that one more time."

Nellie could feel Fin looking at her, so she glanced at her daughter. *She's such an interesting mix of both of us.*

"Auci never leaves you, you know?" Nellie said. "He checked on you every day of your life. Sent people to protect you. To watch over you." She gave her daughter a lopsided grin. "And he really did want to do a lot more than just break the arm of that idiot boy who broke your heart at thirteen."

"Really?" Fin's eyes twinkled.

"Oh, yeah. He's very protective."

Fin's face held a swirl of questions but also happiness.

She'll grow close to Auci.

Fin asked, "Are you able to watch me, too? See me grow up?"

Nellie rubbed her belly again. "No. The Council won't allow it. Auci can do as he wishes. They can't limit him. But humans and bounty hunters have limits. Obviously."

Fin tilted her head. "You really love him, don't you?"

"Deeply."

"Gunnar said yours is a storybook version of love."

"I suppose it is." She looked across the sweeping lake and felt at peace as fond memories flickered through her mind. She faced Fin. "You'll see."

Auci appeared beside Nellie and placed his hand on her lower back. "It's time to go."

With a hint of desperation, Fin said, "When will I see you again?"

"Turn around," Nellie said, spinning her finger in a circle.

Fin did and Nellie dug through her backpack, pulling something out before asking her to turn back around.

Nellie handed the butterfly that Fin had sculpted from the mud of this lake to Auci. "Honey, would you?"

He waved his hand with the turquoise ring over it. Nellie couldn't see anything, but Fin's eyes widened.

"Is it glowing?" Nellie asked. Fin smiled as Auci handed it to Fin. "Whenever you need us, just hold this in your hand and ask. And we'll come as soon as we can."

Tears spilled down Fin's cheeks as she clutched the figurine and nodded.

Auci said gently, "Fin, you've been called to stand before the Council."

Fin sucked in a breath. "Because of Carl?"

Auci nodded. "And Ice. And Halo. And Lily. Quite a mess."

"I'm sorry, Auci," Fin said.

"You have nothing to be sorry for," he said with a dose of pride. "I'll go with you. Riggs and Sophie will be there as well. We'll do everything we can to help."

"How much trouble am I in?"

"We'll get you out of it. For now, go home. Rest. I'll come for you later."

Nellie pulled Fin into a hug, fighting past the emotions threatening to close her throat so that she could speak. "Before you were my daughter, you were my friend. I think that's what I love most. That fifteen-year-old girl became someone strong because of you."

"I feel the same way." Fin's voice cracked.

"I love you. My beautiful girl."

"I love you, too, Mom." Fin buried her face in her mother's hair.

After a moment, Nellie pulled away, rubbing her stomach and beaming with pride. *She'll be okay.*

Dawson wandered over and said, "Looks like all's well." He gave a slight hello wave to Auci and Nellie.

"Dawson." Nellie reached over and hugged him briefly. "You are equally impressive, nephew."

"Thank you." He grinned.

Fin collected herself and asked Dawson, "Ready to go home?"

"I am." He grasped her elbow.

Before they left, Nellie exclaimed, "Fin?"

"Yeah?"

Nellie thought for a moment. *What can I possibly say to the daughter I had no hand in raising but love more than anything?* "Just . . . be careful."

"I will, Mom," Fin said quietly.

"And always take a sweater with you!" she added frantically.

"A sweater?"

"You know, in case it gets cold or . . . something."

Fin dashed back to Nellie and wrapped her in a fierce hug. Nellie held onto her child for dear life.

As Fin pulled away, she said with a gentle understanding, "I'll make sure I always have a sweater."

Emotion choked Nellie as she said, "Thank you."

Fin held out her elbow for Dawson, who took it.

After they disappeared, Nellie looked at the father of her child and then lightly touched her belly. "Promise me you'll always keep an eye on them both after I die."

Auci grimaced. "I don't want to talk—"

"Auci," Nellie interrupted. "Promise me."

"I will always have my eye on them, I promise." His hand pressed warmly onto her swollen belly.

Nellie gripped Auci's hand, entwining their fingers.

"How does she take it? When you tell her about her brother?"

He kissed her instead of answering. A move she was familiar with by now. There were answers even she was not allowed to know.

"It's time to go." He squeezed her hand as they disappeared from Newcross.

51

Did You Do it for Me?

Lily cautiously followed Ice into the back room of a small bar in downtown Cincinnati where her boots stuck to the tacky floor. The stench of old cigarette smoke and booze invaded her nostrils as some bullshit song about somebody doing something wrong to someone played on the jukebox.

This shithole smells like Russell.

Her lip curled in disgust as she took in the riffraff dumping shots down their throats and whining to each other about their sad lives.

Pathetic.

A dart flew past her face, slamming into the bullseye on the board. Vicious anger ripped through her chest as she glared at the thrower. Heady fantasies of breaking the asshole's nose floated through her mind. She'd been itching for a fight since being stripped of her knife, her pride, and the Grim after another failed confrontation with Fin. Resentment boiled in her gut as she forced herself to turn away from the guy.

I'm the hunter not the hunted.

Understanding her vulnerability in this situation, she stayed on full alert, meeting the curious glances in the darkened saloon with intense hatred to keep everyone at bay.

Why couldn't I beat Fin?

The dart player hollered, "She's here."

Lily whipped around and found herself looking into a pair of thoughtfully wicked light eyes that had no color and every color all at the same time. The young man didn't look much older than her. His red hair was long on the top and cascaded over his thin, interesting face like a waterfall. His body was lean but muscular, and she was very aware that she liked looking at it. The pulsing she felt wasn't the killing kind. It had a destination different from anything she'd experienced in her seventeen years.

She asked him, "Who are you?"

Instead of answering, he closed the distance between them and yanked out a knife from its sheath on his side. Instead of attacking him, she took a questioning step backwards and put up a defensive hand. A smug look crossed his face as he lightly intertwined his fingers with her raised digits. The feeling of his skin against hers sent a warm tingle through her body.

This must be what it feels like to want a man for something other than killing.

Intoxicated, she watched as he took his knife and held the point to her arm. He possessed her gaze as he dragged the blade across her skin. She gasped with a delight she didn't know she could feel.

He pulled her to him and whispered in her ear, "My name's Stone." Sliding his knife into her coat pocket, he gave her a sexy smile.

Ice shoved Stone out of her way and grabbed Lily's arm. She tugged her in front of a huge man, who was bigger than Grayson and old enough to be her uncle. The giant stepped out from behind a pool table and walked toward her.

Ice said, "This is her, Halo." She took a swig of the beer he handed to her.

Lily jerked her arm away from Ice with a look that promised murder before facing Halo.

"Nice eyes," he said in a smooth and seductive way.

Reacting to his tone and his gold tooth, Lily sneered at him. "Gross."

Tempered humor suffused his large face, which grew facial hair like her father used to have. She remembered how Russell's skin felt like sandpaper when he'd tried to rape her.

I'm glad he's dead. Mother fucker.

And she wasn't fond of this asshole, either, dressed in a brown leather duster, combat boots, and a cowboy hat. He was loaded with weaponry from his head to his toes.

Lily asked, "What do you want with me?"

The only sound in the bar was a quarter sliding into the jukebox. Everyone was looking at her as a new song started. She'd never heard it before, but when she saw that Stone was the one who played it, the lyrics suddenly had a delicate feel to her ears.

Some people call me the space cowboy, yeah, some call me the gangster of love . . .

Stone stalked up behind Halo, captivating her with a stare that only another predator would recognize. A smiled toyed with her lips.

Halo said with pride, "You're a new recruit."

She knew that bloated bone bag didn't realize what was coming, but Lily did. She'd made the face Stone was making many times, and Grayson had to bury the results. She gave no warning to the idiot as Stone advanced.

"Recruit for what?" She looked around at the scarred and worn faces, a few of which were letting out nervous laughs.

"We used to be bounty hunters," Halo said. "Had a different way of doing things. We were a disgrace to them. They exiled us. So, now we want to destroy everything they touch and steal back the objects they're hiding."

Lily clocked the exits as her new favorite song played on.

You're the cutest thing I ever did see . . .

She scoffed. "What makes you think I'd help you?"

Halo whipped out a knife and flipped it under her chin. "What makes you think you'll live if you don't?"

Stone's face twisted with rage as he got into position behind Halo.

I'm a joker; I'm a smoker; I'm a midnight toker. I sure don't want to hurt no one . . .

Stone pulled out a large hunting knife and slid it through Halo's throat like it was hot butter.

People keep talkin' about me, baby. Say I'm doing you wrong . . .

As Halo dropped to the floor, Lily grabbed Stone's knife out of her pocket. She turned and jabbed the knife into Ice's chest, putting her down like a dog as everyone in the bar scattered.

Don't worry, mama, 'cause I'm right here, right here, right here at home . . .

Stone grabbed Lily's hand as everyone and everything in the club suddenly froze. He said nothing as he pulled on her through the statues. She wasn't sure what was happening, but she didn't care because she was enamored with him already.

Finally, someone who understands.

Her eyes devoured his body as he lead her through the musty bar and out the front door.

She was breathless and giddy in the cool night air as they stopped next to a parked motorcycle with a silver body and pale blue trim.

Reading the words on the side, she asked, "What's Ducati?"

He cracked a smile at her, and her insides warmed as he said, "Don't worry about it."

He handed her the knife's sheath, so she put away the bloody blade and clipped it to her waistband. When she looked up, he kicked a long leg over the bike and tapped the empty seat behind him, signaling for her to get on.

She took a step back. "Not until you tell me how you made everybody freeze like that."

His eyes roamed her face and figure with a smoldering slowness that pulled on something deep in her core. He held up a small red stone in his hand. She reached out to touch it, but he yanked it back and dropped it into a small, black sack he put in his pocket.

Playing coy, she asked, "Did you do it for me?"

He flicked a demanding glance at her. "Get. On."

The last man who talked to her like that was in her freezer, but she was enjoying this new game. She reached up and grabbed her coat as she held his stare. With smoldering eyes, he watched her strip off the heavy trench coat. She revealed a figure that was only a few months away from being, as her mother would say, "A woman of legal age."

Pffft, legal.

She lowered her eyes to his lips and asked, "What do you plan to do with me?"

His colorful eyes burned with excitement. "You're the Bonnie to my Clyde."

With a grin, she stepped toward him and slid her body against his as she sat on the back of his bike. She couldn't wait to explore these sexual feelings with him. As the bike's engine roared between her legs, she wrapped her arms around his waist.

He pulled out a small vial of honey-colored liquid and handed it to her. "My gift to you."

"What is it?" She tipped the gooey liquid back and forth.

He captured her stare over his shoulder. "Got anyone you want to bring back from the dead?"

Her insides thrilled at the thought. "I'm sure I can think of someone."

"They come back worse for wear. Evil."

Lily laughed as she put the vile in her pants pocket. "Exactly how I like them."

"That's what I like to hear." He revved the engine. "Let's ride."

52

I Feel That, Too

New York City, 2020

When Fin and Dawson opened their eyes, they were standing in the middle of Fin's apartment. She took in a sharp breath as she caught a glimpse of herself and Auci disappearing from earlier in the day.

So strange to see that now, after everything.

The clink of a toothbrush falling into the sink and Hodge saying, "Shit," brought up a swell of affection for him. But it evaporated when she remembered one of the reasons she needed to come back to New York.

I have to tell him the truth.

Hodge called out, "Fin?"

She winced at his voice. Now that he'd called out to her, it meant she had to respond. They had to have the talk where she'd tell him he wasn't the guy she'd give anything for.

Forcing herself to sound normal, she said, "I'll be there in a second."

He hollered back, "Okay. We need to get going though."

"Got it."

Fin glanced at Dawson, who returned her guilty look with a comforting one.

He said, "He'll be okay. It's better for him to know than to string him along."

"I'm really gonna miss you, cousin," she said.

And she really meant it. Who knew a bookworm like Dawson could work his way into her heart and make a home there?

He adjusted his glasses as a blush crossed his cheeks. "I'm not quite sure what to do next."

"Me either."

She peered out her windows into the city and touched her compass bracelet. The same feeling she had when a case wasn't right or when a suspect felt off weighed on her chest. She was in the right place but everything felt wrong somehow.

Her face must have communicated something because Dawson asked, "What?"

She turned to him. "Do you feel like we shouldn't have left?"

"You're probably just missing them," said Dawson. "I feel that, too."

"Hmm." She chewed on her lip as her gut continued to nag her. Something was off when she was touching her mother's pregnant belly. *It felt too strong to be one kick. Or maybe it was both of my feet at the same time?* She tried to shake off the foreboding feeling but couldn't. *This doesn't feel over.*

Forcing herself to think about something else, she asked Dawson, "You're sure you want to fly back to Ireland? You know I can take you like that." Fin snapped her fingers.

"I could stand to have a regular form of travel." He chuckled as he rearranged his bags and grinned. "No offense."

"None taken." She moved toward him and the door.

He faced her, letting out a long exhale. "I guess this is where we say goodbye, then?"

She put her hands on his arms and squeezed. "I suppose it is, for now."

His eyes warmed with sincerity. "You've changed me, Fin Baker. And perhaps changed my life."

She pulled him into a tight hug. "You did that all on your own."

He squeezed her back, and they both let go. "I think they're proud of us."

"Me, too," Fin said quietly.

A quiet second passed before Dawson said, "Well, then, I've got your number."

"Use it anytime." She patted his shoulder as he opened the door and hung for a moment in the doorway.

He smiled at her. "I will."

He walked out the door, and she gently shut it behind him.

She walked over to her bag and pulled out the letter she got when she turned eighteen, taking the note out of the envelope and smoothing it out on her desk. She pulled Nellie's address from her back pocket and laid it side-by-side with the note.

"Oh." She stared at the handwriting on each of the notes. *Not even close.* "Shit." *Who's handwriting is it in this note?*

The bathroom door opened.

Hodge.

Squaring her shoulders, she walked over to him as he was putting on his rumpled navy blue suit.

He glanced at her and frowned. "What are you wearing? You're all sweaty and dirty. We have to go to the scene." He straightened up. "Wait, did you go out?"

She stopped in front of him. "We need to talk."

He searched her face as a torrent of emotions flooded his eyes. "Don't." He yanked his gray tie on and grabbed his gun and badge. "Don't fucking even, Fin."

"This isn't working, and you know it."

"It's not working because I love you and you tolerate me, right?" He snatched up the few things he had brought with him.

"That's not true. I do love you. I just—"

"Just not in the same way?" he asked sarcastically. "Fuck you. That's bullshit." He stormed out the bedroom door.

"Hodge, wait," she yelled and followed him.

He had already made it to the stairs when she caught up with him as they raced down the steps at a dangerous pace.

"Fin, we've been together for six months. We could have had this conversation at any point. Why now?"

"I'm sorry, I didn't know how I—"

"What changed?" He interrupted, stopping abruptly on the landing and whipping around so that she ran into him. He looked down at her, giving her a front row seat to the pain she was causing him. "Tell me. What changed between last night and this morning?"

Speechless, she stared at him. *So many things.* "I don't know."

"You know, my buddies, they warned me about you." He pointed at her as he continued his justified tantrum down the last flight of stairs.

Even though his smackdown was warranted, irritation bled into her guilt. *Fuck his stupid fucking friends.* "Warned you? What the fuck does that mean?"

He burst through the front door onto the quiet, early morning sidewalk.

"Daddy complex, they said. Abandonment issues, they said. I didn't listen. I kept saying you were different. And I was right. You are different. You're worse!"

His venom injected deep into her, making her flinch. She didn't mean to hurt him, but it hardly mattered in this moment. Or at all. In his mind, he had loved her and given her everything, but now she was spitting on all that.

"Hodge, please let me explain. Just wait and I'll tell you everything."

Spinning to face her, he said, "I love you so much." He backed into the street. "And it wasn't, and never will be, enough."

As bright headlights lit up his face she yelled, "Get out of the street!"

From out of nowhere, a sleek, black Mercedes Benz slammed into Hodge's body, throwing him like a crash test dummy twenty feet. The car came screeching to a halt.

"Hodge!" Fin screamed. She sprinted to him. Finding his pulse with one hand, she reached for her phone with the other. But she didn't have it. "Fuck."

"Quite sure you left it in your apartment." The driver arrogantly sauntered toward her from the expensive killing machine. The young man was dressed in black from head to toe with wickedly slick bleached white hair and icy clear eyes. He sucked on a vape pen and exhaled calmly. "Pity."

Confused, she yelled, "Call 911!"

"Sorry, can't. Daddy's looking forward to this one. A right strong soul that ought to give Pops a nice little burst of energy. T'would be irresponsible not to deliver as promised."

Her stomach dropped as she stared at him and felt Hodge's pulse stop. She slowly stood and faced the man realizing whatever he was, he wasn't completely human.

Or maybe not human at all. "Who are you?"

"Sorry, my manners are dreadful. I'm Balor. Balor Alexander. Our dads go way back." His eyes twinkled with glee as he took another deep hit from the vape pen.

Out of the corner of her eye, Fin noticed that the flowers on the sidewalk between them were wilting. Dying before her eyes.

She rocked back on her heels. "Impossible."

"Oh, come now, haven't you seen the memes? It's not 'impossible'; it's 'I'm Possible'." The humor on his face transformed into a simmering rage. "And I am possible. Thanks to your dad wanting you to live, it opened an opportunity for my dad to procreate. Something an entity like Death should never be allowed to do." He made a tsk-tsk motion with his index finger. "Think of the possibilities." He held out his arms and spun in a slow pirouette. "Voilà."

Fin stood slack-jawed as her mind raced to catch up.

He ambled back to his car and opened the driver's side door, giving her one last defiant look. "We'll meet again, Fin Baker." He slid into the seat, slammed the door, and the car sped away.

She looked down at Hodge's broken body as ambulance sirens screamed in the distance. They would be too late. And she couldn't fix it. Panic built a nest in her gut.

Not knowing what else to do, she yelled, "Auci, help me!"

Leave a review!

Did you love *Newcross* and its unique and exciting cast of characters? Let other readers know by scanning the QR code below and leaving a review.